T0171171

I sat with an ornate carpetbag full of cash on my lap, keeping a hand on it at all times. It was money thrown to me at the last minute back in Missouri, by my cousin, Jesse Woodson James; and there was no doubt in my mind that he intended for me to hold it till we met again come spring. There was nearly thirty thousand dollars in the bag. I didn't like carrying it around. . . .

The thirty thousand dollars was just the beginning of his troubles. For Jeston Nash, drawn into a world of greed, lust, and deadly desire, hiding a cache of money robbed by the James Gang was small time compared with the greedy machinations of a deadly mountain clan that has him dancing on a knife's edge, with the law on one side—and the evil temptations that turn men's hearts to darkness on the other. . . .

KILLERS OF MAN

Praise for Ralph Cotton's Previous Jeston Nash Adventures

WHILE ANGELS DANCE

"A rich adventure novel . . . Cotton's blend of history and imagination works because authentic Old West detail and dialogue fill the book."
—Gregory Lalire, *Wild West* magazine

(continued . . .)

POWDER RIVER

"Entertaining . . . Historical personages and details are authentically re-created. The book will delight readers already acquainted with the roguish Nash. . . ."
—*Publishers Weekly*

"A rollicking tale of the James boys that hurtles you along at breakneck speed . . . Ralph Cotton writes the sort of story we all hope to find within us: the bloodstained, gun-smoked, grease-stained, sweat-stenched yarn that yanks a reader right out of today and flings him down into a well-worn saddle as the bullets snarl past his ear and your heart rises to your throat."
—Terry Johnston

"An innovative, rewarding, and well-researched historical western."
—*Kirkus Reviews*

"When readers delve into the western world of Ralph Cotton, they often find themselves between a rock and a hard place, so real is the picture Cotton paints with his words. . . . Reality and imagination go hand in hand in a wonderfully woven tapestry of fact and fiction."
—Ginny Fleming, *Southern Indiana Writers Review*

Books by Ralph Cotton

While Angels Dance
Powder River
Price of a Horse
Cost of a Killing*
Killers of Man*

*Published by POCKET BOOKS

KILLERS OF MAN

RALPH W. COTTON

POCKET BOOKS
New York   London   Toronto   Sydney   Tokyo   Singapore

This book is a work of fiction. Names, characters, places and incidents are products of the author's imagination or are used fictitiously. Any resemblance to actual events or locales or persons, living or dead, is entirely coincidental.

An *Original* Publication of POCKET BOOKS

POCKET BOOKS, a division of Simon & Schuster Inc.
1230 Avenue of the Americas, New York, NY 10020

Copyright © 1997 by Ralph W. Cotton

All rights reserved, including the right to reproduce this book or portions thereof in any form whatsoever. For information address Pocket Books, 1230 Avenue of the Americas, New York, NY 10020

ISBN: 978-1-4391-9669-4

First Pocket Books printing January 1997

10 9 8 7 6 5 4 3 2 1

POCKET and colophon are registered trademarks of Simon & Schuster Inc.

Cover art by Robert McGinnis

Printed in the U.S.A.

For Mary Lynn, of course . . . and to Terry C. Johnston and Matt Braun, whose words of praise got me out of the chute and helped me stick the full eight seconds. What a ride it is. . . .

And a very special thanks to Professor Wade Hall (that keen-eyed ole word hawk), who sifts the meaning, layer by layer, knowing wherein lies the story within the story, within the story, within the story.

And special thanks to Robert Earl Keen and his bunch of Texans for all the fine crazy music. *The road goes on forever, the party never ends.* . . . You can't beat that.

I said in mine heart concerning the estate of the sons of men, that God might manifest them, and that they might see that they themselves are beasts. For that which befalleth the sons of men befalleth beasts; even one thing befalleth them: as the one dieth, so dieth the other; yea, they have all one breath; so that a man hath no preeminence above a beast: for all *is* vanity. All go unto one place; all are of the dust, and all turn to dust again. Who knoweth the spirit of the man that goeth upward, and the spirit of the beast that goeth downward to the earth?

—Ecclesiastes

PART I

LORD
OF THE
MOUNTAIN

CHAPTER

1

———•———

We rode out of the north toward Rawling Siding, both of us still damp and cold from the morning rain. Our long dusters clung heavy and dark wet across our shoulders, smelling musty of horse and of wood smoke from last night's campfire along Little Dog Creek. We'd been carefully checking the ground—getting a feel for it—searching for any holes or sodden ruts that might snap a horse's leg, should a horse have cause to come back this way in a hurry.

Tops of wet wild grass licked at our stirrups as we moved forward on the rolling prairie. "What do you think?" Quiet Jack asked, working his brule gelding back and forth in front of me. Mud sloshed around the horses' hoofs. Grass swayed limp, full of rain, leaving wet seeds and bits of chaff on our boots and along our horses' sides. "I hate this weather," he said, gazing up at the sky before I had time to answer.

"It'll have to do," I said, looking out, around at the broad swells of grassland that seemed to overlap off to the far edges of the earth. We rode on for another half hour beneath a low hanging sky the color of iron ore, our damp tack and leather swollen, steam wavering from our horses' flanks. "A man'll never get anywhere if he lets the weather stop him," I added. Jack didn't answer. He must've known it was my nerves talking.

3

Ahead, we heard the flat crack of a small-caliber rifle, then another, and another. The shots came spaced apart with no sound of urgency. We glanced at each other and reined down for a minute, listening. A rifle shot popped every few seconds, steady and unhurried like the sound of a Sunday target shoot.

"What do you think?" Quiet Jack asked me for the second time that morning.

I just looked at him. "Why do you keep asking me what *I think?*" There was a slight tension in the tone of my voice.

"Humph." He swung his head to the side and spit a stream of tobacco juice. "Beats me," he said. He ran a gloved hand across his mouth and we nudged our horses forward, continuing on, watching the town rise up beyond a swell of wild grass. From a distance we studied the rooflines with wary eyes.

Closer, we heard the squeal of many hogs; then the rifle shots stopped for a few minutes and the hog squealing lessened some as we rode in, past a broken-down freight wagon and a pile of scrap iron and whiskey bottles at the edge of town. A skinny cat curled around through the debris, saw us, and slipped down out of sight behind a broken wagon wheel.

"Hog killing, railroad style," Quiet Jack said, sweeping his eyes across a rail chute full of squirming, sour-smelling hogs, as we drew closer to it on our right. The wooden chute trembled with the thrashing of the pinned animals. Watery mud sloshed out between the boards. "I hate a lousy hog worse than anything," he added. He hiked his duster collar up, spitting again as we heeled our horses on and rode slowly past the chute.

"Me too," I said, just going along with him. Ordinarily I might've asked him why he hated hogs worse than anything, but I decided not to right then. Nerves sing high and tight in a man's head right before a robbery. I figured Jack was just talking to keep the pressure down. Although I'd never seen a sign of Quiet Jack having any frayed nerve endings, this seemed an odd time and place to talk about hogs *or* the weather.

The rifle shots started again. In a nearby corral, mud-

4

streaked horses craned their necks against the top rail, staring blankly at the hog slaughter. They quivered and flattened their ears at the crack of the rifles, nickering low, shaking out their damp manes and scraping their hoofs in the mud. Yet they kept watching, milling, sidling, bumping one another and swishing their matted tails.

A boiler whistle shrieked from the siding platform ahead.

Perched atop the hog chute a few feet away with his muddy boot heels hooked on the next rail down, a young boy looked up, picking a small-caliber shell from a single-shot rifle. He flipped the spent shell away and grinned at us across teeth too worn and broken for his age. "Y'all want some of this?" He nodded his shaggy head toward the squealing hogs and shoved another bullet in the rifle.

We shook our heads. Jack wallowed the cut of tobacco in his jaw and spit a stream, eyeing the boy as we drifted past, our long oval hats mantled low across our foreheads. "You orta try it a little," the boy called out. "I been shooting all morning. It's as much fun as it looks!"

"I bet it is," Jack called back in a flat tone.

At the far end of the chute, another small-caliber rifle barked. Two old men moved backward straddle-legged, bowed at the waist, dragging dead hogs from the chute to a bleeding rack. A dozen dead hogs hung by one rear hoof, their other rear hoof bobbing stiffly out to the side. They twisted back and forth in the breeze like dancers in a stage show from hell waltzing slowly, upturned on an empty sky. Blood dripped from their slit throats into rusty lard tins.

"See anybody?" I asked Jack in a hushed voice, scanning the rail platform ahead and the flat land beyond it. A wagonload of hog trimmings sat near the bleeding rack where an Indian woman stood in it knee-deep, picking among steamy entrails as if searching for precious jewels.

"No," he said, "do you?"

"Not yet. Reckon everything's all right? Reckon Jesse called it off? Something mighta gone wrong. You never know about railroads."

I knew I sounded more tense. My words seemed to rush out. There was a part of me wishing Jesse *had* called it off. But there was also a part of me that was as drawn to

5

outlawry as the devil's drawn to darkness; and though I'd grown more and more aware of the error of my long-rider ways, I wasn't yet ready to give them up.

Jack just turned his face toward me, looked me up and down through a veil of steaming breath, and said, "Damned railroads." He was silent for a second, then added, "Wanta know why I hate 'em?"

"Who?" I said, watching for anything out of the ordinary from the long train of freight and stock cars as we rode closer, closer but staying wide of them. At the head of the train, black smoke pulsed from the engine stack. I wasn't sure if we were still talking about hogs, the weather, or now perhaps railroads.

Jack chuckled under his breath. "Hogs, damn it." He spit again. "What do you think we was talking about?"

"Well, Jack. You seem to be hating a lot of things today. I thought I better check and make sure I wasn't hating the wrong thing with you." I felt myself winding tighter and tighter each step we took into Rawling Siding. Still I saw no sign of Cousin Jesse or Frank, or any of the others.

"I hate a hog because they've got no better sense than to just stand there squealing like idiots and let somebody put a bullet in their head."

I slowed my horse a step, still scanning the platform and the train. "I doubt if it's something they look forward to. I reckon a dumb hog don't even know what's happening to him till it's too late."

"They see the other hogs getting shot. That oughta let them know *something's* wrong. Seems like they'd wanta try to make a getaway."

"Maybe they are trying to, Jack. Maybe that's what all the squealing's about."

"Squealing won't get them nowhere. They could quit squealing and start figuring a way out," Jack said. He nodded. "That's what they *could* do."

"Where would a hog go, even if he got away?"

That stopped him for a second. I glanced at him and saw the chilled breeze lift at the edge of his damp hat brim. Then he tugged at it and said, "They could cut out to the woods and become wild hogs."

"Yeah, you'd think so," I said. Talking seemed to take the

6

sharp edge off my nerves. I took a breath and let it out slowly, feeling myself settle some.

Off to our distant right, we saw three figures in long dusters lopping up over a low rise, hats appearing first, then the rest of them coming up into view as if rising out of the earth. Their wet duster tails flared about them and slapped at their horses' flanks.

"So," I said quietly, "you're just hating *tame* hogs, but not wild hogs?"

The middle rider rode ahead of the others by three or four feet. It was Cousin Jesse, his big dun stallion prancing high-hoofed and quarter-wise as Jesse rose in his stirrups and gazed toward us across the flatland.

Jack said, without looking away from the riders, "Hell, I don't hate hogs, not really. They got a right to die if they want to, the way I look at it."

"But you just said—"

"I know what I said, but now I wish I never brought it up."

We swung wide of the railcars now and stepped our horses closer to a ramshackle livery barn with its doors thrown open and resting on their hinges in the mud.

I started to say *me too* again, but I stopped myself. Instead of saying anything, I ran my hand beneath my duster and across the forty-four strapped up under my arm. Still there. Always there. Just checking it.

I glanced about the mud strip of a town—four buildings, a livery, and a rail siding. If a person had to pick what men would look like who came to rob a train in a town such as this, it would be Jack, myself, and the three riders risen up from the grassy flatland. *No doubt about it.*

An old dock man wearing leather leg aprons leaned into a wheelbarrow of bulging grain sacks and forced it along the mud-rutted street. If he looked up right now, he would know, I thought. Anybody looking up right now, from whatever they were doing, would *know.*

"There's Clell and Hibbens," Jack said just above a whisper as we drew sideways and put more space between ourselves and the long train of cars.

The two of them came out of nowhere, strolling quickly across the mud street like two businessmen gone to dinner, except Clell Miller carried an axe over one shoulder and Early Hibbens swung a shotgun back and forth beneath his duster. They angled their path toward the express car where a uniformed guard stood gazing off in the other direction. A rifle lay at port arms across his chest.

"Jesus," I whispered, "hurry up," watching them, trying to hurry them along with my mind, my mind starting to race a bit now while the rest of the world started moving slower and slower. Clell grinned at us from thirty yards away, a broad, dumb-looking, what-the-hell-do-I-care grin, as Jack and I reined up beside the livery door and sat our horses with our hands near our pistols.

Beside Clell, Hibbens' face looked wide-eyed and drawn tight as fence wire. The shotgun swung from beneath his duster in clear view with each step. Dim sunlight glinted off the black barrel. Perhaps no one noticed it but me. To me, it stood out like a flag waving.

"Why don't they just carry a sign," I hissed. Again the tension began to boil in my forehead. But a freight clerk glanced up from checking a bill of lading as they passed by, then looked back down, touching a pencil stub to his tongue without noticing them.

"Ease up," Jack said in a near whisper.

I let go a tense breath. "Where's Joe Macky? See him anywhere?" Beneath me, my horse stepped about nervously in place and bumped into Jack's brule gelding.

"Will you *please* settle down some?" Jack glanced at me. "He's here somewhere, keeping watch. Just ease up and let this thing happen." He scanned the roofs of the buildings, then moved his gaze off toward Jesse, Frank, and Cole Younger as they closed in from the far side of the train. "I wish you'd look what J.J.'s wearing." He chuckled. "Can you imagine a man wearing a hat like that in public?"

I turned my gaze from the rooftops and the mud street and noticed that Jesse had removed his long oval Stetson and replaced it with a tall fur hat. Loose earflaps hung bouncing against his cheeks. Then I saw the bulky article he carried across his lap, just before the three of them dropped out of sight beyond the line of railcars.

"What's he carrying?" I craned my neck, rising slightly in my stirrups.

8

"Who knows," Jack said. "He's your cousin. You oughta say something to him about that hat, first chance ya get."

"I will," I said, knowing full well that I wouldn't; and we sat watching the street, and the rooftops, and the muddy trail in both directions.

I'd never heard of robbing a train while it sat at a siding, and as far as I knew neither had anybody else. But train robbery in general had become far more difficult than it had ever been in the past, and anybody in the robbing business—if they wanted to stay in the business—was always looking for the new and unexpected angle, the thing that would get them in and out of a situation, hopefully without bloodshed, before the railroads knew what hit them.

I'd been riding with the boys since the last year of the great Civil Conflict, and if there was one thing I could say for certain about my cousins it was that they had become masters of the *unexpected.* Still, I sat my horse more tense than usual that day, hearing the peal of single-shot rifles from the slaughter chute, and the squeal of dying hogs.

I eased down a bit when the express guard turned and faced the half-raised shotgun in Hibbens' hand. Seeing the barrel only two feet from his chin, he let the tip of his rifle slump toward the ground without moving another muscle. *So far, so good.*

"That-a-boy, Hibbens," I whispered. Clell doffed his hat to the guard, smiling as he reached out his free hand and lifted the rifle from him. Then he lifted the guard's sidearm, spun it on his finger, shoved it in his waist, and doffed his hat again. "Come on, Clell, don't fool around there," I added under my breath.

"Why don't you be still," Jack hissed. "You're starting to get on my nerves something awful." He shook his head. "Bad enough I gotta listen to them pig shooters."

Our jobs that day were to stay back and keep watch. If all went well, we'd take a head start out of town, just far enough ahead to lead Jesse and the others to a spot inside a strip of woods, five miles back near Little Dog Creek. There we had stashed a string of fresh horses and left them in the care of Whiskey Ed Ryan. We'd swap horses there, split up, and disappear like smoke. I'd had my doubts at first, but

9

now, as the guard stood frozen under the wide muzzle of Early Hibbens' shotgun, I saw it was all going as planned.

Jesse, Frank, and Cole Younger had rounded the front end of the train and started back toward the express car, spreading out with six feet of mud street between them. When Clell saw them closing in, he glanced around once, then stepped back and swung the axe against the heavy iron lock on the express car.

The sound of metal against metal crashed along the street loud enough to jar window frames, I thought; but as I tensed and shot a glance in both directions, nobody seemed to notice, save for the old man pushing the wheelbarrow. He stopped and looked over, then just stood watching without saying a word. *That's it, ole man, just stand there, keep quiet . . . keep quiet.* My hand tightened on my reins.

"Come on come on," I whispered, all of it moving too slow, Jesse and Cole Younger taking too long to drop from their saddles as Clell's axe swung and crashed again. Now the clerk looked up from his paperwork across the street. His mouth dropped open. Frank held the reins to Cole's and Jesse's horses, and turned staring at the clerk with his rifle raised slightly from his lap.

"They're robbing the *Bine-cod* train!" the old dock man shouted, coming alive, yelling, running backward in the mud doing a crazy sort of jumping-jack trot.

"Here we go," I said, stepping my horse away from Jack a few feet. Jack's rifle slipped quickly from his scabbard into his gloved hand. It swung back and forth once with a sharp click, levering a round into the chamber. The heavy lock fell to the ground. Clell dropped the axe and slid the car door open.

Jesse had already bounded into the car with his pistol in one hand and the bulky article he'd carried across his lap in the other. I saw now that what he carried was an ornate carpetbag. Cole looked around, then stepped up and into the car. *Come on, come on!* My mind raced.

"You can't do this," the clerk called out. His clipboard and pencil fell to the mud. He started across the street with his hands held chest high. "That's railroad money."

"We're *doing* it!" I heard Frank from sixty feet away. He

10

leveled his rifle toward the clerk. "Mind your own business," he added.

The clerk stopped, stood still biting his lip. It was at that second that I caught the first dull glint of metal from atop the rail station; and at the same second I felt the tension leave me, replaced now by the steel-hard calmness that comes when all fears are realized.

"Jack," I said, my voice going flat now that I saw what was come upon us.

"I saw it," he said, cutting me off.

He spun his reins one turn around his saddlehorn and stood in his stirrups with his rifle up, fanning the rooftop, watching, knowing it was coming. I swung the forty-four from beneath my duster and cocked it on the upswing, gigging my horse forward, pirouetting him in the mud. I'd just started to call out to Frank, when I saw a man in a derby hat and a long duster running from the same direction Clell and Hibbens had come only moments before. It was Joe Macky, our other lookout man.

"Ambush!" He screamed as he ran, waving a big Russian forty-four above his head, his duster tails fanned out behind him, mud splashing up on his black wool suit.

"Cover me, Jack!" I yelled, gigging my horse into the mud street, turning him toward Joe Macky just as rifle barrels filled the rooflines on both sides.

"Lord God! No!" I heard the clerk say as I charged past him. He dropped into a ball with his arms wrapped over his head. The world stopped, held its breath for just a second before it exploded above the squeal of hogs from the slaughter chute.

"Jooooe!" I leaned low to the side and saw his eyes shining with fear as I pounded toward him in a spray of mud. My arm dropped low and hooked out, ready to catch into his as I ran past him; but at fifty feet I reined back hard, seeing Joe Macky stop, spinning and jerking, as the bullets pounded into him from the rooftops. Chunks of him blew out of his black wool vest and sprayed red about him in a mist of blood. He went down hard, his cheekbone blown away, his derby hat sailing through the air. More shots thumped into his body and into the mud around him.

11

My horse slid sideways beneath me, thrashing, backpedaling wildly. I felt him going out from under me, and jerked my boot from the stirrup, sliding with him, sinking my boot heel into the mire, feeling it splash around us. Bullets whistled down, spitting into the mud. Behind me, the sound of gunfire answered them, cracking against the rooflines, spraying down a rain of splinters. A scream rose through the hail of fire. A rifleman bounced off the porch overhang and splashed facedown in the mud.

I was up now, pulling the reins, seeing my horse struggle to right himself. But he slipped, floundered in the mud. "Damn it!" I turned him loose and ran for the shelter of the boardwalk. When I leaped up on it, sliding, unable to stop, I barely had time to cover my face with my arms before crashing through the glass window of a mercantile store.

Bolts of cloth and shards of glass showered down around me. A woman screamed; a dog barked. I slammed face-first into a post and felt something ring in my head like a church bell. Outside, horses ran wildly from the livery. Rifle fire volleyed from the roofs.

"They've got our horses," one of the riflemen yelled from the rooftop.

Good, I thought, running, stumbling, crashing through the store with a fat little lapdog snapping at my heels. A woman stood behind a counter with her head ducked, her hands covering her face. The back door crashed open when I shouldered it; and when I jumped out, my muddy pistol was up, waving blindly at the sound of a horse pounding toward me.

"Don't shoot, it's me," I heard Jack say.

"Jack! Jack! I can't see a thing." I scrambled up behind him on the brule gelding, wiping blood and mud from my eyes. My nose throbbed.

"I found their horses and turned them loose," he yelled. We bolted forward and turned, sliding into an alley and back toward the street. "Jesse and the others pulled over to the corral. We gotta get outa here!"

"Where's my horse?" I raised a hand to my nose—*Broke, bigger than hell.* We reined up at the corner of the alley facing the street. The firing lulled.

"He's dead in the street," Jack said. He tapped the brule

12

forward a step, venturing from the alley, looking in both directions. At the corral a hundred yards away near the hog chute, Clell waved his hat to us above the wooden rails, then dropped it down as bullets spit from the rooftops and blew chunks of wood in the air.

"We gotta run for it. Will that pistol fire?"

"I doubt it," I said. My breath hammered in my chest. My broken nose throbbed.

"Then take mine. We gotta make a move."

I shoved my muddy pistol in my holster and slipped Jack's forty-four from his. "Waiting on you," I said. "Stay on the boardwalk as long as you can. It'll cover us some—"

"Don't tell me how to make a getaway. I *know* how to make a getaway."

"Then make it," I said, "and quit talking about it. Who are those guys?"

"I don't know. But they don't seem to think twice about gunning down freight clerks."

"Bounty hunters then," I said, scanning the street, seeing Joe Macky's twisted body lying there, facedown in the mud in his dandy black suit with his duster torn to shreds and blood-soaked. Ten yards away lay the freight clerk, still rolled in a ball, only now on his side in the mud, the top of his head missing.

"Yep, they hire their killing done. That's what I hate about railroads," Jack said.

"Me too," I said quietly, seeing my horse lying there dead, dark blood pooling in the mud around him.

Jack stepped the brule gelding out and up along the boardwalk as rifles pounded once more toward the corral. I knew Jesse and the boys would cover us as soon as we made our move, but knowing it didn't still the trembling in my stomach, nor would it shorten the distance between the end of the boardwalk and the thirty-yard dash beneath a hail of rifle fire.

But we made the dash.

Jack stalled the horse a few feet back from the end of the boardwalk, making sure Jesse and the others saw what we were going to do while the rifles above us pounded toward the corral and the slaughter chute. Two riflemen had come down from the roofs across the street and tried to take

13

position on us from around the corner of a building, but I turned and kept them pinned with Jack's pistol. The whole town smelled of burnt powder.

Jesse and the others held their fire for a second, making a full reload. Then, when they opened a heavy fire on the rooftops above us, Jack and I leaned low and braced ourselves. He spurred the big brule hard in the flanks, and we sailed out off the boardwalk, slipping, sliding, spinning, then pounding through the mud toward the slaughter chute while bullets whipped past us like hornets.

The mud-splattered brule raced past the corral and hog chute without even slowing down. Jesse waved us on toward the grassland with his fur hat in one hand and his pistol blazing in the other. When I looked back, the rest of the gang were mounted and moving out behind us, firing back at the rooftops.

We'd managed to get out of town one step ahead of the ambushers. Jack had spotted their horses reined up inside the livery barn, and he'd turned them loose and spooked them away when the shooting started. That's all that had saved us—that, and the deadly accuracy of Jesse, Frank, Cole, and Clell's pistol fire. Four bounty hunters lay face-down in the mud.

But Joe Macky and Early Hibbens also lay dead in the street, and Clarence Carter, who'd ridden in with Jesse and Frank, had taken a small-caliber bullet in his head on the way out of town. I couldn't help but think that dumb-looking boy shooting pigs must've hit him with a lucky shot, a wild shot made most likely from the cover of the hog chute, but something the boy could talk about the rest of his life.

Jesse and the others caught up to us along the trail back to Little Dog Creek. When we got there, Frank and Cole dragged Clarence Carter from his horse over to a tree and propped him against it. Jack helped Whiskey Ed and me bring up the fresh horses while Clarence laughed and coughed and babbled in a slurred voice. "It don't hurt none," I heard him telling Frank and Cole as I walked up leading the horses.

Behind me, Jack and Whiskey Ed quickly stripped saddles from the tired horses and set them free, fanning them away with their hats. Clarence looked up at me and said, "I'm shot in the head, you know it?" His eyes swirled. He shivered hard and tried to grin.

"Yeah," I said, "I know it." I glanced at Frank and saw him shake his head slowly. "Sorry, Clarence," I added.

"Aw . . . it don't hurt nothing like you'd think. It's like a bee stung me at first, then it just went numb. I'm fine, except things ain't so clear now." A trickle of blood pumped out above his ear, ran down, and dripped from his earlobe. "Just glad you and Jack made it out all right. Hell, I can still ride, shoot, and all—"

"You've had it, Clarence," Cole said, cutting him off.

Clarence sniffed, shivered hard. His face cramped and twisted tight on one side; then it settled and he said, "Hell, I know it, Cole. Just leave me a gun with ary one bullet in it. I know what to do."

"But will you do it?" I saw the dark expression in Cole's eyes, saw his hand rest on the pistol in his belt. "You won't be thinking straight before long. Don't wanta lay here saying something you shouldn't, do ya?"

"I understand," said Clarence Carter; and that was the last thing said until Jesse stepped up and handed me the carpetbag when Jack and I started to leave.

"Remember what it's cost us to get it," Jesse said, nodding at the bag. I just stared at him a second, then stepped up atop my black stallion, Buck, and reined away.

As Jack and I crossed the creek and headed up the other bank, we heard the sharp bark of Cole's forty-four. "Damn Cole," Jack said, gigging his horse on. I clenched my jaws tight and cursed under my breath. But neither of us looked back. Dying was just a part of the game. For Clarence Carter, the game had just played itself out.

15

CHAPTER

2

———•———

I stared out the window of the rattling railcar at a wall of jagged rock, at crevices streaked by skiffs of snow and laden with icicles. Now that we'd slanted upward and begun the last steep stretch up the mountain, the world outside the window moved past slower and slower. The engine at the head of the train pumped harder. Steam swirled. Such a small engine, I thought, for such a large mountain.

I sat holding the ornate carpetbag full of cash on my lap, keeping a hand on it at all times. Rawling Siding had cost the lives of three good men, and though our gains were ill gotten, they were also *hard* gotten. Being such, it was my duty to see to it they were *hard* kept. Clarence had been the bagman. Now his job had been passed to me. When Jesse had handed me the bag, I knew he meant for me to hold on to it till spring, when we'd meet again and divvy it up. This I would do at all cost.

It had been two weeks since the raid on Rawling Siding, and Jack and I had been hiding from pillar to post ever since. My broken nose was mending, but it was still the color of fruit gone bad. The dark circles had faded beneath my eyes, but they were still visible—too visible, I thought, for a man on the run who wanted to go unnoticed.

At the foothills to the mountain range, Jack and I had slipped into a small town, took on a change of heavy winter clothes at a trading post, and purchased train fare heading up to a mountain retreat called Lodge Pole. We counted on the place being nearly empty this time of year—a good place to rest, hide out, and let things settle here on the lower plains.

"Beware any endeavor that requires new clothes," Jack had said, chuckling, looking us both up and down in our mackinaw coats and thick wool shirts, the day we caught the train up to Lodge Pole. He was quoting from a leatherbound book of philosophy he'd been carrying around in his saddlebags. The book was titled *Walden's Pond,* by a man named Henry David Thoreau. Jack read it every chance he got, and quoted from it time to time when the spirit moved him.

My reply when he'd said it was simply "Beware of any endeavor that requires reading philosophy."

Yet I thought of Jack's words that day, still hearing the sound of Cole's big pistol as I gazed out into the wall of rock, snow, and ice, listening to the small engine struggle upward in a swirl of gray steam and wood smoke.

Jack's book told the story of a man gone off to the wilderness seeking retreat from the rigors of society. Supposedly Henry Thoreau found some spiritual enlightenment in building a cabin and communing with nature. More than once I'd skimmed through the book, but it didn't hold my interest near as much as, say, Shelley's *Frankenstein,* or some of Samuel Clemens' work.

I'd built more than one cabin in my life, and gotten no more from it than a dry place to sleep and two hands full of calluses. I'd communed with nature *many* times, usually by chewing on a stale biscuit and a cut of jerked beef, huddled near a low flame, somewhere deep in the woods. If these things had enlightened my spirit to any great extent, I'd never noticed it. But then, who was I to question Mr. Thoreau in what—to him—seemed such a noble undertaking?

I sniffed and touched a fingertip to my broken nose.

The other passengers had gotten off the train farther back down the mountain, at a strip of a town called Elk Ridge. Now the only other person in the car was a chunky feller in a striking plaid coat and a brown derby hat. He'd swayed in

17

through the front door only a moment earlier, and smiled as he rocked back and forth along the aisle.

I figured him to be a whiskey drummer, and as such, paid him no mind. He'd already started snoring, making sounds like bubbling tar and wood flutes back there, four seats behind me. Jack had gone out to the stock car to check on our horses. He'd been gone quite a while.

I'd just stood up to go see what was keeping Jack when all at once the rear door opened and down the aisle came the bluest eyes and palest blond hair I'd ever seen. She swayed back and forth with the rhythm of the rails, shielding her face with a dainty handkerchief. So sudden and striking was her appearance that I just stood staring as she stopped at the seat behind me and sat down in a soft rustle of petticoat. She glanced at me, then looked away quickly, but not before I caught a glimpse of the red welt across her cheek.

"Excuse me, ma'am," I said, slipping my hat from my head, "but are you all right?" I swayed with the rails, holding the carpetbag at my side.

"Oh," she said, looking up now as if having just noticed me there, "I hope I'm not disturbing you."

I looked into those blue eyes, caught a faint scent of lilac, and said, "Why, *no* ma'am. Not at all." I shot a glance around the car and wondered why she'd picked the seat right behind me. "But I couldn't help notice that you seem . . . distressed?" I nodded slightly at the handkerchief near her cheek. "Is there something wrong? Anything I can do?"

"Thank you, but no . . ." A nervous smile flickered, then vanished. She sighed, turned her cheek away from me, and dabbed at her eye with the handkerchief.

I stood there for a second wondering what to say next. Finally, I smiled and bowed slightly at the waist. "Permit me to introduce myself, ma'am. I'm Mr. Beatty . . . James Beatty."

I'd gotten so use to the name James Beatty that I sometimes forgot it was only an alias. My real name was Jeston Nash; but I'd changed it to Miller Crowe after the war. No sooner than I'd changed it to Miller Crowe, I'd killed a crooked sheriff and had to change it again.

18

Beatty was my *third* name, in a world were so few had so many.

"I'm Laura . . . Laura Larr." She glanced around nervously. "It's kind of you to inquire, Mr. Beatty, *very* kind. But there's nothing you can do. I'm afraid there's really nothing anyone can do—"

She stopped talking as the sound of the steel wheels grew louder through the open rear car door. I looked up as a husky young man in a suit too tight for him stepped inside and closed the door behind himself. Everything about him said *hired help,* as he swaggered forward. I saw the long holster strapped to his leg, barely hidden by his wool suit coat.

"There you are," he said, staring at her as he stepped closer. I saw a lot of belligerence rolled into that tight wool suit. He reached out a hand and grasped her firmly by her forearm. "Boss says, get on back there, right now. Says he's sorry. So don't make a fuss, okay?" He spoke in an offhanded manner, as if he'd just as soon crack her skull with a gun butt.

"Let go, Eldon, you're, hurting, me." She wrenched her arm away; but he leaned over, reached for her again as she cowered away across the seat.

This time as he reached, my hand caught his wrist before his hand caught her. He stopped cold. "That's far enough," I said, keeping my voice calm, my hand wrapped firmly around his wrist.

He raised his face around slowly toward me, still leaning, looking the way an animal of prey might look before making a lunge. He gazed at my hand on his wrist, saying, "The hell is this?"

"No, Eldon," she pleaded, "he's only trying—" He stared back into my eyes, straightening up, way up.

I stared right back, raising my eyes up there with him and letting my hand slip loose and fall to my side. "Leave the lady alone, amigo," I said, still holding the carpetbag of money in my other hand. He hadn't looked that tall before, but now I realized, looking up at him, that his chin was about level with the top of my head. His shoulders were broad enough to shade me on a sunny day.

"Did you just *touch* me, *boy?"* His expression was be-

19

mused but harsh; his cheeks turned dangerously red. I saw stringy yellow hair tremble beneath his small-brimmed hat. He smelled of cigar smoke and whiskey.

"Yeah," I said. "But that's just the first of *many* if you don't leave the lady alone."

"Eldon! Please!" Her voice quavered. He'd jerked a step toward me, but stopped as she caught him by the coat sleeve. My right hand rose instinctively and poised on my chest, a familiar poise near the handle of the Colt in my shoulder harness under my left arm. Pledging allegiance to hell, I always called it.

He glanced at my hand, then let out a breath and eased *his* hand away from the holster beneath his coat. "You're a lucky little snip." He sneered down at me. "I could fan you away like a popcorn fart."

Little snip? Fan me away? I glared at him, clenching the carpetbag in my left hand.

He looked back down at her as if I wasn't there, and said, "Boss says come on back there. You coming?"

"Yes," she said in a low and shaky voice; and she started to rise.

"Hold on," I said. I felt my hand growing moist around the handle of the carpetbag. "Ma'am, you don't have to do nothing you don't want to." I lowered my right hand, hooked my thumb in my hip pocket, and stared up at the big man, *Eldon,* she'd called him.

"Please, Mr. Beatty. It's . . . it's all right. He works for my husband, Ben Larr. I'll go with him."

"Yeah," *Eldon* said with a strange ugly grin. "I work for her husband. She's coming with me." He glanced at the carpetbag as he raised her by her forearm. "Go fold your nightshirt or sumpin, little *Angel boy.*"

Angel boy? What I felt like doing—what I *really* wanted to do, and could see myself doing plain as day, was to start beating his big head right down into the floor. Beat him with the carpetbag even, until the bag busted and dollars flew all over the car, then grab something else and keep right on beating him. But instead, I clenched my jaw and said to the lady, "Whatever you say, ma'am. It's your decision."

I reminded myself that Jack and I had just spent the last

20

two weeks hiding out in the woods. I didn't want to do something to draw attention to us and send us back out there.

As she stood the rest of the way up, I heard the door open once more and saw a well-dressed man standing there with a long cigar in his mouth. His necktie hung loose and his collar blared open. He looked mad-drunk, wild-eyed, swaying back and forth with one hand on the car door. "Eldon . . . Laura," he barked in a gravelly voice. "What's the holdup there? Both of you, get back here."

"I'm coming, Ben," she said. She looked terrified, turning and swaying away toward him. Something about her struck me that she was not a woman who tolerated abuse, yet she was doing so. Why?

"Then get a move on!"

But Eldon stood staring at me for a second until she was out of hearing range, puffing his chest in and out, straining the buttons on his *too*-tight vest. Then he leaned slightly toward me. I smelled his breath, like something dead had festered and turned green under his tongue. And there, close to my face, just between the two us he said, of *all* things, "Your nose looks like a goat's pecker, *Angel boy."* He glanced at the carpetbag with a nasty smirk, then turned and sauntered away.

I just stood there, stunned and seething, clenching and unclenching the handle on the carpetbag, my face red, knowing that the bag *was* embroidered with little purple angels that appeared to be fluttering around long willowy reeds. I swayed with the car and watched him stop as he started through the door. The other man took out his cigar, gestured it toward me, and said something to Eldon. But I couldn't make it out above the noise of the train. Big Eldon glanced over his shoulder, shrugged, and swiped a hand back toward me as if swatting a fly. Then the door closed.

"I saw that," said the man in the plaid coat. "Saw the whole thing." He wiped sleep from his eyes, leaned forward in his seat, and whipped off his brown derby. "It was a vulgar display of rudeness if you ask me." He ran a hand back across his hair. It was sleek with oil and finely parted in the middle.

21

I nodded, still seething, touching the tip of my sore nose as I turned and sat down. I swung the carpetbag onto the aisle seat beside me and kept my hand on it; but no sooner than I'd gazed back out the window, I caught a glimpse of the plaid suit coat reflecting in the glass. "If you ask me," he continued, leaning beside me, "we're getting far too lenient of rudeness in this country. I'm afraid it'll have a dramatic effect on our whole society, in time."

I looked around and up at him. He stood with one hand on the back of the seat beside me and the other on the seat in front, rocking back and forth. A pudgy little man. I nodded. "Yes we are, I'm afraid."

"If you'll permit me—" He reached a hand toward the carpetbag, but I smoothly swept a hand in under his and lifted it away. I placed it on the floor between my boots. "I'm Beam . . . Brerton Beam." His voice was somewhat strained above the clack of the rails and the heavy chug of the engine only two cars away. "I'm a traveling—"

"Drummer," I said, smiling as I finished his words for him.

"What? Oh, a *drummer?* Why yes! Indeed I am. But how did you know?"

I raised my eyes to his hat, then down to his plaid jacket. His face flushed slightly. "Oh, of course. How obvious of me."

"What do you sell, whiskey?" My voice also rose as the engine seemed to struggle harder.

"My, my, what perception you have, Mister . . . Beatty? Did I hear you tell the lady?"

"Yes, it's Beatty . . . James Beatty. I'm a horse trader out of Missouri."

I shook his soft warm hand, glanced back out the window, then back to him as he said, "Seldom do I have the pleasure of meeting a man with such perception and . . . might I dare say, sensitivity as yourself, especially on this last stretch up to Lodge Pole."

I just looked at him curiously until he glanced down at the carpetbag, then back up with a smile as he added, "After all, that certainly is quite a—how should I say it—*gentleman's* commodity valise? Isn't it?"

KILLERS OF MAN

"Beam, Beam," I said, shaking my head slowly. "This belongs to a friend of mine. He's checking on our horses. He's quite ill." I jiggled the carpetbag. "Would you believe that this is full of all the tonics and medications he has to take, and I mean, take *daily!*"

"That poor man." He made a clucking sound. "I suppose he's here for the cold weather? The healing properties of clean mountain air?"

"Exactly," I nodded, "I'm here to care for him as best I can. Until—" I let out a sigh. "—Well, until such time as he no longer needs mortal help." I gazed upward.

"What a true friend you are. And apparently you've been in an accident of some sort yourself?"

I touched my fingers to my nose and nodded. "Yes. I accidently smacked myself with a hammer . . . building new pews for our church back home."

"My, my." He shook his head. "And to think that a blackguard like that one a while ago had the audacity to chastise you in such a manner."

"Yeah," I nodded again, "did you *hear* what he said to me?" I cocked a brow.

"No, not very clearly I'm afraid. What did he say?"

"Well, I won't repeat it, but it was very crude and coarse," I said. "Let's just put it that way." I glanced back out the window, caught myself rubbing my nose, and stopped. *I'll see that son of a bitch again. Yep, I'll get him.*

Outside the window, thin icicles had turned into ice swords as we traveled higher. The skiffs of snow now turned into thick white drifts that drooped over the high edge of the wall and sloped down from the rock crevices. Some drifts had given way with the vibration of the train and had poured down and spilled onto the tracks. Now a gray slush streaked the window as we chugged and rocked, swaying ever upward.

Over the next twenty or so minutes I learned everything a person could possibly want to know about the brewing, aging, bottling, and distribution of malt beer, bock beer, scotch, brandy, bourbon, whiskey, gin—Beam apparently

23

enjoyed his work—schnapps, tequila, Russian potato vodka. Then he went on to explain the vineyard processing of French wine, German Rhine, Italian rosé; and why good champagne could be dangerous in a crowd if not opened properly. Twice I tried lying to him, telling him I didn't even drink. But it didn't faze him.

I was grateful to see Quiet Jack stumble and sway through the forward door of the car and stomp over to the potbellied stove in the front corner. "Lord have mercy!" He batted his arms across his chest. "It's colder than a whore's heart!" Flakes of frost danced in the air about him. He stared at me wide-eyed and shivering. "Didn't you hear me yelling my lungs out?" His nose was red and shiny, as were his cheeks and ears beneath his drooping hat brim.

"No," I said, "about what?" I rose slightly, looking for any reason to get away from Beam. The man's eyes had glazed over as he droned on and on above the rattle of the train. "Excuse me," I said, standing, picking up the carpetbag, stepping past him and into the aisle. He stopped talking, but kept his thumb and finger in the air, still showing the proper length of a cork.

"This is your sick friend?" He spoke softly as if not to disturb the dying, then lowered his fingers. I only nodded and walked to Jack, steadying myself with one hand from seat back to seat back, carrying that damned carpetbag.

"Man oh man! I'm out there locked in the damned stock car, and you can't hear me hollering? I could've froze to death."

I stopped, facing him as he bounced on his toes with his arms folded. "How in the world'd you get locked in?" I looked him up and down. "How'd you get *out?*"

"Bolt must've fallen and locked." He turned, laid his shivering red hands near the top of the glowing stove, then pressed them to his face. "Had to pull a slat loose to reach through and lift it. You didn't hear me yell?"

"Jack. If I *heard* you, don't you think I would've come running? I couldn't hear nothing for that damned—" I stopped myself from saying *whiskey drummer,* and said *engine* instead. I glanced back at Beam and saw him stand up and sway toward us.

"Perhaps, I have something here that would help." I saw him pull a silver flask from inside his plaid coat as he rocked toward us. "That is, if your condition will allow—"

"God-yes-give-it-here!" Jack snatched the flask from Beam's hand, untwisted the metal cap, and threw back a long gurgling drink.

"This is a very fine brandy, made by a hostel of priests, who devote their lives to the—"

"This is Mr. Beam," I said, keeping Beam from going into a spiel. I spoke to Jack's upturned chin. His Adam's apple jumped and dropped.

When his head came back down, he let out a long hiss and ran his hand across his mouth. "God bless those wonderful holy men and the fine work they do."

Beam reached for the flask, but Jack turned it up again. I heard it go empty with a metallic pop; then Jack handed it back. "What *condition* were you talking about?" He looked at Beam with a curious turn of his head.

"I told him you were ill," I said quickly, before Jack could offer something to the contrary. "Told him how I was bringing you up here, hoping the cold would do you some good?"

Jack stalled for a second, then said, "Uh . . . that's true, Mr. Beam—" He stifled a cough with his hand, then held his hand out to Brerton Beam. Beam hesitated, but then shook hands. "Nobody knows what it is, but folks back home are dropping like flies from it. Contagious as hell."

"My goodness!" Beam rubbed his hand on his trouser leg, then pulled a handkerchief from inside his plaid coat. He wiped his hand and nodded at the carpetbag. "I hope you have plenty of medicine in your bag for it."

Jack glanced at the bag with its purple angels and willowy reeds, then at me, then back to Beam. "Actually, it's *his* bag." He nodded toward me. "He's just been gracious enough to carry my medicine in it." He shot me a dark glance, and added, "I carry my belongings in saddlebags . . . *leather.*" He made a fist. "Very *strong* leather saddlebags." Then he opened his hand, swiped it toward the carpetbag and shook his head. "I don't know why he carries some-

25

thing like *that."* He turned back to the stove, smiling. "Crazy, I guess."

"Yes, well—" I cleared my throat, feeling my face burn. "—it belonged to my mother before she died. I can't part with it."

"Oh, I see," said Beam. He seemed relieved about something. "I dare say, gentlemen, for just a second there I wondered if perhaps . . ." He turned a hand in the air, smiled, and glanced back and forth between us.

"So, Beam," Jack said after a second of pause, "how much brandy did them ole *holy-boys* make?"

"Huh?" Beam looked bewildered, then caught on and said, "Oh, you'd like another drink?" He raised a finger. "I'll just be a moment . . . have more in my kit." He pointed back toward his seat as he turned and rocked away down the aisle.

Jack leaned close and spoke just above a whisper. "The hell's going on here? Why'd you tell him I'm sick? Do I look sick to you? You oughta see *your* nose. Anybody can tell by looking that you ain't exactly a *nurse."*

"Jack . . ." I stopped and wondered for a second just how to explain it, about the woman, her husband, big Eldon and his vulgar description of my nose. *Yes sir, I'll get that big ole boy.* But then I only said, "Forget it, Jack. I'll explain it later."

We watched Brerton Beam rise up slowly from his seat and start back toward us, swaying, grinning, carrying a bottle of brandy in his stubby hand. Beside me, Jack stood shivering, rubbing his hands together. At the rear of the car, the door opened slowly and big Eldon stepped inside.

"I hope I don't have to thump this big idiot," I said to Jack, under my breath. Jack shot me a curious glance; but before I could say anything else, there came a tremendous crash that slammed Jack and me backward, bouncing us off the potbellied stove and tumbling us against the front wall of the car. *"Holy!"*

Beam came rolling forward in a dizzying ball of plaid and a spray of brandy. I heard Eldon sliding across the top of seat backs like someone running a hand along a picket fence. Then I felt my breath gush out, hard enough to loosen roof shingles, as Beam slammed into my chest. *"The brandy!"* I heard Jack yell, saw his hand grab the bottle before it hit the wall.

In a few seconds the world settled, and seemed to right itself. I lay on the floor staring up, trying to breathe deep. Beneath me, I felt the slow solid pulse of the steam engine, then the long hiss of steam as the engineer released it from the boiler.

"One minute I'm freezing to death . . . next minute I'm burnt all to hell," I heard Jack say.

"What happened, Jack?" I raised myself up and looked around, at Beam who'd bounced off me and landed upside down in the front corner, at big Eldon's feet sticking up over the back of a seat, one boot hanging off his foot.

"If I had to guess, I'd say we struck the side of the mountain. You all right?"

"Yeah," I said in a strained voice, "I think so. You?"

"Burnt my hand on the stove," he said, slinging his hand up and down. "Not bad, just enough to hurt good. Lucky that stove is well secured or we'd be slapping flames right now."

"Yeah," I said wryly. "It's always safety first with these railroads, I reckon."

I stood up, picked up the carpetbag from against the wall, stepped over, and tipped Beam down from the corner. He was knocked cold as a wedge. A short-barreled Merwin Hulbert revolver had fallen out of his plaid coat. I picked it up, checked it, and shoved it down in his waist.

"Mr. Beam's gonna have a hell of a headache," I said. Then I nodded back to Eldon's feet sticking up above the seat. "I hope that big ugly bastard's dead."

"Who is he?" Jack stepped beside me and threw back a shot of brandy.

"Some jake-leg, who works for some other jake-leg," I said. "The one in charge is called Ben Larr. He's a wife smacker, evidently."

"How do you know that?"

"I met his wife while you were attending the horses. She's got a welt on her face . . . looks like *somebody* smacked her one." I nodded again toward Eldon and heard a low groan

27

from down in the seat. "That one's a low, vulgar-mouthed bastard."

Jack chuckled. "Take it easy. What'd he ever do to you?"

"What'd he do to me?" I reached down, picked up my battered slouch hat, slapped it against my leg, and dropped it on my head. "Let me *tell* you what he had the nerve to *say* to me. . . ."

CHAPTER

3

I'd slapped Beam's face back and forth gently, until he blinked his eyes and touched his fingers to the knot on top of his head. "What happened?" His eyes swam around the railcar. I pitched him his brown derby hat. Jack and I walked back toward the door at the rear of the car. We heard big Eldon groan, and saw his feet twitch as we passed him. I hoped he'd be stuck there for the rest of the day.

Jack looked down, shook his head, and chuckled. "He really said something like that to you?"

"I don't think it's so funny, Jack," I said; and I walked on ahead carrying the carpetbag.

"No, but it's fairly original, don't you think? *I've* never heard anybody say something like that. It's almost like a schoolboy remark."

"You'll never hear *him* say it again either, not to me. One more nickel's worth of his mouth, and I'll beat his head down between his shoulder blades. Look at him. Don't he just look like somebody you'd want to beat the hell out of every time you passed him on the street?"

"Yeah, he does . . . but why're you so damned worked up about it? It ain't like he spoke ill of your mother or something. There's lots of things been said about ya before. I never seen ya like this over it."

"There was just no cause for his saying it, Jack." I stopped

29

at the rear door and turned to Jack. Back up the aisle I saw Eldon's boot fall off his foot, then saw him struggling to right himself and get out of the seat. "I've been called nearly everything from a horse's ass to a buck baboon, but nobody's ever said anything like that to me. It was a very personal sort of insult."

"I don't see that much to it. But if *you* do, you shoulda busted his head right then, not let it eat at ya."

"I figured I better let it go for now. To tell you the truth, it kind of caught me off guard, hearing him say something like that right out of the blue." I almost raised my hand to my sore nose, but I stopped myself and opened the door. "Does it really look that bad?"

Jack chuckled and shook his head. "I've seen ya look better. Let's just put it that way."

A cold wind rushed across us as we stepped over through crusty ice to the next car. It was a fancy car, painted glossy black. Elaborate brasswork trim lined the upper edge and down the corners. Icicles hung above a large brass plate that displayed the words COL. BENJAMIN LARR RET. engraved in fancy scrolled letters.

"Anyway," I said, as I reached out and knocked on the door, *"Why?* Why would a man say something like that? Why not just call me a bad name or something like anybody else would? I figure he's gonna be on me the rest of the trip if I don't settle with him."

"You're really making too big a deal of it," Jack said; and he'd started to say more, but stopped when a peephole slid open an inch and a voice inside said, "Yeah? What do you want?"

I shot Jack a glance, then said to an eye staring through the hole, "Just making sure everybody's all right back here. We just hit something."

"We know that," said the eye, searching us up and down through the small brass hole.

Behind the eye, I heard another voice say, "Tell them to get the hell away from here."

"You heard that," said the voice behind the eye. "Now get on away from here!" The peephole snapped shut.

I looked at Jack and shrugged. We'd started to turn and walk away, when we heard footsteps crunching through the snow and saw a breath of steam curl up around the corner of the car.

"Be-jesus," said a voice, "it's colder than an I-don't-know-what out here." Behind the breath of steam, a rough hand caught the corner rail on the car and an old man in striped overalls swung up beside us. He stopped at the sight of us and looked us up and down, rubbing a gloved hand over his jaw. "Y'all all right here?"

"You the engineer? What the hell happened?" I looked at him as he stepped between us and knocked hard on the door. He smelled of wood smoke and oil.

"Fireman, brakeman, and oiler, all three," he said. He shook his head beneath the floppy railroad cap. "Think I'd be walking back here in this cold if I was a full-time engineer? *Hell* no!" He knocked harder. "I'd be back up *there,* my feet warmer than Aunt Lucy's ass, letting some other poor sumbitch do all this—" His voice kicked up a notch: "Open this damned door! I'm too old for this kinda malarkey!"

He turned back to me as the peephole snapped open again. "We just hit a big drift, is all, young fellers. But we'll be the rest of the day getting shed of it. Gotta expect this kinda stuff, this time of year."

"Keep your shirt on, old man," said the same voice I'd heard a moment before. A bolt clicked inside the door and it swung open, crunching ice beneath it on the metal deck. A tall man in a buckskin coat looked at Jack and me, then at the old fireman. "Boss ain't feeling so good. He wants to be up the mountain before dark. Do what it takes to get us going again . . . and be quick about it."

"What it takes?" The old man leaned forward. "What it takes, Renfrow, *my fine, warm friend,* is everybody out there on a shovel, getting this blasted snow off the tracks. If you think I'm doing it all by myself, you're outa your *egg-sucking* mind! I'll quit this job in a flat minute and go to picking grit with the chickens before I'll—"

"What's all the commotion out there, Dallas?" said Ben Larr's voice; and I leaned just enough to see him standing there, halfway back in the car in a long nightshirt, weaving, one hand grasping a handsome wing-back chair for support. "Get him on in here and shut that door."

31

"Now you've done it," the man in buckskin hissed at the old fireman.

"Horse squat. I'm too old to worry about upsetting people." The old man shoved himself inside the car, even with the other man's hand on his chest. I shrugged at Jack and we stepped in also.

"Mr. Larr, we're in a bank out here ten feet high," said the old man, stepping forward. The man in buckskin tried holding him back near the door. Jack and I stepped to the side. Another man stepped before us with his hand on his holstered forty-four.

"Let him go, Dallas," Ben Larr said. The old man glared at the one called Dallas. He shook his coat and took another step closer to Ben Larr.

"I tried telling him, it's gonna take everybody to get us shoveled out of here," the old man continued. "If we dick around long enough, we'll catch a blizzard and that boiler'll freeze and bust. Then you'll be out a railroad—"

The man standing before Jack and me looked us up and down. He looked like more hired help, of the same caliber as big Eldon, I thought.

"I see," said Ben Larr. He looked from the old fireman to Jack and me, nodding toward us. I thought he was being friendly, and I started to nod in return, but then he said, "And who are these yardbirds?"

Yardbirds? "Now, just one minute—"

I'd started forward, but the man before me stood firm, blocking my way. "Easy," he warned.

"Let him be, Brace," Larr said to the man. "We'll hear him out."

I looked at Jack. His thumb hooked in his belt near his holster. His expression had turned flat and hollow, staring past the others at Larr.

"I'm Beatty . . . James Beatty," I said. "And that's the *only* name I respond to." I looked from one to the other.

"The hell's he getting at?" said the one before me to the one in buckskin. I gazed past them and at Larr, standing there red-eyed in his nightshirt behind a polished wooden table.

"I'm saying, if you expect me and my friend to shovel this

train out, you best keep a civil tongue in your heads." I glanced around. "All of you."

"I don't recall asking you, Mr. Beatty . . . *James* Beatty," said Larr in a mock tone. "I own this rail line from Elk Ridge to Lodge Pole. I say who shovels and who doesn't."

That stopped me for a second. Was he saying he wouldn't let me help shovel us out? All right, I could live with that. I gazed around the car as I stood there thinking of what to say next. It was as plush as a suite in a New York hotel—inlaid oak bar, walnut sculpted picture and chair rail, richly colored tapestries, Oriental rugs, fine furniture.

I saw that this car looked shorter than the others, but then realized it was partitioned off. Beyond the rear door would not be the cold blowing wind and the smell of steam and wood smoke, rather the warm bed of Laura Larr, in which she might be lying this very moment. I almost let out a breath thinking about it.

"That's fine with me," I said to Larr, back now to who would or wouldn't shovel snow, but still catching glimpses of her in a warm bed, maybe with a silk sheet draped halfway up her creamy pale leg, back there beyond the dividing wall. "We've got horses, my friend and I. We can ride on from here and *leave* you to your shoveling."

"That's certainly your free decision," Larr said in an offhand manner.

"Damn right it is." I turned to the old fireman, who stood scratching his head beneath his cap. "How much farther to Lodge Pole?" I asked.

He shrugged his thick-shouldered coat. "Hell, seventeen, eighteen miles." Then it seemed to dawn on him what I was talking about and he snapped his eyes to mine. "Why, you worthless piece of chicken shit. You'd leave us here to freeze over, let that boiler bust, rather than bend your back a little and help us get out?"

I stared at the old fireman, hearing Jack chuckle under his breath. "You heard Mr. Larr," I said. "He doesn't want our help. Right, Larr?" I turned back to him, and saw that a cigar had appeared, was lit and curling smoke up the side of his face as he blew out a thin gray stream.

"That is correct. I do *not* want your help. I only desire people around me who are interested in the good of all. If you're not that type of person, feel free to dismiss yourself. You *will not* be missed."

I heard Jack say quietly to me, "Maybe we oughta help out, if it'll get this train going—"

"Naw, naw, naw!" I shook a finger and spread a sly grin at Larr. "I see what you're doing . . . but it won't work. You ain't horning us into shoveling snow off *your* railroad. Not us *yardbirds."* I turned to Jack, flipping up my coat collar. "Come on, let's ride outa here."

I couldn't help turning back to Larr from the door. "Maybe you need to learn how to talk a little more civil to folks, *Mister* Larr. It's a big world, and none of us are any better than the other. We all need to show a little manners. Think about that while your toes go numb shoveling snow."

Again I started to leave, but once again I had to stop, turn, and say, "Oh . . . and your boy, *Eldon?* He's back there learning to walk upside down. Get *him* a shovel!" I stepped out and slammed the door behind us, not really feeling any better because I hadn't gotten the proper response, I thought. They'd just stood there staring at us blank-faced, Larr exhaling smoke and studying the end of his cigar.

"Guess I straightened them out, huh?" I leveled my hat, hefted the carpetbag closer to my chest, and stepped down off the platform into the snow.

"No," Jack said. "All you did was call attention to us. We coulda just gone along with him. You didn't have to make a big thing of it."

"Jack. Nobody has the right to act the way that man was acting. *Yardbirds?* Then that *Eldon* saying what he said about my nose? Where do these people get off?"

Jack had stepped down beside me and leaned on his hand against the wall three feet away. "Okay, maybe you're right," he said. He nodded his head until I stopped raving, then gestured his free hand along the side of the train. "But now, how do we get our horses?"

Aw naw. I gazed along the narrow corridor between the train and the wall of rock and ice, a width of three feet or less where we stood, even more narrow up by the stock car. Snow flurried off the wall and swirled back in my face.

34

KILLERS OF MAN

I swallowed hard, stepped under the car with that damned carpetbag against my chest and out on the other side. *Whooa!* I caught myself, and jerked back flat against the car. Less then a yard away lay a drop of over three hundred feet. White clouds of snow swirled and danced above the swaying tops of pine, aspen, and spruce across the valley below.

I leaned on the shovel for a second, then took off a glove and wiped a hand across my brow. Behind us, the engine thumped and pulsed, bleeding off enough steam now and then to keep the pressure low and steady. I looked back at it, there at the end of the high piles of snow on either side of the cleared tracks.

Before us lay another fifteen-foot stretch of high drifted snow, mixed with chunks of rock and dirt that had spilled down with it from the crevices in the steep wall. I knew how much farther we had to clear, because I'd been the one to climb the drift and crawl to the other end, just to make sure before we'd started. My knees were wet now, as were my forearms.

Big Eldon stood near the front of the engine, walking back and forth with a wool muffler wrapped around his head from under his chin, tied up over the crown of his hat. He carried a rifle cradled in his arms. Behind him, leaning against the train, another of Larr's men stood sipping coffee from a steaming tin cup.

"This must be what a chain gang feels like," I said to Jack and the old fireman. "Look at that foulmouthed bastard strutting, back and forth, back and forth. For two cents I'd choke him with his muffler. I'd take his rifle and shove it down his—"

"Why don't you settle down and quit picking at everybody?" Jack stopped shoveling and rested both hands on his shovel handle. "All you're doing is aggravating yourself. Him saying what he said had nothing to do with us shoveling snow."

"Well . . . I'm demanding our money back," I said. "It's Larr's railroad. We paid to ride it. If we shovel snow, Larr should at least have to refund us our fare. That's no more than right, is it?"

35

"Ha," the old fireman said. "Good luck collecting what's *right* from the colonel. Larr's got the first dollar he ever screwed anybody out of—all rich men do. That's the way they got to be so rich."

"I've got nothing against *rich,*" I said. "But something tells me he was born a turd, and all money did was make him smell worse."

"Hell, you don't know nothing." The old fireman laughed across empty gums, save for two crooked teeth and a wad of tobacco.

"You might be surprised what I know," I said. "I know he smacks his wife around. I saw that clear enough."

"Ha! Smacks Laura? *Laura Larr?*" He shook his head and spit. "Don't you ever fret about little Laura, she knows which side of the bread the butter's on."

"What's that supposed to mean?"

"You boys quit talking . . . and keep shoveling up there," Eldon called out from within his warm muffler. I pictured myself walking back there calmly and slowly, and ringing the shovel upside his big head. But I let out a breath. I'd get him, yes sir! When the time was right . . . I'd get him.

Before we'd started, I'd checked on the horses, Jack's silver-gray gelding and my black stallion, Buck. I found them huddled close together at the front end of the stock car, grinding hay in their mouths and shaking out their manes. Steam snorted from their nostrils; heat rose off their backs.

Good, I'd thought; and before going to work on the snowdrift, I'd taken the bound stacks of money from the bag and lined them around my waist beneath my shirt. I'd told Jack that now at least we could get rid of that damned carpetbag.

"Jesse'll want it back," Jack had said. "I think it's a keepsake."

"Damn it!" I'd stuffed the bag behind some hay in the corner of the stock car before we left. On the way out, I looked at the lock on the car door and wondered how a man could get himself locked in there. As I'd stood there looking at it, Ben Larr had stepped out of the next car back, puffing his cigar. Two of his men came out behind him.

"So, you've managed to break a slat off my brand new stock car, I see." Larr spread a sarcastic smile.

I looked down at the broken slat Jack had managed to bust loose to get his hand out to the bolt. "I didn't break a damned thing," I'd told him. "My friend got locked in and had to break it."

"Locked in? Why, that's preposterous." He laughed, turned to the man in buckskins and the other one beside him. "Hear that, Brace, hear that, Dallas? His friend locked himself in the stock car."

The other two chuckled; Larr spun back to me. "Beatty, how you *do* go on." He let go a puff of smoke, leaning close, cocking his head at a jaunty angle. "Tell me . . . do you ever take the responsibility for anything you do? I bet not." He'd winked and stepped down off the platform. He was clear-eyed and chipper as a squirrel. A wake of cigar smoke drifted behind him.

The man in buckskins, Dallas Renfrow, had smiled and dropped a shovel at my feet. "Don't get too cold," he'd said.

I shook my head now, thinking about it, and leaned back to shoveling snow off the tracks. By the time we'd neared the end of the drift, the flurries had stopped by some twist of nature and the evening sun came out, peeped down over the edge of the wall above us, and streaked across the valley below in long golden rays.

Eldon had moved up closer to us, still cradling his rifle and pacing back and forth. I avoided even looking at him; I couldn't put my finger on why I thought it, but somehow I got the idea that he held me to blame for him having knocked himself out in the railcar.

"We're here to hunt bear," he'd said, to no one in particular. I just kept shoveling, figuring there were probably many times when big Eldon just blurted out something like that for no reason. "Anybody ain't man enough to *hunt* bear, ain't man enough to *eat* bear," he added.

Shoveling beside me, Jack rolled his eyes, grinned, and kept working. I let out a breath and leaned into shoveling. I'd try to ignore Eldon if I could. But I'd get him . . . when the time was right.

"Ever eat bear, Beatty?" Eldon stepped over beside me as

37

he spoke. I saw his boots. A dark wet line had spread across his toes and halfway up to his ankles.

"No," I said, lying, without looking up. "I don't eat anything of the canine family. It'd be the same as eating a cocker spaniel, far as I'm concerned."

"Whaaaat? I've never heard of nothing like that."

I smiled to myself, and said, "There's probably a long, long list of things you've never heard of, Eldon." I felt my hand close tight around the shovel handle, could picture *and* hear it whooshing through the air. "I bet you've never heard of a man my size, lifting a big sumbitch—"

"That about cleans it up," Jack said, seeing where I was headed, cutting me off before I got there. He straightened up, rubbing his gloved hands together. Ahead of us, the drift was now only a foot-high pile of loose snow and dirt. "Good thing, too." He glanced up at the ever-graying sky above us. "We'll soon be out of daylight."

I heard footsteps walking up behind us and turned to see Ben Larr and his other two *hired hands.* Larr stopped, slapped his gloves together, and gazed all around the narrow pass, out across the valley, then back to me. "Well, Mr. Beatty . . . *James* Beatty." He smiled around his cigar. "It's all done. We can go on. Now, did it really hurt you so bad . . . being a part of a joint effort? Pitching in . . . doing something good?" He made a fist and feigned a brotherly poke at my stomach.

I just stared at him. "You owe us money, Larr. I was just telling my friend . . . your train . . . your problem. We paid for passage up to Lodge Pole, not to shovel *your* snow off of *your* tracks for you."

"Boss," said big Eldon, handing his rifle to the man beside him. "Why don't I bat this little sucker's head against that wall a few good licks."

He leveled his shoulders and stepped toward me. I raised the shovel with both hands tight around the handle and drew it back. "There's nothing I'd like better, *Eldon,* than to change your whole outlook."

"Gentlemen!" said Larr. He stepped forward, spread his arms between us. "This is what's wrong with the world! Nobody wants to get along anymore—" He looked at me. "—make sacrifices and work together!" He rocked slightly

38

on his right foot. Dallas Renfrow threw out a hand to steady him, but Larr waved his hand away and said, "Mr. Beatty. I'll gladly see to it your fare is refunded, if you wish."

He looked around at everybody. "But I didn't come out here to argue. It's nearly dark . . . and I came to thank you *all* for your help, and to tell you that we have a nice hot steak dinner awaiting you in my dining car." He spread a smile. "Just my way of saying a heartfelt *thanks.*"

Damn it all. I felt my face turn bloodred and I ducked my eyes away. "As you well know, Freddie," Larr said to the old fireman. "It pains me that I couldn't be out here lending my back to the effort—"

"Aw yeah?" I blurted out. "Then why didn't you? Your leg ain't broke."

"Leave it alone," I heard Jack say beside me out the corner of his mouth. But it was too late.

Ben Larr's men glanced down, shaking their heads slowly. "Indeed it isn't broken," Larr said; and he raised his trouser leg just enough to show me the polished wooden prosthetic beneath it. "I'm afraid the Sioux have resolved any chance of that ever happening."

Jesus. I felt like turning the shovel around and smacking myself in the face with it.

"I told you to leave it alone," Jack said quietly as Ben Larr and his men turned and walked away.

Big Eldon swung a step wider than the others, leaned toward me, and said in passing, "Ain't you about the lowest horse's ass ever lived."

What could I say? Jack and I walked back to the car with our shovels over our shoulders. Old Freddie had walked along with us until we got to the engine; then he'd looked at me, grunted, and shaken his head, as if still thinking about what I'd said to Larr. He spit a stream and hefted himself up the steel ladder rungs.

"Getting dark quick," he said. "We best be hauling as soon as I pressure up and charge some running lights. One of ya bring me up a plate of dinner, if ya would." He glanced at me: "That is, if your *leg ain't broke.*" He grunted again, still shaking his head as he swung into the engine.

We went back into the car where Brerton Beam sat holding a handkerchief full of snow against his head. He'd

39

lit and trimmed a small oil lamp and hung it above a window for light. "Sorry I wasn't able to help out there," he said. "I've been dizzy, blurred vision, gosh, I hope I won't be needing medical attention—"

I waved a hand. "Think nothing of it, we knew you were hurt."

"Because I would've been right there on a shovel, cheerfully doing my part. I hate a shirker . . . or someone who constantly complains about doing their share."

"I said it's all right, Mr. Beam." I sat down, hearing Jack stifle a laugh. "If you're feeling better, we're all invited to dinner in Mr. Larr's dining car."

"Oh, my! What an honor. What a truly gracious man to offer such hospitality after all that's happened here."

"Yeah, yeah," I said. "Anyway, I'm glad you're feeling better, after that bump on your head."

"Well thank you for both your help, and concern." Beam smiled. "I hesitate to ask you this, but in the stir of things I seem to have lost my wallet." He held up his thumb and finger. "Black wallet? This size? I know someone found that dreadful pistol I have to carry. I hope you also saw my wallet lying about. Nothing of any importance in it to anyone, except me." He shrugged. "Only a letter from my precious daughter, Elly, a photograph of my wife, Vera."

"Haven't seen it," I said. I glanced at Jack, he shrugged.

"Oh, there might have been a couple of dollars in it. But I'd gladly consider that a reward for anyone who returned it."

I detected his slight implication, and I raised a hand. "Hold it, Mr. Beam. I found your pistol, shoved it in your waist, and that's that. Had I found your wallet"—I nodded at Jack—"or if he'd found it, we would've put it back in your pocket. Are we clear on this?"

He bit the knuckle on his thumb and said, "I'm afraid I didn't handle that very well, did I? What I meant was, I know things happen, things get misplaced, sometimes even with the best intentions we forget. . . ."

"Beam," I said more firmly. "We haven't *seen* your wallet. Now, without going into a long-winded spiel, just answer me yes or no. Do you think we have it?"

40

KILLERS OF MAN

He studied our eyes for a second, his eyes darting nervously from one of us to the other. He appeared to be sitting on straight pins. It must've been killing him to say just *one* word. Then he let out a tense breath and opened his mouth.

"BURRR-RARRRRRR-UUULLL!!!" He bawled out in a voice deeper than cannon fire. The whole car quivered. I nearly jumped over Jack and into the floor before I realized it wasn't Beam's voice at all, but the sound of something huge, something monstrous and angry just outside the window beside me.

There came another, shriller scream—this time it *was* Beam's voice—and as I turned to the window, glass crashed into my face and something foul-smelling and hairy knocked me across the railcar.

Once again I was surrounded by a world of plaid, Beam atop me and Jack, Jack struggling to draw his pistol with Beam pawing us and screaming. The car rocked dangerously high on one side as I saw a bear paw bigger than *any* I'd ever seen. Claws the size of steel winch hooks spread out, and ripped the back off the seat where I'd sat a second before. "God almighty!"

Jack shoved Beam away, snatched out his pistol, and got off two rounds. We heard another terrible growl like thunder, and saw half the seat pulled out the window. Then silence fell upon us like the cold hand of death; and I stood there shaking, feeling my hat brim flutter like the wings of a bird.

I heard a rifle shot, then another, one of them ricocheting off the rock wall. "Good, it's Eldon!" I yelled. But then we heard the rend and ripping of wood coming from the direction of the stock car, followed by the high-pitched whinnying of Jack's silver-gray gelding.

"The horses," Jack yelled, "let's go!" And I raced with him along the aisle, out into the cold. A shot whistled past our heads as we jumped off the platform.

"It's us, damn it!" Jack yelled. We raced on, hugging close to the cars, hearing bullets sail past us like hornets.

"Stay down!" Eldon yelled, but we ran on, our shoulders swiping against the car until we reached the stock car and

41

hurled ourselves up the platform. Two more shots ricocheted off the wall. "I missed him, Boss! That damned idiot got in my way!"

Inside the car, Jack's gelding kicked and snorted, racing around the car, slamming the walls. Even in the dark, I saw the dark red blood dripping from its face and felt it splatter on *my* face as the big silver-gray slung its head. Jack leaped out and grabbed the gelding around the neck, wrestling it. It screamed, stomped and settled. "Easy, boy," Jack said, running his hand along the horse's neck, soothing it.

My black stallion, Buck, stood cringing, backed into the far corner of the car, scraping a hoof, snorting, but with no sign of cuts on him. I looked down at the wide rip in the side of the car, at long deep scars in the wooden floor where the big bear had made a snatch for the horses and missed. "Is he okay, Jack?"

"He ain't even cut! How's Buck?"

"I don't know yet, he won't let me near him. Where'd all the blood come from?" I looked all around the dark floor. "I don't understand it."

"I do," said Jack, his voice going quiet. "It ain't horse blood we're looking at here."

I walked over where he'd kneeled down and pointed out through the hole torn in the wall. "Take a look at this."

"My God," I said, looking through the hole in the wall, down at the ground, at the dark pools of blood in the snow, and at the mangled, shredded remains of the man named Brace.

CHAPTER

4

———•———

"What do you say, Beatty? Was it a *cocker spaniel* that did all that?"

"Things ain't gonna get no better between us, are they, *Eldon,*" I said. I rose up slowly from beside the mangled body, still staring down at it, an *it* now, now that the left arm, left shoulder, and half the chest were gone—an *it* with its eyes glassed over and blank, the neck snapped like a piece of kindling.

Big Eldon sneered. "That's right, *Angel boy,* things won't get no better at all. You caused me to miss killing that bear. If you hadn't been out there in the way, Brace would still be alive. So I owe you one . . . a *bad* one."

"A *bad* one? You're crazy, Eldon," I said. "The bear got him before you ever stuck your head out."

"Just the same," he said, "I've had it with you, you and your *cocker spaniel* bullshit—"

"What are you talking about, Eldon?" Larr's voice had a crisp hard edge to it.

"Beatty here says a grizzly's the same as a flea-scratching mutt."

I looked up at Eldon; he spread a nasty grin and tapped a finger to his nose. I felt my hackles swell across my back.

"Take a good look, Beatty," said Ben Larr. "That's what a

grizzly will do. This is no joking matter. Brace Denton was a good man."

"Never said otherwise," I murmured under my breath, following the bear's tracks with my eyes in the glow of the lantern ole Freddie the fireman held up. Blood lay thick and wide beneath the body. Red paw prints, as big around as a water bucket, led off along the cleared rails. They disappeared into the rock wall beneath moonlight the color of spun gold and coal dust.

"You just as well have," Eldon said. "Going on about *eating a dog,* and all that."

"About *what?"* Larr glared at me as I took off my coat and hung it on one of the broken boards of his brand-new stock car. "I don't know what the problem *is* between you two, but we've got plenty more to worry about here than who *will* or will *not* eat a dog, for crying out loud!"

"One thing had nothing to do with the other," I said quietly. I took off my hat, adjusted the dents in the crown, and hung it beside my coat. "I'm sorry your man's dead, Colonel Larr. But it had nothing to do with what I said about bears."

"The hell it didn't!" Eldon stood with his rifle cradled in his arm. "Everything's got something to do with everything else, far as I'm concerned. Your getting in the way killed Brace just as surely as the bear."

I shot Jack a glance, ran my hand in my back pocket beneath my wadded up handkerchief.

"Is Buck all right?" Jack asked.

"Yeah, he's fine," I said, still in a quiet voice, "just bloody and wild-eyed." I stepped in front of Eldon, and said to Jack and Larr over my shoulder, "Beam's all right too. I think he's drying his trousers over the woodstove."

I looked up and grinned at Eldon as Jack and the others smiled at my little joke—grim smiles owing to the circumstances. Eldon even made a flicker of a smile as I gazed at him, nodding my head. Then I snatched my hand out of my pocket, working my fingers, adjusting them. I spread my feet, crouched, snapped my shoulder back, and swung my full weight behind the brass knuckles, burying them into Eldon's lower belly on the upswing.

Whoooo-ooooosh! Breath exploded from his lungs. Buttons shot off of his tight vest. I jumped to the side to keep him from slamming down on me when he jackknifed forward. The blow raised him high up on his toes and bent him into a strange deep angle, his jaws down there between his knees.

"Easy, Colonel." Jack spun his pistol out and pointed it at Larr. He shook his head, and Ben Larr lowered the rifle he'd swung toward me. "Better let him get it out of his system," Jack said. "It's a personal matter."

"You're insane, Beatty," Larr hissed. I reached over, slipped the rifle out of Eldon's arm while he wobbled there, clutching it, bowed deep but raising his face now, his knees tight together but his feet wide apart.

I slipped the brass knuckles off, into my pocket, and patted Eldon on his back. He made a long strained sound that would've called in moose had we been farther north. "Now, listen real close, *Eldon*. I don't want you thinking that once this is over we'll make up and be friends anytime soon, all right?"

He couldn't speak, couldn't move. I didn't know what was keeping him on his feet. But I reached down and picked up a long broken length of board from the stock car, and hefted it in both hands, judging the weight and strength of it.

"I demand that you stop this!" Larr tried to take a step, but Jack cocked the pistol in his hand.

"I want you to remember that I coulda killed ya and didn't, *Eldon,*" I said, leaning down, looking up in Eldon's twisted face. "Know why? It's so you'll be alive to think about this tomorrow and get *real* mad about it. Then I want you to go get yourself a knife, an axe, a gun . . . get a *cannon,* whatever you want, then come looking for me with it, okay?"

"Don't! You'll kill 'im!" ole Freddie yelled at me. But I'd already stepped back. I broke the board over Eldon's head and dropped the shorter piece to the ground as he fell.

"What manner of man *are* you?" Larr's eyes were wide and shiny in the light of the lantern. "That is the single most barbaric act I've ever seen."

"I don't enjoy personal remarks," I said, stopping Larr short, wiping a finger across my sore nose. I reached for my

45

hat and coat and saw Jack grinning. Dallas Renfrow came running up carrying another lantern. "Oh my God! *Man! What happened here?"* He looked down at Eldon, then at Brace Denton. His face went pale.

"Where were *you?"* Larr demanded.

"I heard the shots, Boss. I was down the tracks a ways, relieving myself." He kneeled slightly. "Lord have mercy." He looked up at Larr and rubbed a hand across his face. "Was it *him?* The big grizzly, you think?"

Jack and I stared at Larr. "Of course it was him," Larr said. "What else would do this?"

I looked back toward the platform and saw Brerton Beam venturing out of the car. His hat was off and strands of his oily hair stood straight up. "Are we still invited to dinner?"

"Stay inside," I called back to him. I looked at Larr. "This bear ain't acting like any I've ever seen. What's this about? A big rogue running loose?"

"He's been around here for years," said Larr, scanning the darkness along the upper ridge. "Waiting, always waiting. He's the devil's own demon. Nobody's ever been able to stop him . . . *nobody."* I saw his clenched fist at his side, his other hand squeezing tight around his rifle. "He's a man killer. The worst I've ever seen."

Eldon groaned, and I reached down with Dallas Renfrow and helped pull him to his feet. He still couldn't straighten up at the waist. "The bear got 'em both?" Dallas looked Eldon over.

"No." I let out a breath. "I had to bust ole *Eldon* one, for the sake of good manners."

Eldon squeezed out a long string of saliva; it dangled and dropped in the snow.

"He told me what he said to you, Beatty." Dallas struggled with Eldon's crooked back and leaned him against the car. "Can't blame ya for busting him one, I reckon."

"What was this? What did he say?" Ben Larr looked back and forth between us. I heard Jack chuckle.

"It ain't important now," I said. I looked at ole Freddie. "Can we get on up the mountain? This place gives me the willies."

He cocked an eye at Larr for approval and said, "We do

need to make some time. We could be in worse trouble if there's more drifts twixt here and Lodge Pole."

Larr seemed to consider something for a second, then waved the old fireman toward the engine. "All right, let's roll." He turned to Dallas Renfrow. "Load Brace inside the car, and let's get hauling," he said. "Nothing more we can do here."

Because of all that had happened, it was only natural that we didn't join Ben Larr for dinner. Instead, after we loaded the body and patched the side of the stock car, Jack and I calmed our horses down and joined Beam back in the car full of broken window glass. Beam had pulled down the window shade over the broken window and tacked it at the bottom—tacks he'd gotten from his kit, I learned.

We felt the engine tug forward and begin forcing its way upward, trembling against gravity until it got its steam up and its weight moving. I went back to Larr's dining car and brought back some food for Jack, Beam, and myself; and we ate lukewarm steaks and drank wine from coffee mugs while the engine chugged on up through the night.

Beam only picked at his food nervously for a while, then took the seat right across from us and went to sleep with a wet rag on his swollen forehead. I noticed he now slept in the aisle seat and leaned away from the window.

"You know," Jack said in a low voice, still holding a piece of rare steak in his hand, sipping the red wine. "I didn't really think you'd make your play on Eldon back there."

"Neither did he," I said. "That's why I did it. He knew it was coming, he just wasn't expecting it right then—the big ole b'hoy." I threw back a drink of red wine, trying not to picture Brace Denton's blood in the snow and the bloody paw prints of the monster. "I figured I needed to get it done in case we run into more bear trouble. I wanted a clear head. Besides, after that close call with the bear, I hated thinking I coulda died and never got the chance to bust ole *Eldon* up a little."

"I know." Jack nodded and sipped and gazed out into the darkness. "Bear nearly got ya back there."

"Yep. It scared the hell out of me." I stretched and sank down in the seat. "But a miss is as good as a mile, I reckon."

"Speaking of a miss," Jack said; and he took a bite of the steak as he continued. "I know I hit that big bastard. Had to hit him both shots."

"How do you know?"

"Have you ever seen me miss anything I shoot at?"

"No, but you mighta been rattled when you shot."

"Ever seen me rattled? About *anything?* Especially when I shoot?"

"No, but come on, Jack. It's only human to miss *sometimes.*"

"Not for me, it ain't. I don't miss, not ever. But that damn bear still got away and killed that ole boy . . . quicker than a cat can scratch its behind."

I looked at him. "I figure he killed Brace Denton before he came after us. I just can't imagine him being so quiet about it. That bear works fast, faster than anything I ever dealt with."

"Faster than a *cocker spaniel?*" Jack grinned over a working jaw full of steak. "Ole *Eldon.*" He shook his head.

I grinned too. "I flat put it on him, didn't I. Laid the iron to him, then boarded him down."

"Yeah, you did. Feel better now?"

I paused and thought about it. "Funny thing is, now that I've beat the hell out of him, I can't really say that his remark was all that bad . . . do you think?"

"Naw, not really. I didn't in the first place. I've sure heard worse. You just let it grate on you. I knew you had to get him if you was ever gonna put it out of your mind."

"And I got him . . . got him good."

"Yep, and I got that bear—*twice.* But he's still up."

We rode on in silence, swaying back and forth, two seats back from the broken window with the canvas shade tacked down, billowing back and forth as if being shaken by invisible bear claws out in the night. Then Jack said, "It's turning into a strange trip. We ain't even got where we're going, and I'm already wishing we'd never gone there." He eyed me curiously and his voice dropped again. "What're you gonna do when he comes back?"

"Kill him, if I have to," I said quietly, feeling strange as I said it, not sure if we were talking about Eldon . . . or the bear.

48

"That's what I thought," he said; and the way he said it let me know that he wasn't sure either. I watched him take the last bite of steak, lick his fingers, throw back the wine, and pull his hat down over his eyes.

In the sway of the car and the clack of rails, I dozed restlessly, and jerked forward with a start when I felt a hand come down on my shoulder. I looked up at Dallas Renfrow, wearing a thin smile that let me know he'd startled me intentionally. "Boss wants to see ya," he said.

"Can't it wait till morning?" I said it, but I was already pushing up from the seat before he answered, steadying myself to the sway of the car.

"It can, but it won't. So, come on. I think he just wants ta pour you a drink. We'll be in Lodge Pole in a couple hours. What's the harm?"

"All right." I stepped into the aisle.

He stood there and said before turning, "He's been hitting the sauce pretty hard, so don't let him get to ya. The colonel can be a little hard to take sometimes."

"He's got more twists and turns than a rattlesnake, ain't he?" I said it to see his reaction.

"Yeah. He's like the weather up here, changes about every few minutes. Just go easy," he said; and I followed him, swaying and rocking back to the fancy car.

When we stepped in, Dallas slipped to the side and leaned against the wall by the door. I saw Ben Larr sitting at an oak table wearing a dark night-robe. The table hadn't been there earlier. On it lay a sleek-looking rifle of a brand and model I'd never seen. Walnut stock and brass frame glinted in the glow of an overhead lamp.

Beside the rifle sat a bottle of bourbon and two shot glasses. The light above formed a soft circle about the table and left the rest of the car in darkness. The bourbon quivered and glistened in the bottle.

"Sit the hell down, Beatty," said Larr. His eyes were once again red-rimmed and wild. An anger seemed to swirl in them. "Dallas. Go read or something . . . check on Eldon. Get the hell on out of here."

I shot Dallas a glance, saw him turn his eyes to the ceiling and walk toward the rear of the car. I wondered if he was

49

going into that warm bedroom I'd pictured, the one where Laura Larr's warm leg lay half covered in silk. I stepped over, slipped out from under my hat, and pulled out the only other chair at the table. I saw his artificial leg leaning against his chair. "What're you looking at?"

I stared at him and said bluntly, "Your wooden leg, Larr. Or am I supposed to act like I don't see it? Act like it ain't really there?"

I saw the anger swirl in his eyes. *Mad as a scalded wildcat,* I thought. But then he licked his pale dry lips, and I saw his chest shake slightly. Something changed in his streaked eyes, and he let out what would have to pass for a laugh.

"You're a brazen son of a bitch, Beatty, you are." He raised a hand, seeing my hackles flare, I suppose. "Don't reach for your pocket and make me kill you," he chuckled. "I like a *brazen son of a bitch,* so it's a term of respect. Not at all like insulting your nose."

I had to grin a little at that. I reached out and tipped a drink into both glasses, hearing velvet bourbon kissing against crystal, watching the trickle of amber glow in the soft light. "Here's to *brazen sons-a-bitches* then," I said, raising one glass and nodding down at the other. He picked it up and threw it back without toasting. I shrugged, did the same, and hissed it smoothly into place.

"You ever seen this rifle before?" He stared at me.

"Not till now—"

"No, no, you idiot! I mean this *kind* of rifle. Ever seen this *kind* of rifle before." He patted it hard with his hand, but then stroked his hand along it gently as if smoothing out soft wrinkles.

I reminded myself that Dallas Renfrow *had* warned me about his mood; and I took a deep breath and said, "No . . . I can't recall ever seeing one like it." I reached my hand over toward it, just to touch it. I didn't know why. "But it looks like a fine piece."

"I didn't say you could touch her, did I?" He jerked it back toward him, leaving my hand there above the table. "Did I?"

I rubbed my thumb and fingers together and drew them back. "Did you ask me here to drink, or to fight, Larr?" I glared at him. It was late and I was tired. I wasn't going to take much more of his abusive craziness.

"Do you really *care* which?" He slung his jaw back in a gesture of arrogance and glared right back. I saw what he was doing. After me hammering Eldon into the ground, Larr must've figured he had to act nasty just to show me he wasn't impressed. I would play along with his tough talk a little.

"Makes no difference to me," I said, shrugging. "I've never whipped a man with his own wooden leg before. Might be an interesting thing."

The anger rose and flared in his eyes, but he checked it down, staring at me; then a grim smile twitched on his lips and he chuckled deep in his chest. "The way you buckwheated Eldon with those knuckle-dusters? Was that *interesting?* You know you hurt him pretty bad . . . could have killed him."

"I sure hope I hurt him *pretty* bad. I meant to. But kill him? Naw . . . he's too big and thickheaded to kill that easy."

I poured us both a shot from the bottle, and said, "He shoulda expected something after what he said to me. Dumb as he is, I reckon he's used to somebody hanging a board on his head now and then. He'll get over it, till the next time."

"I hired him because he's the best muscle out of Denver . . . saw him rip a man's arm off in a straight-up fight." He watched my eyes to see if that kind of information would make any difference.

I raised my glass. "Maybe the man's arm was loose to begin with," I said, tipping my glass toward him slightly. "Thanks for the warning though. I don't plan on ever fighting him *straight up."*

"Then plan on him killing you," Larr said, gripping the shot glass in his hand. "He'll tear your head off as soon as he's able."

"He ain't going to get that *able,"* I said. "I plan on taking off another chunk of him every time he gets within four feet of me, just enough to keep him sailing at half mast. Call it a precautionary measure."

51

I tossed back the drink and wiped my lip, thinking it peculiar that this man's conversation was littered with all sorts of missing limbs—ripped-off arms, torn-off heads. I glanced at his wooden leg, then back to his face. "He brought it on himself."

He slapped his palm down on the table. "By God! I like a man who knows his mind and doesn't mind speaking it. I bet you know how to get a job done, Beatty. I believe you'd be a good man to have on the payroll . . . you and your friend."

"I don't think so," I said, shaking my head. "We don't like shoveling snow."

"Let's not jockey around here. You know the kind of work I mean. I'm a wealthy man, Beatty. Like all wealthy men, I need things done on occasion. Things that keep my business interests running smoothly."

"Hired thugs . . . *gunmen,* is what you're saying you need, Larr. The kind it takes to run a railroad." I sat the glass down and pushed it away with my fingertips. "And that ain't my kinda business."

"This small railroad is more of a hobby of mine. I have many interests." He tossed a hand. "I never keep all my eggs in one basket."

"Well. Eggs, railroads, shoveling snow. You've already told me what you're looking for. I'm no hired gun."

"Oh?" His raised his brow. "And what kind of business are you in? I know you're not simply traveling with a sick friend, as rumor has it."

I smiled slightly. "Word travels fast on your railroad."

"What did you expect?" He tossed a hand. "I've never known a whiskey drummer who doesn't gossip like an old maid, have you?"

I shrugged. "I don't care what Beam told you, or what you want to believe. I'm still not interested in a job offer. You might want somebody shot that I don't feel like shooting. Then you and I would wind up shooting each other. It wouldn't be a good idea." I stood up slowly. "But thanks for the drink. I better go get some shut-eye."

"Wait!" There was almost panic in his voice. "Who said anything about shooting somebody? I can get anybody shot for fifty dollars. That's no problem. What I need is somebody with nerve enough to face a grizzly." He picked up the rifle, pitched it to me and I caught it. "Here, you can handle her, just do it gently."

I looked the rifle over, turning it in my hands and hefting the balance of it. It felt perfect, almost too smooth and perfect to hold. "I've got no fight with that big grizzly," I said.

"After you saw what it did to Brace? You wouldn't kill it?"

"Not unless I had to. Bears don't come looking for ya by name, just by nature. I've been around grizzly and never had trouble with them. You just have to walk wide around them and show some respect."

"But that one's a man killer, Beatty. It tried to snatch you out the window! It's got to be stopped."

"Then you and your men hunt it down and kill it . . . or hire a professional hunter. But I didn't come here to hunt bear. I want no part of it."

I held the rifle back toward him, but he wouldn't take it. Instead, he reached across the table leaning on one hand and ran his other hand along the rifle stock. "Go on, run your hand along her . . . just see what she feels like."

I ran my hand across the stock just to humor him. "Yep, it's a fine piece all right."

"Fine piece? If that's all you can call her, maybe you are the wrong man for the job. This is a precision-made instrument," he said, taking his hand back, but pointing at the rifle. "A man holding that rifle has nothing to fear—" His words stopped, and he stood there with a blank stare as if some dark memory had just taken over his thoughts.

I almost leaned over to see if he'd died. But then he seemed to snap back from some distant place, and said, "I'll pay you well, of course. Let's say . . . two hundred dollars?"

"No thanks." I laid the rifle down on the table and let out a breath. "If you can get a man shot for fifty dollars, you can surely get a bear hunter for two hundred—"

"I want you, Beatty. The bear made a move on you and missed. Something tells me you can kill it . . . kill it where others have failed. I saw how you handled Eldon. Calm, calculated. You had it all laid out in your mind before you made a move. You knew the outcome before you ever reached in your pocket. That's what it'll take to kill this bear." He leaned on both hands now and gazed across the table with a knowing glint in his eyes. "You're a killer, Beatty. Don't even try to deny it."

I looked away, getting a flash of things I didn't want to remember, knowing that he was trying to make me remember them, things from the war, and things since. I shook my head. "I'm really tired, Larr. Maybe we could talk tomor—"

"Damn it, man!" He slammed a hand on the table. "You heard *my* offer, now make yours. What will it take to get you to kill it?"

I just shook my head. "Maybe you oughta get some sleep yourself, Larr. It's been a long day."

"I don't sleep. Not up here. Not this close to that bear." His hand disappeared into his robe. I tensed, then settled as he pulled out the gold cigar case, laid it on the table, and flipped it open. "Here's my sleep," he said, his voice gone back to purring again. I saw the sparkling powder, and seeing it, I realized it was what lay at the core of his craziness. He poured more bourbon quickly, some of it dashing over the top of the glass; and he took a large pinch of the powder, dropped it in the glass and threw it back. "Canadian 'edge,'" he whispered in anticipation. "Take some for yourself."

"Huh-uh," I said as he slid the glass and cigar case to me. "The only edge I carry is on my knife."

He picked up the cigar case, stuck his nose down, and inhaled the powder. Then he wiped some off his nose, licked it from his hand, and worked his tongue around on his gums. I just watched, knowing now where he got all his twists and turns, his snappy words and winks—how he could be waxed drunk one minute and chipper as a squirrel the next. *Hophead . . . a rich, crazy, crippled hophead.* So used to getting his way that he came apart at the seams when somebody denied him.

I stepped back, once more ready to turn and leave. "Where you going?" He stood up now, bracing himself with a hand on the table, swaying to the car on his *only* leg. "Here." He shoved the rifle across the table. It left a long scratch, tumbled to the floor, thudded on rich carpet, and lay there. He started to fall; I jumped forward and caught him across the table.

"Holy cobb." I eased him down in his chair. "You're on a bad one, Larr. Settle down before you hurt yourself."

He grasped my sleeve, panicking now and trembling. "Listen to me! Listen! Beatty, you've got to kill him for me. Kill him because I can't! Kill him because he has to die! Has to! Do you hear me? You don't want money? What do you want?"

"Easy," I said, pulling free. "Here, I'll get it for ya." I reached down and picked up the rifle.

"No! You keep it! For killing the bear."

"I don't want it." I laid it back on the table; and he snatched it up, ran the bolt back, and slammed a round into the chamber. I saw his finger slip in across the trigger. I tensed as he swung the tip of the barrel toward me.

"Let's take it real easy, Larr," I said in a cautious whisper. I reached out a hand and slowly moved the barrel away. Then I wrapped my hand around it and took it from him.

He trembled turning it loose, staring wild-eyed through a cocaine glow. "Whatever you want, Beatty. Anything I've got. You've seen my wife. Do you want her? She's yours. Do as you please with her. I saw how you looked at her. I can tell you want her. Any man in his right mind would."

My face reddened. "Shut up, Larr. You're saying things now that you'll regret in the morning." I slipped back the bolt, unloaded the rifle, and leaned it against the table.

"No, listen," he said, "I mean it. You can have her . . . have her for the night. Nobody but us has to ever know."

"You're crazy—"

"She's back there in the dark, just waiting for me to say the word." He turned his head and called out over his shoulder. "You're there, aren't you darling?"

Good Lord . . . is this happening?

"Yes, I'm here," said a soft voice from the darkness. And as I snapped my eyes up, I saw her.

Laura Larr stepped into the circle of dim light wearing a black silk robe, open down the front and revealing her nakedness beneath it. I realized she'd been there all along, watching, listening. This had been arranged, as calmly and as calculated as I had been about laying Eldon out cold as a

55

wedge. Ben Larr had set it up for reasons only known in his drugged mind. He thought he already knew the outcome. But he was wrong.

"Whoa now." I raised my hands chest-high. "This is . . . I mean, this *ain't*. I mean, *Jesus! I got to go!"*

"Why?" she said flatly, closing her robe slightly. Her eyes were there, but not quite there, the pupils tiny, too tiny, and lost somewhere inside her head.

She stood close to the table, swaying slightly to the rails, the mark on her face darkly defined in the dim light. I couldn't look at her, yet I couldn't look away. "He's giving me to you, to kill the bear. He can do that, you know. Can't you, Ben?"

"Yes, I can," he hissed. He threw back a drink from the bottle and it ran down his chin, down his throat. He slammed the bottle down. The train took a small bump that rocked me forward and rocked Laura Larr against the table.

"Show him what he wants to see." He grabbed her roughly, down there low, spreading the robe open. She gasped at his touch; and he kept his hand there as he turned his face away and stared at the wall. "For God sakes, man, take her! Don't be a fool." He kneaded her flesh with his hand. "She wants you. She wants every man . . . every man but me."

Her eyes were blank, blue ice, lost somewhere, staring straight ahead. She swayed naked with his hand there on fine hair the color of sunlight. "Come take her, touch her," he said, hoarsely now. "She's all yours. Just kill the bear."

"Yes," she said, turning her face to me now, "touch me. Do what he wants you to do." She nodded down at him as he sat there staring away, gripping the table edge with his free hand. Her eyes riveted into mine. "Kill the bear for him." Her lips parted slightly, wet, glistening in the light. An ever-so-faint smile touched her lips, her eyes deep and pulling me. She reached a hand up and slid the robe off one shoulder.

"Well? What are you waiting for," Ben Larr said. "What more can I offer you?"

"No . . ." I shook my head, still staring at her. "I've got to get some . . . air." I wiped a hand over my face, snatched the bottle of bourbon, and turned and ran out on the platform into the biting cold.

I stood there, breathing hard, leaning back against the wall of the fancy black car with the brass plate on it; and I felt ice crunch beneath my feet as I rocked back and forth. My hands trembled as I threw back shot after shot and thought of how close I'd just come to doing what both of them were asking me to do. I felt the cold already pinching my ears and nose. My nose, the one Eldon said—

I shook my head, drank bourbon, pictured the partition wall in there, and beyond it the warm naked leg half draped by a silk sheet . . .

Whoooiee! I let out a nervous laugh. *Some strange birds, the Larrs.* I leaned there swaying, hearing the rails clack and screech beneath me. Although the train was not traveling that fast, I could hear the steady thud of the engine struggling against the mountain, winding through its twists and turns up the wall of rock. The beat of it permeated me, thumping inside my chest, a thick metal heartbeat. *Something about trains.* Yes, something about trains, I thought; and I stood there for what seemed like the longest time.

CHAPTER

5

———•———

"**W**here've you been?" Jack stretched and looked up. I stood there weaving, swaying with the bottle hanging from my hand. The train moved faster now and more level. I stared at him. I was drunk, I supposed, although I was in no condition to judge right then. "You don't drink like this." He snatched the bottle, looked at it, and swirled it around. "*I* drink like this." He tossed back a shot and hissed it into place. "You've been carousing with the big boys, huh?"

I nodded, and sat down, staring ahead at the flapping window shade. It had pulled loose a bit, and one corner waved like a maiden aunt gone on a visit. "Jack, let's don't pick hideouts anymore unless they come *highly* recommended by somebody, okay?"

"The hell's the matter with you?" He looked me up and down. "You ill?"

"No," I said. I wasn't about to tell him what'd happened. I wouldn't. I couldn't—no way in the world. But then I did.

When I'd finished telling him, he grunted the same way the ole fireman had grunted earlier. "Well, I haven't seen the woman. But let me ask ya this, are they—?" He rounded his hands out before his chest. "I mean, if you don't mind saying."

"Jack. Just picture the most beautiful woman you ever

58

saw, then imagine her *better*-looking sister." I rubbed both hands on my tired eyes.

"Umm-umm. Then you probably shoulda gone ahead and made a deal with the man."

"Jack, Jack." I shook my head. "I couldn't do something like that."

"Hell, *he* wanted ya to, *she* wanted ya to, right?" He turned his hand back and forth. "The right time, right place. I don't know." He seemed to be considering it. "Think maybe if I walked back there . . .?"

"I shouldn't have told you about it."

"Why not? I would've told *you*. We're amigos." He threw back a shot of bourbon. "I been sitting here listening to that little *Beam* grunt and snore? You're back there ready to bump your roscoes with a fine, doped-up *blonde?* Something ain't fair about that."

"Something ain't *right* about it either," I said, feeling the whiskey start to lap on my brain like calm waves on a beach. "I think Larr's been powdering down too long—both of them have, I reckon. They're on the verge of snapping. I don't wanta be around when they do."

"Then put 'em outa your mind and let's just lay low. That's why we came here, ain't it? Chances are, they'll both sober up and not be able to face ya . . . if they even remember it at all."

"Yeah. You're right. They'll likely not even remember it." I sank back in the seat with a long sigh. "What a long strange trip it's turning into."

In minutes I dozed off again, this time with the help of the bourbon tide rising slow and soothing inside my head; and I barely heard Jack saying something as he stood and stepped past me into the aisle. I scooted over and slept with my head near the window and my hat down over my eyes.

When I awoke, I did so slowly, drifting back from a warm cloud, from a world devoid of crazy rich men, naked blondes, bodies mauled by bears, and big rude men who make remarks about a man's facial features. The clacking sway of the train had helped lull me off, and the ceasing of it helped just as well in waking me.

A long breath of steam let out beneath us, and for a second I still lay there beneath my hat wondering if all that

59

had happened had only been a bad dream. The train had squeaked slowly to a halt and now sat still, save for the pulsing of the idling engine.

From under my hat brim, I saw a faint glow of grainy sunlight streaking across the car. *All right now. Breakfast, coffee, mounds of hotcakes oozing butter and syrup . . .*

I straightened up, leveled my hat, and watched Jack at the front of the car stirring the woodstove. There was a scraping sound outside the railcar window, but I paid it no attention as I stretched and rubbed my face. "I see we made it all right," I called out to Jack, turning and lifting the canvas window blind. "Looks like a good day to—*Yiii!*"

There, only inches from my face, stood the bear! I let out the yell and fell back, out into the aisle, seeing it scrape its paws on the window.

"What's wrong?" Jack jumped into the aisle with his pistol drawn. I'd drawn mine as well, had it pointed and cocked; but then the bear licked a long wet tongue up the dirty glass, and a weathered hand reached out from the side and pulled it away by a leather collar.

"Damn it to hell!" I ran a trembling hand across my face, glancing all around. Beam stood crouched up on his seat against the other wall. His face was stark white. Jack spun his gun back into his holster with a grin, looked at the two of us cowering, and shook his head.

"What kind of fool would do something like that?" I stepped back between the seats and looked out, at an old man in a ragged coat and a gypsy skullcap. He tugged at the bear's collar and appeared to be chastising it. This bear was in no way akin to the likes of last night's grizzly monster. It was smaller, much smaller; and as I watched it, I chuckled a little as it stood up, there on the wooden platform, and started turning in a circle with its paws spread. A furry, clumsy ballerina.

"A dancing bear," I said over my shoulder. The old man looked in at me, opened a mouth of broken teeth, and said something through steamy breath near the window. I couldn't make it out, but I knew what he wanted when he held out a palm and rubbed his thumb and fingers together. I shook my head.

60

"No," I said through the glass. I'd seen enough *bear* to last me a while, dancing or otherwise. He shrugged, then turned to a man and woman who walked wide around him, keeping their eyes on the bear. They shook their heads and hurried along the platform as if late for the train.

"My, but you certainly gave me a start, Mr. Beatty," Beam said, stepping down from the seat and straightening his coat. "I nearly—Well, let's just say this whole journey has been one for the books."

I smiled at him. "Did you ever find your wallet?"

He looked a little embarrassed. "Yes, I did, in spite of all the commotion."

"Good, then," I said. "I hope you'll have a profitable day here. I suppose you'll be heading back down this evening before dark, won't you?"

"No, actually, I thought I'd spend a couple of days here, get to know the bartender. Make some contacts. This business is all about who you know." He winked. "Granted, I carry the finest lines of whiskeys, bourbons, malts, and such. But nothing sells as well as *friendship.*" He raised a finger. "Always remember one thing, Mr. Beatty—"

"I will," I said, before he could finish. I could tell he was on the verge of breaking into a spiel, so I shook hands with him, leaning away as I did so, and said, "Have a good visit." I buttoned my coat as I walked past Jack and reached for the door. "I'll go get our horses."

I stepped out into the crisp cold air and off the platform. The town of Lodge Pole was no larger than Elk Ridge, but it looked better attended, with walk planks leading off toward a small street lined with modest storefronts. At the end of the street stood the big lodging house where we'd be staying. It was a two-story house of stone- and logwork, a little out of place there among the other, smaller buildings. Snow dust scurried and swirled across the wide front porch.

Ole Freddie the fireman had already lowered the loading plank when I got to the stock car. I watched as Dallas Renfrow and an old Indian in a blanket coat carried Brace Denton's body off the car. Strands of straw spilled from the plank and tiny bits of it swirled in the breeze. I smelled something rank and looked down beside me at a big dirty

61

Airedale who stood sniffing my boot. His coat was grown out long and ragged. Long matted clumps of fur hung from him.

"Get out of here, you stinking dog," yelled a voice from the stock-car door; and I looked up at an old man wearing a sheriff's badge. He was short, slim, and had on a thick pair of eyeglasses. He grinned beneath a long gray mustache and hooked a thumb beside a long Colt Dragoon shoved down in his belt. His belt was wrapped around the outside of his gray mackinaw, and he wore his trouser legs inside knee-high miner boots that looked too big for him.

He lifted the boots one after the other, slowly, and stepped down the loading plank. "Kick that stinking mutt away, mister, or you'll be stuck with him your whole trip."

I looked down at the big Airedale, but I didn't kick him. Instead I nudged him away gently with the side of my boot. "He ain't bothering me," I said, never being one to kick a dog, especially one this big and this ugly. He looked like a bar swamper's mop, with legs. He eased back toward my boot as I stepped away toward the sheriff.

"There's two strays hangs around here," said the sheriff. "Him and a one-eyed Catahoula." He spit tobacco and adjusted his crotch. "Neither one's fit to be shot." He eyed me up and down, taking in the long-barreled forty-four on my hip and the shorter one hanging from my shoulder harness. "You're Beatty, ain't ya?"

His words stopped me for a second. He might have noticed me hesitate, because he went on to say, "Freddie told me your name. Said you's the one found Brace's body?" He tapped the badge on his coat. "I'm Till. I'm the sheriff here, more or less."

I nodded. "Yes, I'm Beatty . . . James Beatty. We all sorta found the man at the same time."

"I understand," he said. "I know it's hard on ya, come up here to relax, maybe eat an elk," he spit again, "then something like this happens. But I try to get all the particulars down on something like this in case family members inquire."

"Sure, I understand," I said. "The bear broke a window, my friend and I took off to see about our horses, and there we found him." I spread a hand. "That's about the long and short of it. The bear tore him up something awful."

"That's what Freddie told me." He spit again, aiming for the Airedale. But he missed. The dog took a step back and sniffed at the puddle. "Damn strays. Boss says walk them out and shoot 'em. I say they ain't worth a bullet." He looked back at me, his eyes large behind the thick spectacles. "Go on and get your horses, Beatty." He nodded toward the car. "It's too cold to stand here jawing. We'll talk later once Mr. Larr gets here."

"Thank you, Sheriff," I said; and I walked up the plank with the dirty Airedale beside me. "Why don't you get the hell away," I said down to him. But he stayed close, sniffing at the straw on the car floor.

I had to keep shoving him away with the side of my boot as I bridled Buck and Jack's silver-gray. He followed when I led both horses off down the boarding plank and hitched them to a nearby rail. I could smell him, even in the cold air; and I wondered how he'd look and act if somebody clipped his fur down and gave him a good hot scrubbing. He looked up at me and licked both sides of his mouth. Both edges of his mouth were brown-stained, as if he'd chewed tobacco all his life.

Quiet Jack hopped up into the car when I went back to get the carpetbag from behind the hay. "The hell's that smell?" he asked, looking around. I glanced around with him and saw the Airedale lying on my saddle in the corner. "Damn it! Get off there." I walked over, slapping my hands together until he stood up grudgingly and slinked away. "Now I'll smell like a dog for the next week." I reached down and shouldered up my saddle. Jack chuckled and did the same; and we walked off the car and to our horses, carrying our gear and the carpetbag.

We stood saddling our horses when Ben Larr, Dallas Renfrow, and the old sheriff came walking up. Across the street, big Eldon walked along stiffly, hobbling from one support to the next, headed toward the lodging house. He appeared to be gagging, each step he took. Snow dust swirled about his feet.

Twenty feet ahead of Eldon, I saw *her,* Laura Larr, walking quickly, the fur collar of her coat pulled up and a

63

fur hat covering her head. She sidestepped around Eldon, passed him without a glance, and continued on as if he weren't there.

"There you are, Beatty . . . *James* Beatty," said Ben Larr, walking up. His walk didn't look much different than that of a man with two good legs, although as I glanced down I noticed for the first time that there was no sign of crease or wear on top of his left boot. He wore a wide smile—just wide, not friendly—and I marveled at the clearness of his eyes and how energetic he appeared after such a bout of drinking and using the powder.

"I need a decision from you," he said, stopping, flanked by the other two men on either side. I glanced at him, then back to drawing my saddle cinch, a little uncomfortable around him after last night's bizarre incident. But he seemed unabashed, as if nothing had happened—perhaps not even remembering. "We need to take down that bear for once and for all, before somebody else dies."

"Good luck then," I said, darting my eyes past him and back to my task. I dropped the stirrup and tested the saddle by shaking the horn. Buck scraped a hoof on the hard ground.

"I'm afraid I must insist that you come with us. Now then. We need to be leaving quickly, if we're to pick up his tracks—"

"Sorry," I said, "but no way." I glanced at Jack and saw him shake his head slightly. Then I looked at Larr, right in his eyes now, figuring if what had happened last night didn't bother him, it sure shouldn't bother me.

He slapped his gloved hands together, turning back and forth impatiently, and said, "As many shots as Eldon fired, that bear's more than likely wounded. You must never let a wounded grizzly get away."

"If Eldon hit it, then let *Eldon* go find it."

He pointed at Jack. "Your friend also fired at it."

"Nobody hit it," I said, "or we'd have seen more blood in its tracks. I know a little bit about bear hunting. It would've been bawling its head off . . . probably would've turned and fought us."

"There's two families of Utes living up there. Their lives will be in danger as long as that rogue runs loose. It's our

64

duty as men to go find it and destroy it. You don't understand that, do you, Beatty? You don't seem to—"

"Maybe one of us doesn't understand," I said, cutting him off again, "but I don't think it's me. I've got no fight with that bear, nor do I hold any grudge with him. I'm sorry your man got killed, but I reckon he just snagged his toe on Mother Nature's hemline . . . and she et him up. It's too bad, but it happens." I shrugged.

"How darkly philosophical," Larr said. I watched him look at the other two, then back at me. "But you've put me at somewhat of a disadvantage here. I lost one good man—" He pointed a gloved finger at me. "—and you've put poor Eldon on the sick list, as it were."

"Tough break for Eldon," I said. "But I ain't going, and that's final."

"Very well then." Larr turned to the old sheriff. "Arrest him, Till."

"Yessir, Boss." The old sheriff stepped forward, laying his hand on his pistol.

"Hold it!" I braced and raised a hand toward them. *"Arrest* me? Arrest me for what?" The old sheriff saw my other hand go instinctively close to the gun in my holster. He swallowed hard, but still looked determined.

"Why, for assault of course," Larr said. "Eldon has asked me to act on his behalf, to bring charges against you. I could possibly persuade him to drop the charges, if you were more willing to—"

"Assault charges, hell! He's twice my size. I only knuckled him once in the belly and cracked a board over his head. You call that *assault?* That was more like a *harsh lecture."*

The old sheriff took another step forward with a bemused look in his eyes. "Why, yes, son! Indeed, we do call that assault. That was no less assault than if you'd hung a blade in him or shot him with a gun. Maybe I need to check you out a little once I get you locked up. Where'd you say you're from, Beatty?"

"Missouri," I said flatly, staring at him. There was no way I was going to jail. Jail would mean discovery, discovery meant death.

"Well, that explains your liberal attitude toward *assault,* but by God, son! Up here, you don't wear a man out with

65

knuckle-dusters and a wood slate, then act like you did no more than give him a strong *talking* to." He shook his head and spit. "Come on with me. I'll explain the law to ya."

"Law?" I shot Ben Larr a sly glance, then looked back at the sheriff. "I ain't going to jail, gentlemen. A lot of things might happen here and now, but me going to jail ain't one of 'em."

The old sheriff leveled his shoulders and started to raise his pistol. I heard Jack take a step and stop beside me.

"Hold it, Sheriff," Larr said. He must've seen that this particular strategy was only going to get somebody killed. "On second thought, I don't think it would be wise to take a man like Beatty with us. He obviously cares about no one but himself. I think we'll be better off without him, unless he can show a little more concern for others."

I stared at Larr for a second wondering just how many shifts and turns the cocaine had etched into his brain. Then I grinned and raised a finger. "I see what you're doing, Larr. Figure you'll make me feel guilty. Figure you'll make me want to prove something here. But it ain't gonna work."

"We could ride along," I heard Jack say behind me.

"No way in hell," I said. "We're going over to that lodging house, get a warm meal, hot bath, and prop our boots up on a brass rail. I ain't going to jail and I ain't killing no big animal." I turned and pointed at the lodge house. "There's where we'll be." I turned back toward Larr and saw that a cigar had appeared in his hand, lit, and he blew a stream of smoke and studied the end of it.

"Aw naw," I heard Jack say in a low tone. Dallas Renfrow and the old sheriff just stood staring at me with blank expressions. I turned back toward the lodging house, and for the first time read the large sign swaying from the edge of the front porch. It read LARR LODGING HOUSE, in bright bold letters.

"Is there *anything* you don't own, Larr?" I asked, lifting my hat and running my hand back across my head.

"No," he said matter-of-factly, cocking the cigar at his chest. "Not up here, there isn't. Up here it's my way or no way. It may be a *big world,* fraught with the perils of Mother Nature, but this is mine up here, and on *my* mountain, she better hike up her *hemline* and step aside."

"Damn it," I said to Jack under my breath, "looks like we're stuck with it."

I looked back at Larr, raised a finger, and said, "One day is all you get from us . . . *Boss*. If we don't get the grizzly, don't expect us to go after it again. Are we clear on that?"

"But of course," Larr said, offhanded. He turned to Dallas Renfrow and said, "Send word to the lodge. Have them prepare food, quickly. I wouldn't dream of anyone riding with me without providing the best accommodations."

"That's just how Boss is," said old Sheriff Till, as once again I felt the railcar swaying beneath me. We'd turned the engine around, dropped off the other cars except the one for stock and Ben Larr's private car, and headed back. We would take the train as far as we could, then go by horse, up around the wall of rock before the tracks ran down beneath it. "Anybody sides with Ben Larr gets the royal treatment." We'd seen Beam on our way back to the train and told him what we were about to do. He'd looked Jack up and down with a sympathetic expression, patted his shoulder, and walked away toward the lodging house.

"I feel like I've had a royal *something,*" I said, gazing out the window of Larr's private car as I cleaned my Henry rifle and checked the lift sight on it. I hadn't used the lift sight for a long time, nor had I *ever* fired the type of cartridges Larr had Dallas Renfrow pass out to us. When he'd handed them down to me, I'd shook my head and said, "Even his ammunition's first class, huh?"

"That's right," Dallas had replied, holding one up. "Solid silver slugs. Ever seen what they do, with a high-grain load behind them?"

"No," I'd said, letting out a breath. "I can hardly wait."

"At two hundred yards it'll make a hole the size of my fist."

I looked at his fist and nodded. "Why so far away? Two hundred yards? Hell, much farther, we coulda stayed at the lodge and shot him from an upstairs window." I smiled at him.

"You're not taking this very serious, are you, Beatty?"

"I don't like being horned into anything, especially kill-

67

ing, whether it's man or beast. If I lay sights on the bear, he's dead. But I can't get all *worked up* about it."

"After seeing what it did to Brace? You don't think it deserves to die? That coulda been you laying there, shoulder torn off, blood running out the—"

"I get the picture," I said. "It's just that I came up here to rest and enjoy the air, not shovel a rich man's snow or shoot his bear for him."

"I see," Dallas said. "I take it your having a drink with Boss last night didn't change your opinion of him much."

I looked into his eyes, wondering if he knew about last night's madness. If he did, his eyes didn't give it away. "You would've had to be there," I said. "I think your *boss* has quite a few things stuck in his craw . . . killing that bear is only one of 'em."

His eyes narrowed into mine. "What're the others?"

I shrugged and said, "That's his business."

Dallas Renfrow leaned down near me. "Beatty, take some good advice. Help Boss get the bear. For some reason he thinks you can do it. Don't ask me why." He shook his head. "But if you're smart, you'll do like he says, *take* whatever he offers and *give* whatever he asks for. This really is *his* mountain and his world. Don't cross him."

"Is there a personal warning in there somewhere?" I stared closer at him.

"No. Not unless he calls on me. I don't give two hoots about what you did to Eldon—wish somebody would've done it sooner. But I do care about Boss . . . and Laura. All you gotta do is walk through this. Kill the bear if you can." He shrugged. "If you don't, at least he'll see that you tried. Ain't so hard, is it?" He glanced up and down me. "For a man who packs a lot of hardware and a carpetbag with purple angels on it, I'd think this is a piece of cake."

I just stared at him. "Like I said, I only came here to rest up and enjoy the air."

"Good then. Let's just play this thing on out." He smiled, tipped his hat brim, stood, and swayed away toward the rear of the car.

I sat sipping coffee and checking my rifle until the train winded a turn and started drawing to a halt. "We'll be getting off up here aways," said the old sheriff. He stood and began buttoning his mackinaw. "Just betwixt us, Beatty. I didn't want to have to arrest you back there. I was just doing what I's told. Hope there's no hard feelings."

I just grunted, stood, and drew my coat around me; and with my rifle under my arm and a bandolier of ammunition over my shoulder, I walked back to the stock car, where Jack stood checking the horses. The dirty Airedale stood up from a pile of hay and sniffed toward me as I entered the car. Next to Buck, and Jack's silver-gray, three more horses stood, saddled and ready, one of them a big brassy bay gelding. Larr's, I figured.

"What's he doing here?" I asked Jack, pointing at the Airedale.

"I don't know. He must've snuck in and hid when they loaded their horses. That's the worst-smelling dog ever lived. I fed him some jerky, so I reckon he thinks we're friends."

I looked at the Airedale as he shook out his matted fur and walked over to me. "Might not be a bad idea having him along. Airedales are good bear hunters, you know."

"I've heard it." Jack turned to his silver-gray and fed it a piece of a biscuit. He glanced at me over his shoulder. "What do you know about hunting bear? Ever gone after any?"

"Yeah. Black bear . . . back in Kentucky, when I was a kid. What about you?"

"Nope." He shook his head and turned back to the silver-gray.

"Worried about it?" I watched him shove his rifle down in the saddle scabbard.

"Nope. Just wondering how it works is all."

"That's hard to say," I said. "A rogue bear's unpredictable. He shoulda already laid down for the winter, but he's still up. No bear I've ever seen woulda done what he did last night. Usually a bear'll scent a man from a mile away and take off, unless he's guarding something he's killed. This one's different. If he's been around as long and done as much killing as Larr says, there's a possibility he's acquired a taste for man. Once they do that—"

"A killer of man, huh? I always liked that term. It covers a lot of things. We've been called that ourselves a time or two."

"Yeah, but it ain't a name I'm proud of," I said.

"Neither am I." Jack grinned. "But then again, maybe the bear ain't either."

"The bear ain't thought about it one way or the other. Maybe that's the difference twixt man and beast."

"If there's *any* difference twixt man and beast, I ain't seen it," Jack said. "Whichever one you corner, you gotta kill. That grizzly's killing for the same reason—the *only* reason—you and I always have. He's just staying alive."

"He didn't have to attack the train, Jack. That had nothing to do with him living or dying."

"To him it did. He thought it did, someway. That's all that matters. That's all it ever takes to start the blood spilling."

I felt the train rock to a stop beneath us and heard the loud hiss of steam. "Yeah," I said, "I reckon so. But I doubt we'll see that bear again. I figure all we'll do is spend the day freezing our roscoes off till Larr gives up, gets waxed drunk, or falls off his horse and breaks his rich crazy neck. The bear's long gone."

"No, I think you're wrong there," Jack said; and he turned to me with the reins to both horses in his hands. "I put two bullets in that bear. He's somewhere right now, waiting to get even. That's what I'd be doing if I was him."

"Jack, we'd have seen more blood if you hit him. I ain't questioning your shooting, but this is one time you're wrong." The Airedale walked over and sniffed at the car door as I stepped over and took Buck's reins from Jack.

Jack held up two gloved fingers and said through a breath of steam, "Twice I shot . . . twice I hit him. Just remember that." I shook my head, reached out, and slipped the bolt on the loading door.

CHAPTER

6

---•---

"That worthless cur ain't going," said Sheriff Till, pointing a finger at the big Airedale. Till led his horse down the loading plank, still watching the dog, still pointing his finger, his spectacles streaked with steam. The dog sat near Buck's hoofs in the thin snow, scratching and shaking his long dirty coat. I sat atop Buck next to Jack on his silvergray. Steam spun in our breath and the breath of the animals.

"Don't tell *me,*" I said, "I didn't invite him. He just slipped in someway."

Till pulled his pistol from his belt as he stepped his horse off the plank. "Well . . . I'll just *un*invite him, right now. He can *slip* back out, for good."

"Whooa now." I stepped my horse around between Till and the Airedale. "No cause for shooting him. He ain't doing any harm here. You said yourself, he ain't worth a bullet."

"He stinks too bad." Till held the pistol half raised. "Now move aside."

"Huh-uh." I shook my head. "If I killed everything that stunk twixt here and Missouri, there'd be no polecats and damn few preachers. Now you just lower that ole smoker before one of us gets our feelings hurt. You ain't about to shoot that dog while I'm around."

71

"Then I'll wait until you're *not* around."

"What the hell's going on out here?" Larr asked, stepping his big bay down the loading plank. He wore a long bearskin coat with the collar up. A wool muffler covered his face beneath a wide-brimmed hat. His eyes were shiny and full, lit by the first stages of a dose of cocaine.

"Beatty's taken it upon himself to bring that stinking Airedale along."

"No. I didn't bring him along." I shook my head. "I just ain't letting you hurt him—"

"Why'd you bring him, Beatty?" Larr cut me off. "You think he'll actually hunt bear? I've never seen anything out of him, except to hang around and smell up the town."

I shot Jack a glance, then said to Larr, "I've used dogs before. All he has to do is sniff the bear up. Could keep us from getting ambushed in a thicket . . . if that bear's wounded like you seem to think. I say bring him along—"

"Horseshit," Till said. "That dog couldn't sniff up his own tail running in a circle."

"If Beatty wants to bring him along, so be it," said Larr. "We don't have time to argue about it." He turned to me pointing a gloved finger, and added, "But he's your responsibility. You watch that he doesn't get in the way."

"Well shit," I said to Jack under my breath, turning Buck. Jack turned his silver-gray along beside me, and we rode away slowly up along the rising edge of the wall overlooking the tracks. The Airedale waddled along between us, the stink rising up even through the cold air.

In a moment Larr and Dallas Renfrow rode up beside me, their horses' breath swirling steam. Larr held the big Swiss rifle over to me. "Use this, Beatty," he said. "She's loaded with high-grain silvers." His eyes were shiny and wide. "I think you'll like the feel of her."

"Thanks, but I've got a rifle," I said, nodding at the Henry shoved down in my scabbard. "It's served me well in the past. It'll do the job."

"Not from as far away as this baby will," Larr said. "Here, take her." And I detected a faint reminder in his voice as he shoved the rifle to me, and added, "I know you saw her. Don't you wanta know what she can do?"

I hesitated, glancing past him at Dallas Renfrow. Only

when Renfrow nodded his head toward me did I reach out my hand and take the rifle. Larr laughed and shook the rifle before turning it loose. "It's not everybody I make such an offer to."

I jerked the rifle from him and laid it across my lap. "There now, we're all set," he said; and he gigged the bay forward into the lead, his artificial leg sticking out slightly farther than his other one. He raised a hand like a cavalry officer and waved us forward. Dallas Renfrow shot me another glance, then gigged his horse ahead of us by a couple of steps.

I looked back at ole Till scanning the higher ground to our right with his rifle propped up from his saddle. "It's gonna be a long day," I said to Jack, smelling the Airedale. Already, the cold had pinched my cheeks and started to throb deep in my sore nose.

We rode along the edge of the wall until the tracks were far below us. Twice I'd looked back. Both times, ole Freddie waved at us from the pulsing engine. Now only the tops of the railcars were visible as we climbed higher. In a few more minutes we'd topped onto a flatter level of ground and the train was no longer in sight.

On our right lay some of the roughest, most difficult terrain I'd ever seen—jagged upthrusts of rock dusted with skiffs of snow, and thickets of brush along the bottom of cliff breaks and gullies. Drifts of deep snow lay frozen over into spills of ice where last evening's sun had partially melted them, and the cold night had frozen them solid.

"Bear country," I said absently to Jack as I scanned the rise and fall of ridges and gullies.

"Yep." He nudged his silver-gray to the right and rode off slowly, studying the ground. Forty yards up ahead, Ben Larr raised a gloved hand. "Here's his prints," he called back to me. I gigged forward and called the information over to Jack; but he waved me on as he leaned from his saddle and studied the ground near the brush thickets.

I rode ahead and reined up to the others. They'd stepped down off their horses and stood circled around a set of wide bear tracks coming up from the wall across a skiff of snow.

"This is him," said Dallas Renfrow, pointing with his rifle barrel, "and his tracks are clean."

73

Larr grunted, swung back into his saddle, and stepped his horse away from the others, following the tracks back and forth across the frozen ground.

"See," I said, pointing down. "If he was wounded there would still be blood showing. All he had was Brace Denton's blood on his paws, and he wore it off making the climb."

"I think you're right," said Dallas, "but we might as well follow, as long as we've got good tracks."

I let out a breath and looked around at the rough ground on our right. "All right. There's more snow over that way. Only way we'll track him is if he cuts across snow or through some broken brush. The ground's too hard for him to leave prints."

We turned toward Jack when we heard him let out a short whistle. "I've got a print here," he called out to us. He waved us back toward him. The Airedale disappeared into the heavy brush as snow flurried from it.

"Better hope that damn mutt don't scare him away," said Sheriff Till, swinging up on his saddle. "Or I *will* put a bullet in his stinking hide."

"If that grizzly's in heavy brush, you better hope that dog runs into him before we do," I said, turning Buck. "If we come upon him close-range, he won't be planning to retreat, wounded or not."

I fell in behind Larr and followed him back to where Jack sat his horse. He'd drawn his rifle and held it one-handed, pointing out across the top of tangled brush sloping down into a wide gully. The brush rustled back and forth, spilling snow in the wake of the Airedale.

"He came through here," Jack said, "but who knows how long it's been." Then he pointed his rifle barrel back at the ground.

There beneath us, as if branded through the snow and deep into the earth, we saw the first in a trail of paw prints. A few feet ahead lay another, then another just inside the line of brush.

"Too thick for the horses," I said; and I'd started to swing down.

"No," Larr said. "Stay mounted, and follow me. We've got him this time."

"Wait a minute, Larr! I ain't cutting my horse all to hell, maybe cause him to break a leg—"

"We don't know how far he's gotten since last night, Beatty!" Larr shouted, turning his horse just before it stepped into the brush. "This is no time to slow down on us. I brought you to kill the damn bear! Now come on!"

"No way, Larr. You're out of your head!" I shot Jack a glance, then looked back at Larr.

"Beatty's right, Boss," said Dallas Renfrow. "It might take longer circling around, but it'll be hell to pay if we get in there on horseback and jump that bastard up."

"Are you refusing a direct order, Sergeant Renfrow?" Larr's eyes widened, lit high on the powder. He leaned down, jerking the reins and pulling his bay back and forth. The horse nickered, confused by the hard play on the reins.

Sergeant Renfrow? I glanced from Jack to Dallas Renfrow, then back at Larr.

"No, Colonel," said Dallas Renfrow. "But you need to consider what's at stake here. We'll only lose twenty or thirty minutes by going around. If he's in there somewhere, and sees that dog, he'll *tell* us where he's at. We'll have him circled."

Larr seemed to settle, considering it. "Perhaps you're right." He took out a silver flask from inside his bearskin coat, uncapped it, and tossed back a long drink. I stood watching him, realizing how difficult it would be, telling him from a bear in the deep brush. *A bear coat on a bear hunt?* I shook my head.

Larr held the flask toward me when he finished his drink, but I waved it on. He held it toward Jack; Jack did the same. "All right then." Larr twisted the top back on the flask and pointed with it. "We'll split up in twos. Two of you go around one end, two around the other." Then he swung down from his saddle, put the flask in his pocket, and pitched Dallas Renfrow his reins. "I'll go through on foot."

I started to say, *Are you trying to die?* But remembering last night, I realized there was a good possibility that was *exactly* what he was doing. Larr was so haunted by his demons, dying might be his only relief. I'd make it a point to keep him in front of me at all times, but not be led by him. The cocaine might have him brain-screwed, and crazy enough to want to die, but it might also have him crazy enough to not want to die alone.

"Boss," said Dallas Renfrow. "That's not a wise idea, going in there—"

"Damn it, man! Do, as, I, say!" Larr snatched a Spencer carbine from his saddle scabbard and swung it in the air. "I'm *still* in command here!"

Jesus! I darted a glance back and forth between them. Dallas Renfrow jerked the reins of Larr's horse and pulled it around beside him. "Yes sir," he said in a clipped tone. He looked at Sheriff Till. "Come on, we'll go around the far end, let **Beatty** and his friend take the other—"

"Be waiting for me on the other side," Larr said, his voice now fully back in uniform and at the head of a battalion.

"I will, sir," Renfrow said, steam bellowing in his breath. He avoided my eyes as he turned his horse and gigged it away, leading Larr's bay.

"Well, Beatty," Larr said, when the other two rode away. "Now that we've established the pecking order. Will you accompany me afoot?" His eyes swirled in madness, madness made madder by bourbon and dope. He nodded at the big Swiss rifle across my lap. "Do you have the nerve to kill the bear?"

"Go to hell, Larr," I said. "Don't bait me along. I don't care who can piss the farthest. You want to die, go on. Maybe you'll luck out and stump your toe on that big grizzly. But whatever crazy game you're dealing . . . deal *me* out." I started to turn Buck and step him away, but I heard Larr snap the level back and forth on the Spencer carbine.

"Don't even think about it!" I yelled and swung the big Swiss toward him, seeing Jack's pistol already out, cocked and pointed.

Larr laughed, a nasty, cocaine-whiskey laugh that came up from some dark place inside him. "You fool! Do you really think it matters who lives or dies here? No, it's about the *bear!* Killing the bear is all that matters. The rest is all a *game,* but killing the bear . . . that's real, more real than anything you'll ever do. Before this is over, killing the bear is all you'll live for. All you'll think about."

"That's *you* talking." I nodded toward the brush. "So go

76

find it, if it's there. But I ain't going in there with you." I glanced at Jack, still pointing his pistol. "Come on, let that fool do what he wants to."

We rode away, cautiously watching him over our shoulders until he'd disappeared into the brush. Jack threw back his coat and holstered his pistol. "Crazy, raving lunatic," he said. "What the hell was all that about?"

"I don't know, Jack. I'm starting to think he's wanting to die and just needs the bear and the rest of us to set it all up for him."

"Yep. He seems determined that something's gonna kill. He's already got it playing out that way in his mind." Jack shook his head. "He's on dope. Who really knows what he wants. Probably don't know himself."

"Maybe," I said, glancing back once more. "But either way, he's a crazy bastard, drunk and on dope with a big Spencer carbine." I ran my gloved hand idly along the stock of the sleek Swiss rifle. "I'd hate to kill a man just because he's crazy. We better keep an eye out."

"I already am," Jack said, checking his gun.

I adjusted the stacks of money in my waist beneath my shirt as we circled the gully of brush. Riding with it there was uncomfortable, but I'd no time to hide it anywhere before we'd left Lodge Pole. I didn't dare put it in the carpetbag and leave it in the stock car, and I sure didn't want to carry the carpetbag along on a bear hunt.

"If we *ever* get to stay at that lodge," I said, "I'm gonna soak in a hot bath till my toenails turn to butter."

It was over a mile around the gully, and by the time we'd circled and started back along the other side, we could see Till and Renfrow riding down slowly along a trail through a stretch of rocks, coming back toward us from a mile away. There was more snow laid up along this side of the gully than there was on the other. We scanned it for any bear prints as we rode along.

"He coulda slipped back out the other end without leaving a track," Jack said, nodding down at all the snow along the gully, "but if he came out on through here, we're bound to see something."

I touched my sore nose carefully with my gloved fingers.

77

"I'm so damn cold, I almost wish Larr and that grizzly would butt head-on out there . . . one kill the other, so we can get outa here."

No sooner than I'd spoke, I heard a loud roar out in the brush halfway between us and the other two riders. "Jesus!" I said, and I snatched hard on the reins, pulling Buck up short. He reared slightly.

"Careful what you wish for," said Jack. "That was no Airedale!"

We gigged our horses and rode quickly toward Till and Renfrow, who'd heard it too. They came sliding their horses down the narrow trail in a flurry of snow and dust. Damn Larr, I thought as we ran our horses along the fringes of the brush. I heard brush breaking somewhere deep in the gully and I looked down across it as we rode.

Tops of brush thrashed back and forth. I thought I caught a glimpse of brown, silver-tipped fur; but I couldn't see it clearly enough to know if it was Larr's coat or the big grizzly.

I had seen enough to make me slide Buck down to a halt and swing out of the saddle. Jack saw what I was doing and checked down the silver-gray a couple yards ahead. Just as I slapped Buck's rump to get him out of the way, something came running toward me from the other direction, down out of the rocks.

A deep growl resounded, and I swung around with the Swiss rifle coming up to my shoulder. But as I cocked the rifle and steadied myself for a shot, the Airedale came charging out of the rocks, snarling like a panther. He streaked past me into the heavy brush. His back was covered with wet brown mud.

Aw man! I took a deep breath to still my trembling knees, and stepped into the brush as Jack ran up beside me. "That damned dog nearly scared me to death," I said in a hushed tone. Behind us, I heard Till and Renfrow checking down their horses along the edge of the brush.

Ten feet inside the thicket, the brush was up over our heads, so thick we would barely have room to swing our rifles if we were come upon suddenly. "Damn Larr to hell," I said. "He had *no right* to jeopardize everybody's life like this."

"Listen," Jack said in a whisper. We stood stone-still and

78

listened to the sound of deep heavy breathing off to our left, only a few yards away. Behind us, we could hear Till and Renfrow coming through the brush, but we couldn't say anything to warn them.

"The Airedale?" I whispered to Jack, six feet away.

He shook his head. "No. It's something big, whatever it is."

I raised a hand back toward the other two when they got close enough to see me, and they stopped cold. Then Renfrow ventured closer, one quiet step at a time.

I motioned for Jack to step away a little; and when we'd spread out, we moved slowly and quietly toward the sound until I caught a glimpse of steam curl and disappear. I raised a hand without looking around and waved Renfrow up. I took a step around a short upthrust of rock and saw the Airedale there, lowered on all fours, staring at the heavy breathing in the brush straight ahead. I crouched beside him and ran a hand over his dirty head and down under his wet matted chin.

Jack was five yards away, moving along with me when I rose up and stepped forward. The Airedale stayed beside me, doing the same. I took another step, and before my foot touched the ground I heard a sound to my left and swung toward it, just in time to see Larr's bearskin coat rise up from the thicket.

He had the Spencer rifle up and aimed. Then the growl and bawl of the bear shattered the silence of the woods; and as it rose up in the brush in front of us, I swung back at it just as Larr's shots began to explode.

The Airedale charged forward; the bear went down with a hoarse scream, then came back up swinging its paw back-handed. The dog let out a loud yelp, and went sailing through the brush. I could tell by the sound that Larr's shots had struck the bear. Now the big Swiss was locked on the bear as it turned facing me through the brush, thirty feet away. I squeezed the trigger, not wanting the big animal to drop down and charge, not this close.

The shot hit the bear in the chest. Blood sprayed. It rocked back, then forward. I heard Jack and Larr fire at the same time, one on either side of me. The bear crashed backward in the brush and let out a long terrible bawl. I

79

raised a hand. Jack stopped, but Larr yelled, cursing, and fired twice more.

The bear bawled out again, then fell silent. The thrashing in the brush stopped and the whole gully became as silent as a tomb.

We stood waiting for a few seconds; then I stepped forward cautiously. The Airedale did the same from the brush where he'd landed, shaking out his matted coat, limping slightly. We moved toward the large lump of silver-tipped fur there in the pile of broken brush.

"He's done for," I called back to the others, still pointing the big Swiss rifle at the dead bear.

When they moved up closer, we all three stepped through the broken thicket, watching the Airedale sniff the big carcass and wag his tail. "Well, Larr. Looks like you finally got your rogue grizzly." I spoke quietly, looking around again as Renfrow stepped closer. "Where's the sheriff?"

"He's back there. Didn't have the stomach for it, after all." Renfrow offered a nervous smile.

I watched Larr, seeing him walk through the brush like a man in a trance, limping slightly, his eyes glassy and fixed on the bear.

"At last! You rotten . . . lousy—" He raised his Spencer once again and fired a round into the dead bear's belly. Dust swirled where the bullet thumped into it. *"Eat* that, you devil!" He fired again. "How does that taste? Hunh?"

"Better stop him, Renfrow," I said. "I think he's over the edge."

"He's waited a long time," said Renfrow, letting out a breath. "Let him go. That's the bear that ate his leg off."

I looked at Renfrow as Jack stepped in and kneeled over the bear. "I thought he lost his leg fighting the Sioux?"

"No. They just caused it. The bear ate it." He raised a hand. "It's a long story."

I just slumped down in the brush and watched as the three of them examined the bear. "Doesn't look so big now, does he," Renfrow said.

Jack had raised the bear's head with both his hands on its ears and leaned close, looking around under its neck. "No," he said. "It's a lot smaller."

"They always look smaller, dead," said Larr.

"Yeah," said Jack, "but that ain't the reason. The reason is, this ain't the same bear."

"What? You're insane." Larr jumped down beside Jack, his artificial leg still straight and stretched out to the side, his eyes glazed and lost. "Why do you say that? Damn your hide! How can you say such a thing?"

"Because if it was, there'd be two bullets in him about here," Jack said. "I never miss. Not a bear . . . not a man, not any damn thing I shoot at." He dropped the bear's head and dusted his hands together.

"Don't be saying that," Renfrow said to Jack. "Of course it's the rogue grizzly."

Jack shook his head. "Huh-uh. No pistol-shot wounds. It's the wrong damn bear. Sorry, boys." He looked at Larr. "I know how much this meant to you, but I have to tell you, you're just shit out of luck."

I stood up, took a breath and stepped over to them. "Jack. It is the bear. Why can't you just admit that maybe once you didn't hit exactly what you aimed at?"

"Because I hit it," he said. He stepped back, lifted the bear's rear leg, then dropped it. "Damn thing smells worse than that Airedale." When he said that, I glanced around and noticed the Airedale had left. Jack lifted the bear's rear leg again. "There you are, Larr," he said. "Now you tell me. You said that grizzly last night was a boar. Does this look like a boar bear to you? If it does, one of us needs to go back and rethink a few things."

"No," Larr said in a low tone. He stepped back, shaking his head. "No, please, God!" His voice began to tremble. "Noooo!" He jumped on the bear, kicking, screaming, sobbing. "It's not hiiiimmmmm!"

"Told ya." Jack just shrugged.

I jumped in with Renfrow and pulled Larr off the dead bear. He wailed like a maniac. Somewhere off in the brush I heard the Airedale growling deep. We settled Larr down beside the dead bear, took out his flask, and poured a stiff drink down him.

"Wanta hear something else?" Jack said.

"What?" I looked over at him as he leaned down, raised the bear's head a little, and looked under it, at its neck.

"This bear was nearly dead when we shot it—"

81

"What the hell?" I walked around and leaned down with him. Long streaks of blood ran down from the bear's neck. There were deep wounds there, deep enough to sink my finger in.

"Jesus," I said. "What could do something like that to a grizzly?"

Dallas Renfrow stepped around beside us and looked for himself. I heard Larr let out a resigned breath as he sipped from the silver flask. "Only another grizzly could've done that," Dallas Renfrow said.

"I've never heard of a boar grizzly doing something like that to a sow."

"This one will. This one'll do anything. He thinks this mountain is his. He'll kill anything that threatens his food source."

"Well . . . evidently he has nothing to fear from us today. Far as I'm concerned he can have this mountain, lock, stock, and barrel." I stood up and walked over to where the Airedale stood with his hackles up, growling low, off toward the rocks in the distance.

I stooped and patted his stinking back until he settled down and whined under his breath. "You did good, boy." I wiped brown mud from my hand and led him back with me. "As well as the rest of us, I reckon."

CHAPTER

7

———•———

We'd only stopped long enough to rest our horses and chew some jerky on the way back to the train. Larr had demanded that Till ride ahead and have Freddie stoke up the engine. I saw no need in it, since the engine took no more than half an hour to build itself up. It appeared to be more a matter of Larr needing to wield authority over someone.

"What about the bear?" Till had trembled at the thought of riding alone. "I don't see as well as I used to, you know. I wouldn't have a chance if he came upon me alone—"

"I have no room for cowards, Sheriff," Larr said. "Don't forget who you work for here! After all those wild and woolly towns you *supposedly* tamed, *single-handed.* I should think this bear means nothing to you."

There was both fear and shame in the old sheriff's eyes when all eyes turned toward him. Glancing away from Till, I said quietly, trying to keep it between just Larr and myself, "I'll ride on down. No sense in pushing a man. If his eyes are bad, I'd just as soon go . . . if it *really* is necessary."

"You'd rather ride back in his place?" Larr purposely raised his voice. "Did you hear that, Sheriff Till? Our Mr. Beatty here has decided to take you under his wing and do your job for you."

"Stay out of this, Beatty," said Till. There was no iron in his tone or bite in his words—just an attempt at saving face.

"Yes," Larr snapped in a wild drunken voice, "stay out *indeed.* When a man works for me, he does as I ask. Right, Sheriff?" He swung his head back to Till.

"Yes sir, Boss. I'll get right on down there." Till turned his horse and rode away without another word.

"What a rotten hopheaded bastard," I'd said to Jack as the old man disappeared past a stand of snow-covered pine.

Jack and I rode behind Renfrow and Larr, listening to Larr rave on and on, out of control. Twice I saw the flash of the gold cigar case, saw Larr duck his head down for a second as Renfrow looked away. I figured Renfrow had to know what was going on, but just didn't *want* to see it.

"We'll push straight through, back to the train, and get on back to the lodge," Renfrow had said when he rode back beside Jack and me for a second. "Boss is taking this pretty bad." He shook his head. "I sure wish that hada been the right bear."

"Boss might take things a little better if he'd get his head clear and keep it that way awhile," I said.

"Hell," Renfrow said, trying to offer a smile that didn't quite work. "A man needs a nip now and then to keep from freezing."

"Little nip, huh?" I stared at him. "Is that all you see going on here?"

"Yes, it is," he'd said with a final tone to his voice. Then he'd turned his horse and ridden back up to Larr.

"I almost wish you hadn't said anything, Jack. Maybe he'd never known the difference. At least it would've taken a day or two maybe. By then we mighta got a hot bath and thawed out some."

"Maybe you're right. A bear's a bear, I reckon. He mighta *never* found out, drunk as he is." He spit a stream of tobacco. "But I agree with him about these folks living up here. If there's a wounded bear running loose, they oughta at least be warned about it."

"You ain't gonna admit that you mighta missed that bear, are you?"

"There ain't nothing to admit. I shot it." He spit a stream of tobacco and gigged his silver-gray ahead.

The Airedale followed beside me, looking up and begging with his eyes until I took out more jerky and threw it down to him a piece at a time. "You earned something outa this mess," I said down to him, watching him spring up and catch the jerky in midair.

His matted coat bounced in heavy clumps. Now the brown mud on his back was caked, either frozen or dried, and he looked more like a filthy sheep than a filthy Airedale. I grinned. "Guess you showed 'em you're worth something, huh?" He cocked his head as if trying to understand me.

There was something about him showing up covered with mud that I couldn't understand, and although I couldn't put my finger on what it was, I knew it had something to do with the bear—not the dead one, but the big rogue who had Larr's mind so torn apart.

"Wish you could talk," I said to the Airedale. Then I looked up to see if anybody had seen me talking to a dog. I shook my head, and gigged Buck forward. So what? I thought, glancing ahead at Larr and Renfrow as Jack rode up toward them. There were worse things than talking to dogs.

We rode steadily on as the afternoon sun darkened behind an encroaching gray sky that hung low and heavy, clouds drifting in from the northwest. Cold wind began licking at our coats and hat brims. I felt my sore nose starting to go numb.

At the top of the ridge leading down toward the train, we stopped long enough to check the sky and look around once more at the rough terrain. Larr had grown sullen and quiet, slumped down in his saddle with the flask in his lap.

As we descended along the edge of the high wall, I could see Sheriff Till's horse hitched near the stock car. A full thick cloud of wood smoke rose from the stack on the engine and hung low beneath the swollen gray clouds. "I see Till made good time and got the engine stoked and ready," said Dallas Renfrow. He glanced up and around the sky. "A good thing too. Looks like we've got a norther heading in."

"Then let's get on in," I said. "I've had enough bear to last me a lifetime."

"He'll want to come back, you know." Dallas spoke to me

in a low tone, just between the two of us. "Once he gets sober, and gets over his disappointment, he'll want to come back up here."

"Then he'll come back by himself, far as I'm concerned." I gigged Buck and started on down along the edge.

We rode another twenty or so minutes down toward the three-car train; and as I rode closer, ahead of the others, ole Freddie looked up toward me from fifty yards away, then ducked his head back inside the engine. In a second, his rifle barrel reached out the window, and before I could do anything, I felt a bullet thump the ground before me, followed by the loud crack of the shot.

"Freddie!" I yelled as loud as I could, reining Buck sideways toward an upshot of rock. "Hold your fire! Damn it!"

He poked his head out the window. "Didn't know it was you, Beatty," he shouted. "Get down here quick!"

"Something's sure got *him* spooked," I said back to the others, kicking Buck into a trot, as fast as I dared on this rough sloping grade. I looked all around, riding down to the engine. When we reined up, one after the other, I jumped from my saddle and ran to the engine. "What the hell were you shooting at?" I called up to him above the sound of the idling engine.

"Thought you was that damned bear!" His hand trembled when he shoved it out the window and waved it across the rough land alongside us.

"Do I look like a *bear?*"

"He's out there, man, sure as hell!" He waved his arm again. "I heard him, smelt him, and saw him, right along that ridgeline." He pointed off to the right.

"You're crazy, old man," I shouted. "Where's Till? What's going on here?"

Jack and Dallas Renfrow ran up beside me. Larr sat atop his horse with his head bowed beneath his wide-brimmed hat. "Till's dead," Freddie yelled. "The bear et him! He'll be eating us too. You're lucky I didn't haul out of here." His eyes were red-rimmed with fear.

Dallas Renfrow jumped up on the engine and snatched Freddie by his coveralls. "Listen, you old coot! Where's

86

Till?" He shook Freddie back and forth; the old man shielded his face with his weathered hands.

"Till's dead. I told you. I heard him scream! Over there! Look at his horse. Look at it, I tell ya!"

I stepped quickly over to Till's horse, already seeing blood on the ground around its hoofs as I snatched its reins and spun it around. "My God!" Four deep slashes ran down the horse's rump, each of them more than an inch deep and gaping. White bone glistened. The horse pitched its head up, staggering in place, and nickered in a weak pitiful tone.

Larr came alive, but like a man moving slowly in a bad dream. He slipped down from his saddle and nearly fell. Then he hung there with a hand on the saddlehorn, just staring.

"Jack! Quick!" I pulled the wounded horse toward the boarding plank. "Help me get some rags and water, before he bleeds to death!"

"Where's Till?" I heard Renfrow shouting at the old fireman as Jack gathered the reins to both our horses, spun their reins on the stock car, and ran up the boarding plank.

"Whatever's left of him's up there." Freddie pointed along a tree line high atop a ridge three hundred yards away. "I seen him get et, I tell ya!"

I pulled at the horse, but it weaved and faltered. I tugged hard to keep it on all fours, but it sank down on its rear haunches and let out a painful whinny. "Up, boy," I bellowed. "Up, damn you!"

He tried to stand but his rear legs gave out. He sank again. Jack ran back down with a handful of loose straw and a canteen of water. "Keep him up, Jack," I shouted, handing him the reins; and I snatched the straw and tried pressing it against the steady flow of dark blood streaming down the horse's rump.

"God," I said. There was too much blood; it flowed through the handful of straw and down my arm, warm and steaming in the cold air. "Why didn't you do something?" I raged at the old fireman.

"I was scared, damn it to hell! You didn't see that big bastard! Throwing Till around like a rag . . . carried him off under one arm."

"Jesus," I said under my breath, pressing the red soppy

mess of straw into the deep gashes. The horse was too far gone to even flinch. "Get some thread! Some needles!" I pushed and cursed and tried holding the gashes closed with my hand. "Somebody help, get some—"

I stopped short at the sound of Jack's pistol, and felt the horse sink the rest of the way to the frozen ground. Steam rose from the blood around him. I stood covered with warm blood, felt it drip from my fingers, my chin. "Come on," Jack said. "Let it go." I felt his hand on my arm, and I stepped back, my breath heaving.

"That filthy bastard!" I yelled, turning toward the high ridge. "I'm going back, right now. I'll kill him this time."

"No. Come on," Jack said. "There's bad weather blowing in. We gotta go." I jerked my arm free.

"He's right, Beatty," I heard Dallas Renfrow say. "He'll have to keep till another time. We can't even go get Till's body. It's too risky."

I caught a glimpse of Jack leading our horses up the boarding plank as I studied the ridgeline. "We got to get his body and take it back," I said.

"He's gone," Renfrow said. "There won't be enough left of him to make up a funeral."

I glanced around, saw that Larr had staggered off and up onto the train. "It's that bastard's fault." I pointed a finger and yelled, "Larr, you got him killed! Him and his horse. Hear me? You killed 'em both! You and your damned bear."

"He can't hear you," Dallas Renfrow said. "Now let's get going."

Somewhere high up in the distance, above the low-hanging sky, in a silver mist that had dropped and spread like swirling spirits, we heard the low long bawl of the bear. From the door of the stock car, the big Airedale raised his head and answered with a mournful howl, as if conceding this battle to the bear, but grudgingly and with a promise of battle to come.

It was the rogue up there . . . and none other. I knew it down in my marrow—knew it was him because he seemed to be calling out to me, reminding me of what he could do, reminding me that he'd be waiting, warning me that this was his mountain, his world . . . that it would always be so.

* * *

KILLERS OF MAN

We chugged back through the dim evening light, darkness closing early, gray and thick and streaked with mist, mist that swirled and howled outside the windows of Larr's private car. Snow pelted the windows and ran sideways, turning to slush, then to water against the heat of the woodstove inside.

I sat solemnly at the oak table, sipping coffee, inspecting piece by piece the big Swiss rifle and making myself better acquainted with its weight, its balance, and its lift-sight mechanism. I'd taken the rifle apart down to the stock and had it spread out on the table.

"Boss won't like you doing that," said Dallas Renfrow, nodding at the row of bolt, barrel, and trigger assembly laid out before me. He carried a bottle and a shot glass in his hand.

I took a breath, let it out slowly, and said in a resolved tone, "Then *Boss* can go straight to hell, far as I care." I picked up the bolt and examined it in the light of the lamp, the same lamp that had spilled light soft and golden on the scantily clad body of Laura Larr only a night ago. I pictured her body now, perhaps to take my mind off the blood, and the pitiful pleading of the dying horse. Thought of her face rather than the face of the old sheriff whose mangled corpse lay back there somewhere in the face of all elements, unfeeling and cold, as cold as the earth beneath it.

"He's resting, finally," said Dallas Renfrow, easing down in the chair across from me. He sat the shot glass and whiskey bottle on the table. Jack sat nearby in the wing-backed chair, drinking from a bottle of bourbon with his boots off and his feet propped up on the lift handle of a glowing woodstove.

"Why do you do it, Renfrow?" I looked up from the precision-milled, highly polished metal that had come out of the earth in the form of rock, and been honed by man into an instrument for killing.

"What?" he said, then he stopped for a second, stared at me, and added, "Oh . . . work for him?" He shrugged. "We've been together for years. I served under him against the Comanche and the Sioux. When he hung it up, so did I. Been with him ever since."

"That don't tell me a thing," I said, laying down the bolt

and picking up the trigger assembly. I blew into it and inspected it closely. "I asked you *why,* not how long."

"Maybe it's none of your business," he said. But there was no heat in his words, only reluctance.

"Yesterday it wasn't. Today it is. There's been an old man and a fine horse killed because of his obsession with that damned bear. I was there, taking the same chance as Till. I think I've got a right to ask whatever I damn well please—"

"He wasn't always like this," he said, before I could finish. "It started after he lost his leg . . . then the whiskey, then the dope." He saw me raise my brow. "Sure I know it. But I look the other way. I knew him when he rode taller in the saddle than any *ten* George Custers or Bill Sheridans . . . and he would've proved it if it hadn't been for that bear."

I gestured with my eyes about the fancy car. "I'd say he carved out a pretty healthy chunk for himself."

"Yeah, but most of it was his father's. Getting the rest was just a way to make up for what he thought he was lacking."

"Lots of men lose an arm or leg. It doesn't ruin 'em. They pick up and go on. He's got it all . . . wealth, a beautiful wife, his own mountain, a railroad. Too much to throw away for a bellyful of whiskey and a headful of cocaine. Sometimes you just have to be tough enough to see what it takes to—"

"Tough? He invented *tough,* Beatty. The man laid still while that same grizzly devil ate his leg off . . . never even whimpered. Could you do that?"

"I hope I never find out."

"Damn right, you hope it. But he did. Then he laid there afterward, made a tourniquet of his belt, and crawled seven miles, till I found him and brought him back to the regiment." He poured a drink, snapped it back, and set the glass down.

He let out a slight hiss and said, "We'd been cut off from our regiment for two days, eleven of us fighting on the run. I was sergeant of scouts then. The colonel and three men came looking for me when I held up for weather. Imagine that, a *colonel* risking his neck for a damned scout. But that's how he was. And him and the other three got

90

avalanched, lost their gear, guns, horses." He poured another drink, threw it back.

"Then when they were walking it out, they got hit by that
grizzly. Bear pinned them in a tiny cave in a box canyon,
crippled them down and took his time, picking 'em out like
sweet berries, one at a time . . . and eating them in front of
the others."

Renfrow shook his head slowly. "Colonel had to watch
him eat the others alive while they screamed and fought—
couldn't do a thing. Then, when it came his time, he played
dead. Had to lay there while it wallowed on him like he was
carrion . . . then not make a sound while it tore chunk after
chunk of nerve, meat, and muscle off his leg, and ate it to
the bone."

"Lord God," I said under my breath. I glanced at Jack
there by the woodstove, saw him listening with narrow-eyed
fascination.

"So," Renfrow said, *"obsessed with the bear?* You might
say that. I don't reckon there's enough bourbon and dope in
the world to wash that bear from his mind. I imagine it puts
him to sleep of a night and wakes him of a morning. What
do you think, Beatty?" He threw back another shot, hissed,
stood up, and looked down at me. But he swayed away
toward the back of the car before I could answer.

I sat there listening to the clacking of the rails and the
wail of the wind, until Jack cleared his throat and said,
"Now that was one *hungry* bear, I'd say."

"Yeah, Jack," I said, examining the big Swiss rifle more
closely, thinking of Laura Larr, seeing her as I'd seen her the
night before in the glow of the lamp. I wondered what part
she played in all this as I put the rifle back together
carefully, perfectly, and checked the action on it. When I'd
finished, I looked at Jack, saw him watching me intently.
"How long does a grizzly live, Jack?"

"I wouldn't know," he said. "Pretty old, if Larr has been
chasing this one since the last Sioux campaign. Why? You
thinking about going back and throwing that one a birthday
party?"

"No." I leaned the rifle against my leg, took up my Henry
rifle from the floor, and laid it out to break it down and

inspect it the same way. "I'm thinking about going back to Missouri and spend a restful winter dodging posses and fighting bounty hunters. I think it might be safer."

"We might be doing the same thing here if we ain't careful. Larr seems to have a way of holding something over everybody's head, then dropping it on 'em ever now and then . . . the way he hit ole Till with that line about *supposedly* taming some wild and woolly towns. What else could the old man do at that point?"

"Well . . . Larr ain't holding nothing over our heads—"

"You're wrong." Jack cut me off. "The whole world has something over our heads. It's just up to us to keep anybody from dropping it on us."

"You're saying Larr would draw in a posse on us? If we don't do his beck and call?"

"Ain't a doubt in my mind." Jack leaned back, studied the ceiling, and added, "The way I figure it, Larr died inside the day that bear ate his leg. He's gone crazy, looking for that *leg*, or something to take its place ever since. Until he finds it, he'll crush everybody and everything around him. He was right about one thing. He is the *lord* of the mountain . . . but it's a *hell* of a mountain he's lord over."

I listened, considering Jack's words while I polished the barrel on the Henry rifle. "Sorta like your book, ain't it. Thoreau took to the wilderness looking for something he lost. You *could* say society et *his* leg, and he went looking for something to take its place—"

"Since when did you start reading philosophy?" Jack looked surprised, stunned perhaps.

My face reddened. "Hell, Jack, I read . . . *some,* when I feel like it. I ain't a *complete* idiot. I've skimmed through it enough to get the jest of what you're saying here. Jeez!" I shook my head and started putting the Henry rifle back together.

"Yeah. Well, I'm not comparing Larr with Thoreau. But they lost something that would destroy them if they didn't replace it somehow. Only Thoreau lost it in the whirl of the city and ran to the wilds to find it. Larr lost his leg *to the wilds.* Where else in hell can he go to find it? Thoreau communed with nature and found what he'd lost. The only thing Larr has left to commune with is the bear."

"And the whiskey. And the cocaine. And lording his will over people, I reckon. Anybody weak enough to allow it."

"So there you are," Jack said. "The man's been dead inside for years. He just ain't fell over yet. He's a dangerous man. Don't be surprised at anything he does."

"Maybe I ain't read much philosophy, Jack. But I ain't surprised at *anything* man does . . . haven't been in years."

A silence passed, then as I laid out the Henry and the big Swiss rifle side by side on the table, Jack asked in a quiet tone, "So, what did you *think* of the book?"

I laid my pistol alongside the rifles and ran my hand along each instrument of death laid there before me. Light from the lamp flickered, dancing along the polished brass and steel. "The book's all right, I reckon. It's just too heavy to carry around all the time."

Jack grunted and shook his head. I grinned, shrugged, and said, "I just ain't a big reader, Jack. What can I tell ya. I'm more drawn to the *visual* arts."

"Okay." He nodded. "Then picture this. Two men high up on a mountain, minding their own business . . . spending the winter drinking good whiskey and watching the sun rise and set, day after day . . . without getting involved with killer bears, or crazy rich men."

"Now I can see that," I said, picking up the pistol, shoving it into my shoulder harness. "I can see that clear as a bell."

PART II

DEN OF DOGS

CHAPTER

8

It was dark when Jack and I led our horses off the stock car into the empty street at Lodge Pole. The sky was low, dark, and gray. A biting wind full of sleet and snow licked at our coats and hats and blew the night sideways. Our horses leaned into the wind with their heads ducked and their manes and tails whipping in circles.

The Airedale leaped from the stock car and ran up to a black Catahoula cur who appeared to be waiting for him, wagging its tail and trembling in the cold. The two dogs sniffed, circled one another, and took off down the windy street.

"Nice to have somebody waiting," I said to Jack above the wail of the wind.

"What?" He yelled from only four feet away. I just waved it off.

A fancy buggy with its top up was waiting near the higher end of the platform, and I looked back and saw Dallas Renfrow leading Larr toward it. Larr's left arm lay looped across Renfrow's shoulder and a bottle dangled from his right hand.

"There you go, Boss," I heard Dallas Renfrow say beneath the roar of wind. Then he doffed his hat up to the buggy as Larr spilled into it. The buggy turned and started off past us, wind whipping the ribbed leather top. Laura

Larr sat in the darkness beneath the covered buggy, but I pretended not to see her as Jack and I hiked our collars up, held our hands on our hats, and led the horses off to the livery stables.

But I continued watching the buggy until it pulled over in front of the Larr Lodging House. There, an old Indian trotted out to the passenger side of the buggy—the same Indian who'd helped carry Brace Denton's body off the train that morning. He reached up and helped Ben Larr spill down against the side of the buggy, then looped Larr's arm across his shoulder and guided him toward the lodge. Snow spun into a mist around them.

"All I want is food, whiskey, and barrels of hot water," Jack yelled beside me, above the wind. "Anybody denies me that, they're taking their life in their own hands."

We walked the horses to the stables. Each of us paid a skinny kid fifty cents to grain, water, and bed them down. Then we walked on over to the lodging house with our rifles and saddlebags over our shoulders. I'd taken the empty carpetbag from the stock car where I'd stashed it, and carried it now, with the wind trying to pull it from my hands.

I'd noticed, walking along the street, that although the storefronts were neat and well maintained, through the dark windows they all appeared to be empty. A lone mannequin stood in a window wearing a woman's black cape and a fashionable flat-brimmed hat. It seemed to watch us as if wondering what sort of fools would tread this weather.

As soon as we'd signed the register at the lodging house, I asked the desk clerk about the stores and he ran a hand back over his bald head and told me that they closed in early autumn and stayed closed until spring.

"They cater to the summer trade, Mister—?" He turned the register halfway around and cocked his head toward it. "—Beatty, is it?"

"Yes," I said; and before he could turn to a young blond-haired man who'd slipped up to the counter beside me, I added, "My friend and I will require hot baths and some hot food. As soon as possible—"

98

"Excuse me, seer," said the blond-haired man to the clerk, before I'd finished talking. "Do you theenk the snow weel be appropriate by the mornick?"

I just looked at him, hearing his unfamiliar accent. "Hope I didn't *interrupt* you," I said, before the clerk could answer him.

His face reddened. "Oh, forgive me, seer. I am so—how you say?—excitabled about the cooming sneow. How rutde of me."

He offered an apologetic smile, his finely trimmed mustache spreading into a straight line above his lip. A close-cropped goatee came to a dangerous point on his chin. He wore a high-collared wool sweater that could warm the dead. I felt like stripping it off his back.

I nodded. "Well . . . perhaps I'm a little testy tonight. No harm done." I gestured him toward the clerk.

"Yes, well—" The clerk cleared his throat. "Mr. Kriz*leg*ber*zthe?*" The clerk's tongue seemed to twist and knot in his mouth. "All indications are that the snow should be deep, and I dare say, *slick and fast,* by morning." The clerk darted a glance past me as if embarrassed. I just stared.

"The hell's he talking about?" I heard Jack say quietly behind me. "Are we any closer to getting rooms here?"

I shrugged.

"Awwww!" the blond-haired man said, looking as if he might collapse in ecstasy. Then he straightened, clicked his heels in a bow, turned, and took off up the stairs, two at a time.

The clerk's eyes followed him, then turned back to me. "Snow makes him that way." His voice lowered; he leaned closer across the counter as if sharing a secret. "A skier, you know."

"I see," I nodded, thinking only of hot soapy water and mounds of steaming food. The heat of the place caused my cold nose to thump with each pulse beat. I touched a finger to it.

"Of course the bear being out there has everybody a little tense." He grinned. "Can you imagine, that young man sliding down a hill with a couple of bed slats strapped to his feet—all of a sudden a big hairy paw reaches out, and

99

blaaaam!" He pawed his hand through the air, then slapped it on the countertop and laughed until his breath wheezed in his chest.

"Oh my . . ." He patted a hand on his chest. "These *zany* foreigners! They *kill* me." He ran a finger beneath his nose and breathed deep.

I shot Jack a glance and saw him shake his head.

"Why, only last winter," the clerk continued, "I had one who thought—" His voice stopped. Jack's rifle barrel had swung up and pressed against the tip of his nose. The clerk's eyes turned wide and crossed, staring down the barrel.

Jack said, "Do I have to clip something off your face to get a room here?"

"Easy, Jack!" I laid a hand on the rifle barrel and nudged it away.

The clerk's face went pale; he swallowed hard. "Last two—on the left—second floor—no charge, compliments of Colonel Ben Larr, enjoy your stay!" Two brass keys hit the countertop and rang like small church bells.

I snatched them up and pitched one to Jack. "Thank you," I said with a narrowed gaze; and I followed Jack up the stairs.

But no sooner had my foot hit the third step than I stopped when I heard big Eldon say, *"Angel boy!* You red-nosed son of a—"

"Eldon, please," the clerk said quickly. "You know Boss doesn't allow trouble in here!"

I turned slowly on the stairs and looked over at him, steadying himself with a hand on the far end of the counter. He stood slightly bent, wearing no gun. A thick bandage circled his head; another showed through the open buttons on his shirt.

"Why, *Eldon,"* I said quietly, "look, at, you." A beaded curtain swayed behind him where he'd stepped through from a lobby area.

"Yeah, you bastard! Look at me! You did *this* to me." He pointed a shaking finger at himself, then at me. "Broke my damn ribs, busted my damn head. I'm *seeing* double here! Can't take a *jake* without passing blood—can't even spit without *spitting* blood. *You* . . . did all this!"

"Thanks for telling me, *mi amigo.* I've gone around all day, worried that I hadn't hurt ya near as bad as I wanted to—big ole *b'hoy like you."*

Eldon trembled all over. "I'll . . . *kill you,"* he said, and started scooting along the counter, still steadying himself with one hand. I heard Jack chuckle, two steps up; and I let the carpetbag drop to the stairs and eased my hand around to my back pocket.

"Come on, *Eldon—!"* I shouted, taking a step down and slipping my fingers into the brass knuckle-dusters. "Let me bat your big head around some more. You dumb *cocker spaniel!"* I dropped the rest of my gear on the stairs.

Eldon trembled all over, scooted quicker along the rail, and raged: *"I'm coming—I'm coming!"*

"Please, gentlemen!" The clerk threw his hands over his face. Brerton Beam and the old Indian peeped through the beaded curtain at the sudden commotion. I drew back my fist as Eldon tried to spring toward me from the counter, throwing his guard up. But then I ducked straight down as his fist swished over my head; and I cracked the brass knuckles as hard as I could into his right shinbone just below his knee.

Big Eldon bellowed like a newly neutered bull. He danced a crazy broken dance on his left foot, trying to reach his shin but unable to because of his tightly bandaged ribs. I straightened up slowly and slipped the brass knuckles back in my pocket, watching him hop and scream, first sideways, slamming into the counter, then spinning along it, then off the far end and backward through the beaded curtain.

He took out the curtain with a sweep of his arms, thrashing in it as it wrapped around him, strands of it lashing at him like snakes. He swiped his hands at it, grabbing it, jerking at it; and he wrestled with it across the lobby, until he flipped backward over a low sofa.

"Jee-hee-sus!" I heard Jack say. There was a loud thump as Eldon smacked the wooden floor. Sparks flurried in the hearth. Beam stood gawking with his mouth dropped open.

"And now, our boy *Eldon's* down again," I said quietly. The old Indian walked over to the sofa and stared down, scratching his head.

101

"I hope this whole trip ain't gonna be just one damn thing after another," Jack said, turning and heading up the stairs.

The old Indian's name was Ponce, I learned, as he carried up bucket after bucket of steaming hot water and poured it into the high-back metal bathtub. Each trip he carried up two buckets, took one to Jack's room, and brought one to mine. There was no way to hurry the process. Each time he finished pouring the bucket, he would stop and talk.

"Heard what the bear did," he said, shaking his head, holding the empty bucket. He looked a hundred years, but carried himself in a sturdy—if slow—manner.

"Yeah," I said. "It's been a rough day. I'm really looking forward to a good hot—"

"Shoulda taken the Catahoula," he said, not seeming to hear me.

"The Airedale was along," I said, leaning against a wardrobe and pulling off my boots. "He did what he could."

"Needed both." He looked up from the floor and into my eyes. "Airedale draws him out. Catahoula takes him down. Two work as one." He held up two fingers, then closed them together.

"I ain't sure it'd work," I said, cocking an eye. "I've all the respect in the world for Catahoula curs, Airedales too . . . but this is a hell of a bear."

"Not just bear . . . a *rogue grizzly,*" he said. "Big difference. Airedale track him on ground. Catahoula track him on *wind.* Airedale, *big* and *bold.* Catahoula, *fast* and *smart.* Two dogs work as one, on a rogue grizzly. Seen many good dogs work together that way . . . even when I was a child."

"That's interesting," I said. "I'll consider that while I soak in a hot tub." He nodded and left.

"Can I get some *damned* hot water?" I heard Jack yell as the old Indian stepped out the door.

I slipped off my shirt, took the money from my waist, and put it in the carpetbag while I waited for the next bucket of hot water. When Ponce came back, he emptied the water in the tub, then stood there with the bucket hanging from his hand. Steam curled up around his wrist. "Good job you did on Eldon," he said. I saw a trace of a smile. "How you trade the brass knuckles?"

"Can't," I said. "It's the only pair I've got." I looked at the tub of steaming water, only two buckets deep, then back to him. "I'm cold to my bones here. Do you suppose I'll ever get a hot bath?"

"Soon," he said. He looked down at the tub and back at me. "Those are *my* dogs. They know how to hunt grizzly."

"Till said they were just a couple of strays. Said they weren't good for nothing but bumming food."

"He said that because they are mine. These white-jakes know nothing about grizzly, or dogs. Maybe you will listen."

"Maybe," I said, "but I could listen a lot better after I get a bath."

I heard Jack pound on the wall next door. *"—Some water!"*

"If I owned brass knuckles," Ponce said, paying Jack no attention, "I could hit somebody the way you hit Eldon."

"A club wouldn't do?"

"Did it for you?" Again the trace of a smile.

On his third trip, he told me how the dogs had been given to him by an older trapper, and how they'd been looked down on as strays simply because they were his, and because he let them run loose and fend for themselves. He told me that he talked to the dogs and made them realize how much they needed each other, needed to work together, each with their own strengths, each making up for any weaknesses the other might have. By this time, I stood shivering, barefoot, with my arms folded across my naked chest, listening to Jack beat the wall and curse in the next room.

"Thank you, thank you, *Jesus!*" I said, when he made his last trip and poured the steaming bucket into the tub.

He stuck a finger in the water and said, "Still hot."

"Good!"

I walked him to the door and opened it for him. But he stopped and turned. "Will you get the bear in the morning?"

"Don't think so," I said, jiggling the knob and nodding him toward the hallway.

"Because the snow will help you find him—"

"I just want to spend the day resting, maybe crack big Eldon in his other shin."

103

"That would be good." He nodded. "But when you go to get the bear, take my dogs with you."

"If I do, I will. But I might forget about hunting the bear," I said, ready to shove him out if I had to.

"Do you believe in tipping Indians?" he asked quietly, raising a palm.

Man oh man! I went and took some money from my trouser pocket, came back, and gave it to him. "Now, will you please—"

He nodded back across the room at the carpetbag with the purple angels on it. "Maybe you *should* forget about hunting grizzly." Again, the trace of a smile as he stepped out in the hall. "I will bring you some salve for your nose."

The nerve . . . I hurried to the bathtub, snatching the carpetbag on my way. I dropped it on the floor beside the tub and hurried out of my trousers. I stuck my toe in the tub, then my whole foot.

Lord! That's good. . . . I waited just a second, feeling the hot water travel up my calf.

"Beatty? Are you there?" *Jesus!* I heard a knock on the door.

"Yeah, go away," I called out from the edge of the tub.

"Can't do it," said Dallas Renfrow at the door. "Boss sent for you. Wants to see you right away."

"Ten minutes?" I felt steam curl up around my thigh, my foot hanging there in hot water. I knew that ten minutes would mean an hour once I got settled in the tub.

"Right now," he said. "The colonel don't get kept waiting."

"He wasn't able to stand up an hour ago. Surely he can wait while I get—"

"I'm just following orders, Beatty."

"Five minutes?" I heard sort of a pleading in my voice.

"Beatty, do you realize who *owns* this place? The *only* lodge in town?"

Why me? I gazed up, shook my head, raised my foot from the tub, and shook it as I reached for trousers and that damned carpetbag.

"I'm coming," I said, "just hang on."

"I'm headed back to the train," he said through the door.

"Just go to the suite at the far end of the hall. It's the Larrs'."

"All right, all right . . ."

I threw on my shirt, half buttoned it, and walked barefoot to the door, carrying the carpetbag. *To hell with dressing.* What did they expect, getting a man out of a hot bath?

I passed the blond foreigner in the hall, and he said in an excited voice, "Tomorrow mornick, we weel give it *heel,* eh?"

"You bet," I said, barely looking at him as I walked to the wide door at the end of the hall. I raised a brass knocker, tapped it a couple of times, and stood there, tense, debating whether or not to give Larr a piece of my mind. But it was Laura Larr who opened the door and looked out at me. "Excuse *me,*" I said, pulling my shirt closed with my free hand. "I thought . . . I mean . . . Dallas Renfrow said—"

"Please come in, Mr. Beatty," she said. "Yes, my husband sent for you." She wore a long, flowing evening gown. Immodest, I thought, but perhaps not in bad taste for folks in the Larrs' circle. *Certainly more than she had on last time.* "He'll join us in a moment." She smiled. "But tell me, would you have come so quickly if *I* had sent for you?"

I just looked at her, not wanting to get into a conversation about what I would or wouldn't do, not while a hot bath lay waiting for me. "I'm here, ma'am. What more can I tell you."

"Yes, of course." She glanced at the carpetbag, and down at my bare feet as I stepped in. "Why is your foot so red? Are you all right?"

"It's nothing, ma'am," I said. "I'm fine."

"Good then." She led me across a finely furnished room and swept a hand toward a velvet sofa. "Please sit down. Would you like a drink?"

"Nothing for me, thanks." At first I hesitated to sit, owing to the way I'd dressed—the only two buttons I'd buttoned were buttoned wrong—but then I shrugged to myself and eased down on the edge of the sofa, setting the carpetbag between my feet. I was a little curious, wondering how she would face me after what had happened last night. I didn't have to wonder long.

"I want to thank you for what you did yesterday on the train." She turned with two crystal brandy snifters and held one out to me, apparently not having heard that I didn't care for one. "That was very chivalrous of you . . . Eldon's a *big* man."

I took the snifter, and smiled slightly. "He's growing smaller every day, ma'am."

"So I hear." She returned my smile, tipped her snifter of brandy toward me, and sipped it. "Also, I want to ask you not to feel differently toward me over what happened last evening. I'm afraid I wasn't at my best. My husband is a man of bizarre taste and habits. Often I weaken and fall allured by them. We destroy one another, I'm afraid." She smiled, a smile built on irony or cruelty, I wasn't sure which. "Call me wicked, but I enjoyed standing there last night, vulnerable, feeling your eyes on me. I was ready to do anything, right there, right then—in front of *him* if need be. Him and his *bear* obsession." She nodded toward the wall separating us from her husband, then back into my eyes. "Were you excited by it?" she asked casually, as if asking the time of day.

I reddened slightly but managed to hold her gaze, knowing she was playing with herself somehow, by playing with me. "I wasn't as shocked as you might think, ma'am," I said, leaning back, swirling the brandy in the snifter. I sipped it and crossed my legs, my bare foot looking pale and small there in the fancy suite. "I've been around some. I know that dope makes a person do peculiar things."

"Yes. I seldom use it, but when I do it's *anything* goes." She smiled above the brandy snifter. "Would you like *some?*" She let her eyes and voice toy with the word *some.* But I knew she was teasing me, and I let it pass, shaking my head.

"Never use it."

"Of course. Now I remember. The only *edge* you want is on your knife blade?"

"Must sound pretty trite to you, ma'am, but it's true. I know what the stuff does to a person." I took a deeper sip. "Now, if you don't mind, I know you didn't bring me here to *thank* me, because you're probably used to men falling all over themselves being chivalrous for you. Now that I've

106

seen you—and I mean, *seen* you—I'm sure you think that no matter how coarse I found you and your husband's behavior last night, the only *difference* I could feel toward you is to want to see more." I threw back the brandy and finished it. "But you're wrong, ma'am."

"Call me, Laura," she said, "if you don't mind." I noticed the faintest sign of cocaine start to show in her eyes. Maybe she had taken it just before I arrived.

"I'll call you Mrs. Larr," I said, smiling, "if *you* don't mind."

She tossed her head. "Most men would've been, as you say, 'falling all over themselves' at the opportunity you had before you. You could have taken advantage . . . and yet you turned it down."

"Call me old-fashioned, but a husband offering another man his wife, to get him to kill a bear—?" I shook my head slowly and swirled the brandy in the snifter. "Kinda chills a romantic interlude." I smiled. "Last night showed me about all of you folk I need to see. You're rich, doped, and crazy. Skillful at playing dangerous games with one another, and leaving somebody else to straighten out your mess. The only part I don't understand is you letting him slap you around. For some reason I'd have never guessed you to be the type." I tipped the snifter toward her. "But to each their own, I reckon—"

"Listen to me," she said, leaning toward me, her voice suddenly lowered. She shot a glance toward a door, then back to me. "He wants you to kill the bear so bad, he's willing to do whatever you ask. Do you hear me? But whatever he offers you to kill the bear, just remember this— I'll double it if you'll . . . kill *him* instead."

"Whoa now." I raised a hand, seeing that the cocaine was beginning to talk through her. "Let's just forget you ever said that. People get a little doped or drunk, they say things they don't mean."

"But I do mean it!" Her voice rasped with insistence. "Kill him, and I'll pay you anything. Take him out as if you're hunting the bear, and simply blow his head off. No one will ever question it. You're walking along, you trip, your rifle goes off. *Whoops,* he's dead, and I'll do anything! Do you hear me—"

107

"Forget it!" I just stared at her. "I want nothing more to do with the bear, or you, or your husband. I don't know what you think I am, but you're wrong."

"Just remember," she said, whispering hoarsely. *"Double,* whatever he pays you to kill the bear. Double!"

"No way," I said, "and that's the gospel."

I heard the door across from us open and I turned toward it. "Careful what you call the *gospel,* Mr. Beatty," said Ben Larr. He stood in the doorway in his dark robe, weaving, red-eyed, with a haunted look on his face. "Peter called the Gospel one thing, Paul called it another . . . and of course we all *know* what it did for Jesus." I could tell he was drunk, but his drunkenness was tightly wrapped in a cocaine glow.

"Darling," said Laura Larr, standing. I stood up also, as Ben Larr staggered across the room using a fine hickory cane with a silver-inlaid tip and handle. "I was just telling Mr. Beatty how persuasive you can be when you want something done."

I shot her a glance, saw her guarded expression plead for secrecy. "And I was telling her, I'm not going back after the bear, no matter what." I said it with finality and threw back the glass of brandy. "So if you'll excuse me." I started to set the snifter down, ready to turn and leave.

"Sit down, *Mister* Beatty . . . *James* Beatty!" His voice hissed, but it was a loud hiss; and it stopped me and drew my eyes back to his. He had a cigar in his hand, lit, with smoke curling up as he cradled it near his chest and weaved over to me. "Of course you're going after the bear. Dallas said you were ready to go back after it today, when you saw what it did to Till's horse."

But instead of sitting, I picked up the carpetbag and said, "I get upset at the sight of innocent blood. Sure, I was ready to then, but not now. I can't blame that one on the bear. He just acted in his nature. You're the one who sent the old man back there alone, knowing what could happen—him scared stiff. He nearly begged you not to make him go."

Larr spread a twisted grin. "That was just me acting in *my* nature. It's a man's nature to command. But I suppose you're less tolerant of man than beast."

I stared at him for a second, realizing there was no talking to a doped-up drunk. "Say what you will, Larr. I'm out of

108

your game." I glanced at Laura Larr and added, "Yours too. You're both gonna have to find somebody who's got more at stake than I do. You've got some nerve, forcing me on that bear, making me do your killing for you." I spoke to Ben Larr but shot Laura a glance, hoping she got the same message. "I've got nothing to do with—"

"Let me show you something, Beatty," Larr said before I could finish. He stuck the cigar in his mouth; his hand darted inside his robe. I tensed until he pulled out two folded pieces of paper. He tapped them in the air and narrowed his brow. "Just a little something I do in my spare time." He pitched them to Laura Larr. "Show him, dear." He turned back to me as she unfolded one of the papers. *"This* is what makes me think you'll do my killing for me."

I watched Laura Larr's blank expression as she smoothed it in her hand and held it up before me. Cocaine swirled in her eyes now. "A wanted poster, of Jesse Woodson James. My husband collects these—a bizarre hobby, I think. Does it look familiar, Mr. Beatty . . . *James* Beatty?"

I took a deep breath and let it out. "So that's what this is about. Y'all think I'm him." I chuckled, shook my head, and looked back at Ben Larr. "You're wrong . . . wrong, wrong. Wrong enough to hold public office."

"Oh?" He raised his brow and puffed his cigar. "Then you're not him?" He gestured a hand toward her, and she unfolded the other piece and held it up. "Then, here, I'll give you a choice—pick one."

I stared at the poster of me, me under the name Miller Crowe. I tried to chuckle again, but it didn't have quite the same depth to it. "Larr, Larr, haven't you heard? That feller Crowe died at Powder River a few years back. Got himself skinned and gutted by a band of bloodthirsty—"

"James or Crowe. You look enough like either one. Whichever one you are, you're going after my bear for me—" He weaved slightly, but caught himself. "—and you're not coming back until you've killed it."

I hesitated for a second, thinking of a way out. Then I let out a breath and said, "Even if I was Jesse James *or* Miller Crowe, would that make me a *bear* hunter?"

Larr shook his head slowly. "No, it only means you're a killer. I saw how you were today, calm, cool, just like you were with big Eldon. You don't rattle or freeze at that second when the flesh splits and the blood spills. Your shot hit the bear dead center. You're a killer of man, Beatty . . . and that's what's needed here. If you can kill a man, you can certainly kill a bear for me."

"I ain't killing nothing for you, Larr." I felt heat rise up my neck; I took a step toward him.

"You do realize that we have a telegraph line from here to Elk Horn? Don't you?"

"No," I said, stopping, feeling the flash of heat on my neck turn to a chill. "But what's that got to do with anything?" I knew exactly what it had to do with *everything*. One message from him and Jack and I could spend a hard winter ducking a posse in this mean country.

"Nothing at all if you're not Jesse James or Miller Crowe. Nothing at all if you *really* have nothing to hide." He nodded at the carpetbag. "But unless you carry that around for your health, I'm willing to bet that you do."

There was no point in denying anything, coming off with some weak excuse for myself. I just stared at him and said, "Careful, Larr. If I was either of the two men you've accused me of being, I'd tell you that you're getting close to stepping over a line."

"Oh! Now we see where your heart lies. Now you've shown your tender spot—" He weaved, steadied himself with his cane, and spread a crafty cocaine smile.

"Nothing tender here. You've just put your nose in my business. My friend and I came here to rest a couple weeks, then go on our way. It would be best if you just let us do that. There're other pawns who'll play your games for you. Believe me, you're teasing the wrong dog."

He puffed the cigar, shrugged, and added, "True, there are others. But you're also the most expendable. If the bear gets you, what have I really lost? Dogs have never frightened me, Mr. Beatty. I've teased many of the wrong ones. You turned down my most generous *offer.*" He gestured his cigar toward his wife as if she were a prize in a shooting match. "Now, I'm afraid you'll have to accept my *proposition.*" He reached out with his cane and tapped the tip of it against the carpetbag. "Kill the grizzly, Beatty . . . and I'll match whatever you pull out of there. That should make even your life worth something."

"You're a dirty bastard, Larr," I said, gripping the carpetbag in my hand.

He smiled, weaved some more, and said, "Yes, and just think, you have no choice but to do as I say." He turned to Laura Larr. "Show our dear Mr. *Beatty* to the door, darling." He turned and staggered away, back across the room. I stood seething as he closed the door behind him.

"You see," she said quietly, her blue eyes narrowed and turned to ice. "He doesn't care if the bear kills you. He doesn't care about anything or anybody. Kill him for me." I felt her grip my forearm. "Just kill him, please." She stepped forward, almost against me, and watched my eyes, waiting, her eyes telling me that last night's offer was still good. "Make a choice," she whispered near my ear. Now I felt her against me. Close and warm against me. Somehow I felt that she knew it wasn't much of a choice. Who in their right mind would rather face a *rogue* grizzly than simply kill a *crazy* man?

CHAPTER

9

—◆—

I'd left the Larrs' suite with a lot on my mind, and walked back down the empty hall to my room. The carpetbag seemed to weigh a ton. I should have realized that Jack and I didn't look like the types to carry such a thing. I'd guarded it too close to *not* be noticed; and since everybody from Beam the drummer to Laura and Ben Larr *had* noticed it, and commented on it in some fashion, I had to wonder just how many others had taken notice of me between Missouri and Lodge Pole.

By the time I'd reached my room, I could picture thousands of fingers pointing toward the mountain and thousands of lawmen and bounty hunters looking up here as they jacked a round into their rifles. *Jesus.* Now, to boot, I felt like I had to make a decision, whether to kill Ben Larr or kill the big grizzly. I could play along with the Larrs' craziness until Jack and I slipped away, but where would we go—deeper into the cold frozen wilderness? At this time of year that might be worse than taking our chances against a posse; and if we did flee into the wilds, like as not we would end up facing the bear anyway.

I thought of the conversation Jack and I had had earlier. He was right. There was no doubt Ben Larr would sic the law on us if we didn't go along with him, and I had no doubt that Laura Larr had only mentioned killing the bear because she figured—given a choice—that I'd just shoot her husband for her and be done with it.

These things ran through my mind as I walked back through my room to the bathtub, dropped the carpetbag to the floor, undressed, and stuck my foot into the water. "Well, hell." Now the water was turning cold.

I bathed anyway, wondering how hard it would be to locate the telegraph line and cut the wires. But that would only buy us so much time, and soon the clerk down in Elk Horn would send somebody to see what was wrong. No, I thought, that was a bad idea.

When I finished my tepid bath, I put any notion of a hot meal out of my mind and crawled off to bed, tired to the bones and with the carpetbag under my arm. I fell asleep thinking about the Larrs and their dope and the strange world they lived in. Before I'd left their suite, I'd asked her why she didn't just grab what she could and leave him. Why did she have to have him killed? "Grab what I can?" She'd laughed. "And give up what's rightfully mine?" Why should she? "Can't you see my husband's a coward? If he wasn't he would have already blown his own head off," she'd said bluntly. "You have to do the killing. My husband obviously doesn't have the nerve it takes to pull the trigger on a dumb animal, let alone himself."

More than once that night I saw the faces of her and her husband near me in my sleep, their eyes glassed and swirling in madness, and behind them the grizzly, its big paws spread, ready to devour them both. And larger than all of them, I saw the dancing bear I'd seen at the rail siding. He turned and curtsied around and around, all at the prodding of a weathered hand.

I awoke restless the next morning with the sun already reaching through my window and across the floor. I dressed quickly, took the money from the bag and shoved it down in my waist, and headed down for a hot breakfast. As I stepped outside my door, I almost tripped over a wooden box of ammunition. There beside my door stood the Swiss rifle, just a reminder from Ben Larr that he had me where he wanted me and I'd better do as he'd said. I glanced down the hall toward the door to their suite, picked up the rifle and ammunition, and headed downstairs.

113

I walked down, through the lobby that was now minus a beaded curtain, and back into a small dining room where Quiet Jack sat picking at a steamy plate of food and sipping coffee. The only other person in the dining room was the blond-haired young man, and he sat over near a window, gazing out with a forlorn expression, his chin in his palm. His plate of breakfast sat before him untouched.

"Thought you died in your sleep," said Jack, dropping a biscuit on his plate.

"I'm going to die pretty soon if I don't get some hot food," I said, dropping down in the chair across from him. I rubbed my hands together. "What's good here?"

"It's all good—" He sighed and pushed his plate away. "—but I woke up without an appetite this morning."

"That ain't like you," I said. "Feeling bad?"

"No, just ain't hungry. They quit serving breakfast a few minutes ago. Said if you showed up, they might throw down some jerky and hardtack from the supply room."

I glanced around. "Damn it! What kinda place won't serve a breakfast to a hungry man? It ain't like they're too *busy!*"

Jack chuckled. "Just telling you what the old Indian said. He's the cook here, and he had to cut it short so he could go down to the engine and help clear the tracks. If I was you I wouldn't press the issue. Never have somebody handle your food once you've made them mad at you."

"Man!" I rubbed my hand across my mouth. "I've gotta eat something."

"Here, I've barely et any off it." He slid his plate over to me.

"Are you sure?"

"Yeah, I'll eat something later."

I dug in, glancing over at the blond-haired man, eyeing his plate of eggs, meat, and flapjacks covered with butter and syrup. "What's his problem?" I nodded toward him. "He ain't eating either."

"Big storm blew over and missed us last night. He's disappointed about it, I reckon." Jack shrugged. "He wanted to slide down some hills. The old Indian says it hit hard twelve miles down the mountain."

"Ain't that a shame." I grinned and threw back a mouth-

114

ful of gravy and biscuit. "Now then. If I can just get some hot coffee to go with this." Jack shook his head and slid his cup of coffee over to me.

While I ate, I told him about the strange conversation with the Larrs, about Ben wanting the bear killed and Laura Larr wanting *him* killed. I told him about Ben Larr's deal— his offer to match whatever was in the bag if I killed the bear for him, and his threat of turning us in to the law if I didn't. When I'd finished, Jack just shook his head. "Well, we've seen he ain't got the nerve to pull the trigger on that bear— that much is true. Do you suppose he meant it, about matching the money in the bag? Think he'd do that?"

"The man's on dope. You can't count on nothing he says. Except I do believe he'd turn us in—"

"Thirty thousand is a lot of money for killing a bear. Even *that* bear."

"Yeah, I know. I hate getting any deeper involved with the Larrs in any way, shape, or form. As soon as we can, I think we best get out of here. But for now, I reckon we've got no choice. Looks like I've got to try and kill that bear."

"Or—" Jack's eyes fixed on mine. I saw the dark question in his eyes without him finishing his words.

"No, Jack. I ain't killing Ben Larr," I said.

"Didn't think you was. But it won't hurt for me to check now and then . . . make sure you ain't changed your mind."

"Yeah," I said quietly. I threw back the coffee and finished it; and we stood up and walked over to the stables to check on our horses. On our way there, we saw Brerton Beam step out of a building with a sign that read LARR TELEGRAPH OFFICE. He'd started toward us with his head down when I raised a hand and called out his name. He looked startled and stopped in his tracks.

"Good morning, Mr. Beam," I called out to him. Then I chuckled, seeing the look on his face as we came closer to him. "What's wrong, Beam? You look like you just saw a ghost."

He sighed. "To be honest, Mr. Beatty, after what happened in the lodge last night, I'm just a bit beside myself." He glanced toward Jack and added, "You look a little pale. I hope your condition has improved."

"I'm much better," Jack said, smiling through a steamy

115

breath. "Nothing like hunting a mean bear in the cold to straighten a man out."

"Indeed." Beam leaned slightly toward Jack, searching his eyes with a concerned expression. He reached inside his coat and pulled out the silver flask. "I'd like for you to take this along with you. If you don't mind my saying so," he said to Jack, "this brandy might do more for you than all your other medicine."

"Well, thank you." Jack grinned and took the flask.

"You needn't worry about what happened last night, Beam," I said. "Eldon and I just have some problems we're working out between us."

Beam turned to me and spread his hands. "I saw how rudely he treated you on the train. But my goodness, Mr. Beatty, hitting a man with such an instrument as you had on your hand. I dare say! That makes me a little afraid to be around you."

"Then I apologize," I said. "But you needn't fear. From now on I'll try to beat the hell out of him in private." I nodded toward the telegraph office. "Wiring in an order of whiskey, are ya?"

"What?" He looked dumbfounded, then caught on and said, "Oh no, not yet. I just had to send a wire to Vera and little Ellen. How they worry when they don't hear from me." He shook his head. "Being a family man has its drawbacks at times, I'm afraid. Not that I would trade places with a bachelor . . . no sir!"

"That's good, Beam," I said, moving away before he went into a spiel. "I envy you the comfort of hearth and kin."

He called out as Jack and I headed on toward the stables. "Will you be going back after that vicious creature? I heard what it did to the poor sheriff."

"Yep, we're going after him," I called back to him. "Wanta come along with us?"

"Now, I know you're only jesting with me," he said.

We walked on to the stables through the crisp morning air. I'd already decided to leave Buck here and take one of Larr's horses. Jack decided the same. Our horses were tired from the cold and trudging the snow; and I didn't want to risk Buck ruining a leg while I did another man's hunting for him.

When we'd grained and watered our own horses, we closed their stalls and led out two of Larr's big riding horses. In the midst of our preparing them for the trail, Ponce the Indian walked into the barn flanked by the Airedale and the big Catahoula. "Take these dogs with you," he said, as we looked up from drawing our cinches.

I dropped the stirrup and tested the saddle; the dun gelding crunched on a mouthful of cracked corn. "If they go, they could get killed," I said, looking down at the Airedale as he stepped forward and sniffed my boot. The Catahoula stayed back, watching, wagging his tail cautiously, and sniffing the air toward me. One of his eyes was dark brown, the other as blue and clear as seawater.

"I have talked about these things with them," Ponce said. "They tell me they would like to die like good dogs." His wrinkled face split into a proud smile. "It is better they die fighting a bear, than to die here on the street, when they are old and have no teeth to chew their food." He reached a hand down and scratched the Airedale's head. "If you were a dog, how would you want to die?"

"I see your point," I said. "Are you coming with us?" I checked my Henry rifle and slipped it into my saddle scabbard. The Swiss rifle leaned against a stall door beside me.

"No. I am more important *shoveling snow* off the tracks." His face took on an ironic twist. "Who ever heard of an *Indian* hunting a bear?"

Jack chuckled. "Sounds un-American, all right." He led the brule gelding around toward the door. The horse high-stepped and shuffled, and snorted a breath of steam.

I gathered my reins and followed him. As I passed the Catahoula cur, I reached down a hand. "C'mon, big boy, looks like we're gonna—"

The dog snapped at my hand with a hoarse growl and sprang to his feet. His hackles flared and he snapped at my boots. I jumped back. The dun snorted and reared. *"Jesus! Call him off!"*

Ponce reached down and poked a finger in the dog's ribs. The dog settled and walked stiff-legged in a circle, watching me with his back still high. "I forgot to tell you. He does not like people touching him."

117

I rubbed my hands together, keeping an eye on the black Catahoula. "Anything else I need to know about him?"

Ponce raised a finger. "Never kick him. Catahoulas do not like being kicked. They have killed men for kicking them."

"I already know that," I said; and we left the barn and walked over to the rail siding, where the engine sat waiting with smoke rising from its stack.

"We'll take ya as far as we can," ole Freddie called down from the engine. "But I'm only stopping for as long as it takes ya to get off."

I nodded and waved a hand. Jack dropped the loading plank; and within minutes we'd loaded the horses and dogs. Dallas Renfrow walked up, leading his horse from the stables. "Hold it," he called out, seeing Jack start to raise the loading plank. "Boss says I'm going with ya. Is that all right?"

"Suits us fine," I said. "You know the country better than us."

He looked the horses up and down. "Those are his horses."

"That's right," I said. "It's his hunt. He can provide the transportation." We swayed slightly as the stock car creaked and drifted forward with the pull of the engine.

Renfrow nodded, then looked at the Swiss rifle hanging from my hand. "As long as I've been with him, he's never lent me that rifle. He must think a lot of you, Beatty. I hope you don't let him down."

I shot Jack a glance, and said, "I'd sure hate to."

The three of us stared out the open door of the car as the car slowly, gradually began to roll past the siding dock. I saw Eldon standing on the boardwalk outside the telegraph office as we swayed and rolled out of town. His right leg was wrapped in a heavy bandage from his knee to the tips of his toes. I grinned and shook my head. He stared until we rolled out of sight around a bend in the rails, leaning on a crutch with a bitter expression.

Once we'd settled into the car, and the train headed out along the winding rails, I poured two cups of hot coffee and walked from the warm fancy car back to the stock car, where Ponce sat on a pile of hay, his collar up against the cold and a shovel across his lap. The dogs lay curled at his feet and only lifted a curious glance toward me when I stepped inside. I swayed back and forth and walked over to him. Steam swirled up from the cups of coffee. "Thought you could use something hot," I said above the rattle of the rails.

"You thought right." He reached up with both hands and took a cup.

"Sorry there's no whiskey, but I want everybody clear-headed today."

"Good idea. Coffee is better, for now. When the bear is dead, you and I will drink whiskey together."

"Sounds good to me." I sat down beside him in the hay and sipped the coffee. "Why don't we take about an hour and you tell me everything I need to do to hunt a grizzly."

He grinned. "In an hour I can only tell you what you better *not* do. The rest would take many years to tell you."

"Fair enough," I said. "Keep in mind that I *have* hunted black bear, so I know a little."

"Very little." He shook his head. "Hunting black bear will only teach you enough to get you killed hunting a grizzly. If there were ten black bears feeding on an elk, they would all leave without a fight if *one* grizzly came upon them and wanted it."

He must've seen a flash of fear cross my brow. "But if you listen to these dogs you will do well." Then he stopped talking and gazed off through the wall slats at the frozen countryside.

"Is that it? That's all you're going to tell me?"

He spread a crafty grin. "I would tell you more, if you trade me the knuckle-dusters."

I shook my head. "Can't do it. I told you, it's the only pair I've got. I might need them to jar ole Eldon around some more."

"That's true," he nodded. "But when all is done, trade them to me before you leave the mountain. You can get another pair down in the lower plains."

I considered it a second, and said, "Okay. When I leave they're yours. I'll give them to you."

119

"No. Not *give* . . . trade them to me. By then I will have something you'll want."

"Fair enough then, we'll make a trade." I stared at him.

He sipped the coffee and said, "Don't *hunt* the grizzly. Let the dogs hunt him. You hunt the dogs. You will know the difference in the dogs' voices when they have bayed the bear, or when they have him running. The Airedale will bark all the time, but pay him no attention until you hear the Catahoula. The Catahoula will make no sound until he is ready to do battle with the bear. Then you move in fast, because the bear will fight his way past them." He raised a finger. "But don't go near the bear on horseback. He will charge the horse and make you miss your shot. If he stalks you, don't try to outrun him on horseback, because he will catch your horse and kill it—"

"Whoa now. *Stalk me?* He won't stalk me. I'll have the dogs on him."

"He is smart. If he can get far enough ahead of the dogs, he will circle, then he will be the one stalking, not you." He shook his head. "That is when you are in trouble. The bear can smell you from a mile away. If you lose the dogs, he will track you."

I sipped the coffee and shook my head. "Sounds more like we're hunting a man than a beast."

"Grizzly is smarter than a man . . . out here. He stays here on the mountain and remembers every rock and gully of it. He is smart enough to watch you and stay hidden until he gets you and your friend alone. He will let you track him, and *he* will backtrack *you,* and lay in wait beside his tracks. Then he will spring out and kill you, without making a sound." He raised his finger again. "With only one blow. Then he will drag you away and wait for your friend to come looking for you. He will kill him the same way."

I shot him an askance smile. "Now, wait a minute. No animal does all that. You make it sound like he can *think and reason.*"

He turned his eyes to mine. "He does. No animal is like the grizzly. He has no enemies except man. He fears nothing and no one. He takes on the spirit of all he kills, and he rolls in its smell after its flesh has gone bad, so he can remember it. He knows no illness, and pain does not stop him . . .

120

only makes him rage. To kill this one, you must think like he does and become what *he* is."

I shook my head, seeing my hands tremble slightly around the coffee cup. I threw back a drink and said, "It almost sounds like you're trying to talk me out of going."

"No. I don't tell you these things to trouble you. I tell you so you will come back alive, and trade me the knuckle-dusters as you say you will."

"I see," I said, nodding. "Don't worry, I plan on bringing them back to you. If I don't, my friend will. He'll come back—if only to kill Larr for causing all this."

"Good then." He sat silently for a second, then said, "Larr thinks the bear cannot die unless it is killed by a silver bullet. He thinks he and the bear are of the same spirit— that one cannot die unless the other dies also."

"That's interesting." I ran my hand inside my pocket and felt the silver bullets there. "I brought some along. If he's right, then I guess I'm prepared." I studied his face, hoping he'd offer more.

"The bear turned him into a coward. He has never been able to face his shame. He laid in a cave with a loaded pistol and watched the bear eat his men—too afraid to shoot the bear, and too afraid to shoot himself. That is why he is crazy."

"I heard the bear ate his men and his leg, but I never heard about the *loaded gun.* I can't believe he laid there and did nothing. How do you know all this?"

He raised his coat and shirt slowly. I saw the terrible scars on his wrinkled stomach, and I winced at the sight. "I know because I was one of those men." He lowered his clothing and smoothed a hand down his coat.

"I was one of his scouts. Do not tell him that I said these things to you," he said softly. "But I was there that day. The bear turned from eating me, and I crawled off behind a rock. I saw what a bear does to a man when he kills him. And from that day on, I have seen what a bear does to a man when he leaves him *alive.* Because of what I witnessed, Larr is ashamed to have me around, yet he is ashamed to tell me to go away. He will see no peace until the bear is dead . . . because he thinks the coward within *him* will die too."

I sat quietly, watching his face turn blank, as he stared

back out through the wall slats at the rough terrain drifting by. He threw back his last drink of coffee and huddled down inside his blanket coat.

Whew . . . I stood up, took the empty cups, and swayed back toward the warm car where Jack and Dallas Renfrow waited. I stopped for a second at the stock-car door and said, "Why don't you come on back where it's warm. Maybe we *could* rustle up *one* drink of whiskey before we—"

"You go. I will stay here with the dogs and tell them what they must do to hunt the bear."

I walked back into the car and saw Dallas Renfrow holding a coffeepot beside the oak table. Jack sat napping near a window with his coat open and his boots off. "How's Ponce and his dogs doing back there?" Dallas asked, looking up from pouring coffee.

"They're all right." I shook my head, smiling. "I invited him back here but he turned me down. Suppose he's allergic to heat and good company?"

"Ponce is a strange one, even by *Indian* standards. Don't know why Boss keeps him around."

"I bet I know," I said. I told him what the old Indian had said about Larr and the bear.

When I'd finished, Dallas looked up from his coffee cup and tapped his fingers on the oak table. "I reckon anyone who was there would tell a different version. Ain't that how it is when something terrible happens?"

I just stared at him, watching his eyes. He shrugged, raised his cup, and said, "I bet if George or Tom Custer was still here there'd be a whole other story about the Little Bighorn." He offered a weak smile.

"I met George and Tom Custer once," I said. "They mighta gave a different version, but the outcome would still be the same. Larr might tell a different story about what happened with the bear, but he'd have a hard time making me understand why a man laying there with a *loaded* gun would let a bear eat his men . . . and his own *leg.*"

"So, you'll just brand him a coward?" Dallas sipped the coffee as steam swirled around his cheeks.

"I ain't branding him *nothing,* except a man who slicks everybody into doing what he wants . . . even his killing."

I waved a hand about the fancy car. "All this—everything

about the man, is nothing but whitewash to cover up what he really is. *Brand him?* Hell, all this *brands* him, once you look through it and see what he is—a rich, doped-up drunk who's still searching for something that ate him up years ago."

"I reckon we all do a little of that," he said, his eyes fixing on mine. "Some of us hide what we know we are behind railroads, dope, and money—some of us behind a carpetbag with angels on it. Either way, it's the very thing we try to hide that exposes us in the end." He sat the cup down. "Everybody's hiding something, eh, Beatty?"

"Careful," I warned him quietly. I stood swaying with the motion of the train, looking down at him, hearing the rails clack beneath us. "Don't invite yourself into my world and close the door behind you."

He made it a point to lean both hands out on the table and folded them. "The way you did, coming into Larr's mountain?"

"I mighta found my own way to his mountain, but everything on his mountain found its way to me. I plan on killing that bear if I can. But whether I do or not, once this hunt's over, my friend and I are pulling out of here. Anybody tries to stop us—" I paused to let my words sink in. "—they'll *wish* all they had to face was a bear. Think about it before you let Larr sic you on us. There's been no problem between you and me. Let's keep it that way."

"I understand," he said. "You have my word."

CHAPTER

10

When the train wound down to a halt, the sky was grainy and gray but moving away slowly. Although the full weight of the storm had hit farther down the mountain, it had swept through here and spilled its cold breath. Drifts of snow lay in crevices of upthrust rock and in smooth sloops up the base of tree trunks. Streaks of ice lay heavy in the drooping branches of pine and aspen, and capped the tops of brush thickets.

I looked across the land from the stock-car door, glad that we'd left Buck and Jack's silver-gray back in Lodge Pole. Fine white powder swirled in sharp gusts of wind.

Ole Freddie had stopped the train alongside the remains of Sheriff Till's horse, where we'd left it the night before. We walked our horses over to it once we'd checked our gear and led them down the loading plank.

Ponce walked along with us, a shovel over his shoulder and both the Airedale and the Catahoula running short circles around him. The Airedale kept its nose to the ground, but the Catahoula only sniffed the ground for a few seconds, then began widening the circle with his nose to the air.

"He's been here since the storm passed," I said, looking down at the half-eaten remains of the horse. Snow had been brushed off of it by large paws. Part of a rear quarter had

124

been eaten, and a tamped-down patch of ice and gore lay around it.

"Yeah," said Dallas Renfrow, squatting down near the carcass. "Hadn't been for the storm coming, we coulda posted ourselves off thirty yards and settled this whole thing come morning." Our eyes followed the large red tracks leading off up the ridgeline. "Filthy bastard," he added under his breath.

"No," said Ponce. "If you had stayed and laid in wait for him, he would not have come back. He has more than one kill hidden nearby." He nodded off toward the higher ledges of snow-streaked rock. "He has what's left of Till up there somewhere. He can choose where he wants to eat, for now. He will go where he thinks he is most safe."

"How do you know so much about what he thinks?" Dallas Renfrow said, a bit harshly.

"Because if I was him, that's what I would think," Ponce said.

"Yeah, well . . . why don't you take your shovel and hop back on the train, old man," said Renfrow. "If you'd knowed your business years ago we wouldn't be hunting this bear." I glanced back and forth between the two of them, then looked at Jack. He rolled his eyes slightly and stepped away from the dead horse.

"Soon . . . when you talk to me that way," Ponce said to Renfrow in a tight voice, "I will crack your head open with my fist." He shot me a knowing smile, made a weathered fist, and tapped it against his palm.

"Yeah, yeah." Dallas Renfrow brushed him away with his gloved hand. "Meanwhile, go on with Freddie and get the tracks cleared down to Elk Horn. That's what you do best."

Ponce ignored him and turned to me. "Once the dogs have the bear, they will not leave until someone kills it. They will drive him in a circle back to you, until you call them in." He raised a finger. "Be sure to call them in. When you call them in, do it like this." He raised a hand high over his head and whistled in a shrill tone. The Airedale turned back to him quickly, but the Catahoula made one more circle, then narrowed in beside us.

Jack led his horse away alongside the bear tracks as Ponce leaned down and spoke to the dogs in Indian, half words

125

and half sign. They looked around at me as if he'd just instructed them to follow my orders, then they turned and loped away.

"I have told them what to do," he said. "Now you follow them, and find the bear." The dogs ran ahead past Jack, circling wide of the bear tracks and scouring the ridgeline. In seconds they were out of sight, the Airedale already barking.

"He will talk to you enough to let you know where he is." He raised a finger. "But the Catahoula only speaks when he has something important to say. When you hear him, be prepared to meet the bear." Ponce walked away with his shovel over his shoulder.

I turned to Dallas Renfrow and said, "Ready when you are."

Renfrow chuckled, nodding toward Ponce as the old Indian walked away. "Think you can remember all that?"

"If it'll save our lives, I will. I reckon I can whistle as well as the next man."

We mounted and rode up to where Jack stood studying the tracks, but when I asked if he was ready to ride, he pointed down at the tracks and said, "Did you notice any dirt scraped away back by Till's horse?"

"No," I said. "Why?"

"Look at this." He leaned and pointed his rifle barrel to one of the paw prints, at a streak of brown mud now frozen into the thin skiff of snow. "As stiff as this ground is, where do you suppose he got his paws muddy?"

I glanced at Dallas Renfrow; he shook his head. "Who knows. Maybe scraped some dirt up between his claws coming down the ridge?" He looked from one of us to the other. When neither of us offered no more on it, he gigged his horse forward and headed up the ridgeline. I looked around when the train began rolling slowly away beneath a cloud of steam and wood smoke.

"There goes our last warm memory for a while," I heard Jack say as he stepped up in his stirrup and swung into his saddle. I nodded, watched him turn the horse and gig it toward Dallas Renfrow on the ridgeline. I couldn't help but feel a slight twist in my stomach watching Larr's warm fancy car chugging away from us, knowing we'd spend the night somewhere up here in the freezing darkness.

"Yep," I said. "But maybe we'll get lucky. Maybe that bear will slip on a patch of ice and break his damned neck." Then I gigged my horse, fell in behind him, and upped my collar against the biting cold.

This time when we topped the ridgeline, instead of following the same path we'd taken the day before we followed the barking of the Airedale and swung right, away from the ridge and upward into a tangle of leaning spruce and ancient pine that stretched farther upward along a jagged ledge. The Airedale's bark was steady, but not urgent, just loud enough to keep us following, and to know where he was headed.

"What's up this way?" I asked Dallas Renfrow as our horses climbed upward, leaving a breath of steam in their wake.

"Nothing for a while," he said. "Past the ledge and back down the other side, there's one of the Ute families Larr told you about. It's about seven miles though."

"Good," Jack said, pulling his horse up beside mine. "The dogs are headed that way anyway. This is a good time to stop by and warn them."

I looked at him as I nodded, and noticed that his eyes looked red, puffy, and weak. "Jack, are you feeling any better? Did you ever eat anything?"

"No," he said flatly; and before I could say any more, he looked away and gigged his horse forward.

Mercifully, sunlight began to peek down through the shifting sky by the time we'd cleared the high ledge and started down the other side into a rough rolling valley. The voice of the Airedale had led us from a half mile or more ahead, clear and strong.

More than once we spotted the black Catahoula working silently in a wide circle around us, in and out of rocks and brush thickets, his head up and his nose probing the air. Seeing him offered a certain amount of comfort. At least we'd know if the bear was anywhere near.

We'd spread out single file with ten yards between us down the winding steep path, our rifles out and propped up from our laps. Each of us scanned the terrain, alternating from one side to the other. Within an hour we reached a level relief in the land, where we stopped to rest the horses; but as we sat there I noticed the Airedale had grown quiet and the Catahoula had disappeared. Even the wind and the land around us had grown still.

"What do you think?" I said to Jack, almost in a whisper, scanning the small valley as I spoke.

"I don't know," he said. "It got awfully quiet, awfully quick, didn't it."

"Too quiet . . . too quick," Renfrow said in a hushed tone. And we sat there, still as stone, until all at once the hoarse deep voice of the Catahoula shattered the silence. Unexpected, the sound of his voice caused us to jerk our horses sideways. Mine nearly bolted. We all three looked at each other in surprise.

"Whoa!" I sat back on the reins, listening for only a second, then realized what old Ponce had told me about the Catahoula. "He's got him! Let's go!"

I gigged the horse out, off the narrow trail, cutting back and forth through jagged rock along the edge of the narrow valley. The Catahoula's voice blared like a coarse trumpet. Rounding a turn nearer the sound of his voice, I remembered what Ponce said about being on horseback, and I reined the horse down on his haunches and slipped from his back.

Beside me Jack did the same, and behind him I saw Renfrow slide his horse sideways, coming down from his saddle as I saddle-spun my reins and ran toward the sound of the dog thrashing and baying in a thicket at the edge of a cliff.

I slowed down and walked forward cautiously, slightly crouched with my Henry rifle locked to my shoulder. Searching the brush, I spotted the Catahoula amid the thicket, down on his front paws and barking at the top of his lungs. "Spread out," I called back to Jack and Renfrow, hearing them running up toward me.

But when they'd done so, we stalked forward until I could tell there was no bear in the brush ahead of the dog, only the sharp edge of a cliff above a narrow ravine. "Easy, boy," I said to the dog. I looked down into the ravine. *Nothing.*

"There he goes," Jack yelled from over on my right. I

spun toward him, then looked down in the direction of his pointed rifle. The big grizzly was moving fast along the bottom of the ravine, cutting around, and up and over rock, as surefooted as a mountain goat. A distance of two hundred yards lay between us and the big monster.

"Save your shot," Renfrow yelled, just as I'd begun to take aim. I stopped and let out a breath, knowing he was right. Two hundred yards was nothing for a Henry rifle, but the bear was moving fast in and out of rock cover. I lowered my rifle as the bear disappeared around a turn in the rock wall on the other side.

"Now *that* was him," Jack said above the low growl of the Catahoula. I stood beside the dog, staring down into the ravine. "That's the biggest bear I've ever seen in my life." He stepped over beside me, his breath heaving in and out, swirling steam.

I checked the direction of the cold breeze sweeping past us, realizing we'd been downwind of the bear all morning. "What do you suppose has him on the run?" I looked from one to the other of them.

"I don't know," said Jack. "But it ain't us." He glanced around, then said, "I figured the Airedale would be coming in by now. Why do you suppose he quit barking?"

Renfrow snuffed his nose and spit. "You boys are putting too much faith in them curs if ya ask me. I've known Ponce for years. He's all wind and tunnel."

"Dogs have been hunting bears since time began," I said. "The Catahoula sure seen him before we did, just then."

"The colonel's been after that bear for years," Renfrow said. "If he can't kill it, I doubt if a couple of Indian curs will. Unless you're saying Ben Larr ain't as smart as a dog."

"I'd trust a dog's senses in the wilds quicker than I would a man's any day," I said. "As far as Larr goes, he ain't impressed me a lick." I hiked my rifle up under my arm and turned back toward the horses.

"Then why are you out here?" I heard Renfrow call out, and I turned and looked at him. He shook his head. "What's the colonel got on you? It ain't just because you stove ole Eldon up. I don't buy that."

"You don't, huh?" I stared at him, realizing that Larr *hadn't* told him what he was holding over me.

129

Jack had looked him up and down and started walking toward me. Renfrow followed him, turning his collar up against the cold. "No, I don't," Renfrow said, stepping along. "You don't strike me as the kinda men who'd be pressed into this unless there was some higher stake involved."

"Keep talking," I said to Renfrow as Jack walked past me and picked up his reins. "Whatever needs saying, you better get it said and understood before we lock horns with that grizzly."

Renfrow stopped three feet from me and looked me in the eyes. His breath plumed in the cold. "I figure you're out here because you've struck up a deal of some kind with Laura. That's what I figure."

"Then you've figured wrong," I said, watching his eyes, trying to discern what was working behind them.

"Just so we understand one another, Beatty," he said. "Miss Laura and me go back a long ways, same as me and the colonel. Whatever problem they've got, I won't have some outsider stepping in and making things worse." He swung his rifle from under his arm and shoved it down into his saddle scabbard. Then he turned back to me, adding, "That's my say on it. Walk easy with them, Beatty."

I watched Jack step up into his stirrup and swing onto his saddle. He looked down at Renfrow and stepped his horse back, back to where we were both facing Renfrow. Renfrow took note of our position and raised a hand cautiously. "Alls I'm saying is—"

"We heard what you've got to say, Renfrow," I said, cutting him off. "But we're only out to kill a bear. Anything you add to that is just your mind working overtime." I stepped across the front of him between him and Jack, took up my reins, and stepped up into my saddle. "Now, let's ride," I said, tightening my hat down against the wind.

The only way to stay on the bear's trail was to keep on the way we were going, swing down around the base of the cliff and pick up the ravine. I'd had to call the Catahoula up to get him away from the ledge. Once he'd looked away from the ravine, he lowered his hackles and took off ahead of us probing the air. We rode on for another fifteen or twenty

130

minutes, still noticing the quietness that had settled over the land.

"The Ute family's just below the next rise," Renfrow said, after a long silence. "The Airedale probably got there and they hushed him."

Jack and I followed him; and when we'd topped the trail through a jagged rise of rock, we saw beneath us a small cabin built partly of pine log and partly of rough-cut plank. Thin gray smoke curled from a stone chimney. "This is Yamat Two Shirts' place," Renfrow said. "If we're lucky we'll catch him in a good mood."

"And if we ain't lucky?" I glanced from the cabin to Renfrow.

Renfrow grinned. "All he shoots is an old muzzle-loading trade rifle. We'll feel him out before we get too close." He tapped his heels to his horse's flanks and stepped him carefully down the steep trail.

"Hello, Two Shirts," he called out when we neared the bottom of the trail. We stopped and listened, then nudged forward a few steps. "It's Dallas Renfrow, Two Shirts. We're tracking a grizzly. He might be wounded." Again we waited; again we heard no response.

Sunlight peeped through the gray sky and glistened on the snow surrounding the cabin. The Airedale trotted around from behind the cabin and came up to us whining under his steaming breath. "Something ain't right here," Renfrow said. He stepped his horse to the side, letting Jack and me spread out beside him. The Airedale circled near me, whining and nudging toward the cabin.

"Wait here," I said to Jack and Renfrow; and I tapped my horse forward, making a wide circle around the cabin, following the dirty Airedale. The Catahoula came down out of the rocks a few yards from the trail. He circled the cabin from the other side. Behind the cabin, a blood trail led to a plank cellar door amid red bear tracks and footprints. The door was battered and deeply scarred. "Come on back," I called out to the others as I stepped down from my saddle. The two dogs ran to the cellar door, sniffing and scratching at it.

"You can come out," I called out toward the door. "The bear's gone." But I waited as Jack and Renfrow circled the cabin and stepped down from their saddles, and still heard no response.

I eased forward to the door, saying, "Don't shoot, now, ya hear? We're tracking the bear."

I peeped between the cracks on the door, and saw a pair of frightened eyes looking back at me through the darkness. I heard a child's voice say something in Indian. "Unlatch the door, now," I said. "We mean you no harm."

Renfrow stepped up beside me, nudging the Airedale away with the side of his boot. "Two Shirts? It's me, Renfrow. Are you hurt in there?"

I stepped back and watched the outside of the latch lift slowly. Then the door opened an inch. I reached out and opened it the rest of the way, seeing the small Indian boy look up at me, squinting against the light of day. I glanced past him at the blood-soaked figure of an old man leaning against the earth wall of the cellar. A wadded-up feed sack had been pressed into a terrible wound, stuffed down inside his stomach to stay the flow of blood and intestines. "Jesus, Renfrow, look at this."

"It's Two Shirts," he said quietly, reaching in and taking the boy by his arm. "This is his grandson." He pulled the boy from the cellar and I stepped in and over to the old man. One close look and I stepped back outside the cellar and shook my head.

Jack had stepped closer, and he saw the look on my face. "How bad is it?" he asked. Not wanting to say it too loud in front of the boy, I lifted my eyes to Jack's and waved him to the side.

"Looks like he was nearly eaten alive," I said.

Jack stepped past me into the cellar, then back out. "We've got to catch that bastard and kill him," he said. His voice sounded weak, and he staggered, catching himself against the cellar door.

"Jack, are you all right?"

"Yeah," he said. "Maybe I shoulda made myself eat something before we left the lodge."

Renfrow walked toward the cabin, leading the boy by the hand. "Go on inside with them, Jack," I said. "Get warmed up. I'll tend the horses."

"Yeah, I'll see if there's any coffee," he said. He raised a hand to his forehead as he walked off toward the cabin. I'd never known Jack to be ill except for a hangover now and then. It worried me. I watched him until he'd stepped inside the cabin; then I gathered the reins of our horses and led them to a lean-to stable across the yard. The snow-streaked yard was covered with bear prints, and two rails were freshly broken from a small corral around the stable. There were hoofprints where an unshod horse had fled the corral.

I spun the horses' reins around a rail beneath the stable overhang and walked to the cabin with my rifle cradled in my arm. The dogs sniffed and circled and headed out along the hoofprints leading away from the corral. Although I'd seen the bear running away through the ravine nearly an hour ago, I couldn't help but feel his presence here.

Walking across the yard, I felt as if I walked in the grim wake of a terrible storm. I'd now seen the bodies of three men who'd been killed by this rogue grizzly, and I realized how easily it could've been me he snatched out through the railcar window instead of the seat.

Inside the cabin, Jack and Renfrow had sat the boy before an open stone fireplace and were rubbing feeling back into his arms and legs. The boy stared into the low flames through dazed and hollow eyes. "There's coffee heating in the pot," Jack said over his shoulder to me. "It's old, but it'll do."

Renfrow took off his buckskin coat, wrapped it around the boy, and said, "I figure the bear must've hit here at about daylight. It got Two Shirts, but he managed to get the boy to the cellar before he died."

"He could've ripped that cellar door to shreds if he wanted to," I said.

"Yeah, but he ain't hard up for food." Renfrow glanced up at me then back down, tucking the coat snug around the shivering boy. "He's got kills strung out all over this side of the mountain now. This attack was just pure orneriness. Just to show everybody he could." He patted the boy on the shoulder and straightened up.

I heard the Indian boy whisper something in a quavering voice, and I walked over and leaned down beside him.

"What's he saying?" I looked at him closely and judged him to be no more than seven or eight years old. "Does he speak English?"

"Yeah, he does, but he's too rattled right now. Lucky to say anything at all." Renfrow took a step back and glanced around the cabin. "We can't leave him here alone, and it's too risky taking him with us—"

"What about his folks? His ma and pa?"

"His pa's been dead since early last winter." His voice lowered. He gestured me to the side, and when I'd stepped away with him, he said, "I figure his ma is what kept the bear from ripping off the cellar door. We won't know till he can tell us, but if she ain't around here somewhere, I got a feeling the bear snatched her and drug her off."

"Jesus," I said, letting go a breath. I walked over and looked out through a cracked dirty window, at sunlight shooting a thin golden ray across bear tracks and blood, dark red blood staining white snow, and blood turned frosty and pink where it had been trampled into the snow-covered earth.

"Then we'll stay here till morning," I said quietly. "The train will be back through from Elk Horn sometime tomorrow. We'll take the boy back to the ridgeline and meet it. We'll just have to be careful every step."

"This bear doesn't like to wander very far," Renfrow said. "Most big old boar grizzlies will range out twenty or thirty miles. But not this one. He's staying close. He's got a taste for humans and he knows there's none past here till he gets all the way down the mountain."

"Good then," I heard Jack say; and I looked toward him, saw his dark smile as he ran his hand along the rifle across his lap. His face looked pale, his eyes traced with dark circles. "That means we'll be the only meal left in his meathouse. Sooner or later he's got to raise us to the top of his menu. He's got to come to us."

CHAPTER

11

---·◆·---

Near dark the weather had turned biting cold once again, the sky dropping low and swollen, blustering, the color of a bad dream. A wind whined in harder and harder from the northwest; and I felt the weight of it pressing me sideways as I quartered our horses and brought in armloads of wood for the hearth. Renfrow had taken down a cut of antelope that hung from a rafter. It sizzled in its juices, skewered above the licking flames as he turned and basted it with a mixture of herbs and pepper.

The Indian boy sat on a stool near the hearth, wrapped in Renfrow's buckskin coat. His toes barely touched the dirt floor, brushing back and forth absently as he watched Jack boil down chunks of the meat and stir flour into the broth with a wooden spoon until it bubbled into a dark rich gravy. The boy's stomach made a low whining sound.

Jack raised the spoon, blew on it, and held it out to him. Yellow and blue flames glittered in the boy's eyes. He shied back for a second, then sniffed toward it cautiously, like a woods critter, until finally he drew off a bit of it and licked his lips.

"You're gonna be all right, kid," Jack said, more to Renfrow and me than the boy. "We'll just get some hot food in ya." He glanced up at me and nodded. I noticed that his eyes looked weak and had taken on a blue pallor beneath them.

"What about you, Jack?" I asked. After I'd laid down the load of wood, I leaned against a post in the middle of the cabin, unloading the Henry rifle to clean it and check it. "You feeling any better?"

"Yeah, I'm fine," he said, turning back to the hearth. But he sure didn't look it . . . and I sure didn't believe it. I thought about what he'd said, about the bear having to come to us sooner or later. It was an unsettling thought, but it was true. If the grizzly had a particular taste for human flesh, we were quickly becoming his only bill of fare.

I wiped down the rifle, inspected it, and leaned it against the post, thinking it peculiar that of all the times I'd been hunted and tracked by man, I'd never felt so small and vulnerable as I felt knowing that something was out there ready to kill us—kill us not because we were wanted men with a reward on our heads, or because killing us would right some wrong that lay between us.

This bear would kill us as we would kill a beast of the field, dispassionately. The render of our skin and sinew held for him nothing more, or nothing less, than the core of his primal existence. There was no compromise, no deal to strike, no threat of who or what we were to hold before him in some final showdown to unsteady his thought or intentions. His focus on us would be singular, with no fear, regard, or respect of character. We were simple substance, fuel and strength against the harsh elements of his domain.

I looked around at us in the circle of firelight from the open hearth, seeing us as ground squirrels in a burrow, knowing that beyond the door in the shadows of coming night, something could unearth us at any time, root us out with sharp claws, taste our blood and tear the warm flesh from our bodies. *Jesus.* I bit my lip.

"You don't look so good yourself," Jack said. He and Renfrow looked up at me from before the hearth. Jack chuckled, eyeing me curiously. "What the hell are you thinking about?"

I had to shake myself loose before I could step forward toward the sizzling roast. "Nothing," I said. "Just tired, I reckon. Tired and wishing I was someplace else."

136

"We got food for the day and shelter for the night." Jack chuckled. "A man starts wanting more than that he could develop a tick in his jaw."

"Ain't it the truth," I said halfheartedly. I caught a glimpse of the Indian boy's eyes, polished black stones asking nothing nor offering anything in return; and I pulled the glades knife from my boot and raised it, stepping to the fire. We ate in silence, listening to the wind groan and spin in the dusty rafters. It grew in intensity, pressing, then pulling on the cabin roof, causing the hearth to pulse and glow. Flames stirred, rising and falling like devils' breath beneath the stick of meat.

By the time we'd finished eating, the Indian boy had dozed off sitting on the stool. Renfrow stood up from near the fire, quietly gathered the boy in his arms, and carried him to a pallet of straw just outside the circle of firelight. I noticed that Jack looked better now that he'd eaten. I watched him take out the flask of brandy Beam had given him. He sipped from it and passed it up to Renfrow when Renfrow came back and stood with his foot propped on the stool.

"What's the story on the silver bullets?" I asked Renfrow, watching him sniff the brandy and raise it close to his lips. He stopped and looked before taking a drink. "Does Larr think this bear has some supernatural powers or something?"

"Maybe," Renfrow said. He leaned on his raised knee, studying the flask in his hand. "As much as the bear's put him through, I don't blame him for whatever notions he has of it." He shrugged, started to throw a sip, then stopped again.

"Tell me something, Renfrow," Jack said. "What do you do, what time you ain't defending that crazy sumbitch?" He reached a hand up toward the flask, and Renfrow handed it to him. Renfrow's face reddened.

He shook his head. "I ain't making no excuses for him. I know he's got his problems. But I also know the kind of man he was before that devil nearly destroyed him. Don't judge a man just because he's met the thing in life that's bigger than him. You never know when you'll do the same. For Larr, it was a bear."

He handed Jack the flask without taking a drink. Jack took it, turned back a drink, and held it propped on his lap.

"Every man runs into something that can cripple him," Renfrow added. "What will it be for you? A woman? A bottle?" He nodded at the pistol on Jack's hip. "A faster gun?"

Jack ran the back of his hand over his mouth slowly. "A woman?" He considered it for a second. "That might be a good crippling, if crippling's what I was looking for . . . but it ain't. A bottle? I doubt it. A faster gun? There ain't one, and there ain't gonna be. The day I stop *knowing* I'm the best is the day I'll fall. That's something I worked out a long time ago, back when I decided *my* living was worth more than the other man's dying."

"That's false confidence if you ask me," said Renfrow. He spit into the fire; it sizzled and vanished. "The kinda thing keeps a man living an illusion."

"Some say it's all illusion." Jack grinned. I hoped he wasn't gonna quote something from his book of philosophy. "But it ain't false confidence to believe in yourself. *False* confidence is when you take faith in silver bullets because your faith in yourself is lacking. Illusion? That's just the right move you think you're making, to justify the wrong move you made before."

Jack's gaze deepened into Renfrow's eyes. "Like thinking it takes a silver bullet to kill a bear. Like thinking cocaine can bring back a missing leg. Larr has you blinded, Renfrow. You can't see past his illusion. If you did—"

"I ain't blinded by him. That's nonsense!" Renfrow turned, leaned down and stoked the glowing embers with an iron poker. "We'll see how cocky you are when it comes to killing the bear," he said.

Jack pitched the flask to me. "I've never been *cocky* about killing . . . just confident, knowing I can." He winked as I raised the flask, and said to me, "Does that make you feel any better? Or are you gonna spend the night thinking 'how big the bear, how small the man'?"

"I ain't worried," I said; and I'd just started to throw back a drink when something slammed against the door. I dropped the flask, jumped over, and grabbed the rifle as the sound of big claws scratching on the wooden door filled the

138

room. Then I stopped and let out a breath when I heard the low whining of the Catahoula and the bark of the Airedale. "Damn dogs," I said.

Jack picked up the flask of brandy before much of it poured out in the dirt. He chuckled, let out a breath, examined the flask, then capped it and put it away. "Nothing's ever worth getting *this* worried."

I banked the fire good and high before we turned in, and the next morning at daybreak, I awoke wrapped in a blanket near the open hearth with the Catahoula curled against my back. He growled low when I stirred and stood up, then scooted closer to the low fire and curled back up again.

The wind had settled overnight, but it left a line of snow filling the crack beneath the door and had blown it in a thin skiff across the dirt. A thick white frost scalloped the window inside and out.

The Airedale lay by the door like a pile of greasy rags. Puffs of steam swirled in his breath. He stood up stiffly, stretched, and yawned, his tongue reaching out then rolling back inside a damp curtain of fur. His yawn ended in a sharp whine, like an old man's; and he circled slowly near the door as I walked toward him.

When I walked out to the horses with my rifle cradled in my arms, both dogs scoured the yard close to the house, their muzzles bellowing steam, kicking up low swirls of fresh snow. They scented the ground and left their yellow marks the way a drummer might leave a calling card.

There was something settling in watching the dogs work the yard. I took comfort knowing that theirs was a business of instincts, spinal creatures unfettered by moral interpretation, given to the kill for the sake of killing, with no regard to consequence. Man had removed them from the wild, yet they ran with one foot in the primeval past, their guttural voices far-reaching, a warning—dark requiem to those who dared stir their senses, I thought; and in the matter of the bear, I envied them *that.*

For all the wind and bluster, the night had only left behind a couple of inches of new powder—enough to cover the old tracks and streaks of dirt and blood. The Airedale scented the spot and wallowed in it. The Catahoula marked it as if for future reference.

I hayed and readied the horses, and returned to the cabin as the scent of wood smoke and brewed coffee drifted in the morning air.

Renfrow, the Indian boy, and I finished off the left-over roast from last night's meal. I noticed that Jack only sipped a cup of coffee. Once again his face looked drawn and weak. I started to ask how he felt, then changed my mind, watching him lace the coffee with a shot from the brandy flask. Hangover, I figured; and I shook my head as he looked up, smiled wearily, capped the flask, and shoved it inside his coat. "Ready when you are," he said.

We pressed on through the fresh snow as steadily and as quickly as we could. Now that we had the boy with us, the farthest thing from my mind was tracking the bear. That would keep until later. We kept the two dogs working a circle around us, not to pick up the bear's trail, but simply to have them out there between us in case we came upon him. Sunlight peeped out and glittered like diamonds across the ravine where we'd last seen the bear.

There was no doubt in my mind that he was still over there somewhere. It was rough country that I would avoid going into if there was any way around it. I asked Renfrow if there was another way in. "You could swing down along the rails and come in where the ravine ends, but it's thirty miles out of your way."

"That might be better than risking our horses and our lives crossing those rocks and brush." I gazed across the ravine as we wound along it. It was iced now and covered with new snow. If a bear ever wanted a place to ambush man and horse, he could find none better.

"Ain't that why you brought along those two mangy curs . . . to keep from getting ambushed?" He glanced at me, then gestured his eyes toward the sky. "You don't have that kind of time. Don't let this little surge of sunlight fool you. By evening there'll be another storm blowing past. It's just been playing with us night after night . . . but there's a big one coming . . . coming soon. It'll shut this mountain down for a month or more. Don't be out here when it does."

He chucked his horse forward with the boy on his lap. I just stared at his back as he rode ahead, and when Jack caught up to me, I turned the dun in beside him and we rode on. "Everybody knows so damn much about what to do, seems like they'd have killed that bear a long time ago."

"They all know what to do," Jack said. "That bear's just got 'em too scared to *do* it." I noticed his voice sounded weak. "Most bear-shy bunch of boys I've ever seen."

Although the distant northwest horizon was streaked dark gray and broadening slowly toward us, above us the sun was out all the way, spilling in broken rays through towering pine and aspen. It loosened pillows of snow that lay swaying in the high treetops, sending them falling through lower branches, crumbling and spreading downward in a long white spray.

A hawk swung across the sky chastising us in a sharp voice, then circled and disappeared. The dogs bounded ahead and around us, lurching through drifts as high as their haunches and scrambling across sheets of ice.

By noon, the dark sky out of the northwest had nearly reached us. Our horses were heavy-winded and we rested them in a clearing lit by remnants of sunlight before pushing on the last few miles to the rails. We'd crossed a stretch of loose jagged rock beneath a cover of snow on our way to the clearing, and Renfrow's horse had gone down on its front legs in a spray of snow and shale. He'd led it limping into the clearing and stood examining its hoof as Jack and I sat huddled with our reins in our hands.

The Indian boy stood beside me, flanked by the dogs. They sat like sentinels, their steaming breath frosting on their flews. Their tongues lolled and dripped; their chests pounded.

"His hoof's split deep," Renfrow said; and he let the horse's fore hoof down gently, patted its leg, and stepped back, raising his hat brim. Beside me, Jack grunted, shook his head, and ran his eyes across the changing sky.

"That settles who's going, or staying," I said, standing up.

"I can camp near the rails and have Freddie bring me back a horse." Renfrow turned to me, dusting his gloved hands.

"Hunh-uh." I shook my head. "You said yourself, there's a big one coming through anytime. If the train gets snowed in, you'd be in poor shape—"

141

"Larr wants me out here," he said. "I ain't letting him down."

"Then ride in, get a horse, and come back. Larr will know that's the smart thing to do. You wouldn't catch him camping out there waiting for a train that might not come. There's not even any shelter around there. What if the bear shows up?"

"You're awfully concerned about my well-being, Beatty." He shot me a skeptical glance.

I squared my hat and stepped into my stirrup. "Do what suits ya then." I swung into my saddle and reached my hand down toward him. "You can double with me and lead your horse, if he's able to make it. Jack'll carry the boy."

Renfrow looked away for a second and studied the sway of wind in the distant treetops. Then he picked up the reins to his horse and said without facing me, "I'll just walk him awhile." I looked at Jack as he swung up to his saddle and raised the Indian up behind him. He shrugged and spit, and we watched Renfrow lead his limping horse out of the clearing and onto the icy trail.

The wind grew sharp. The afternoon sun had disappeared behind the encroaching cloud by the time we'd started ascending the ridge that would overlook the rails. Moments before, we'd seen a stream of wood smoke drift away on the skyline, and knew the train had made it up from Elk Horn. Freddie would wait at least an hour or so to see if we showed up.

We had plenty of time, but we hurried anyway, pushing the horses as hard as we dared on the slick trail. Renfrow lagged behind leading his horse. Once Jack and I made it to the train we would tell Freddie what happened and wait for Renfrow. Such was our plans.

But as I gigged my horse close to the crest of the ridge, we saw both dogs duck back from the edge with their hackles up and growling low. I reined up hard and slid from the saddle, holding my rifle up, signaling Jack to stop. Their voices didn't sound the same as when they'd spotted the bear.

They ducked farther back from the edge, looking back at me as if in warning as I crept closer. Ice flakes brushed my cheeks as I stilled the horse with my hand, reached down and spun the reins around his leg, and moved toward the edge in a crouch.

There sat the train, the engine quietly letting off a trickle of smoke from its stack. Freddie stood beside the engine with his hands on his hips, watching as six men unloaded horses from the stock car. *Damn it!* I looked back as Jack came leading his horse up cautiously.

"What is it?" he asked, crouching down beside me.

"It's trouble," I whispered over my shoulder, still watching them down there, moving around, smaller creatures in a smaller world from our lofty perch above. One of the men unfolded a flap of cloth and took out a slender brass-trimmed object. "Trouble carrying scopes," I added.

"Yep," Jack said, beside me now and scanning them as they led down horse after horse from the car. "Trouble carrying scopes, and led by Dandy Dan Silks."

"Dandy Dan? Are you sure?" I felt a chill run up my back, scanned them again quickly. "The old man in the stovepipe hat? The one leading the big paint? That's him?"

"Count on it," Jack said, inching back from the edge, checking his rifle. Past him, the Indian boy watched us without question. Renfrow walked up leading his lame horse. Flakes of ice and snow swirled in sideways.

"Why would they send in somebody like Dan Silks?" I pushed up my hat brim and slumped on the ground. "I mean . . . in this weather, any fool could track us through snow. They didn't need *him*. I thought he quit working for organized law posses?"

"He did," Jack said. "That's a bounty posse. Didn't you see the gunnysacks hanging from his saddle?"

I glanced back down, saw wind stir two empty feed sacks tied to the saddlehorn on the paint horse as it stepped away from the loading plank.

"What's going on?" Renfrow asked, stopping back beside the boy.

"A posse," I said, turning to him. "Your *boss, Larr,* has jackpotted us. That's what's going on." I stared at him, letting him know I now wondered if he might have known about it. He saw the question in my eyes. Snow swirled. Grains of ice tapped on my hat brim.

He raised his hands chest high. "If you think I had

143

anything to do with it, shoot me right here right now. I don't work that way. I don't think Larr would either. He wants the bear killed—"

"Somebody told them," I said; and as soon as I said it, I pictured big Eldon leaning on the crutch outside the telegraph office. "Eldon . . . that rotten bastard."

"Naw," Jack said, gathering his reins. "Eldon wants to eat your brains for breakfast. It would break his heart if somebody else killed ya." Steam curled in his breath.

"Who then?" I scooted farther back from the edge and stood up dusting my knees. "Laura Larr? I doubt it."

"So you both really *are* wanted men." Renfrow glanced between us. "I figured as much—"

"Then figure this also," I said, checking the cinch on my saddle. "They're here to take back our heads in a gunnysack. You'll have to stay here with the boy. But if you fire a shot or warn them in any way before we're out of sight, I'll turn and put a bullet in ya."

"I told ya I don't work that way," Renfrow said. He dropped his rifle in the snow and raised his pistol with two fingers. He pitched it to me; I caught it. "I'll take the boy and wait in the trees till they get here. You've got about a half-hour start. They'll see your tracks for a ways till the snow covers them, so I can't lie for you. But I won't warn them. That's my word."

I hefted his pistol in my hand and looked at him and the boy. If the bear happened upon them before the posse got here, they were dead. I looked into the boy's dark blank eyes as the wind whipped a strand of hair across his face. Then I pitched the pistol back to Renfrow and said, "When you get to Lodge Pole, do me a favor. Don't let them hurt our horses."

"You got it all," Renfrow said, nodding, dropping his pistol back in his holster. He squinted against the grains of ice and the swirl of wet snowflakes. "I'll do what I can."

"Thanks," I said, and I stepped up into the stirrup. The two dogs stirred at the sight of me mounting the horse. They pulled back and circled quietly behind us. Jack had mounted. He took out the flask, raised it to his lips. Renfrow looked at him and said, "Just for the hell of it, can I ask who you really are?"

KILLERS OF MAN

Jack lowered the flask, capped it, put it away, and crossed his wrists on his saddlehorn. He stared at Renfrow with a blank expression. Flakes of snow lit on his gloved hand and turned into dark spots like drops of cold teardrops from the cold eyes of God. He looked at me and shot a glance toward the rough terrain behind us, the way from which we came.

I pictured jagged stems of rock piercing gray heaven, and dreaded the turn of hoof and tap of heel that would carry me back against it, back where the fear of a beast had permeated all else, but where now the beast no longer mattered. In place of sharp claws I dreaded now the click of a metal lever, the close hot breath of man. Fire-driven lead replaced the bawl of the bear as the hunters became the hunted.

"I'm Miller Crowe," I said, letting out a breath as Jack turned his horse and gigged it away.

"Lord God," Renfrow said in a hushed tone. "Then I reckon big Eldon's lucky to even be alive."

I stepped the horse back, feeling the wind sweep in, moaning low, hard, and cold against my shoulders. Snow stung my neck beneath my hat brim and I raised my collar against it. "Ain't we all," I said, shrugging up inside my clothes against the cold. My breath swirled and drifted away on the cold air. The boy stepped closer to Renfrow as I turned my horse slowly; and I rode off behind Jack into the raging silver mist.

PART III

BEST-LAID PLANS

CHAPTER

12

The most natural thing to do would've been to circle wide, double back once the snow covered our trail, and follow the rails either back up to Lodge Pole or on down to Elk Horn, then cut clean and make a getaway from there. Even better would've been to slip around the posse, take possession of the train, and make our getaway while the posse foundered in the snow. But this was not the time to do the obvious. I'd seen at first glance that these boys knew what they were doing. They'd reduced the train to a slow idle knowing that if we caught them off guard and snatched it, it would take us a good half hour to build up enough steam to pull the mountain grade.

They were professionals, and if having Dan Silks as a tracker was any indication of the type of men we had on our trail, Jack and I had our hands full. Silks had led posses for years, and worked as lead scout for Crook during the Apache campaign. His reputation stretched from the Montana high country to the west Texas border. Now he was working with bounty hunters, men whose sole purpose in the hunt was to cut our heads from our bodies and deliver them for cash money, the way a trapper would deliver a pelt to market.

I wondered what our heads were worth these days as Jack and I kicked our horses on through the swirling storm.

There was no room to consider backtracking on Silks and trying to ambush the posse. He'd be ready for that; and it would only cost us precious time if we tried to create a false trail for him to follow.

Our only chance was to press deeper into the harsh weather, get under the storm and keep as much frozen ground between us and them as possible. Our only allies were the cold, the snow, the wind, and the mountain, and until we could figure a way around them and back to civilization, I hoped that whatever our hide was worth to them in money was not enough to make them brave such merciless elements.

"Look at it this way," Jack said, when we'd drawn our horses up along the ravine where the Catahoula had spotted the bear only a day before. "Jesse and Frank's worth twenty thousand each. We're probably only worth half that." He shuffled his gloved fingers. "There's six of 'em. Hell, that only comes to a thousand and change apiece. They won't stick long for that kinda money, would you?" He smiled a weak smile. His red-rimmed eyes looked hollow behind his steaming breath.

"We don't know what kinda money's being offered," I said. "If it's railroad money it could be a lot. For all we know they might think they *are* tracking Jesse and Frank."

"Can't ever look on the bright side, can ya," Jack said, scanning across the ravine, studying the other side, where the bear had fled deeper into the wilds.

"Bright side?" I shook my head. "Besides, a man like Silks ain't in it just for money. It's a matter of pride, reputation, all that kinda happy horseshit."

"Naw. You're wrong there. It mighta used to be, but I reckon he got his fill of all that on the proper side of the law. He's bountying now. So it's a matter of the amount of dollars returned for the amount of work involved. All we gotta do is keep upping his cost of doing business. He'll break. Everybody does at a point." He glanced at me from beneath his hat brim as he turned his horse. "Everybody except me—" He grinned. "—and maybe *you.* In our business we have to keep our heads . . . just to *keep* our heads."

"Thanks Jack," I said wryly. "I feel a lot better now." I

started to turn my horse in behind him when the Catahoula and Airedale came thrashing through the brush and snow. "Look at this. They must think we're still hunting the bear."

"Then let 'em think it if it makes 'em feel better," he said over his shoulder. "I know *I'd* feel better still thinking it." He reached out and slapped the reins against his horse's flanks, and I rode behind him on toward the empty cabin.

At the cabin we stripped the blankets off the three straw pallets, took down what was left of the dried shank of antelope hanging from the rafter, gathered what other small amount of food was there, and carried everything out into the snow-covered yard. I went back inside, took the globe and lid off of an oil lamp, and slung the contents all about the cabin while outside Jack rolled up the blankets and packed the food in our saddlebags.

I dreaded what we had to do, but with a posse on our trail in this kind of weather, we couldn't afford to leave anything behind that would aid them—couldn't allow them the shelter and comfort of a warm hearth while Jack and I weathered the wilds. It gave them too much of an edge.

I stood looking about the cabin for a second, and thought about the Ute family who'd lived here, picturing the silent face of the Indian boy, thinking of how the bear had stepped into his life for only a brief second. Now, life as he'd known it would never again be as it was.

I let out a breath, struck a match, watched the sulfur sizzle and flare, and pitched it into one of the straw pallets. Low blue flames shot across the floor and up the walls, tracing the wet line of lamp oil.

The dry straw turned black and curly beneath yellow dancing flames. Then I turned around and walked out as the fire already began to crackle and spit behind me. Jack looked up from tying down the blankets behind our saddles.

"It's nothing but wood now," he said, seeing the expression in my eyes. "The boy would've never came back here. If he did it would've been nothing but a bad memory."

"I reckon," I said quietly, turning around and watching the flames roll out the door and lick up toward the roof. Across the yard, flames reached up from the small barn where Jack had started a fire as well. The two dogs had circled into the yard and sat in the snow with their tongues

151

lolling, steaming. They watched the fire and looked back and forth at Jack and me as if questioning our sanity.

"Why don't y'all go home," I said; and I stamped my foot in the snow at them. "Go on, git!" But the Airedale only swallowed hard and shied back without moving. The Catahoula raised his bristles, growled low, and sat staring as I stepped up into the stirrups and turned my horse.

Jack chuckled, looking down at the Catahoula as he snarled and showed his teeth up toward me. "Ponce must've raised him on gunpowder and rattlesnake meat."

I leveled my hat brim and looked down at them. They were both covered with burrs and streaked with ice. "I hope they don't give us away if the going gets close." Steam smoldered low against their backs.

"I don't think they will. They don't care which end of the hunt they're on, so long as they can keep a foot in the game." Jack stepped his horse closer to the big Airedale and the dog sidled back a step and sat back down in the snow. The Catahoula had a brush cut across his muzzle that had frozen over black and thick and cracked on one end, oozing a trickle of fresh blood.

"Look at 'em." Jack spit and wiped a hand across his mouth. "That's us a million years ago." The Catahoula raised a wet icy paw and rubbed it across his muzzle. Both dogs' eyes shined, wide and wild, like wolves'.

"Yeah? You maybe. I'd like to think my folks came from more of an upright species."

"And so they did . . . but they were no less wild or their senses no less keen than the wolf or any other predatory critter. I reckon they spent a few thousand years growling, running in circles, and sniffing each other's behind before something dumbstruck 'em and civilized them. They didn't always say *please* and *thank you*. And they're still growling and sniffing today—just doing it in different ways."

"Says you," I murmured under my breath, sweeping my eyes back along the trail behind us, judging distance, judging time, my senses pressed and attuned to the arcane forest, longing to discern by sixth sense what forces might lie in wait. But nothing came of my effort, nothing save the cold in my nostrils and the low hollow roar of the wind.

We headed out, and risked riding back, a hundred yards above the trail, along icy cliff lines and around rock spurs and ledges deep with drift, until we came to a narrow path leading down across the trail. We followed it down, crossed the trail with wind-driven snow pressing against us, and stepped off carefully onto a steeper path that cut down into the ravine. I was thankful to see the fallen snow had covered our tracks toward the cabin. With any luck, it would now also cover what few tracks we left crossing the trail. Nobody in their right mind would risk descending the ravine in this weather, I thought, none but wanted men—the hunted with nothing to lose but their lives.

"Lead 'em," I said over my shoulder, stepping down from the saddle and steadying myself on a thin sheet of ice.

"Easy boy," Jack said gently, stepping down behind me. He held the reins close to the horse's muzzle as it shied back and nickered. Jack coughed deep in his chest, and bowed from the force of it, still holding the reins tight. His cough sounded like gravel rattling in a bucket of water.

Perched on a narrow ledge halfway down the wall of the ravine, we stood for a moment in the cold wind, watching the dogs weave downward around juts of rock and through streaks of ice and snow. "You ain't feeling worth a damn, are ya?" I asked without facing him.

"No. To be honest I'm sicker'n hell," he said in a rasping voice. There was a clinking sound, and I glanced at him as he turned up a shot from the flask. "But I ain't complaining."

"Damn it, Jack." I turned and squinted out across the swirl of white beneath a gray sky. "I've been asking for three days how you felt. Now that we're one step ahead of the law, you finally tell me."

"So? What was you gonna do about it? Take me to a doctor? I'll be all right." He capped the flask and put it away. "You caused it anyway, telling little Brerton Beam how sick I was. I been getting sicker ever since. Never felt nothing like it."

"Maybe you oughta lay off the sauce a couple of days. See if that helps."

"That'd be real smart," he said. "It's the only medicine

153

I've *got,* and you want me to quit taking it. Maybe you oughta take a shot or two yourself. Maybe it'd loosen your nerves a little."

"My nerves are all right. I just don't know what we'll do if you get all the way down sick."

"Well, I'll be damned," he said. "You act like it's my fault or something. I didn't pick it, it picked me." He muffled a cough with his hand. "I told ya I'll be all right."

I looked at him and gathered my reins close to the horse's bridle. "Sorry," I said, "maybe I am a little tense."

"Then quit being. It don't help. Besides, we've been in worse spots than this, ain't we?"

"Yeah," I said, leading the horse carefully forward, "reckon we have." But I couldn't really remember when.

"I've been squeezing this brandy ever since Beam gave it to me, hoping to make it last. Once I run out of it, that'll be the time to start worrying. That's when *they* better start worrying too. I might just decide to make a stand and kill every one of them, the way I feel."

"That's the spirit," I said, smiling to myself. "Reckon that's what'll bring the beast on in *you.* Your ancestors would be glad to hear it—while they were running around on all *fours."* I picked the best footing and stepped down sideways against the high pitch of the icy wall.

We weaved a broken serpentine path around rock and patches of ice for nearly an hour. My toes were numb in my stiff boots when we finally reached the flat stretch of land at the base of the ravine. My fingers ached and pulsed in my gloves. Before us lay a stream no more than twenty yards wide, partly frozen but still running in shallow ripples across thin gravel bars. Pieces of broken boulders skirted the banks and lay strung throughout, iced over and patched with snow. "I hate crossing cold water." I stooped down with my reins dangling from my hands and felt a weariness deep in my bones.

"There's nothing like a brisk spray of cold water after climbing down a wall of ice." Jack chuckled and stooped down beside me, shaking all over. We'd have to cross, climb the other wall, at least as high as the broad ledge where we'd seen the bear running; and we'd have to take shelter and risk a fire, posse be damned. Jack was coming down hard whether he realized it or not. One cold night could finish him.

Jack took my reins. I stood, walked out to the edge of the stream, and searched the upper edge of the wall behind us. They would not see us from there, unless they left the trail as I had when I followed the Catahoula's barking. They would ride straight on toward the rise of smoke from the burning cabin.

The smoke was a natural lead that any tracker would have to investigate. It was the place from which their search would start; and by now our tracks were covered by fresh snow. We'd carefully kept from breaking any branches or leaving any sign when we passed through the sparse woods above the trail. I had to figure they would follow the trail on past the cabin.

"Let's chance staying the night down here, Jack," I said, studying the sky above the edge of the ravine. "At least it's down out of the wind. We can go up the other side in the morning before light."

"That'll be real interesting, dragging these horses up that wall before light. Once we do, then what?" He looked at me, then looked away and spit.

"I don't know. Circle back wide some way? Get into Lodge Pole, then cut out with our own horses and get off this mountain?"

"We could get snowed in down here. Then we're screwed." His eyes searched the high climb before us across the stream. The two dogs had crossed, and they ran back and forth along the far bank, sniffing and scraping at the frozen ground.

"We're outa sight—getting less snow down here than we would up there," I said. "They can't surprise us down here. You got any better ideas?"

"No." He huddled inside his coat, trembling. "But you shoulda planned better. I always believe in taking the high ground when I can."

"Take the high—? Jesus, Jack!" I spread my arms and stepped toward him. "What the hell do you want from me here?"

He sliced a hand through the air. *"Hush!* Listen. Did you hear that? It sounded Indian."

155

I just stared at him, thinking he was going out of his head. "There. Hear it?"

"No." But I looked around, listening above the rippling stream. The dogs had turned and started along the bank at a cautious trot, staring toward a rise of rock at the base of the wall.

"I damn sure heard it. A voice, speaking Indian." Jack's gun slipped from under his coat as he rose up slowly, handing me my reins.

I drew my pistol too, staring at the rise of rocks as the dogs circled it with their hackles up. "Dan Silks?" I asked in a whisper.

"Not unless he's slid down a strand of barbed wire. It's a woman's voice."

"I didn't hear nothing." I stepped toward the edge of the stream, leading my horse.

"Then you're stone deaf," Jack said, moving along with me but stepping wide and away.

The dogs advanced on the rocks, then backed away. "Good Lord, Jack. Look at this."

We watched, stunned, with our pistols raised and our breath steaming, as a woman in a torn doeskin dress staggered from within the rise of rocks, clinging to them for support. Her dress hung loose down her left side. Her left breast, shoulder, and arm were coated thick and black with crusted blood, blood matted with grass and dried leaves.

She looked at us across the stream, called out in a failing voice, then slumped over the icy rock as the dogs bounded forward and sniffed at her. "Cover me, in case it's a trick," I said, stepping up in my stirrup.

"Some trick," Jack said; and I gigged my horse out across the stream with my pistol raised and cocked, shoulder high.

While Jack had cradled her in his arms, I'd scouted downstream a quarter of a mile and come upon an overhang of rock ten feet above the base of the wall behind us—a deep recess cut beneath the wall by years of spring flooding, but high and dry now, welcome refuge for our sore and desperate circumstance.

By the grainy light of evening, we moved the woman there, and built a small fire of driftwood twigs back under the overhang. I heated water. While Jack dabbed carefully at her face with a wet rag, I strung a rope across the front of the low overhang and draped it with our spare blankets. Then I walked out along the edge of the stream and looked back toward our hidden campsite from both directions.

Only a dim flicker of light shone out on the stream bank. A thin veil of smoke crept out and curled upward, skimming along snowcapped rocks like a long pale ghost. We were safe, unless by some strange turn the posse happened to be down along the stream in the middle of the night in a snowstorm—in which case we'd be dead anyway.

"Take a look at this," Jack said, when I'd stepped around the blanket and over to the fire.

I kneeled beside him, saw the fresh blood starting to run from a deep gash across her shoulder just beneath her throat. She moaned and turned her head slightly as I touched my fingertip to it. "Don't wash her anymore, not yet," I said. "The mud and leaves are all that's kept her from bleeding to death. We gotta sew her up some way." I glanced around in the firelight as if a needle and thread might be lying there somewhere. "Jesus," I whispered.

"What about this?" Jack picked at a sliver of antelope bone in the beaded breastwork of her dress. "Whittle a point on it and notch it on the end. It'll work."

"It's too big, Jack."

"It's all we've got. It's gotta do." He held the wet rag pressed on the open gash with one hand and ripped off the sliver of bone with his other. "I can unravel some thread from my shirt."

"All right." I breathed deep and ran a hand across my forehead. I looked at the sliver of bone and drew my glades knife from my boot. "But if I'm ever hurt this bad, promise me you won't let nobody do to *me* what *I'm* about to do to *her.*"

"Aw, you're just being squeamish." Jack dabbed at the fresh flow of blood that had now widened. He squeezed the wound shut carefully and shook his head. "It's either this or watch her die."

"I know," I said; and I whittled the bone to a fine point, notched the other end, and heated it over the low flames.

As I prepared the sliver of bone, Jack unraveled thread

from the cuff of his shirt. I watched as he wet his thumb and finger in the hot water over the fire and ran the thread between them until it hung straight. He took it by both ends and tested it, then laid it across my knee. "Ready when you are. Don't go sewing up the wrong thing."

"That ain't funny, Jack." I looked at him in the glow of the firelight. Beads of sweat covered his forehead. He shivered all over.

I pinched the thread into the notch on the bone, drew it, wet and doubled it, and twirled it together. I took a deep breath and let it out slowly. "Remember the time we run a string of horses up to Powder River," I said, as I held the gash of soft skin closed and lowered the crude bone needle toward it. I formed a mound of flesh between my thumb and finger and pierced it carefully. Blood welled and trickled down across my finger. The woman moaned, stirred slightly, but didn't awaken.

"Yeah," Jack said quietly. "I remember it was warm. I remember we was lucky to get out of there alive—"

I pushed the bone needle through, drew it up and tied it, then cut it with my knife and reached back down. "Yeah," I said. "What else? Tell me some more."

"Well . . . let's see." Jack dabbed the wet rag on the stitch. "I remember that big colored feller that worked with us. What was his name?"

"Shod," I said. "Big Shod we called him. . . ." I bit my lip and pierced the flesh once again."

"Yeah, it was Shod, Big Shod. Hell of a guy as I recall." Jack made a sucking sound in his teeth as I drew the thread and tied it off. My fingertips were already sticky, and when I finished the stitch, I dipped them in the hot water and swished them around. "I wonder what ever become of him," he added.

"I don't know." I ran my free hand across my forehead and leaned back toward the wound with the bone needle in my wet fingers. "But just keep talking. This is gonna take a while."

A silence passed, and I sensed Jack struggling for something to say as I ran the crude needle through the flesh once again and drew the wound closed. "So," he said finally, as I

158

made the knot and clipped the thread with my knife, "you figure she's the Indian kid's mother?"

"Could be," I said quietly, leaning back to my work. "Whoever she is, she's shook hands with that bear."

"Or one like him," Jack said.

Once more I made a stitch, tied and clipped it, took a deep breath, and said, "Naw, it's him, Jack. He's the *Boss* of this mountain, whether Larr wants to realize it or not. But Larr's right about one thing. He's gotta be stopped. A grizzly's no problem as long as you stir wide of them and show respect . . . but not this one. He's on a killing rampage. Nothing'll stop him but a bullet in his brain." I ran the thread through my bloody fingers, examined it, and went back to work.

We listened to the long howl of a wolf somewhere out in the swirling snow above us. Beside the fire, the dogs raised their heads at the same time, the Catahoula growling low toward the world beyond the wall of blankets.

"We're easy pickin's stuck back in this hole," Jack said. He levered a round up in his rifle and looked around as he laid it across his lap. "Sorry." He grinned. "Just thinking out loud here."

I offered a tired tight smile. "Are you starting to worry?"

"Are you going crazy?" He flashed a smile in return; beads of sweat glistened on his cheek.

I glanced around, saw the horses pressed together, only inches from the low circle of fire, their heads bowed beneath the drifting layer of smoke between them and the low ceiling. "Easy pickin's for what? The posse or the bear?"

Another silence passed; then Jack said, "Just easy pickin's, I reckon . . . for *whatever's* out there."

When I finished the stitching, Jack wiped the closed wound carefully with the wet rag, and we wrapped the woman in a blanket and laid her close to the low fire. We'd looked her over good and found other wounds, but none as bad as the one I'd attended, none that required my crude handiwork at the moment. She'd awakened for a few seconds as we wrapped the blanket around her.

I could only imagine what we looked like to her, two shadowed faces looking at her in the flicker of dim firelight.

159

My face was streaked with her blood. "Ha-sha," she said in a failing voice. Her eyes swam across us, then faded.

"You're gonna be all right, ma'am," I said, brushing back a strand of damp black hair from her face.

She murmured the word again and tried to squeeze my arm. Then she drifted away. I tucked the blanket around her and stepped back, picking up my rifle. "We'll wake her in a few minutes and get some hot broth down her."

Jack nodded. I walked crouched beneath the low ceiling with the Swiss rifle hanging from my hand. At the blankets, I sat down, leaned against the wall and peeped out into the night. And I sat there well over an hour, until Jack stirred broth from the cut of antelope and whispered to the woman as he raised her head up on his lap.

"Drink this," he said to her, and she repeated the word in a soft whimper. "Shhh. Get your strength back first. Then you can talk."

As I watched her sip the broth, I thought of where we were, and why we were here. At some time or another in my life I'd been at odds with either man or beast; but this was the first time I'd ever found myself at odds with both.

There on Jack's lap lay the gruesome handiwork of nature, and it struck me as strange that while we'd worked to bring her life back from the clutches of the wilds, there lay in wait for us somewhere here, atop a snow-covered mountain, a force of man, no less gruesome, no less cruel, than that of the raging beast.

As I dozed on and off throughout the night, I pictured the cold world above us and the men who had brought along feed sacks in which to carry our heads back to civilization, like the trophies of some terrible hunt. And even as they searched for us there above, somewhere here below in the craggy snowcapped world enveloped by rock and earth lurked the bear, the most primitive of all killers known to man. Tomorrow they would be up and about, both man and beast, in a world of ice and rock and brutal elements, both intent, each in their own reason, to lay carnage to their prey.

CHAPTER

13

———◆———

During the night, I got up from my spot at the front edge of the overhang and stepped over where Jack slept with a blanket wrapped around him. My intentions were to wake him and have him keep watch for a while. But as I reached down to touch his shoulder, in the flicker of low firelight I saw how badly he was shivering, and decided to let him sleep.

A few minutes later, the Indian woman began to awaken, moaning, tossing her head back and forth, murmuring under her breath, her voice growing more urgent until I feared she would scream aloud.

"Easy, ma'am," I whispered, moving near and laying a hand on her shoulder as she tried to raise herself up. I pressed her back down gently, realizing she might not understand a word I said. "We mean you no harm."

"Hasha. Hasha?" She resisted, but only slightly; then she moaned again and lay quietly. I raised the blanket and the torn shoulder of her buckskin dress and saw that the stitches were holding and beginning to dry as well as could be expected.

"You're safe here, ma'am," I said. "You probably don't know what I'm saying, but you're safe here with us."

"I understand. . . ." She turned her face to the side, looking off toward the entrance of the overhang where the

161

sound of the creek trickled quietly. "The bear . . ." She pressed upward against my hand, but I held her down as gently as possible.

Her voice trailed as she relaxed back down. "Good." I nodded, laid the torn dress back across the stitches, and laid the blanket edge back over the wounds carefully. Patting her shoulder ever so softly, I said, "Just rest. No bear will bother you here."

Jack stirred for a second, then slept on. He shivered on and off throughout the night; and I sat awake listening above the sound of the creek for the click of hoof against rock, or muted voices, or anything else associated with the coming of man. The dogs lay close by, circled into round balls, their noses resting across their tucked-in hind legs as if keeping watch by scent, even as they slept.

Before dawn, the Catahoula raised his head and cocked his shaggy ears toward the night beyond the hanging blankets. A split second later the Airedale did the same, and growled low in his throat, until I moved over, placed a hand on his head, and silenced him.

With every fiber of my will, I honed my hearing out into the darkness and above the sound of the creek. The Catahoula stood slowly, crept as quietly as a ghost out through the blankets, and disappeared into the night. The Airedale stayed beside me, tense, listening with his nose raised.

Finally, from a long way upstream, I heard the ever-so-slight rustle of hoofs through the brush; and I sat still as stone waiting to hear it again. When I did, it was more clear and closer. *Jesus!* Had they actually ridden all night, past the cabin, and followed the trail around into the mouth of the ravine? *In the dark?* But I only wondered for a second, and even then as I moved over and shook Jack by the shoulder. "Jack," I whispered, "they're coming. Let's go."

He stood and groaned, wiped a hand across his face as he reached for his rifle. "They must be crazy." He faltered once and nearly fell; but he caught himself, rolled the blanket off his shoulders, and stamped out the glowing embers of fire. "How far are they?"

"Close, Jack, too close. Following the stream, I'd say." I looked at him in the last glow of light before his boot put it out. "How're you feeling?"

"I'm all right. A night's sleep must've cured me." I heard the top coming off the flask. "Here goes the last of it," he said; and I heard the flask fall to the ground as I reached down to move the Indian woman close to the front of the overhang.

"They'll find you here," I whispered to her. "You'll be fine."

"No," she said, also whispering. I felt her hand try to grasp my arm.

Before she could say anything more, the Airedale's voice erupted in a fierce growl that turned into a loud baying, and we flinched at the sound of it as he tore off through the blankets covering the entrance. "Damned dog!" Jack said aloud. "There goes our cover."

I hurried toward the entrance, crouched, carrying the woman. "Come on, Jack, come on," I said, easing her down. But I froze at the sound of the Catahoula's voice joining the Airedale's upstream; then a piercing scream filled the darkness, followed by the loud bawl of the grizzly.

"My God!" I started to turn the woman loose, but she held my arm. Upstream, the sound of the dogs and the bear filled the ravine and echoed down around us. Rifle fire barked; the sound of men's voices yelled back and forth in the darkness. Another terrible scream.

"Score one for the bear," Jack said, yanking down the blankets from across the entrance and leading the horses out in a hurry.

"Do not leave me here," the woman said, gripping my arm.

"Ma'am, you're hurt. They'll help you."

"No. The bear. Do not leave me here." Her voice was still weak, but urgent, pleading.

"She's right," Jack said. Rifles exploded less than a mile upstream. The dogs growled and bayed; the bear roared above all else. "Leave her here and she's as good as dead."

I looked at her face in the darkness. "Ma'am, I'll leave you a rifle. We've got to climb the wall up the other side. They're out to kill us. They'll be shooting at us—"

"No." She grasped my arm harder as I tried to pull free. "Don't leave me. I know a way out. . . ." She slumped against me. I glanced up at Jack. Upstream the roar of the

163

bear and the sound of the dogs stilled for a second as rifles exploded.

"Bring her, man! And come on, while the bear's having them for breakfast." Again the bear let out a fierce bawl; one of the dogs yelped. Rifles pounded.

Jesus! I hurried out with her in my arms and handed her to Jack. He held her until I stepped up into the saddle, then handed her up to me carefully. "This is gonna hurt, ma'am," I said.

"Go," she said in faint tight voice, pressing her face against my chest to steady herself against the pain.

We slipped across the stream as the battle raged in the predawn darkness. The woman seemed to stifle a scream, sliced her voice into a hiss, and slumped in my lap. But she forced herself upright when we started to turn downstream. I tried to heel the horse on, but she found the strength to grab my reins, saying, "No, go that way." She pointed a weak hand toward the melee upstream.

I looked at Jack, close beside me in the darkness. "You must . . . trust me," she said, her voice failing, sounding more and more shallow. "The way I came in . . . it is the way out. . . ."

We turned and rode cautiously toward the random flashes of rifle fire, knowing they were shooting wildly at the sound of the animals in the dark. In a few minutes we came to the place where we'd found the woman the night before.

The sound of the dogs and the bear faded away up the side of the ravine and the rifles had lulled. Then the firing ceased altogether by the time we reached the path where the woman had come down through the rocks to the creek. We heard the men's voices when we'd drawn closer and turned upward, our horses climbing and weaving among the rocks.

"Harvey, you alive over there?" someone called out no more than forty yards away. "Tell us something, Harvey. You hear me? You okay?"

I glanced back along the narrow path as we moved up it farther and farther, higher up above the sound of voices and the thrashing of riders scouring the creek bank. We slipped ahead quietly in a grainy break of dawn. "If I was him, I'd hope Harvey didn't owe me any money," Jack whispered beside me. The woman lay against me unconscious, a spot

164

of fresh blood starting to show through her torn buckskin dress.

"Yeah," I whispered back to him. As I looked around in the gray light, it was clear we were heading up through a deep spur canyon leading off the main ravine. The wall on both sides of us stayed tight and close, reaching high above us. "Better hope she knows what she's talking about. If there's no way out of here, they've got us cold, dead to rights." With my free hand, I reached around and raised my collar against the cold morning air.

For nearly an hour we rode on, winding upward and around until we reached an even steeper wall of rock before us. Above it we could see that we'd reached the end of the canyon, and once we were atop this last stretch of rock there had to be flatter land—there had to be. The woman stirred once more and raised herself up on my lap. "A cabin . . . up there, nine more miles," she said.

"Let's hope so, ma'am," I said quietly. Jack slipped down from his saddle. I noticed his face had gone sickly pale again. I lowered her to him and slipped down myself, working my shoulder that had gone stiff from holding her.

Jack carefully leaned her against a broken boulder, and turned to me. He nodded back down the path and said, "So. What do you think?"

"I give them an hour, maybe a little longer. The bear bought us a little time—not much. They didn't spot this path right off. I figure they went on downstream and saw where we camped. They've worked back this way and picked up our tracks by now though."

Jack studied the path for a second. "She said nine miles to a cabin. But once we get there, then what?" He looked up toward the top of the steep stretch to the flatland. "They'll ride us down in no time across good ground . . . us carrying her."

"I know it." We stood silent for a second. "You ride on with her, get her to the cabin, then cut out."

"Cut out? You mean just *leave* you here, alone? Forget it. I ain't going the rest of my life wondering what it was that got you, the bear or the posse." He shook his head.

"Listen, Jack. I can perch up there and pin them down long enough for you to ride double the next nine miles. I'll buy you some time then skin out of here. I'll be all right. There's no time to argue."

"Then you go, I'll stay here." He stifled a cough with the back of his hand. "I'm a better shot anyway."

"Look at you. You look like hell, Jack! Now go on before it's too late. We'll meet up later . . . down the mountain somewhere."

He coughed, hesitated for a second; then, when he saw I wasn't going to be moved on it, he stepped over, slipped his rifle from his scabbard, and pitched it to me. "Keep this then. It'll save having to reload if they get too frisky."

I caught it. "Thanks, now go."

"You're sure? You know you've got a way of always getting in trouble when you're on your own."

I just stared at him.

"Okay, I'll go. But in two hours, you better fire three shots and let me know you're coming, or I swear I'll turn right around and ride right back here. And I mean it."

"Get out of here, Jack." I stood there watching as he mounted. Then I handed the woman up to him, and without either of us saying another word, I continued watching until he'd leaned forward with her in his arms and coaxed the horse forward up into the steep path to the flatland.

When he'd topped out of sight above the wall, I waited a few minutes before leading my horse up there. Once there, I led the horse off a ways and spun the reins around a dried chokecherry bush and walked back to the top of the wall. I sat watching the path and waiting, judging how long it would take to get Jack safely to the cabin before lighting out of here.

I'd placed the posse an hour behind us. When they got here, I figured on holding them another half hour, with any luck. That should do it, an hour and a half. Jack would press hard for the cabin and be there and gone by then.

I sat tense, covering the path below me, listening for the slightest sound, ready to throw down rifle fire as soon as the posse stepped up into sight. But an hour passed without a trace of anything moving below, and I eased up a bit and looked all around the flatland behind me, wondering if they had found another way up and gotten past me or were at that very minute taking position behind me and waiting for me to raise my head like a tin duck at a county fair.

Nothing stirred but the cold wind across scrub grass and brush. *Bear country,* I thought. I hunched up in my coat, feeling exposed from both sides to two deadly forces, man and beast.

The dead silence became eerie after a while; and when nearly another full hour had passed, I rose up slowly, dusted snow off the seat of my trousers, and walked over to the horse, scanning all directions. So far, so good, I thought. Could they have missed seeing our tracks? Had the bear thrown them off so much they'd rode on, found where we'd camped, and continued on downstream from there? Maybe the bear attack had been too much for them. I smiled to myself and took up the reins.

The flatland lay before me, as cold, as desolate, and as still as a tomb; yet when I stepped up into my saddle, sunlight peeped out from between thick clouds and sliced like a golden blade across the ice-streaked land. Steam swirled in my breath. "Let the sun shine in," I said aloud there on that barren mountain plain; and I reined the horse around and heeled him forward. But I knew it wouldn't last. Sunshine up here only seemed to serve as a warning for a coming storm.

I picked up Jack's tracks and followed them like a map through brush and rock and skiffs of snow, continuing to glance back over my shoulder every few seconds while the horse held a strong and steady gait. After four or five miles I'd just started to ease down a little—feeling better about everything—when suddenly, beneath me, a large set of bear tracks had swung out of the brush and fell in alongside Jack's horse's hoofs.

Uh-oh. Sawing down hard on the reins, I spun the horse back and forth, sliding to a halt, staring down at the tracks just to make sure.

There was no doubt. It was the big grizzly. It had fallen in behind him and the woman and was hot on their trail. I could tell by the hoofprints that Jack was moving along at a pretty good clip. But from the spread of the bear prints, he was keeping up. The spread was as long as fifteen feet a stride. With Jack riding double on a tired horse, his arms

167

full carrying the woman, what chance would he have unless he happened to see it coming up behind them?

I'd kicked along at a sharp pace, watching both sets of tracks beneath me. A mile passed, then another half mile; and as I'd followed, I noticed the bear prints began to lessen in spread, dropping down to ten feet, then down to five or six. Then I dropped the horse down to almost a standstill when I noticed the bear prints had slowed down to what looked like a walking pace.

When the prints veered off of the horse's hoofs and back into the brush, I tipped up my hat brim and veered off with them just to make sure it had ceased trailing him.

Off to my right twenty or so yards ahead, the tracks faded deeper into brush, farther away from Jack's trail. The land appeared to drop off into another ravine, so I sat my horse for a minute without going forward, studying a sparse line of pines that ran along the edge. That was as much time as I could give to the bear. There was still a posse somewhere behind. Just because I hadn't seen them didn't mean they weren't back there.

I'd turned my horse and started back toward Jack's trail at a steady trot, still looking back for any sign of the posse. Suddenly, a few yards along, the horse nickered and balked, and jerked sideways. I managed to right him and tried to press him forward; but then I realized he had to have done it for a reason. And that reason sent a chill up my spine as I reined him back hard.

"Easy, boy," I said, trying to settle him, trying to coax him gently onward.

But the horse would have none of it. He stomped, snorted, and racked sideways, high-hoofed and ready to bolt. I jacked a round into the rifle across my lap, reining him hard with my free hand. He reared high and long in the air, twisting as he flayed his hoofs. In the wind I caught the most rancid smell, of soured meat, rot, and defecation, and from somewhere close by I heard the gut-wrenching bawl of the big grizzly.

The earth began to shudder beneath the pounding of large paws. He was coming, from out of the brush. I knew not from which direction. The horse came down hard and spun wildly beneath me. Remembering what Dallas Renfrow had said about not getting caught on horseback, I'd raised my boot free of the stirrup and started to slide off the horse.

But before I could slip down, I caught a glimpse of dark, silver-tipped fur hurtling through the air toward me. It came fast, as if out of midair, hitting with the impact of a field howitzer. Only inches beneath my raised boot, its broad head slammed into the horse's side like a battering ram, the big paws spread wide, claws reaching up on either side of me and sinking into horse flesh as we tumbled.

The horse was knocked from beneath me. I went down— facedown for a second into a coarse and terrible-smelling world of matted damp fur. Then I hit the ground rolling, spitting, still holding my Henry rifle, seeing the bear slash and rip at the screaming, writhing horse beneath him.

I struggled to my knees, ten feet away, my breath knocked from my lungs, my chest heaving to reclaim it. The bear raised the horse high off the ground, claws sunk deep, the horse thrashing and screaming. Then the bear slammed it back down, burying wide-open jaws in the horse's side as it hit the ground.

I got the Henry up, wobbling on my knees, and fired without aiming. The bear stiffened, straight up, turning the horse loose with a loud bawl. It turned slowly toward me with both paws raised. Blood ran from severed horse hide stuck in the bear's teeth. A piece of bloody meat fell from its mouth and flopped on the frozen ground. Steam bellowed.

I jacked another round up, this time catching a breath and raising a knee before me for support. The bear stood staring at me, slack jaws steaming and running red with blood. "Goddamn you devil! Come on!" I threw the Henry up, cocked my elbow on my knee, and leveled in for the shot. The bear lowered his head between his raised shoulders, swinging his jaws back and forth, slinging long strings of spittle.

He crouched, and bawled long and deep toward me. I squeezed this one off, dead perfect on the heart; but something bumped me from behind just as the shot exploded, and the bear reeled back and staggered sideways.

"The hell?" I spun to see what had bumped me. "God Almighty!"

169

Hovering above me was what at one time must've been a man. Only this one's arms had been torn from its shoulders and it staggered there covered with blood, and with brown mud hanging from it on strands of ripped and dangling flesh. I pulled away from under it, yelling, "Good Lord!"

Standing there, swaying back and forth, its one eye swimming about, its face missing a bottom lip tried to say something, but the words were words from a dead man. "Shoooot meeeee," it pleaded. Then it took a step forward and dangled in place, like a lost puppet hanging from the strings of heaven.

Behind me the bear bawled long and terrible, and I jacked another round up in the Henry, turning toward the bear.

Something had come loose inside me. I couldn't focus, couldn't think, raising the rifle, trembling, or convulsing, I knew not which. I aimed at the bear but either the rifle or my vision would not stay in place. I squeezed on the trigger but my finger had turned soft and limp, the nerves and all feeling gone from it.

Jesus! I yanked at the trigger but nothing happened. The bear crouched again toward me, ready to spring; but the remnant of a man stepped forward, swaying sideways, to and fro, and staggered right into the wide-open arms of the bawling grizzly.

The bear threw his big shaggy arms around the man as if welcoming him home to everlasting hell, then reached down, closed his jaws over the torn and bloody head, and lifted the man in the air like a flopping salmon. I'd dropped the useless rifle and was already moving away, backward, my legs spent and weak, watching the bear swing the man back and forth fiercely until the man came apart at the shoulders and flew away onto the ground.

The bear looked back at me as I started gaining footing, looking with his paws hanging at his sides, a *look-what-I-just-did* look, swaying back and forth with the head still between his jaws.

My feet were working now, better and better, pumping like steam pistons, tearing through the brush, pounding across the ground toward the tall trees at the edge of the ravine. Looking back as I ran, I saw the bear cock his head, watching me; and as he dropped down on all fours and let the head fall from his mouth, I pumped harder, knowing he was on his way.

Across the flatland I ran, my breath heaving in my chest, back past where I'd sat my horse only moments before. I remembered hearing somewhere that grizzlies didn't climb trees. The tall pines along the edge of the canyon would be my salvation—my only salvation, here on this barren land with no horse, stalked by a unearthly monster which the weapons of mere mortal man could not kill.

A pistol swung back and forth under my arm and another from my hip, yet I dared not slow down long enough to pull one. If I had it would have only been to throw them away and lessen the weight that held me back. I'd lost all faith in mere powder and lead. Bullets meant nothing. *All* weapons of man were useless now. Only *God* could kill a grizzly . . . this one anyway.

CHAPTER

14

---·---

I made it to the first in a long line of pine trees, and hung against it with my heart pounding. The trunk was bare of any outreaching branches a man could grab and climb up on. *Oh no!* I glanced back. The bear ran lumbering and bouncing through the brush with all the time in the world. I pushed away from that tree and ran, past the second one, which was as bare-branched as the first.

The third tree was taller, slimmer, and leaning out over the edge of the canyon; but it had stubs of broken branches sticking out, as if designed to accommodate a man hunted by a bear. Across the stretch of brush, the bear let out a long deep-throated bawl. Then, somewhere in the distance, the baying of the dogs resounded as if in reply.

I leaped, caught the first stub of a branch, and pulled myself up, digging at the trunk with my boots. Clawing, digging, and scrambling upward from one stub to the next, I felt flecks of bark spill about me. Sharp stubs nipped and tore at my hands and chest. Ten feet up the tree, I heard the brush beginning to thrash harder. I climbed faster, scraping myself, tearing my clothes, feeling the pistol under my arm snag on a branch and flip from my holster and fall. I dared not stop and try to catch it.

Another ten feet, and I swung my leg up around a thick branch, pulled myself up on it, and glanced down. The bear stood twenty feet from the base of the tree, looking up with his big arms spread, bawling his head off. *Bawl, you big bastard! I made it!*

I clung to the tree trunk for a moment, wondering how long the bear would stay down there before giving up. How long before he chalked this one up as a loss and lumbered off, back to the horse, or to that poor bastard lying back there dead. I shook my head to clear it.

Reaching an arm up around another limb overhead, I stood up crouched there like an ape, breathing hard, hearing the baying of the dogs drawing closer below, somewhere down in the canyon. *Jesus.* After the fracas this morning between them and the bear, it was a sure bet the posse would ride along any time. I looked down the other side of the tree as it leaned and swayed above the canyon. The ground stretched downward four hundred feet or more, a long steep slide filled with broken boulders and scrub brush.

So what? I was safe up here, up here in this tree built like a perfect ladder with its stubs sticking out just the right length for a good firm handhold. Then, as I looked down, seeing the bear walk over to the tree and look up it, it dawned on me in a sickening flash.

A grizzly's claws were not hooked round like a black bear's—not made for climbing trees. But my God! *This* tree! Anything or anybody could climb it. I just had!

Below, I saw the bear look straight up at me with his jaws thrown open as he reached up a big paw, wrapped it over the first stub, and pulled himself up. *Oh . . . my . . . God. . . .* I looked up, and back down, and all around, wild-eyed. Down there, far below in the canyon, I caught sight of the dogs moving upward, tumbling and bounding over rocks like two circus clowns, their voices snarling and baying, and looking up toward me swaying there above them.

Hurry boys, damn it! Hurry! I snatched my other pistol from my hip, cocked it, and pointed it straight down at the bear. He'd glanced up once more and slung his bloody jaws back and forth, then set about his climb.

All I saw now was the top of his broad head, the hump of his back, and his thick arms reaching up, one past the other, coming to me quietly now, save for the steady draw and gush of his heavy steaming breath. I moved the pistol back

173

and forth, searching for a clear shot through the many stubs of broken limbs. *God, anything but* this, *I don't deserve this . . . do I?*

I prayed to myself, picturing what I'd just seen this monster do to a man, and to a horse, and to Brace Denton and the others.

My first shot thumped into a thick stub, and the bear looked up at me and slung his slack jaws back and forth. I grimaced, threw a quick glance up to heaven as I recocked the pistol. *God,* I said, perhaps aloud now. *I know I've been a worthless, rotten bastard for the most part*—I pulled off another round; it hit nothing as far as I could tell—*I know now that I was wrong doing what I did to big Eldon . . . to a lot of folks, Lord!*

I fired again, saw the bear's shoulder flinch, but he roared, swung halfway around the tree trunk, and kept coming. Beneath me down the canyon wall, the dogs drew closer, climbing hard. *Hell, half the time I haven't even believed in ya, Lord*—I leaned around the trunk, holding the limb above and swaying as I fired. It went wild and pinged off a stub.

But I do TODAY, Lord! I'm a changed man. Can change. Will change! Please just don't feed me to this fu—I mean raging bear!

Two shots left, and the sound of the dogs seeming to make the bear climb faster. Bark and dust bellowed around him as he swung higher and higher toward me. At five feet away, I pulled off another round and saw it thump into his fur. *Jesus, still coming!*

He roared, and with his next step he bounded upward, slashing a paw that barely missed my leg. My shot whistled past his head as I jerked away. Scrambling up onto the next branch just as he swung around beneath me, I dropped my pistol in my rush, and heard it bounce off the bear's thick furry head. His steaming breath drifted up around me.

The dogs tumbled over the canyon edge and hit the base of the tree, clawing, baying, and bouncing in the air. The bear shot them a glance, bawled loud as I scrambled onto another branch, jerking the glades knife from my boot. *"All right, you bastard!* If it's killin' you want!"

I braced myself on the limb with my legs wrapped around

it, holding around the trunk with one hand, leaning down, ready, with the knife in my other. I slashed at the big paw that reached up for me, felt the blade cut across coarse fur. Fur flew. Blood spewed behind the slash of the blade, and I slashed it back, this time missing as the bear bawled, drew his paw back, and slapped at my hand. He missed; hot blood flew from his paw into my face. He bounded up; I scrambled higher.

Big claws nicked my boot heel. I bolted up to the next branch, three feet above me, still slashing down with the knife, yelling at him. He swung up onto the limb I'd just left, lunging up with both paws just as I swung the blade. My hand hit his paw and the knife fell, bounced off his head, and tumbled away.

Below, the dogs were going crazy. The tree swayed as I swung higher up and around the trunk away from him. *Nothing left!* His big wounded paw wrapped around the trunk and held on, only inches from my face, spewing blood.

I yanked out the brass knuckles from my pocket, yelling as I slipped my fingers into them, the bear bawling, his paw searching the trunk for me, scraping and tearing off chunks of tree. Pounding the big paw with the brass knuckles until it loosened its grip on the trunk, I scrambled on up, feeling him right behind me on the other side.

I caught a dizzy glance of the posse riding along in the bottom of the canyon looking up at us swaying there high above them. *Damn it, why?* Sure they were bound to come, but why now? *Lord, I could've used a couple more minutes here!*

I hooked an arm over a limb and hung there like a wild monkey, my strength waning, my boot soles scratching at the trunk. Steam curled around the tree trunk; and I cocked my arm back. Then, when the big face ventured around into sight, I let him have it, a hard swinging right that buried the knuckle-dusters alongside his big slimy nose.

He bawled loud and long, shaking his head; and I hit him again, getting my swinging weight behind it. He drew his head back, threw his wounded paw around the trunk, and tried to hold on. His paw slid down the trunk a few inches,

175

then held firm. I cocked back a boot and slammed my heel into the big paw, saw it slip some more.

"Fall, you bastard!"

He grunted, slipped some more, leaving gashes in the bark behind his big claws. I kept stomping the big bloody paw as it slid down. *That's it, fall!* Something thumped against the tree trunk beneath me, followed by the crack of a rifle from the canyon floor. The dogs jumped, clawing at the tree in a frenzy, their voices breaking hoarse in their rage.

Anticipating the bear's next move, I hung from the limb by both hands now, the brass knuckles digging into the palm of my hand, squeezing down hard across my fingers. I cocked my knees high just as he swung his whole body around the trunk. A packet of dollar bills spilled from my waist, broke and fluttered away like birds from a magician's shirt. I buried both boot heels in the bear's bawling face.

Steam from his mouth split and puffed in both directions around my boots; and he screamed as he slid down two feet, shaking his head amid a cloud of money. I cocked my right boot and let him have it again, this time swinging up, clipping his chin with my boot heel. His head jerked back, his teeth clacked together. He clawed wildly at the trunk, staggering back from it.

Another bullet thumped the tree, this one higher up. They were honing their rifles in, getting a fix on me. The bear tumbled, bawling, screaming, ripping strips of bark as he went, snapping smaller limbs, bouncing off larger ones, jarring the whole tree. Dust bellowed when he hit the ground . . . and the dogs were upon him.

Dollar bills sailed out on the breeze and showered down the canyon. I swung in against the tree as a bullet whistled past, caught my arms around the trunk and scrambled around it out of the rifle sights. Now they volleyed, their bullets slapping the tree as it swayed back and forth. The sound of bullets zipped past me as I slid down to the next branch and hung there, completely spent, staring down at the whirling, screaming, snarling tangle of dogs and bear on the ground beneath me.

A dollar bill sailed in and stuck on my sweaty nose; I blew it away, heaving, steaming, wiping my face with a quaking hand.

176

KILLERS OF MAN

As suddenly as they'd attacked, the dogs rolled away from the bear and made a stand fifteen feet back, down on their front legs, their hackles up, froth running from their raised flews. The bear stood up slashing and bawling and spinning back and forth. Without giving me a second look he stalked forward toward the dogs.

The Catahoula darted in and out snapping at the bear's legs, drawing the big brute farther away from the tree as the Airedale circled wide, around, and lunged into his back.

When the bear spun, swinging at the Airedale, the Catahoula shot in high, took a mouthful of the bear's neck, and held on while the monster slung him back and forth. *Eat that son of a bitch, boy. Eat him!* I slipped down the tree as the battle raged.

My feet touched the ground and I snatched up my glades knife and the gun that had fallen from my shoulder harness. Glancing once down the canyon and seeing the posse dismounting and firing from behind rocks and brush, I slipped over the edge and ran quickly along, just beneath the rim in the shelter of jagged boulders, needing to put distance between myself, the growling and bawling of the beasts, and the killers of man gathered on the canyon floor.

For fifty yards or more I ran, long, hard and winded, stumbling, falling among the rocks, but catching myself and running on, until the sound of rifles and raging animals grew distant behind me. Then I topped the edge of the canyon once more and continued on, out through the brush of the flatland, searching for Jack's tracks.

I dared not go back for the rifle I needed so badly or for my gear and ammunition that lay spilled out around the dead horse. My only chance at staying alive was to stay ahead of the posse and away from the bear. It would take the men a good hour or longer to climb the canyon wall, if they climbed it at all. They might well circle back and ride up rather than give up their horses and run me down on foot. As for the bear: now that the dogs had him, they would keep him busy for a while, until one killed the other or they all gave up in exhaustion.

I ran on.

Spotting Jack's horse tracks, I fell into them and slowed

to a trot, trying to rest myself without losing any time. He'd said if I didn't fire three shots he'd ride back looking for me. I wasn't about to fire three shots now. Now I *prayed* he'd come rounding across the flatland—prayed for deliverance from both man and beast.

A mile along, I swayed to a stop and fell against a broken boulder beside Jack's trail. My lungs felt pierced by each breath of cold air that sliced into them. Above, the sky had turned dark once more and sharp sleet stung my face as I lay gasping. Now the weather would take its turn at trying to kill me, I supposed. *Why not.* The sound of the animals had trailed away and ceased behind me.

I lay there only for a moment until my breathing stilled; then I rose up onto my knees with my palms on my thighs and looked all around. There was no cover, no place to hide, no place to make a stand. The sleet was turning to snowflakes and blowing sideways in a harsh cold wind. The only escape was to push forward.

I reached inside my open coat, under my belt, took out the stacks of money and dropped them on the snowstreaked ground. The money was now a burden, just more weight to carry. But I wasn't about to leave it lying here in the dirt and snow. If I was captured, it might be the only thing that could save me, a bargaining chip in a last effort at staying alive.

I struggled with the rock until it pulled loose from the cold ground; and holding it with one hand, I brushed the packets of money beneath it and let it fall, hoping I could remember the spot if I lived to return for it. Then I brushed a hand around in the dusting of snow to cover my handiwork, pushed myself to my feet, and moved on. Where the hell was Jack?

Following his tracks, half walking, half trotting, I went another three or more miles, glancing back for any sign of the posse. Jack would've already been coming back for me if he could. Now I had to wonder what had happened to him. Had he made it to the cabin? Had the bear gotten him somehow? No. If that was the case, I would've seen some sign of it along the trail.

The bear had followed him for only a while, then veered off. Jack was somewhere ahead. Had to be. Probably coming back for me right about now—going to show up at any second. Behind me the air had turned white and full, snow blowing straight across, the wind cutting and cold, merciless. I huddled against it with one hand holding my coat tight at the throat, and my other hand pressed down on my hat.

Pushing on, I turned and glanced back. Something moved toward me in the wind-driven snow; and when I turned and crouched with my pistol raised, the big Catahoula came loping to me, steam bellowing from his mouth and his tongue lolling. A streak of blood covered one side of his face. His chest heaved in rhythm to his pounding heart. There was no sign of the Airedale.

"Okay, boy," I said, staggering in place and reaching down to him. "Let's take a look at you—" But I stopped short as he snarled and pulled back from me. "Then suit yourself." I turned and staggered on against the wind and snow. Evidently the Airedale was dead; hopefully he hadn't died before inflicting enough damage on the bear to keep it away from me. I looked down at the Catahoula as he bounded ahead of me, his nose tilted up in the cold air. With him along, at least I'd know now if anything came near us.

By the time we'd gone another mile, my feet were turning numb. So were my cheeks and fingertips. The new snow had covered Jack's tracks, but I stumbled on anyway, seeing the faint outline of jagged peaks through the blowing snow. The woman had said her cabin was in a valley just past the flatland. I had no choice but to try and find it.

We reached the end of the flatland, and as I stood deciding which way to go, the Catahoula cut right, and loped upward along a narrow path sniffing the air. I followed him. A hundred yards along the path, I caught the slightest scent of wood smoke and stayed behind the dog as he turned toward it. Another hundred yards upward and around a wall of spilled boulders, the outline of a cabin appeared like a vision of heaven through a white swirl. I stumbled toward it. The Catahoula ran on ahead, wagging his tail and whining.

I got to the cabin and leaned against the door for a second before opening it. When I pulled down on the latch, the wind swung the door open wide, and I stepped in and swooned in the blast of heat from the blazing hearth. The Catahoula slipped inside, shaking snow off his back, and trotted over to the fire. Snow flurried around me, and I pressed the door closed and slumped back against it.

"Thank God," I said, seeing the Indian woman beside the fire with a blanket around her. Beside her, Jack lay on the floor covered with a blanket, shivering violently. The woman looked over at me, and I saw the rag in her hand as she reached out and laid it on his forehead.

CHAPTER

15

---·---

"**H**ow bad is it?" I asked her. I'd warmed my hands quickly over the open fire, held them to my face, and stooped down beside Jack as she continued pressing the wet rag to his forehead. She looked over at me, her face drawn and weary in the firelight.

"It is bad," she said. "It is like the fever that killed many of my people when I was a young girl."

"Aw naw. Jesus." I wiped a hand across my face, wondering what to do next. Then I realized we had no choice and I said, "Can he ride?"

Her expression went flat. She studied my eyes as she shook her head slowly. "He could die. There is no—"

"We all die sooner or later," Jack said in a trembling voice. He looked up at me with sweat pouring down his sunken cheeks. "But I can ride till then." His fevered eyes swam over me, taking in my torn shirt through my open coat and the flecks of tree bark and scuff marks. "Got in trouble, didn't ya?"

"No," I said, ducking my head slightly and glancing away from his gaze. "Well, yeah, a little I reckon," I added grudgingly. "I ran into the posse, and they're right behind us."

Jack coughed, his shivering body racked and stiffened for

a second. "What else? I knew you'd get yourself in trouble if I left ya there—"

"All right, Jack," I cut him off. "I mighta had a little run-in with the bear. But it's all taken care of. We've got to get you out of here somehow."

"Did you . . . kill it?" Again he coughed; the woman pressed the rag back against his forehead.

"No . . . not exactly. But on a brighter note, it didn't kill me either. It killed my horse. I think the Airedale's dead."

Jack coughed, shook his head, and tried to smile. "Told ya you'd get . . . into trouble. . . ."

His words trailed as he turned his head and drifted out of consciousness. The woman laid the rag over his forehead and looked at me again. Dried blood on her dress outlined the cut beneath it. I reached a hand over to it. "Better let me take a look at that, ma'am."

"No." She pulled back slightly and rested a hand on the rag across Jack's forehead. "You two are what they call desperados?"

"Well, let's just say there are some who speak ill of us here and there."

"The posse chasing you. They are bounty hunters? Men who will be paid money to kill you? Kill you because of terrible things you have done to others?"

"Yes, but there's lots more to it than that, ma'am. You're making it sound so . . . so . . ." I rolled a hand, then stopped, realizing she'd said it about as clearly as it could be said.

"Do not try and explain." She shook her head and adjusted the rag on Jack's fevered brow. "And yet, even with your lives at risk, you stopped to help me?"

"Yes, ma'am. We had no choice. We couldn't leave you out there to die." I studied her dark caged eyes for a second. "And we're not really desperados. It's more like we're just a couple of ole boys who's gotten into some legal complications that would take a whole lot of attorneys a whole lot of years to sift through and get straightened out—"

"Please." She shook her head, stopping me. "I asked you not to explain. You helped me. That is what matters to me. Now I must help you." She looked down at Jack, wiped his

182

brow, then looked back at me. "Who is this man leading the bounty hunters?"

"His name is Silks, ma'am . . . Dan Silks," I said.

Her hand stopped moving. "Oh, I see. . . ." She seemed stunned for a second, then caught herself and continued attending to Jack.

I eyed her closely. "Do you *know* him? Have you ever heard of him?"

"Of course." She dipped the rag in a pan, squeezing it, and turned back to Jack. "Who in this country has not heard of *Dandy Dan Silks?*" She glanced at me, seeing by my expression that I required more of an answer. "Yes," she sighed, "I met him years ago. He is a man who knows his business. Out here, there is no one smarter or tougher than him. A brutal man. It is said that if he is hunting you, it is better that you shoot yourself than to be captured."

"Well, that's *real* encouraging, ma'am. But I plan on getting through this with every part of my body I started out with."

"Then I must help you cure your friend, so the two of you can get away."

"Thank you, ma'am, but the fact is we ain't got time to wait for him to get well. They're right behind me somewhere. We've got to make some time."

She nodded upward toward the sound of the wind moaning and roaring across the roof of the cabin. "If this is the *big* storm, it could last for days. And it will be hard traveling even when it is gone. Dan Silks will not travel in this weather. Would you, if you were him?"

I let out a breath, realizing she was probably right. "If I was him, I'd be just as intent on catching us as we are in getting away, I reckon."

She smiled slightly, a weak but knowing smile, and rose up, steadying herself with a hand on the corner of a table. "Come, help me. You will have to do the lifting. I will show you what to do. We must not waste time."

I stood, reached out a hand, and helped her step around Jack there on the floor. "What were you doing out there, ma'am, if you don't mind my asking."

"I searched for my son, Hasha, but the bear has killed him, as it did my father."

183

That stopped me; I stared at her. "So you *are* the woman the bear drug away from Two Shirts' cabin the other day. I figured as much, ma'am."

She studied my eyes without answering.

"The fact is, we found your son. He's safe, ma'am. He went back with another man, up to Lodge Pole on the train."

She nearly swooned with relief. "Then I owe you for my son's life as well as my own."

"You don't owe us a thing," I said, "but I appreciate any help I can get. We really are in a tight spot here."

"No. I do owe you. I must do everything in my power to help you stay alive. Come, we have much to do."

I followed her and she had me take down a big black kettle from a peg on the wall. I stepped outside long enough to fill the kettle with snow, and we placed it over the fire until it was nearly boiling. Then she took two blankets, shook them out, pushed them into the steaming water with a wooden ladle, and raised them out, letting them drip for a minute while I took the blanket off Jack and undressed him.

His clothes were soaked with sweat and smelling of fever. "We must keep sweating the fever from him, and keep the water going into him, until we burn the sickness away," she said, wrapping the blanket around him.

"Yes, ma'am."

We worked throughout the rest of the day and into the night, wrapping Jack in hot wet blankets while he babbled out of his head and the storm howled and battered the roof. Near midnight, the Catahoula ran to the door, sniffing, whining, and scratching. When I went over and opened the door a crack against the wind, the big Airedale tumbled in and fell at my feet.

He was covered with snow, ice, and blood. A gaping wound hung open along one side. He whined pitifully. I held my breath, scooped him up, and carried him over near the fire. "Looks like the bear wins again."

For the rest of the night the Indian woman and I worked like army doctors in a battlefield hospital. She soaked the blankets, and I helped her with Jack, then I clipped off the Airedale's matted coat with a pair of shears I found in the cabin, and washed his stinking body. The woman held

184

the dog's wound closed and I wrapped strips of cloth torn from an old shirt around him.

When he was bound good and firmly, I laid him close to the fire and went back to helping her with Jack. All the while the Catahoula watched, staying close to the Airedale, poking his wet nose toward his wounded friend as if checking to make sure I'd done everything right.

Near dawn, the woman and I sat slumped across the table from one another. She'd set a bowl of hot water on the table between us and dabbed carefully at her own wound as I watched. "Maybe I should do that for you, ma'am," I said, hoping she'd tell me no—which she did.

"You have done your part. You saved my life," she said. "It is up to me now. No wound completely heals except by the hand of the wounded."

"Yes, ma'am," I replied, not sure what she meant, and wondering if she and Jack might've read the same books somewhere down the line.

So we sat, in a small circle of warmth beneath the swirl of cold outside the cabin. I sipped coffee and watched her, and looked around where the Airedale lay, with the Catahoula lying close beside him. And I looked at Jack, who slept now, still muttering under his breath from time to time, but not shivering as badly as he had been before. Now that he seemed to be past some dangerous stage of his illness, I let out a breath and asked the woman, "This fever he has . . . how contagious is it?"

She looked up from attending her wound. "If it is the fever that killed my people, it is *very* contagious." Then she dabbed at her wound for a second and looked back up. "It travels like a prairie fire. All those who came in contact with the sick caught it. It killed many."

"But not you."

She gave me a serious look. "No, not me. I fled the tribes in time and went to live in the white settlements. The fever is like the bear, it rages and kills all around it. Yet I escaped it. Some would say I should've stayed and helped my people. But I ran . . . and kept running."

I rubbed my neck. "I wish you would have told me how contagious it is first, ma'am."

"If you knew, would your fear of the fever have made you

not help save him? Would you have run from it, the way I did as a young girl?"

"No, ma'am." I nodded at Jack asleep in his blanket. "Him and I are friends from times you couldn't imagine. But I might've kept *you* from handling him if I'd known."

"But, did he not handle me, when I was dying? Should I have turned away, and feared the very hand that had saved me only the night before?"

"Well, no ma'am."

"If I had not handled him, you would not have known what to do."

"That's true," I said, "but I would've done something, or else he and I would've died together."

She nodded toward the two dogs. "They *too* are friends, but all the Catahoula dog could do was sit and whine when his friend was wounded. He could not have bound his wounds and saved him. That is why I ran from the fever before, because I didn't know *what* to do. Since then I have learned *what* to do in all matters. Now I run from nothing."

Only when she'd finished attending her wound and let out a tired breath did she look back at me and ask about her son, Hasha. I told her that the boy was badly shaken when we'd found him, but that he was fine otherwise. I told her that her father was dead, but she didn't seem surprised, and I told her the whole story of how we'd left her son and Renfrow near the train so when the bounty men came, the two of them would be taken to safety.

A silence passed after I told her these things, then she looked at me with a puzzled expression.

"Would it not have been better if you and your friend had kept going farther from the reach of these men, once you left the cabin?"

"Maybe," I said. "But we wanted to make sure the boy was all right, and at *that* time we were only hunting the bear. We had no idea there was a posse coming for us."

"If you are desperados, shouldn't you always have an *idea* that a posse may be coming after you?"

"Well . . . yeah. But like I said, ma'am, we don't really consider ourselves desperados." I didn't feel like justifying Jack's and my actions to her.

186

"You do not *really* consider yourselves desperados, the way the bear does not *really* consider himself a killer."

I just stared at her.

Another silence passed as she seemed to examine our actions in her mind, questioning our wisdom, and not quite understanding it. Then she sighed softly, shook her head, and said almost under her breath, "Desperados . . ."

I felt my face redden. "Well, ma'am, things have a way of sneaking up on ya, then you can only deal with them best you can. We've not claimed to be the *smartest* or the *toughest*—"

"The bear is much wiser. He knows that all who come, come to take his life. He does not wait to see how, or question why they do it . . . or even if they are his friends or enemies. He kills all that come onto his mountain, even other bears, until there is nothing left. He acts with no mercy." She tapped a finger to her forehead. "Then he has *nothing* to fear—" She smiled a weak smile. "—and is he who has nothing to fear not the most feared of all the man killers?"

I studied her eyes across the table in the flicker of firelight, seeing in them the same caged dark glow that I'd seen in her son's. She seemed to be waiting for me to explain why Jack and I had not been more ruthless, more single-minded, in our struggle to stay alive.

"Maybe that's true, ma'am, but we're not *animals.* Sometimes there's more to life than just staying alive. There's being able to live with yourself afterwards."

"Yes, but had you not stopped to help my son, and me, you would have been ahead of the storm. One must live, if only to regret the consequence of one's actions . . . for the dead know neither pleasure or remorse. Is this not also true?"

"No offense, ma'am, but that's not exactly the kind of talking or thinking I'd expect from an Indian woman high atop a wild mountain. It's not only a little top-heavy for me, but it says little about honor—little about caring for your own."

"Perhaps I lived too many years in the white man's world before coming back here. Perhaps the better part of me was lost there." She stared at me as if considering something

187

dark and dreadful from her past, something she had long been at odds with, but unable to discuss. "I learned how things *should* be in the white man's *books,* then I learned how things *are* in the white man's *world.*"

"I had no right saying that, ma'am. I'm not the one to give a sermon on honor . . . or who should *care* about *what.* We all do what we think we have to, I reckon."

"Yes we do." Her eyes studied me as if trying to decide something.

I shook my head and gazed over at the two dogs by the fire, one down and the other badly worn. They were here only for the hunt, I thought, unfettered by any moral judgment, and with no regard for gain or loss. They had followed their nature, and their nature had brought them to this.

I could think of no more to say, so I repeated, "Like I said, ma'am, we're not animals . . . him and I." I nodded toward Jack, then lowered my gaze.

She glanced at Jack also, then at the bear-whipped dogs, then up at the ceiling as the storm raged. "Of course not." She stood, dismissing it, and raised the corner of her torn dress up over her wound, then went and sat closer to the fire.

It was midmorning by the time the storm lessened. When I pulled the door open, the sky was still swollen and churning. A two-foot-high wall of snow stood across the doorway. I tried kicking it away only to see that it was not a drift but the actual depth of the snowfall. A veil of white dust still swirled in the air. It peppered onto the Catahoula as he sprang past me and out the door. Behind me by the fire, the Airedale whined from where he lay with his head raised, watching the other dog bound away.

I struggled through the snow to a woodshed and brought back load after load of seasoned firewood. The snow would be both a blessing and a curse. I took comfort knowing that it held back the posse, but I cursed the fact that it did the same to Jack and me.

Jack was soundly sleeping now. His chills seemed to have stopped for the past couple of hours. When a high stack of wood lay near the hearth, I took his pistol from his holster, checked it, cleaned it, and shoved it down in my waist. I sipped hot coffee.

"Are there any firearms here?" I asked the woman.

"No," she said. "No one has lived here for many months. When the bear killed my husband last season, we went and lived with my father, Two Shirts." She sighed. "And now the bear has killed him also."

"Sorry, ma'am," I said quietly, sipping the coffee. I watched her sew up the torn shoulder of her dress for a moment; then I sat down my cup. "Now that the big storm is ending, I'll have to get my friend up and move on."

She stopped sewing and looked at me. "He is too weak to travel, and this storm was not the big storm." She nodded toward the door. "The *big* storm is still coming."

I rubbed the back of my neck and let out a breath. "Then how do you know when the *big* storm gets here?"

"You do not know when it gets here, only when it has been here. Only when the storm was passed can you say it was the big one."

Jesus. I rolled my eyes upward slightly, stood, walked to the coffeepot over the fire, and poured another cup. "So we've got no idea about this weather. We just know it's here, and we don't know how bad it is till it's over."

"*You* have no idea about the weather, but Dan Silks does, and so do I," she said. "To know how to read the weather is to know how to win this hunt. You must either work *with* the weather, or be at the weather's mercy. And like the bear, the weather has no mercy."

I shook my head, looked down at Jack sleeping there, and paced back and forth before the fire. "Nevertheless—" I stopped and stared over at her. "—I've got to push on. We'll have to take our chances with his fever *and* the weather."

"It could kill him if he has the fever."

"Well, it will kill him no less than getting his head gunnysacked, I reckon—" I stopped short and looked at her. "What do you mean *if* he has the fever? You sounded pretty sure last night."

"I know. But his fever has broken too soon to be the fever my people had, and even though it has broken he is still very sick. When a fever breaks, a person comes to quickly. He has not."

189

"So now you're saying you're not sure what he's got?"

"I only know what I know. I thought it was the fever, but now I wonder if he has simply eaten bad food."

"Naw, we've eaten the same thing ever since we've been up here. If he had food poisoning, I'd have it too." I paced back and forth. "Maybe if I got him out of here, I could get him down to Elk Horn to a doctor." I paced more. "Or maybe . . . I could get out of here and bring a doctor back?" I considered it and shook my head. "No, forget that. That would never work. No doctor would come up—"

"Unless you brought him at gunpoint." She stared at me. "Would you do that, to save your friend?"

"Yes, ma'am, if I thought it would work. But it won't." I shook my head and paced some more. "We've just got to make a run for it. That's what it always comes down to. We've got to run . . . and keep running . . . stay ahead of the hunters."

"In this country there is more to staying alive than outrunning the hunters. You must know *how* to run . . . and you must discover the hunter's weakness and know how to use it against him."

"I don't have time to figure out Dandy Dan Silks' weakness, if he even has one. But I reckon if there's one thing I do know, it's how to run, ma'am." I dealt her a narrowed glance.

"Of course," she replied. "I only say this to remind you . . . not to teach you." But I could tell by her expression that she knew she had just bumped against my pride and was now taking a step back to see what damage she'd done.

"I can't wait until this storm has completely passed. I need a couple hours of fresh snow to cover our tracks. I know that much. And the man leading the posse knows it too. He won't wait till the storm's passed. He'll be coming—might be coming now." I rubbed my hand up and down my trouser leg as I paced.

She watched me in silence for a moment as if considering something, then sighed and said, "I must travel with you."

I shook my head. "No, ma'am, that's out of the question. I know you mean well, but it would only slow us down."

"Did having me with you slow you down when I led you to the high path?"

"That was different, ma'am. Like I said, we couldn't leave you there to die—"

"But in turn, bringing me kept you and your friend from being caught. I know the way through the high passes. Silks will work the trails where he expects you to be."

"I understand. But it'll get rough from here on, ma'am. If those men spot you, figure you're leading us, they'll kill you the same as they'd kill our horse if that's what's helping us get away. I can't take you into that just to save our hides."

"Then don't take me along to save your hides. Take me because there is a bear who will kill me if you leave me here unarmed. Take me because I must go get my son Hasha. Take me because if you do not I will leave anyway—on my own." She stared at me as I stopped pacing and ran a hand across my face. "Find what reason you *need* for taking me with you. While you find it, I will prepare for travel."

I watched her stand up slowly from the table, using her hand for support; and she walked over, picked up a blanket, threw it around herself, and walked out the door into a white swirl. I stepped over to the frost-scalloped window, rubbed a circle of haze from it with the heel of my hand, and watched her struggle over to a small shed that seemed strained to point of collapsing beneath the weight of snow.

Behind me, the big Airedale whined, stood up, and came over as I turned and looked down at him. He looked gangly and thin without his heavy coat, weak and unsteady limping across the dirt floor. The bandage around him showed dark with a streak of dried blood; yet he looked up at me wagging his short tail. A gleam shined deep in his tired eyes. He stood game and ready for whatever lay ahead.

I reached down and patted the coarse-cropped hair on his battered head. "You just don't know when you've had enough, do ya, boy?"

He cocked his head as if trying to understand me. I rubbed my hand on my trousers and walked over to where Jack lay sleeping near the fire. We'd taken up all the time *this* day would allow us; now the hunted had to move on.

191

CHAPTER

16

---•---

The snow still fell as we left, only now it was not wind-driven. The flakes were smaller, peppering down less slanted as the fury of the storm spent itself and moved on. Above us the sky spread gray and low, but settled, and with no sun, save for a wide silver glow deeper up in the heavens.

The woman and I struggled along with Jack between us, his arms looped across our shoulders, leaning more of his weight on me than her, owing to her wound. She'd brought two pair of wide snowshoes—Indian mukluks—from the shed before we left. She'd dusted them off and handed me the larger pair while the Airedale and the Catahoula stood watching us curiously.

In the shed, she'd also found a rusty corn knife and a jar of molasses that had turned to sugar. We boiled it back into a heavy dark syrup and wrapped it in a blanket along with a couple pounds of dried beets and the few remaining coffee beans. These things had been left at the place since her husband's death a year ago. *Deadman's food,* I'd thought as I packed them up and tied them across the back of Jack's horse.

I'd considered burning this cabin as I'd burned the other before we left; but I decided against it on the outside chance that with the snow covering all sign of our direction across the flatland, they could spend some time looking for us before ever coming in this direction.

KILLERS OF MAN

The snow had been deep and difficult on the horse and the dogs when we crossed a flat stretch from the cabin to the small barn, yet as we left and traveled upward behind the cabin, the snow became more shallow where the wind had swept it past the towering ridges and dumped it across the valleys and flatlands.

"This is crazy." Jack spoke in a weak voice, leaning near my ear. Steam swirled in our breath. The woman had turned loose and faltered as we crossed a high mound of snow that had spilled down from a break between two upthrusts of jagged rock. "You know you're gonna . . . have to leave me . . . sooner or later," he said.

"Hush up, Jack." I stopped, panting, staggering there, waiting for the woman to catch up to us. The reins to Jack's horse hung from my free hand, and I dropped them to wipe a hand across my face. Ahead, the dogs bounded back and forth, tunneling the snow with their noses and moving steadily on. The Airedale seemed no worse for his wear now that he was back on the trail.

"It's the truth, and you know it," Jack said, gasping breath. "Just leave me my . . . pistol. . . . I know what to do."

"Shut up. You're talking outa your head. We started this trip together and we'll end it together. I ain't letting you shoot yourself."

"Shoot . . . *myself?*" A weak chuckle came up from his chest, followed by a cough. "You're the one . . . talking outa your head. I meant to hold off the posse. . . ."

"Oh." I wondered why I'd even thought otherwise. "Well, I still ain't leaving ya, so pipe down."

"I'd . . . leave you," he said, "if it was . . . the other way around."

"That's a lie. So hush about it. Save your energy. You're gonna need it."

He glanced down at the wide snowshoes on my feet as if noticing them for the first time. "Beware of any endeavor . . . that requires new *shoes.*"

"I will. Now shut *the hell* up!"

When the woman struggled up to us, favoring her wounded shoulder, I nodded at the horse's reins near my

193

feet and pulled Jack closer against me. "I've got him. Just lead the horse awhile."

She picked up the reins, swooned slightly, and pointed along toward the dogs. "The snow has covered our tracks. Five miles up, there is a cave. We rest there."

I looked at her. "Are you doing all right?" As soon as I asked, I realized what a pointless question it was.

Her eyes met mine, then looked away. She nodded without answering and struggled past us leading the horse.

Two miles farther, the snowfall had dissipated to a thin sprinkling, and we stopped just after crossing another high mound of snow. Behind us I heard a sound, like that of a heavy wind rushing across miles of cornstalks.

The earth vibrated beneath my feet as I turned, swinging Jack with me. A high wall of snow came crashing down from between two peaks a hundred yards back. It spilled out over a ledge like a large waterfall, traveling down the slope of the mountain, snapping smaller pine and aspen, and leaving larger trees shuddering in its wake.

"The hell was that?" Jack asked without raising his head.

"Jesus," I whispered, glancing up and along the thick white cornice of snow overlapping the peaks above us. "It's nothing, Jack." Looking back, I saw the bald ridge where the snow had collapsed and tumbled with the impact of a freight train. "Just one more *damn* thing to deal with here in our mountain retreat." I hiked his arm up across my shoulder and walked on, watching the dogs disappear around a bend and beneath an overhang in the path ahead.

We traveled on, slow, labored, and steady, until the woman stopped in front of us and slumped against the horse's side. I let Jack down against a snowcapped rock and hurried to her as she crumpled to the ground.

"I will . . . be all right," she whispered. She tried pushing me away with a limp arm, but I scooped her up from the snow and leaned against the horse with her in my arms for a second, my breath pounding. I felt exhaustion beginning to take its toll on me.

"Yeah . . . we'll all be all right," I said in a gush of steam; and struggling, I got her up across the horse's back, unstrapped the snowshoes from her feet, and righted her into

194

the saddle. She slumped forward, and I opened her blanket enough to see if there was any fresh blood on her doeskin dress. There wasn't. I let out a breath, hung there for another second, then straightened, shook the weariness from my head, and led the horse back a few feet to where I'd left Jack.

I dropped the snowshoes on the ground and spread out the straps. "Okay, okay, okay," I said to myself, looking all around. *One step at a time here. Just get to the cave. Just rest . . . that's all. We all need . . . rest.* I stooped down, took Jack's arm, and raised him to his feet. "Step into these," I said, guiding him to the snowshoes.

He stirred enough to help me get him standing on the snowshoes, and held both his hands on my back while I strapped the leather thongs around his boots.

"Got it made now . . . don't we," he said.

"Yeah . . . nothing to it now," I replied, breathing hard. I stood up, steadying him, and when I'd hiked his arm up and gathered his weight against my side, we pressed on.

The woman was right about the cave farther along the upsweep of rock. She slumped semiconscious on the horse while I struggled on, near to collapsing, with Jack's arm looped across my shoulder, until the Airedale came loping to me around a turn in the rocks. His bandage was streaked with fresh brown mud along his sides, the way he'd been the day Larr had led us out and shot the wrong bear.

I'd wondered that day about the fresh mud, but now as he bounced back and forth in front of me drawing my attention, it dawned on me that he'd been back somewhere inside the earth, out of the weather where the temperature still remained above freezing.

"Good boy," I said in a weak voice; and I looked back along our path where our tracks were fading beneath the slow but steady sprinkling of snow.

With purpose in his stride the dog led us the next hundred yards, then turned and led us another thirty upward through a maze of twists and turns among jagged rock. He disappeared for a second into what appeared to be a steep rock wall. But when Jack and I struggled closer—half walking, half crawling, me tugging the horse's reins to force him along behind us—we came to a three-foot-wide gash in the wall that stretched up into a narrowing point ten feet overhead.

Inside the narrow opening, the Airedale stood facing us from the darkness, wagging his stub of a tail. "Jack, we've made it," I said, panting, puffing steam as I stepped just inside the opening and slumped against the wall with him beside me.

It didn't matter that all we had made it to was a hole in a wall of rock in the midst of desolate country, or that even this was only a temporary refuge from all that beset us. All that mattered right then was that we'd found a place out of the cold; and I must've leaned there a full ten minutes catching my breath while the horse puffed and blew, and scraped a hoof on the frozen ground.

After resting myself, I managed to get Jack up on the horse and lean him forward across the woman's back. I tied both sets of snowshoes together, slung them over my shoulder, and tugged at the horse's reins to lead him along the narrow corridor. At first the horse pitched his head up and snorted and blew, pulling back, but after being forced along the first twenty or thirty feet into the darkness, he settled and came forward on his own.

We followed the soft sound of the Airedale's paws patting against dirt-covered rock and his breath resounding quietly ahead of us. The path grew steeper downward as we followed it, and I stopped long enough to pull an old shirt from our saddlebags, tear it into strips, and make a torch by wrapping it around the blade of the corn knife. I lit it and looked around the narrow crevice.

Smoke curled up and hovered in the point of the ceiling, drifting and spreading ever so slowly in both directions. We'd have to chance it, I thought, moving ahead and downward, following the dog, glancing up and back, knowing the posse would have an eye out for any sign of smoke in this bitter weather.

Walking farther down, I noticed a faint odor in the still air, and at first thought it to be the smell of the Airedale lingering behind him. But since I'd cleaned him up and clipped his fur, he hadn't smelled *that* bad. It was only when

196

we'd gone another twenty or so yards and the smell had grown worse that it dawned on me with a heart-surging chill. What I smelled was the terrible stench of the bear.

I stopped cold, and stood with the torchlight flickering on the narrow space before us. Somewhere ahead I could still hear the dog patting along steadily. I let out a breath, wiped a nervous hand across my brow, and ventured forward again. If the bear was somewhere in there, the dog would've already let me know it.

Settle down, I said to myself, looking all around. There was barely enough room for the horse to walk along through the crevice, let alone the big cumbersome grizzly.

But I remained cautious, even drawing Jack's pistol as the smell grew stronger. Ahead, I still heard the sound of the dog's heavy breath, although I no longer heard the sound of him walking. The horse pulled back slightly. "Easy, boy," I whispered. And I coaxed him forward until I saw two pair of eyes glowing red toward us in the darkness ahead.

I'd already cocked Jack's pistol and braced myself with it raised and aimed when I heard the whimper of the Airedale and the low growl of the Catahoula. "Come on out here, boys." I spoke quietly, and waited with the pistol aimed until the two of them came loping out of the darkness. Then I went forward again with the torch extended and noticed the crevice widen into a space the size of a small room. "This'll have to do."

I leaned once more against the wall and slumped down to the floor. The smell of the bear was strong here. Across the torchlit space, another passage led off into the darkness, this one wider, wide enough for the bear, I thought. He'd been here sometime recently. There was no doubt. Scattered bones and dried pieces of hide lay about the floor of the cavern. Large paw prints circled the small cavern and led off into the dark crevice on the other side.

But we were here now, men on the run; and I reminded myself that there was nothing the bear could do to us that was any worse than what the posse would do if they caught us. And catch us they certainly would if we didn't take refuge from the cold and the snow, rest the horse, get Jack back on his feet, and fight our way out of here.

197

The woman knew the way through this merciless country, and once she was rested I would follow her lead. The bear be damned from here on, if his path collided with ours.

The cavern floor was littered with twigs and bits of dried brush. Once I had Jack and the woman each wrapped in a blanket and leaning against the wall, I gathered up a small mound of debris and worked the torch into a low fire. The horse stayed skittish, so I took the remains of the torn-up shirt and blindered him with it. If the bear came, I wanted to be ready.

I had swallowed my fear of him and was ready to face him on any terms. Having fought him with gun, knife, brass knuckles, and boot heels, I would now fight him toe to toe with my bare hands if need be. But he would *not* take this shelter from us—not on this merciless night.

The split half of a boulder leaned near the crevice on the other side of the cavern. When I'd poured water from a canteen and set it to boil above the fire, for coffee and cooking water, I fashioned a draw hitch from the rope hanging from Jack's saddle and rigged it about the blindered horse. I led him over, hitched the end of the rope around the heavy rock, and set about the task of tipping the rock over in front of the opening.

The rock was easily twenty times my weight, but with the horse straining into the draw hitch and me shouldering with all my might, the rock finally toppled over with an earth-jarring thud. I crouched for a second as dust and chips of rock showered down from the ceiling. "What's going on there?" Jack's voice sounded weak across the cavern.

"Getting ready for the bear," I said, breathing hard. "Or the posse." I ran a hand over my brow. "Or both," I added. The temperature in the cavern, deep in the earth, was much higher than that of the frozen world outside. Now with the small fire doing its job, warmth spread through me like a lover's touch.

Smoke hovered above us in the darkness and seemed to seep slowly up into cracks in the rock ceiling. I dusted my hands, unhitched the horse, and looked at the split boulder across the opening. It only half covered the crevice. It wouldn't stop the big brute if he wanted in bad enough, but it would slow him down.

I fed the horse a handful of grain from our scarce supplies and checked the Airedale's wounded side, and when our food was ready we ate boiled beets, sipped coffee, and glanced constantly toward the opening across from us whether we intended to or not. Jack said he was feeling better. He sat up on his own near the fire with his arms crossed around his knees, still shivering from time to time, but coming around.

The woman had stirred long enough to get some hot food down, then checked her wound and rolled back up in the blanket on the dirt near the small fire.

The dogs flanked her, the Airedale stretched along one side close against her, the Catahoula wrapped in a ball on her other side with his muzzle across her leg, pointed across the cavern as if guarding by scent. Somewhere above us the world lay wrapped in a cold blanket of snow, but here, for now . . . we were safe.

"We might have to give ourselves up, Jack," I said just above a whisper.

Jack coughed. "Watch your language. You're talking out of your head again."

"No," I said. "Let's think about it. I don't mean give up and just let them cut our damned heads off. I mean give up, let them get us off this mountain, then make a break and get out of here."

"They ain't gonna fool around once they catch us, mi amigo." Jack's eyes looked into mine, searching. "These boys will drop us in a bag right off. They won't take a chance on us getting away from them. Why should they?" He shook his head and coughed against his fist. "No. They've got no reason to keep us alive."

"But I can give them a reason," I said, "if they'll just hear me out. We've got thirty thousand dollars, Jack. It'll buy us out, or at least keep us alive till we can find an opening. Surely to goodness I can talk them into wanting the money."

He shook his head again. "No. The ole *I've-got-money-hidden-near-here* trick won't work on these boys. They've heard it all before."

"Yeah, but they've already seen a thousand dollars flying on the breeze. That's pretty convincing to start with. Once I

199

get their greed working, who knows what it'll conjure up for us. Greed is a killer, Jack. We both know it." I stared at him across the flicker of the low flames.

A silence passed. Then he said quietly, "I know I've let ya down this time, but it ain't because I—"

"No, Jack." I cut him off. "You've never let me down. You've come up sick. It was just the luck of the draw. I don't hold none of it against ya. You oughta know that."

"Yeah." He let out a ragged breath. "I don't know what the hell has come over me. I feel like I've been gut-shot with a load of rattlesnake venom." He reached a hand up and wiped his head. "It comes and goes. I can't seem to shake it."

"Well—" I nodded toward the woman. "—she said at first it was some kind of fever. But then she said she wasn't sure. Whatever it is, it's gonna kill ya if we don't get you out of this weather and get you treated."

"Still, I can't see us giving ourselves up. It ain't our nature. Everybody we know will talk ill of us if word ever got around."

I grinned slightly. "We won't do it unless it comes down to the last straw. But I want ya to know that if it happens, it's just to get us a break. I won't really give up . . . so long as there's a move left in the game. The money's buried in a safe place. As long as we've got it, I figure we've got a chance."

"Then whatever play you make, I'll back it," he said; and he leaned back against the wall, his voice sounding tired once more from just setting up and talking awhile. I watched him turn sideways and tug his hat brim down over his eyes. In a second his body shivered, then settled as he drifted off to sleep.

At some time while we'd talked, the woman had rolled in her blanket, and she lay facing me now, her dark eyes studying me closely, so closely that I realized she'd listened to every word Jack and I had said. I took sharp note of it and cocked my head slightly.

"What? What's on your mind?" I asked her, then waited for her reply. I saw something at work behind her dark eyes, yet after a second of silence passed, she only drew the blanket snug around her and turned back to the fire. There

200

was not a whisper of sound from the world outside the cavern.

The bear came suddenly in the middle of the night, his heavy breath and deep voice awakening me, along with the low growl of the dogs, who'd taken a stand on either side of the low fire. I'd only dozed, knowing he would come, and when I heard him moving closer and closer, slowly toward us down the opening behind the overturned boulder, I snapped the blanket from across me and stood up drawing Jack's pistol from my hip. "Jack! He's here, wake up."

Jack staggered to his feet. The woman sat up. I stepped over and snatched the reins to the horse and pulled him quickly over near the fire. I handed Jack the reins as the horse nickered and shook his head, the blinder still over his face, but all his other senses tuned to the coming bear. "Keep him settled," I said to Jack, seeing the horse pull against his grip. Jack swayed, his strength still lacking.

"Got him," he said.

"We must flee from here," said the woman, struggling to her feet. I helped her up and over to the wall beside Jack.

"We ain't going nowhere," I said with finality, and she stared into my eyes in the glow of the low flames.

"You've gone mad! You cannot fight the bear, not here! Not in his den!"

"Then he better stay the hell away, ma'am."

The dogs had dropped down low on their front paws, their hackles high. Their growl had turned into a snarl. They stalked slowly toward the opening in the wall. Jack grabbed my arm as I started over behind them. "Turn me loose, Jack," I said. "I've backed as far as I'm going to, damn it to hell!"

"Think about what you're doing." He stifled a cough.

"I'm through thinking. We ain't had a break from nowhere ever since we hit this mountain." I shook free from his weak grasp. "I've had it, Jack! And I ain't being chased out in the cold by no *damnable* stinking bear!"

"Stop him," the woman said to Jack.

"Here, take the horse into the crevice," I heard him reply to her. His footsteps scraped behind me as I stalked forward behind the dogs with the pistol raised and cocked. "Don't

201

fire that pistol in here!" I heard the urgency in Jack's voice and I glanced up at the pointed ceiling of rock. Deep cracks ran in more directions than an Arkansas road map. "You'll bring the mountain down on us!"

"Get in the crevice with her and the horse," I shouted to him over my shoulder; and I continued on, seeing the outline of a big shaggy head hovering back and forth above the overturned rock. The dogs darted in and out from the rock, snarling, barking, spinning in a circle.

"Hear that, *bear?*" I shouted like a wild man, aiming the pistol at a big paw that reached over the rock and felt back and forth for the snapping dogs, like a blind man searching out his demons in the dark. "One *shot,* and we'll all sleep here together from now on!"

"Come on," Jack said to the woman. "Let's get the horse in there. He's gone plumb over the edge—we'll have to let him work it out."

I felt the pistol buck in my hand. The sound of it seemed to shake the whole cavern. Bits of rock sprayed close to the bear's paw. He slung it back and forth and let out a bawl. The dogs jumped back, but only for a second, then charged toward the rock again as I recocked the pistol. Dust and flecks of rock streamed from a crack in the ceiling. I saw the big rock across the opening come forward an inch, heard the bear grunt against the other side of it.

"We're in for a night of it, you and me," I yelled at the bear. "We ain't leaving . . . you ain't staying!" I stepped forward, fanned dust from before me and aimed the pistol above the rock into the darkness beyond. "So come to daddy, you big dirty bastard!"

PART IV

COLD
ENDEAVOR

CHAPTER

17

—————•❖•—————

Fear had caused something to snap inside me the day I'd faced the bear and dropped my rifle on the open stretch of plains. Seeing him kill my horse, seeing what he'd done to the man who'd staggered up and begged me to kill him, and knowing that the same fate awaited me in a matter of seconds—all these things had caused my finger to turn numb and go limp on the trigger. I had discarded the rifle and run, run like a rabbit.

But now something else snapped inside me as I stood there in the falling dust and the low flickering firelight, yelling like a wild man at a giant monster.

"Come on out!" I raged, no longer fearing the bear. Fear had given way to white-hot anger. My mind, nerves, and body tittered on a thin wire above a deep abyss, teased to a high jittering pitch by the constant siege of the weather, the encroachment of the posse, and the impending horror of the beast.

Behind me, the horse nickered in fright from within the narrow crevice. Jack called out to me, but his words had no meaning. I only stood there rigid, breathing hard and deep, a stream of dust showering down onto my hat brim. The cavern trembled beneath my feet.

"That's it, *big boy,*" I called out to the bear, as the rock slid forward. "Push it, you big bastard! You can do it! I *knooowww* you can!" The dogs bellowed, darted in and out at the split boulder as a big paw reached around it, swiping long claws at them. I called the dogs back but they didn't respond. They bounded back and forth, stirring a swirl of dust, their teeth glistening, spittle flying.

I let out a loud whistle. They cocked their ears. "Get back here! Let him out!" They charged in once more; I whistled again. This time they backed off grudgingly, back to me, turning, glancing up at me, perhaps wondering, as Jack had, if I'd surely lost my mind. "That's it! Stay back here! Let him come!" Now I talked to the dogs as if we spoke the same language.

The Catahoula started to bolt forward when the bear rounded from behind the rock, but I stomped a foot and waved the dog behind me with the pistol barrel. The Airedale followed him, backing along, hackles still raised, still growling toward the bear. "Call them in there," I shouted over my shoulder to Jack. "Give this bear some room."

"No!" Jack yelled. *"You* get in *here,* before he rips your head off!"

"Call them in, Jack! I'm not running from this bastard anymore."

I turned and faced the grizzly from twenty feet, the pistol raised and cocked. He stretched upward on his hind legs with his arms opened wide, his big claws spread; and he slung his head back and forth, bawling long and deep. The cavern seemed to shiver with the sound of him. But I stayed fixed, and when he'd finished slinging his head he looked back at me, as if surprised that I was still there.

"Remember me, bear?" I said in a low tone. "The one you chased up a tree?" I started to pull the trigger, but I stopped myself when I saw him drop onto all fours and take a step sideways and back. He turned back facing me and cocked his head curiously, like a lapdog. Then he seemed to ease down. He looked about the cavern and scratched a big paw in the dirt. Behind me, the Catahoula growled from within the narrow crevice. "Keep them quiet, Jack," I said.

"Get, your, *crazy ass,* in here," I heard Jack say, slicing his words low.

206

The bear rose slightly as if ready to let out another loud bawl, but then he seemed to change his mind, and dropped back down. I lowered the pistol a bit and took a step back. I saw where one of his flews was cut deep, still swollen from me nailing him with the brass knuckles. His right paw was matted and dark with dried blood. I took another slow step back.

"Yeah, that's right, you remember me. I'm the one did it." He stepped sideways, then, grumbling and blowing, lumbered back and stopped beside the overturned rock.

He swayed back and forth, then stuck his nose forward and let out another long bawl. Dust streamed once more from the ceiling. A breathless silence fell about the cavern save for the steady bellow of the bear's breath and the slight crackle of the low fire behind me. I felt myself ease down, and felt my trouser legs flutter against my trembling knees—residue of the fear I no longer felt, or no longer acknowledged.

"Now get the hell out of here," I said to the bear, under my breath. Behind me, the horse nickered and thrashed in his reins. Jack spoke low and soothing, to settle it. Above, I heard a terrible cracking sound shoot across the ceiling. Dust streamed.

I backed slowly to the narrow crevice behind me and stepped into it as the Catahoula sniffed at my legs and boots. Both dogs were still worked into a frenzy. They trembled and bounced in place. I glanced back at Jack and the woman. They'd led the horse deeper back, and they stood there, squeezed together in the darkness in a wall of rock. "What's he doing out there?" Jack asked me in a weak voice.

I looked out and across at the bear, standing there swaying, grumbling, and tossing his big head back and forth. "Nothing, Jack. Evidently he ain't used to folks standing up to him that way. I think he remembers me busting him in his nose."

"You *what?*"

"Yeah," I said over my shoulder in a hushed tone. "The other day when he treed me. I belted him a couple good whacks, just to let him know I meant business." I couldn't help but feel a little cocky, having faced the bear off and

207

giving him no ground. I took a deep breath and loosened my neck.

"You never mentioned it to me." Jack's voice was as hushed as mine.

"You was too feverish at the time. Besides, you wouldn't have believed it anyway, would you?"

I didn't hear him answer, and after a second I looked back over my shoulder, barely seeing either of them in the distant reach of firelight. Jack had slumped against the wall beside the woman. She looked back at me and shook her head slowly. "He is still very sick," she said quietly. "I do not understand what is wrong with him."

"But I'm getting better," Jack said in a faint reply. I heard him cough. "Just weak, is all," he added. "Thought I heard you say you . . . popped that bear in the mouth . . ."

"I did say it."

"Sure . . ." His voice faded.

Across the cavern in the flicker of light, I saw the bear back around the rock and fade into the darkness behind it. "He's leaving," I whispered over my shoulder, letting out a tense breath. I reached down and nudged the Airedale forward with the toe of my boot. "All right, boys, he's all yours. Go get yourselves some bear."

The dogs shot out of the narrow crevice and streaked through the dim firelight. In seconds we heard their voices echoing back to us from deep within the other passageway. Above them, we heard the long bawl of the bear.

"He will come back," the woman said behind me. "Do not trust this beast. Do not think you have won anything from him just because he has left. He will come back. He always comes back."

I turned before stepping out of the narrow crevice and saw the flicker of firelight glow in her dark eyes. "We'll keep an eye out for him," I said, "but we ain't leaving till we're damn good and ready."

We rested without sleep throughout the remainder of the night, huddled near the crevice, the woman keeping the horse's reins in her hand, Jack wrapped in a blanket, leaning against the wall. He shivered now and then, coughing a deep convulsing cough that drew his body into a tight ball until the tremor passed. Watching him there, I wondered for the first time if he might actually *die* from his illness. *What the hell is it?* I studied him closely as he shivered and turned restlessly. If not some terrible fever like the woman said . . . *then what the hell is it?*

We had no way of knowing when the night had ended, cradled as we were deep in the bowels of the mountain. But after a long period of time had passed, the woman crushed the remainder of the coffee beans with a small rock, and we sipped hot coffee in silence. When we'd finished, we gathered the blankets and the horse and ventured back through the narrow crevice to the white cold world outside.

The dogs had not returned throughout the night. I wondered if the bear had killed them. I commented on it as we neared the sliver of light at the mouth of the crevice.

"As well as they know this bear's stomping ground," Jack said, "they might've all got tired and bedded down together." His voice sounded stronger than it had in days.

"Feeling better?" I asked him. We felt the first sharp bite of cold air drifting into the crevice. Beyond the entrance, sunlight sparkled on snowcapped pine and aspen.

"Yep," he said. "Whatever I had, I think it's gone. If it was some kinda *killing* fever, it must've got tired of killing me and went away."

I nodded, let out a breath and handed him his pistol from my waist. "Here," I said, "it's about time you started earning your keep." I glanced at the woman and saw her watching Jack closely, apparently not convinced that he was past his illness. "How about you, ma'am? Feeling any better?"

She looked at me and nodded, then stepped forward and pointed out across the rise and fall of jagged mountain line. "We must make it to the south pass today and get through it. From there you can drop down to Elk Horn, and I will go up to Lodge Pole and get my son."

"How far are we talking about?" I looked at her.

"Twenty miles, perhaps more. But once we get through there is a settlement there. You can get fresh horses, and get away."

"Pretty rough traveling in this snow," I said, gazing out beside her.

"But we must make it today. If the big storm comes and

closes off the pass . . . we will die there." She stopped and looked at each of us as if to make sure we understood the gravity of her words.

I looked up and out across a clear still sky, and started to say that there could be no storm coming behind such a picture-perfect day, but I reminded myself of where we were, and that the weather here was as unpredictable as the bear.

"Then we best get started." I reached out a hand and helped her up onto the horse.

Our tracks from the night before had vanished beneath the layer of fresh snow. I hated laying down fresh tracks for the posse to find, but there was nothing we could do about it. If the posse was still behind us, all we could do from here on was make a hard push to the pass the woman had mentioned and hope to get through it before they caught up to us. *Twenty miles,* I said to myself, taking the horse's reins and leading him out into the snow as Jack stepped around me and down along the narrow path among snow-covered rocks.

Fifty yards down the path we came upon the tracks of the bear amid a circling crisscross of paw prints made by the dogs on his trail. The tracks cut across our path, and I followed them off a few yards to make sure the bear was headed well away from us. Then I walked back to Jack and the woman where they waited.

Steam swirled in my breath. "They might've come through here any time during the night . . . could be miles away by now."

Jack's pistol was out and half raised as he squinted, scanning the snow in blinding sunlight. "I'd like it better if the dogs were close by." He rubbed his eyes and looked at me. "Of course, if the bear comes back, I figure you'll just bust him in the nose and run him off."

"You don't believe I really did that, do ya?" I narrowed a gaze at him. He chuckled, and coughed slightly against his fist. I felt my face redden and added, "But it's the damn truth. I ain't saying I stood nose to nose and slugged it out with him. He had me trapped and it was the only move I could make, so I made it." I shrugged. "Ain't that the same as anybody else would do?" I glanced at the woman, but she looked away.

210

"While you had him whipped," Jack said, "I wish you'd thought to tell him we wanted our rifles back. They'd come in pretty handy today."

"You really *are* feeling better, ain't ya, Jack." I shook my head and trudged on.

By noon we'd reached the bottom of the narrow path with neither a glimpse nor a sound of the dogs or the bear. The woman sat the horse while Jack and I stepped onto the snowshoes and tied the straps around our boots. We were sheltered by an upthrust boulder, and beyond it lay a low stretch of open ground between this rise of mountain and the next. Nothing stirred on the stretch of land save for the shadow of a hawk that swung down in a slow circle, then batted up and across a mountain ridge and vanished into sunlight.

"If I was that posse," Jack said, looking up as he tied the leather straps around his boots, "I'd lay up along them ridges somewhere and wait till I saw us crossing here . . . then pick us off, wouldn't you?"

I thought about it a second, scanning the land from within the shadow of the boulder. Sunlight glistened. "Yeah, you're right. They could see anything that moves from atop the ridges. Once we get about half across, we'll make easy targets for their rifle scopes."

A silence passed; then Jack said, "So, what do you think?"

I looked up at the woman. "Any other way across there, ma'am?"

"None that would take less than two days," she replied. She nodded off to our right at a towering peak. "Over there is the only other pass, but even in good weather it is difficult." She shook her head slowly. "With the big storm still coming, we would never make it through."

"Ma'am," I asked, finishing with my snow shoes, "is there any chance the *big* storm won't come? Is there any way that maybe—"

"It always comes," she said, cutting me off.

"All right then," I said, rocking back and forth on the snowshoes. "We'll try to hug the shadows as much as we can . . . stay close to some rock cover in case we get fired on."

211

"Why don't I take a position," Jack said. "I can slip down, get around the edge somewhere and keep an eye on the ridges till you two get across."

I scanned the high ridgelines, judging the distance, and shook my head. "No good," I said. "Without a rifle, it'd be a waste of time."

"You'd be surprised what I could do with a pistol once I got it fixed in . . . maybe drop a couple rounds down on them."

"Forget it, Jack." I stepped forward, took my pistol from my holster beneath my coat, and shoved it into my coat pocket. "If they come out on us we'll fight them across the open ground. Other than that, we just cut straight across here and take our chances."

"Damn it, I hate this weather," I heard him say, stepping up behind me. "Next hiding out I do is gonna be on the southern shores somewhere . . . on a *beach.*"

Our only cover, I thought, pressing across the sloping flatland, would be the blinding glare of sunlight across the fresh snow. But halfway across the three-mile stretch, as if my thinking had caused it, the sky once more took a dark turn. A streak of gunmetal gray moved in from across the mountain peaks and dampered the sunlight like a wet blanket.

"Is this . . . is this the *big* one coming in?" I asked her in a rasping voice as a wind began to whip across the land, spinning up snow devils. She looked away without answering, perhaps noting the bitter tone in my voice, as if somehow she could be held accountable for the weather. I trudged forward five yards behind Jack, one hand pulling the horse's reins, the other holding my coat closed at the collar.

We pressed on, hard and steady against the wind as snow swirled up and stung our faces. Behind me, the horse struggled through the snow, his head arched to the wind and his frosted mane blown across his eyes like a veil. At any second we expected the bark of rifles from the higher ridges, yet we reached the other side of the sloping stretch of land without incident. And once inside the shelter of jagged rock,

212

the woman slipped down from the saddle and huddled with us out of the swirling snow.

The horse hugged close to a large boulder, out of the wind, and shook out his mane, blowing and scraping a hoof on the cold ground. Steam puffed in his breath. He staggered in place.

"This country is cursed," I said, breathing heavy, slapping my hat against my leg as the three of us squatted down. "I've never seen such damnable, godforsaken weather in my life."

The woman looked around at us, and at the horse, then lowered her eyes. "The horse is blown, and will not make it unless he rests. But we must go on. To stop now is to die. The storm will close the pass by tonight."

"I ain't leaving him here to freeze and die, ma'am. We'll lead him till he drops . . . then we'll shoot him." I shook my head. "But we brought him here. I ain't walking off from him as long as there's a chance he'll make it."

"If we do not reach the pass before it closes," she said, "we will have to *eat* him to keep from starving."

I pushed myself to my feet, staggered on the snowshoes, and steadied myself with a hand against a cold boulder. "Then we best keep moving." I looked around at the stretch of land we'd just crossed. Our tracks showed clearly, leading to us through the lifting, swirling snow. "I wonder what's happened to that posse," I said quietly. "And the dogs . . . and the bear too for that matter."

Jack pushed himself to his feet, then reached down and helped the woman up. "They've all got better sense than to be traipsing around out here."

I looked at him as I raised my collar and reached for the horse's reins. "No rest for the wicked, huh?"

He grunted without answering, hiked his collar, and he and the woman turned and started upward into a maze of snowcapped rock.

CHAPTER

18

---•---

We pushed on, all three of us walking now, the woman seeming to be drawn toward the distant pass by some uncanny instinct, undeterred by the blinding snow, or by her wounds, still fresh and sore, mending beneath the ragged blanket and her doeskin dress. Jack and I led the horse in turn, both of us knowing that with no more supplies than we had left—a handful of dry fire kindling and a few coffee beans—we'd just as well carry them ourselves. Pulling the horse along was becoming more and more of a burden on us. More than that, it was becoming a hazard.

That which could not keep up—be it man or lesser animal—must be left behind, given over to what predatory element had brought about its condition, be that the hand of its natural enemy, the hand of God, or the conjured forces of hell. Death of the weakened, a fact of survival. While men like Jack and myself had long since chosen to live by such fact, it was not of our creation, but rather that by which all mankind had lived since the beginning, I thought—whether we chose to or not.

I spit, ran a coat sleeve across my cold mouth, and forced myself on. There was no reason to keep the exhausted animal with us, unless perhaps, as the woman had said, *for food,* if we found ourselves snowbanked. I knew it, *of course*

KILLERS OF MAN

I knew it, but I wasn't ready to admit it. Even in our desperate circumstances, there was something about giving up one of our own—albeit a dumb animal—that I could not abide. *It won't come to that,* I thought; then I pushed the thought from my mind and tried to think of it no more.

We took turns wearing the snowshoes, and with the wind whipping our faces, Jack and I followed the woman's tracks. We only glanced up at her now and then as she struggled along, less than fifteen feet ahead, but still barely visible in the gray-white swirl. It was drawing dark when I saw her falter a step to the side and slump against a large boulder. I trudged up to her, seeing her sling a foot back and forth to loosen built-up snow from her snowshoe.

"What's wrong?" I asked, shouting close to her face above the roar of wind.

"Nothing is wrong." She raised a forearm and shielded her brow with an edge of the blanket around her. She nodded ahead of us as she swooned and almost fell. "There is the pass. We made it."

"Thank God." I cradled her arm in mine and helped her stand as Jack came leading the horse up to us. Ahead of us in the swirl, a yawning mouth in a wall of rock beckoned as if it had been waiting for us. "It's the pass, Jack," I yelled, "we made it." Then I asked the woman, "How far, to get through it?"

"Less than two miles." Her voice was weak as she strained above the wind. "But we must not stop until we are at the other end. It will not be open long." She rubbed a snowshoe back and forth in the fresh powder of snow. "Soon this will become heavy . . . spill down from the crevices, and close it off."

"Don't worry. We'll make it now." I turned loose of her arm, and she sank down and rested while Jack took off his snowshoes and gave them to me. When I'd finished putting them on, I took the reins and led the horse; and I followed Jack into the narrow pass.

Fifty yards into the shelter of high jagged walls, we felt the wind lessen against us. I breathed easier. The snow still fell heavy, but was no longer stinging our faces and pressing us back. Farther along, a deep whooshing sound exhaled behind us, and we turned in time to see a billowing cloud of

215

snow roll down from between two crevices and spill across the pass. "Good," I said. "If they even *find* our tracks at all, they'll never make it through here come morning."

I realized just how true my words were when we stopped another hundred yards ahead and looked at the five-foot drift of snow before us. "There will be more ahead of us," the woman said. "That is why we cannot stop . . . not even for a second." She looked at the horse, then back at me. I saw what she was thinking.

"No," I said. "I ain't leaving him. I'll get him through it. We'll *all* make it."

She only nodded, and together we hand-shoveled our way through the drift and continued on, the fresh powder growing thicker against our feet, the cold of night closing around us. Darkness set in, and twice more we struggled through spilled drifts, each one deeper than the one before, each one taking more of our strength. But when we'd struggled through the last one, I led the horse out behind Jack and fell over against a leaning boulder. Snow tumbled down and around me, but I brushed it away.

"Now we seek shelter," I heard the woman say, gasping beside Jack. All that showed clearly in the dark was the steam of our breath and the faintest sheen of our eyes. Ahead in the clouded glow of the moon, the snow-covered world looked like a calm and endless sea. The wind had all but stopped, but the snow still fell, the flakes growing larger, heavier, falling slower now, and seeming to build up around us where we stood.

I gasped for air, slid down the boulder, leaned back and squatted there for a second with my arms across my knees. "So . . . we made it." I looked at the dark outline of Jack, saw his breath billowing.

"We made it to here," he said; and I felt his hand close around my forearm and try to raise me to my feet. "Work don't stop at sundown. You heard the lady. Now we've gotta find shelter."

I felt light-headed and I resisted him pulling me up. "Wait," I said. "Let me sit here a minute. Just . . . just give me one minute here. . . ."

"Can't. Don't have a minute for ya," he said, and he

216

pulled harder. "Come on. You know better than to stop out here."

This time I came up, staggering. "Damn it . . ." But I knew he was right. To stop here was to die here. So I trudged forward, pulling the horse along. "Come on, horse, before they get out the silverware on us."

"I'm hungry enough to," Jack said in a rasping voice. "So don't make jokes."

"Which one, me or the horse?" I staggered forward, my voice faint and breathless.

"Whichever of you falls first," he said. "So keep moving."

The woman led us another thirty yards, around a turn of high rock and along a narrow edge which was no more than a foot deep in snow, owing to the direction of the day's wind. We stopped at an inlet of rock, and I hitched the horse's reins around a jagged edge and followed Jack and the woman as they crawled under an overhang that reached back a mere five or six feet out of the weather.

"It'll do," I said, rising up on my elbows and glancing around as Jack struck a match and held it up. There was not enough room to sit all the way up, not without scraping our heads against the dirt-crusted ceiling. But it was shelter—shelter long overdue; and I brushed aside a long brittle snakeskin with my hand and said, "I'll get kindling off the horse and build a fire."

We spent the night huddled together beneath the overhang and awoke cold in the morning. The kindling fire had lasted no longer than an hour, just long enough to partly thaw the frozen airtight of beets and brew up the last of the coffee beans. Now the fire was nothing but a black spot streaked with snow at the edge of the overhang. The heat of our bodies had saved us.

Through a slit of sunlight glistening between the ceiling of rock and the drift of snow across the opening, I saw the horse's legs step back and forth slowly. His muzzle lowered and steamed against the snow. He blew out a breath.

"Time to go," I said, easing the woman off my chest, my voice sounding strange and hollow there beneath a mountain of rock and snow. They both stirred from their sleep. The woman moaned. I rubbed my cold hands together and

217

belly-crawled to the opening. With my hat over my hand, I shoved away the drift of snow and brushed it back and forth. Then I crawled out, like some creature of the wilds who was born to this harsh existence and had known no other. Behind me, Jack grunted, crawling and scraping across the dirt.

I stood up squinting against the sunlight, rubbing my eyes, and looked out across the land a hundred feet below us. Pine and aspen swayed gently, their boughs thick with snow, limbs drooping from the weight of it. The sky was clear and blue, wavering in the morning sun.

"Jesus," I whispered. "We made it, Jack." I let out a breath and reached down to help him stand up as he crawled out. "We beat Dan Silks at his own game."

"I could eat a polecat," he said, struggling to his feet. He brushed himself off and reached back down, helping the woman up.

"We'll try to find you one." I'd started feeling better now in the glow of sunlight. With my hat, I slapped snow off the horse's mane, and unspun his reins. "We'll have to get this ole boy fed too. Now that we're out here and the posse's stuck back there wondering where it all went wrong, I reckon we can—"

My words were cut short by a ricochet off the rock wall, followed by the sharp bark of a rifle from below us. The horse reared high. *"Get down!"* I yelled, shoving the woman into Jack as he helped her stand. He threw an arm around her and fell with her. A shot thumped the wall where he'd stood. I dropped straight down, barely missing the horse's thrashing hoofs.

He reared again, nickered loud. Then the nicker turned into a scream as he slammed against the wall beside me and fell wallowing in snow. Blood spewed from his neck and splattered my face.

Jack yelled, *"Come on!"* He crawled along the edge of the narrow path, upward, dragging the woman by one arm. More shots pounded against the wall above our heads. Snow exploded in a spray of dirt and rock. I snatched my pistol out, fired two wild shots down the steep slope beneath us, rolled quickly across the dying horse and raced, crawling and scrambling, behind Jack along the upward path.

Jack and the woman rolled behind an ice-covered rock. A shot ricocheted off it, and in a second I rolled up against them. "How the hell did they get in front of us!" It wasn't a question; it was a curse.

"It don't matter *how!*" Jack's voice billowed in steam. "They *did it,* damn it! Just when I was starting to feel better." Two more shots slapped against the wall, one behind us, one ahead. They couldn't see us now. They were feeling for us, trying to flush us out. I glanced around quickly. The path ended into the wall less than thirty feet ahead. From there, there was nothing to do but climb hand over hand to a ledge twenty feet up.

I felt my stomach draw tight. Another rifle shot pinged off the wall. "Is there a way out of here if we make that climb?" I spoke to the woman, gesturing upward with my pistol barrel.

She glanced up, then back to me. "We cannot climb it. They will kill us—"

"Not *us,* ma'am," I said. "We're gonna have to leave you here now. You'll be all right, just tell them you had no choice. Say we made you come with us."

"No, you cannot make that climb!" She strained against Jack's grasp. "Don't you see they are ready for—"

"Sorry, ma'am," he said. "We're going . . . you're staying. If they see you climbing with us, they'll shoot you." Two more shots pounded the wall.

"But you won't have a chance. They'll kill you."

Jack shot me a glance, then back to her. "Ma'am, we've had our run at it. If this is the end . . . we've been expecting it. We'd sooner go out this way than what they've got planned for us." His expression turned almost peaceful. "Thanks for all your help. You'll be okay here till it's over."

The rifles had stopped. She looked at him, then nodded and slumped back against the snowcapped rock.

"Crowe-crowe-rowe—owe." A voice echoed up from the bottom of the steep slope. "We've got you, got-you, got-you-you-you, pinned-pinned-pinned-inned. . . ." There was a pause while the echo leveled out; then the voice added, "Give it up, give-it-up-give-it-up. . . ." I thought I heard a muffled laugh, and then the voice added, "We'll give ya a hot meal first, hot-meal-first-meal-first-meal-first. . . ."

I looked at Jack with a wry smile. "You can't beat that, now can ya."

"Don't even ask," he said quietly. "We both know what's waiting down there for us." He rolled the cylinder of his pistol down his coat sleeve, then spun it, cocked it, let out a breath, and said, "Ready when you are, mi amigo."

Again the voice echoed up. "Well, Crowe-crowe-rowe. What say you, say-you-say-you . . . ?"

I peeped around the rock, down across the slope, saw nothing, then said as I checked my pistol, "Are you Dan Silks, Dan-Silks-Dan-silks . . . ?"

"That's right, I am, am-am-am. . . ."

I looked at Jack, saw him rise up, braced and ready. He nodded; and I turned and yelled out down the slope, "Then fuck you, Dan, fuck-you-dan-fuck-you . . . !"

Rifles exploded. I sprang forward, upward along the path.

"Just *had* to piss him off first, didn't ya." Jack was almost grinning, firing alongside me, both of us half crawling, half running the last few feet to the end of the path. We dove behind a rock while bullets showered us with snow and flecks of dirt. I looked back and saw the woman watching us. Farther down the path, the horse had stopped thrashing, its blood spread thick beneath it, red and steaming in the fresh snow.

Snatching bullets from my belt and reloading, I said, breathing hard, "I always hoped I could get the last word on a son of a bitch like Silks when this time came." The rifles volleyed, then lulled, then volleyed again.

Jack snapped his pistol shut and cocked it. "Sounds like you're worried here . . . like you figure we're dead."

I cocked my pistol, moving around beside him. "I think it's a pretty good bet we are. Don't you?"

He managed to raise his arm over the rock, snapped off two shots, then dropped back down. A shot ricocheted and hissed away above us. "Naw, hell, we'll be all right. It's still early. You've got to learn to think better thoughts."

"Bullshit." I snapped two shots around the side of the rock and dropped back before they got an aim on me. "I heard how you was just talking to her."

"That was just for her benefit. So she wouldn't do something stupid—so she would stay put and not try to tag along." He popped up, fired once and dropped. "I figure I can cover you till you get up there. Then you cover me. Then . . . why *hell,* we'll just be off and out of here, right?" Steam bellowed in his breath.

I snatched more bullets from my belt. Rifles pounded. "Yeah, right," I said, glancing around quickly, shaking my head. "The odds are all in our favor. We're holding the high ground."

I thought about the money hidden back along the snow-covered trail, saw it turning to dust over time, and pictured Cousin Jesse always wondering what became of it. "But if you make it and I don't, tell Jesse I *blew* all that money playing poker, will ya?" I looked into his eyes behind a swirl of breath. "Just so he won't go around—"

"We're getting out of this." He cut me off. "So be careful you don't go saying things you'll be embarrassed about later on." He reached over and took my pistol from my hand. "Now get on up there. I've got ya covered."

The rifles volleyed hard and fast as I rolled across the three feet of snow between the rock and the wall. Then I crouched low against the wall, hesitated for a second until the rifles lulled, and snuck a look up at the hand-over-hand climb awaiting me. Cracks zigzagged, bulged with lines of snow. A jut of rock stuck out above me four feet up, and higher up a scrub of drooping snowcapped brush. Would it hold if I grabbed on to it? At the crest of the ledge a mantle of snow hung perilously, sagging out and down like thick cake icing. How deep would I have to plunge into it to get a hold? Or would it fall first, take me down with it—

"Are you going, or not?" Jack's voice was a low hiss. I looked around, saw him crouched against the rock with a pistol in each hand, his thumbs holding the hammers back. He shot me a tight glance. Rifles pounded hard.

"Yeah," I said, and I waited, listening for the rifles to relent for just a second—just long enough for me to make a leap. "Jack," I said, lowering my voice, sensing my move. I ventured up two inches. "I'm glad you're feeling better."

"Shiiiit." He turned away; and I caught a glimpse of him throwing both pistols out arm's length over the rock, firing as I made my lunge.

Toe over toe, hand over hand I clawed, leaping upward

221

the way the bear had climbed the tree. From one crack to the next, barely stopping long enough to get a firm hold. I streaked up along the jagged wall like a fleeing lizard. Snow spilled around me, above and beneath me, showering out in a white mist. Bullets thumped inches from my face. I bolted on up, a man no longer believing in gravity, no longer climbing a steep wall, but rather, running crouched, low on all fours, up across slick, rocky ground.

I heard a crashing sound above me and saw the mantle break loose; but I only hugged tight against the wall for a second, my hand clenched around the scrub of brush as a heavy pile of snow collapsed on my head and pulled at my back on its way over me. Chunks of ice streamed past me and down my back, pelting me like stones and daggers. Then I was moving up again, hearing the rifles and knowing that by now Jack would be having to reload.

Jesus! My hat had fallen away. Ice and snow filled my coat collar, my boot wells. I could not see, lost in that spinning white mist, snow streaming down and blanketing me. But neither could the riflemen. Their bullets struck blindly, near but getting no nearer. A stone broke loose beneath my foot, and I swung for a split second by one hand before finding footing and scrambling on. There was no pistol fire from Jack beneath me. A bad sign. But in another second my arm swung over the edge where the mantle had fallen, and I dug my fingers into cold rock and earth, heaving myself up and over it with one final, desperate burst of strength.

CHAPTER

19

———•———

Rifle shots whistled past me when I went up over the edge. Rolling over in a swirl of snow and ice, it took me a second to realize that I was still *alive* and that maybe Jack was right, we were going to make it after all! Stretched out atop the ledge, I lay there gasping, blinking my eyes at the clear sky above me. All I had to do was have Jack pitch the pistols up to me, and I'd cover him. *All right, all right.* I turned over in the snow and scuttled back to the edge.

A trickle of warm blood ran down my forehead. I swiped a hand across it and called down to Jack, "Throw me up the pistols!"

He didn't answer. The land below had fallen still and quiet. I peeped cautiously down over the edge, still wiping my hand across my wet forehead. "Come on, pitch the pistols up here!" I yelled, knowing that at any second the rifles would start pounding us again. *For godsakes, Jack, come on!*

But when I looked down at Jack all I saw was his right arm sticking out of a pile of snow and ice, lying lifeless across the top of the rock. I'd buried him in the wake of my frantic climb. His pistol had slid from his hand and turned sideways an inch from his outstretched fingers.

"Noooo, noo-noo-no-no-o . . . !" I heard my voice echo off across the valley, not even sounding like my voice at all

but like some wounded critter calling out a threat to heaven.

"It's over, Crowe, over-crowe-over-ver-er . . ." I heard the triumphant tone to Dan Silks' voice though I couldn't see him; and I glanced again at Jack's arm. It didn't move. The woman had stepped out to the edge of the path and spread her arms and raised them slightly. She turned her head and looked up at me as Dan Silks called out, "We got you, got-you-got-you-you-ou. . . ."

Stunned, confused, I jerked back from the edge and staggered to my feet, moving farther back. My hand was red with blood where I'd wiped it across my forehead. One of my boots had been pulled from my foot by the weight of the snow. *Not Jack! Jesus . . . not Jack.* I turned, swaying in a circle, trying to think. Maybe he was alive. If he was, I couldn't leave him to them . . . knowing what they'd do to him. *Rules of survival,* I thought. *Those who can't keep up must be left behind? But not when it comes to leaving Jack.* There were no rules here.

The vast land ahead of me seemed to spin and tilt, confusing me as I turned with my arms spread. I searched my mind quickly for a plan. *Plan! Think!* But nothing came. I heard the voice below calling up to me to give up, surrender, make it easy on myself, not mentioning at all that my head would soon be dropped into a coarse burlap sack. I pictured that gruesome scene, ran a few steps farther from the edge and stopped, my breath heaving, my heart thumping aloud. *Where to! Jesus! Where to?*

Before me lay a mile or more of snow swells covering rock slopes, ending against an upreaching line of mountains. Whatever passes led through the mountain were closed, swollen with last night's snow, the very snow that we'd counted on to close our route behind us. I had no gun, no food, no hat, no shelter, and I was on foot with one boot missing. I leaned down, my palms on my knees, and tried to breathe deep. There was also the big bear out there somewhere—couldn't forget about him. I slung my weary head back and forth. Blood dripped from my forehead and dotted the snow. I'd had it. There was only one move left to make—a hopeless, desperate one at that.

Turning, I limped slowly back to the edge with my arms

raised at my sides. I knew that for their purposes they could put a bullet through me, then come and get me; but to do so would mean climbing to the ledge like I'd just done, or else making a long ride around through snow-covered passes and search for a way up. *No,* I thought, *they're smart. They'll pitch up a rope, have me tie it off and climb down to them, deliver myself to them.* And why not? Where else was I going to go?

"You win, you-win-win-in," I called down, hearing the whipped tone of my voice echo. "Don't shoot, don't-shoot-shoot-hoot-oot."

Below me, below the path where Jack lay buried, and below the hundred-foot slope of rocky snow, the riflemen stepped out from around drooping aspen and pine and looked up with their rifles aimed and ready. Down on the path, the woman still stood with her arms raised the same as mine, and I thought that if there was a third one of us, we would look like the Holy Trinity from the valley below.

Within minutes all but one of them rounded into view up the narrow path, coming single file, stepping their horses along carefully. One remained below us with his rifle aimed at me, and a steady curl of steam drifting away from his face. He was the one I would have to worry about the most when I made my move.

My plan was to get down to the path, get my hands on one of the riflemen and take him over the edge with me. If I could do it quick enough, I could kill him while we tumbled down the rocks, get his gun, his boots too, hopefully, and go. *Where?* I had no idea, but even a bullet in the back beat what they had in mind for me.

"Throw me up a rope," I said down to the first rider. He stepped down from his horse, twenty feet below me, and looked up.

"Don't worry. We'll have your heathen hide down here lickety-split," he said, sounding like he was about to do me a great favor.

Kind of you, I thought, looking down, watching the top of his hat and the shoulders of his thick coat as he took the rope from his saddlehorn, uncoiled a couple of loops, and tied a spike in the end of it. Behind him, I heard the creak of cold leather as the others stepped down from their saddles.

One of them stepped over to the woman and had her lower her arms. She stared up at me. For some reason I felt embarrassed and couldn't return her gaze. I gazed instead out across the frozen land below, working my move out in my mind, stilling myself, resting, getting ready.

"Stand still up there till I tell you otherwise, or Ernie'll put a slug through your head, fair enough?"

"Sounds real fair," I said, still gazing out, hoping to see some sign of a trail or a break through the distant swells of snow. Below, I caught a glimpse of two men raking snow and ice off of Jack with their rifle butts. For some reason I couldn't look at him either, though I did catch sight of his arm as one of the men picked it up from the rock, held it, and pulled.

It took two throws before the rope came spiraling over the edge and landed across my feet. "Take some up and spike it down," said the voice, then added, "Careful, now," as I reached down for it. "Don't make no sudden moves. Keep one arm out where I can see it. Ernie gets nervous. Wouldn't want that, would ya?"

"No," I said, "I wouldn't want that." His voice chuckled below me; and I squatted down slowly with my left arm still raised, and dug away the snow until I saw the gray rock surface. When I got the spike stuck down a few inches into a narrow crack, I stood up and stomped it down, setting it firmly with my boot heel, my left arm still out and raised. "Good boy," he called up. "Now climb on down here, easy like."

"Want me to climb down with one hand, too," I said, my voice a bit wry.

"Don't be a smart aleck, now," he said. "The Lord frowns on a smart aleck. It'll get ya nowhere."

I nodded, thinking *What's the difference,* picked up the rope, tugged it a couple of times and stepped down over the edge. Struggling against the wall, I glanced down and saw the two men pull Jack from the snow and drop him back against the rock. Just as they took a step back, it appeared that his head turned slightly back and forth an inch, and his right hand seemed to twitch.

My God, I thought, did he just move, or was I just seeing

what I wanted to see? "Get on down," the voice said, seeing me hesitate against the wall. I took a deep breath, and let it out slowly. *There's the difference,* I thought, trying now to rethink everything quickly as I took another step down. If he's alive, it makes all the difference in the world.

I stalled at each step down the rock wall, glancing over at Jack, looking for any slight movement, any sign of life to tell me that my eyes hadn't played tricks on me before. If he was alive I had to change my plan. *What plan?* It was more like suicide. I wouldn't make a break for it if there was any chance in hell of saving Jack . . . although as it stood, there appeared to be little chance of even saving myself. "Come on, come on," said the voice. "It didn't take that long getting *up* there."

"I'm . . . I'm hurt bad here," I said, faking a weak voice and hugging close to the wall. "Think my skull's cracked."

He shook the rope, staring up at me from fifteen feet. "Come on, come on, or I'll shoot ya the rest of the way down. Makes no matter to me how a heathen dies."

"Okay, I'm coming," I said.

I stepped down again and stalled, fidgeted with the rope. If only I could see something from Jack, anything at all. Then, just as I took another step, I heard a low moan and heard one of the men say, "This rascal's still alive!"

"The hell you say," said another voice, and I leaned for a second against the wall and took a deep breath. *Okay!* Making a jump for it over the edge was out now. Now I had to give them a reason not to kill us, a reason to keep us alive long enough for Jack to get on his feet. *The money.* That was it. They'd seen a thousand dollars float down out of the pine tree the day the bear had me trapped. Surely I could get them interested in more. *Greed,* I thought. That's what I've got left to play with here.

I stepped the rest of the way down, clearing my head, thinking of what to say and how to say it. Playing it right was all that mattered now, timing it, reading their eyes, anticipating what they would think, smooth them out, talk to them just right. *Keep us alive,* I thought. As long as we were still breathing, there was always a way out. Jack moaned again. As I stepped off the wall, I caught a glimpse of him. His head was bowed, his chin against his chest, but he was turning his face back and forth. *Good enough.*

"Take a look, Crowe," said the voice beside me, turning me roughly toward Jack. "There's your partner you've killed. May the Lord have his vengeance on you."

I turned back slowly and noticed for the first time that the man was wearing wire-rimmed spectacles, the lenses as thick as shot glasses and streaked with steam. "He ain't my partner, I ain't Crowe, and you're all gonna hang for killing two innocent men here. You stupid bunch of pecker-heads."

Laughter rose from the others, but the one facing me snapped a hard right fist into my ribs and bent me double. "I won't tolerate profanity! God damn your hide!" Then his knee shot up into my face and knocked me back against the wall. I slumped down in the snow, not hurt as bad as I wanted it to appear.

"Hold up, Deacon," I heard another voice say. "I want to talk to this bird first. Maybe he's *not* Miller Crowe. He could be Jesse James himself."

"No. He's not Jesse," said the one who'd hit me. "Jesse wouldn't have given up and climbed down here to us like an egg-sucking dog." He shot me a sneer of contempt.

"Either way. I want to ask him about the rest of the gang. They've all got bounty on 'em. Let's find out what he can tell us."

"You heard him, boy," said the one who'd hit me. "Stand up here." He grabbed my shoulder and pulled me up, shaking me back and forth against the rock wall. "The man wants to talk to you."

"Easy, Deacon," the man chuckled. "He can't tell us much if you break his neck."

"His neck will get more than broke before this day's through. The Lord's vengeance will be wrought upon him."

I just stared at him. *A preacher,* I said to myself, *that's good to know.* Across the path, Jack groaned.

The other man stepped in front of me. I saw Jack's pistol hanging from his hand, covered with flecks of ice. When I looked down and away, he jerked my face to his by my hair. "So you're Crowe, huh?"

"No," I said. "Everybody knows Crowe died over at

Powder River. I'm an innocent man here, and you and your boys are gonna have a lot of explaining to do when it's over."

He grinned. "Bring Dory over here," he called out over his shoulder.

Who? I glanced past him, saw the Indian woman walk over slowly and stop beside him. Her eyes were without expression as she stared into mine. "What say you, Dory Love?" Silks glanced at her, then back to me. "Is he Crowe, or am I barking up the wrong tree?"

I felt my heart sink and my head spin when she smiled slightly and said in a flat tone, "Yes, Dan. He told me his name is Miller Crowe, and if you caught him, you would cut off his head for the reward money."

"So, there," he said to me. "You was telling her the truth both times." Chuckling, he reached an arm around the woman and drew her against his side. "Well, Dory, looks like you've earned a piece of the pie here."

I felt sick, lowered my head and shook it slowly.

"Come on, Crowe, buck up." Silks laughed and shook me by my hair. "This gal and I have known each other since back in Stillwell, back when she was the top hump at Mama Greely's Pleasure Palace." Seeing the look on my face, he feigned surprise. "What? She failed to mention it to you?" The men laughed. Then Silks leaned in an inch from my face.

"You're a dead man standing here." His voice turned harsh. "But you can buy yourself a few hours and a bullet in the head if you give us the names and whereabouts of some of your friends. If not, we'll just get to cutting, slow and steady like."

I stared into his eyes. "I lied to her. I ain't Crowe. If your reputation's built on killing innocent men, I've got nothing for you, except a good-bye and a go-to-hell. Get to cutting."

"I didn't figure you'd tell us anything about the gang." He pushed up his hat brim with one finger. Past him, I saw the one he'd called Deacon step away, take down the gunny-sacks, and slip a small hatchet from a saddlebag.

"Go ahead, Dan," said another rifleman in a Texas drawl. "Do what needs to be done so we can get the hell out of this cold. We've fooled around long enough on this job."

229

"So, you've got us in the jackpot, Dan Silks," I said. "And you're gonna cut our heads off no matter what?"

"Yes, so it appears. All you can do is settle down and ride it out. Believe me, a bullet in the head first would be better. Lot easier on you." He grinned and winked. "That hatchet's awfully dull."

"What about a hot meal first, like you said earlier?"

"That was then, before you shot your mouth off. We're down to bullet or hatchet now . . . nothing else."

"All right then, I'll come clean, if it'll make it quicker." I tugged my head back a little and he let go of my hair. "I might be Crowe . . . the man you're looking for. But I've got nothing to say about the rest of the gang."

"Hear that, boys?" Silks glanced back at the others. "Won't tell us about the others, but says he *might* be Crowe after all." They chuckled. He looked back into my eyes. "If I took the time, I'd have you telling me anything I wanted to know about the others. But this has cost me too much already. Hadn't been for Dory leading ya through the pass to me, I mighta been another week catching you."

"At least tell me it's all about the bounty money." I spoke quickly now, before he made his next move. "I'd hate to die thinking it's just for you to boost your reputation." I shook my head. "God, I'd hate that."

"Don't call on the Lord's name, boy," I heard the one called Deacon say. "For he'll not know you now."

Silks shot him a glance, then back to me with his head cocked curiously to one side. "Yep, it's all for the money. Of *course* it's for the money, ain't it, Dory." He hugged her close; she smiled and nodded as he spoke. "I'm not at all concerned about boosting my reputation." He glanced at the woman with a smug grin. "It don't need boosting. And I can't eat you. That would be uncivilized."

The others laughed under their breath. Steam swirled. But it had to be about boosting his reputation. With all the wanted men running loose, why else would he be hunting a couple of the James Gang across these frozen mountains? "Fetch me the hatchet, Dory," he said, turning the woman loose. She stepped over to his horse and came back with the hatchet in her hands, shameless enough to look me in the eyes as she handed it to him.

230

Silks faced me with the hatchet in one hand and Jack's pistol in the other, like a man ready to kill and dress hogs. "Yep." He ran the hatchet blade across his trouser leg. "For me, it's *only* about the money."

"Good," I said. "Then I'll die feeling a little better, knowing you've screwed yourself and your boys out of thirty thousand dollars." I raised my voice just enough for all to hear.

Silks stopped with the pistol raised, cocked it at my chest, and shook his head. "Nice try. But you're not talking your way out of this . . . so save yourself the disappointment."

"Not me," I said. "You've got me, straight up. But this man ain't wanted nowhere for nothing." I nodded toward Jack. "At least take him back to Lodge Pole and check it out. He's nobody, just an innocent man."

"I know all about this *innocent man.*" Silks gestured with the pistol toward Jack. "He's the one nobody ever recognizes, is all. But you and him are tighter than blades of grass in a pig turd, have been for years. We'll get paid for him." I saw the hatchet twist back and forth in his hand. *Getting restless.* Ready to get things over with, I thought.

"That ain't him," I said, "and it's worth thirty thousand for you to wait one day and find out, ain't it? Take this man to Lodge Pole. When I see he's safe, I'll bring you back to the money. I swear it." I stared deep in his eyes, and said, to cinch it, "Are you so afraid of me that you figure you can't hold me one day? Shame on you, Dan Silks."

He half turned and grinned at the others. "He's a talker. That's for sure." Then he turned back, leveled the pistol with a determined look in his eyes. His knuckles whitened on his trigger finger, and I braced myself for one final lunge at him before he pulled the trigger.

"Hang on, Dan," one of the men said. "They did rob a damn train, and who knows how many banks. What about all that money spilling out of the tree when that bear had him? Why wouldn't he be carrying some more? Somebody has to have it. Why not him?"

"He's nothing but the horse-man, Spurlock," Silks said to him. "Think they'd trust all their swag with this *horse-man?*"

"Hell," the man said, "I don't know about y'all, but if

there's more money to be made here, I'm all for getting it—all the trouble we've been through. Freezing our asses off . . . getting waylaid by that bear."

I saw Silks' expression ease slightly. A crafty smile twitched at his lips. "Well, you've managed to get them thinking, haven't you, Crowe. Just like you intended to do."

"Hell yes, that's what I intended. Wouldn't you? Think I want to die here? My head cut off—yanked off like a damn chicken? An innocent man killed too, and me not doing something to stop it? Think I want to go to hell with that on my mind? Think it ain't worth thirty thousand to get one more day of living?" It was starting to lean my way, so I pressed on. "Damn right it's worth it. Who knows, maybe the train'll wreck and I'll be the only survivor. I ain't afraid to play the odds . . . are you, for one day? For thirty thousand dollars? You ain't that afraid, are you?" I glanced past him at the others, then back to him. "If you are . . . maybe you *should* be concerned about your reputation."

He chuckled, pointed the pistol toward Jack, and said, "Suppose I just ask you where the money is and put a bullet in this *innocent man,* every time you don't tell me?"

I shrugged. "It's your bullets. But it won't get nothing. You can carve my fingers off one at a time, but I'll die without telling you where the money is." I hesitated just a second to let that play across my mind. His thumb let the hammer down to half cock but stayed tight across it.

"No, I figure you wouldn't," he said. He seemed to teeter on the verge of pulling the trigger.

Whatever I said next would have to be strong enough to uncock that pistol the rest of the way. I weighed my words carefully, seeing his knuckles white around the pistol butt. "Maybe you'd like to confer with that whore first, since you can't seem to make up your own mind. You chickenshit little prick!" I said it knowing he'd have to crack my head with that pistol barrel just to look good in front of his men. To do it he'd first have to let down the hammer. It was a dangerous play, but I was right.

"Why, you thieving little turd!" he bellowed. *So far so good,* I thought as the barrel swiped across my jaw. I slammed back against the wall and crumbled down on my knees in the snow.

Over by the rock, Jack rolled his head back and forth slowly, crushed and stunned, but still alive. Things were looking up, no doubt about it. What I had here was a bounty hunter concerned with his big reputation, a greedy Texan tired of the cold, and a hotheaded preacher raining the Lord's vengeance on the rest of the world. Given a combination such as this to work with, if I couldn't scheme Jack and me a way out, I deserved to lose my head.

The woman was one double cross I hadn't seen coming, but I had no time for regrets. For now we were still alive. It was up to me to keep us that way. *Wits and wiles.* I could play that game, I thought. Fresh blood dripped from my face into the snow. I took a deep breath and almost spread a dazed grin. *That-a-boy, Jack. Just hang in there. I'm working on it. . . .*

"Hold up, Dan," said the Texas drawl. "He can't lead us to no money if you've beat his brains out." His rifle turned slightly toward Silks as he spoke. Silks took note of it.

"Damn it, Spurlock," he said. "You've been in this business long enough to know they've all got the ole *hidden-money* story worked down to an art. It's just a ploy, just a way to stay alive and look for a getaway."

Spurlock sniffed, spat in the snow, and said, "Then, you're saying maybe he's right, that maybe you *are* afraid we can't hold him?"

"Alls I know, Dan," said another voice, and a swarthy-looking half-breed stepped forward, "is that there *was* a sky full of money back there where he was treed. I don't ordinarily fall for the ole hidden-money myself, but I know what we saw. *Are* you afraid we'll lose him?"

"No! By *God, no!*" Silks' cheeks reddened. "I can hold anything that walks, crawls or rattles. I'm saying, the *only* money is what fell out of that tree."

"No, Dan," the woman said quietly. "It is true he has hidden much money somewhere between here and my cabin. I saw him count it before we left. But I have not seen it since." The way she said it made me wonder for a second if it had really happened. But it hadn't. She was lying. Why? I stared at her curiously, but her eyes gave no clue as to why she'd said it.

"You heard her, Dan. She's got no reason to lie."

Silks looked at her, then at me in a new light, then back to her. "Dory? Are you sure about this?"

She smiled slightly, her caged eyes fixed on his. "When was I ever *unsure,* when it comes to money?"

Silks stared at her, considering it.

"The report from Lodge Pole said he was carrying a whole *carpetbag* full of money," the half-breed put in quietly.

My ears perked at that, wondering who that report had come from.

"So?" Silks spread his hands. "That was what he lost back in the tree!"

"Horse-splat," said Spurlock. "That was a lot of money fell back there, but it damn sure weren't no carpetbag full. I might be from Nagadoches, but damn, even *I'm* smart enough to know better than that."

"So that's what this is about?" Silks let go a breath and ran a coat sleeve across his steaming lips. "You're still sore about that little Nagadoches joke, ain't ya?" I listened close, seeing what I was dealing with here.

"Well," Spurlock said, "it *was* uncalled for. But that's got nothing to do with this." He pointed his finger up and down toward the ground. "I'm saying, if there's more damn money to be made here . . . let's make it."

"Brethren, brethren," the one called Deacon said, raising his arms, "can't you see that this vermin is doing all he can to divide you one against the other! Smite him! Smite him now, or he'll rain our destruction down upon us." I listened, thinking, *Amen to that.*

"To hell with you, Deacon," said the half-breed. "You're lucky I haven't put a bullet up your ass . . . causing my brother to get et by that bear." He swung back toward Dan Silks, pointing a finger at me. "This man says there's money hidden, and I say it's worth checking on. If you're afraid you can't hold him long enough to get this other man back to Lodge Pole, let me and Spurlock take charge." He glanced over at Jack, then back to Silks. "What if that son of a bitch *is* innocent? Maybe they wouldn't hang you for making a mistake, but I'm half Indian. They'd hang me for farting on a public thoroughfare, and you know it."

Spurlock the Texan nodded his head. "Yep, get the money, I say."

"Jesus Christ!" Silks shook his head, then raised a hand. "All right then, we'll put it to vote." He leaned and looked past them, at a stocky black man standing near the horses. "Sparks, you've been awfully quiet. What do you say?"

The black man turned facing them. "Far as I'm concerned—"

"He ain't got no say-so," said Spurlock, cutting the man short. I glanced back and forth, getting a better feel for this crew by the minute.

"Who says I don't?" Sparks' nostrils flared, blowing steam. His rifle half turned toward Spurlock. Spurlock cowered a step. Then Sparks spoke without taking his eyes off him. "I was going to *say,* as far as I'm concerned, we should take a chance on the money."

"Oh," Spurlock said in a meek voice. Then he looked at Silks. "There ya are, then. We've voted."

"What about Ernie down there?" Silks pointed at the rifleman down in the valley.

"What? *Ernie?* Vote? He's too stupid to raise his hand without you tell him to. He's your nephew. He don't get a vote." He swung a finger toward Deacon. "And neither does this four-flushing Bible-thumping hypocrite son of a bitch."

"Why you—" Deacon clenched his fists and jerked toward him. Silks stepped between them and held them apart. I slumped in the snow, seeing all sorts of possibilities here. I could handle this crew, given the time. With a little luck I'd have them killing each other before we made it back to the train, let alone to Lodge Pole.

I jerked my eyes up at the sound of a gunshot and saw Silks holding the smoking pistol above his head. The others stepped back. "See what he's already causing here?" Silks turned from one to the other, then said, "We're all tired and cold and testy. Don't ya think he sees that? I've held ya together this far, and I ain't letting this outlaw come between us. We'll go back to Lodge Pole if that'll satisfy everybody. But I swear, if he gets away, I'll kill the son of a bitch who's supposed to be guarding him. Is that clear?"

Jack, Jack, I said to myself as Silks raged and cursed

235

above me, *just stay alive. Don't die on me. As long as we've got the will, these boys are bound to provide a way.*

"On your feet, Crowe!" Silks grabbed me and pulled me up with the hatchet still in his hand. Wobbling to my feet, I caught a glimpse of the woman watching me, and I stared at her for a second. What was I looking for in her eyes? She'd led us to Dan Silks like chickens to a chopping block, but then she'd just lied about seeing the money. What was her angle here?

Dan saw me watching her and he chuckled. "Dory put it on ya, didn't she? Well, don't feel too bad, she's an old hand at putting boys in the jackpot." He glanced at her, winked, and added, "I figured that was your cabin he burnt back there. Once I knew he was in *your* hands, I told the boys you'd be bringing him to us."

"Looked to me like she was helping 'em," said Spurlock.

"That shows how little you know," Silks said. "If she wanted to, she coulda held out and kept us looking all winter. This woman owes me. I'm the one what got her to whoring back when she was just a strip of a girl." He grinned. "Right, Dory Love?"

"I do not use that name anymore," she said. She shot me an undiscernible glance, then looked away, saying, "But it is true. I have thought about you ever since I came back here. I owe you, for my becoming a whore."

"See, boys—" He grinned, turning, looking at each of them. "Once a whore always a whore." He tapped the side of his head. "There's more to tracking than just sniffing the trail. You have to know what people are thinking, and what to expect of them."

I just stared between them until the Deacon shoved me forward. "Come on, heathen, the Lord's ready to call you to task."

PART V

NATURE OF BEASTS

CHAPTER

20

It took less than a day's ride downhill through the wide snowy passes to reach the sloping flatland the woman had spoken of. The snow was not as deep on this side of the mountain. We followed the path their horses had made on their way in. I made the ride on a pack mule, with a two-foot shackle chain swinging between my wrists, heartsick in knowing that we'd only been a few hours from freedom when they'd caught us.

Deacon Leecher took pleasure in mentioning over and over how instead of following us through the storms, they'd simply doubled back, took Larr's train around the mountain, and rode in on us from below. The train was held by two riflemen awaiting our return.

The posse had quit bickering, and I studied them closely as we rode, Jack at the rear, thrown over a horse like a sack of grain, the woman up front riding double behind Silks, and, flanking me, the half-breed and Spurlock. In front of me, the skinny kid called Ernie kept looking back, as if it was the first time he'd ever seen a man in chains. Sparks rode beside him.

Deacon fell his horse back beside me now and then to remind me of how God's wrath had fallen upon me, how hell beckoned, and how I'd been betrayed by a woman's cunning. "No man hath knowledge of a whore's cold heart," he'd said. "Those are not the words of the *Lord,* boy," he added, "but they dang sure *oughta* be."

"I'm getting a belly full of that bastard," said the half-breed to Spurlock, talking about Deacon as Deacon rode forward after unloading his bleak sermon. "He caused Harvey's death, and we both know it."

Spurlock only grunted a reply. I sat the mule quietly, knowing that Harvey was the man who'd stumbled up behind me the day the bear attacked me and my horse. I thought it best not to mention it right then. My position was awfully shaky, and these boys were still testy and sore from being out in the weather. Although they hadn't been out in it nearly as long as Jack, the woman, and myself, the cold had taken a toll on them. I couldn't help but think that they would have given up in another day if the woman hadn't double-crossed us.

"If you *are* lying about that money," Spurlock said, leaning near me from his saddle, "you won't believe how long it'll take for you to die . . . or how loud you'll holler till it happens."

I just stared straight ahead, listening, watching, waiting, wanting to look back at Jack and see how he was doing, but realizing that at any second this bunch could change their mind and kill us both.

"There she is, boys," Dan Silks called out when we'd rounded a turn on the sloping land and saw the curl of smoke from the engine stack in the distance. I caught a glimpse of the woman's face as she turned and looked back from behind Dan Silks. I only glanced at her long enough to see the look in her eyes, then I had to look away and take a tight breath.

Back on the ledge, before we'd left, Sparks had pitched me my boot from amid a mound of ice and snow. "Believe this is yours," he'd said with a dark grin; and when I'd slipped my foot inside it, I felt the brass knuckles stuck in the toe of it, held there by snow. They were still there, but of very little use against rifles, I thought, looking out across the frozen land.

At the train, Freddie stood rocking back and forth in his hobnail boots, batting his gloved hands together as we rode up. Seeing me, he stepped forward, but a tall man with a rifle pulled him back.

"Take your hand off me," Freddie yelled, jerking loose. He called out to me: "Will you tell these assholes they got no right holding this train up—" Then he saw the chains and the cuffs on my wrists and stopped short. "Well, I'll be damned. What's going on here? Why's that man chained?" He glanced at Jack across the horse. "The hell happened to him?"

"These are the men we were hunting," Silks said, stepping down from his saddle and pulling the woman down behind him. The half-breed raised a boot and shoved me from the mule. I thumped into the snow face-first.

"There must be a mix-up of some kind," said Freddie. "Hell, I know these two. They's hired by Colonel Larr to kill that damned bear."

"They're outlaws," Silks said, stepping up to the rifleman beside Freddie. Another rifleman stepped down from the train and walked over. Silks added, gesturing toward me matter-of-factly, "That one's Miller Crowe, horse-man for the James Gang."

"That's crazy." Ole Freddie reached down and helped me to my feet. "Everybody knows Crowe got killed and gutted over at Powder River." He eyed me, leaning close as he brushed snow off my shoulder. "You *ain't* him, are ya?"

"No," I said quietly, "but go easy here. This is a skittish bunch."

"There now, ya see"—Freddie spread his hands and called out to Silks—"he ain't Crowe. It's all a mistake."

"Dory and I'll be using the private car," Silks said, ignoring Freddie. He ushered the woman to the train, with a hand under her forearm. She avoided my eyes. "You men get settled in and keep your eyes on that rascal."

"Dory?" Freddie looked confused for a second, but snapped out of it and took a step along behind Silks. "Now see here, Dandy Dan. Colonel Larr lets nobody use that car. You can't go in there—" He stopped short and doubled over as a rifle butt snapped out and hooked him in the stomach. I winced just seeing it.

Dan Silks stopped, looked back with fire in his eyes. "Nobody calls me *Dandy* Dan . . . not to my face." The

241

woman tugged his sleeve until he eased down, took a breath, turned, and walked away. "Lucky I don't have him shot," I heard Silks say.

"Listen, you old geezer," said the rifleman standing over Freddie. "Get this train up and stoking, and keep your damned mouth shut. You got that?"

Freddie kneeled forward with his hands across his stomach, struggling for breath, looking up at the rifle butt hovering above his head. "Why you . . . dirty . . . rotten—"

I slipped down beside him in the snow and pulled him to the side as the rifleman drew back for another swipe. My chains rattled. "He hears ya!" I raised a hand the length of my chain. "Don't hit him again. He's the only one can run the engine."

"Then he best get to running it. I'll split his damned noggin open if he fools with me."

"Come on, Freddie," I said almost in a whisper, "keep quiet here. These boys ain't playing."

"There's . . . lots of snow . . . on the tracks," Freddie said. His eyes were red and watery.

"That's okay. It'll be all right. Just do like they say. Don't get yourself hurt."

Spurlock and the half-breed came past us, dragging Jack between them. "What're you so worked up about, Dutch?" said Spurlock. "We're the ones been up there freezing our asses off."

"How come they're still alive?" The one called Dutch nodded down at me, then over to Jack.

"Crowe says this one is innocent," Spurlock said. "We're taking 'em both back to Lodge Pole."

Dutch looked at Jack and chuckled under his breath. *"Innocent?* Innocent of what? They both look like the kind would steal a hot stove."

"It's a long story," said Spurlock. "Help us get them inside."

Dutch grabbed my chain and yanked me to my feet. "Miller Crowe, huh?" He eyed me up and down. "What the hell happened to your nose, anyway? You don't look so damn big and bad to me."

"Yeah? Well," I said, sniffing, blowing snow from my lips,

242

"maybe I ain't been eating right lately, but there's not a *damn* thing wrong with my nose." I'd managed to get a look at Jack as they dragged him past me. With his head lowered he shot me a glance, just enough to let me know that he was coming around.

"Let's go, *badman,*" said Dutch, jerking me by the chain. He was about the same size as big Eldon; and I limped slightly, feeling the brass knuckles down there in the toe of my boot as he pulled me along behind him. "You wanta know what that nose looks like to me? Huh? Do ya?" He shook my chain and let go a nasty laugh. I just stared at his broad back. Steam swirled in my breath. He wouldn't believe what I'd do to him, first chance I got.

Even with the cuffs and chain hanging heavy on my wrists, even as the big ugly faces of Dutch and Spurlock sat across from me staring, watching every move I made, I succumbed to my exhaustion. With my head dropped over against the window of the car, I slept like a dead man, gathering my strength as the engine chugged and struggled upward around the mountain.

When I awoke the train sat idling. Outside the window I saw Sparks and the half-breed walking along with shovels over their shoulders. Dutch and Spurlock had been relieved by the skinny kid, Ernie. Before I'd wiped the sleep from my eyes, he leaned forward and said, "Did you really fist-fight that bear up in the tree?"

I looked at him, sizing him up, figuring what part he might play in Jack and me escaping. "Sure, kid, you were there in the valley, didn't you see it?"

"I weren't there. I was farther back, still looking for ole Harvey. But Spurlock said you hit that bear right in the jaw." His eyes lit with excitement.

I shrugged. "I'm from Kentucky. We were never known to tolerate sassy bears. What about you, kid? Where you from? Been a bounty hunter long?"

"I'm from Illinois. You ever been there?"

"Aw yeah, many times. I've been everywhere. Started out bounty hunting just like you." I let my expression turn haunted. "But then . . . I killed my first man, feller by the name of Haskins. A horse thief out of Kansas." I shook my head slightly. "I just wasn't the same afterwards. Had to give it up. How about you? How'd you do, first time you had to shoot somebody?"

"Oh, I ain't yet—shot nobody, that is. But I've thought about it a lot." He spread an uncertain smile. "I'll be all right though. Uncle Dan says after the first time, it's as easy as sucking pie off your finger."

"Hell of a pie." I studied his face for a second. "How come your uncle don't like being called *Dandy* Dan? I thought it was his chosen nickname."

"Heck no. He can't stand it no more. He used to be a fool for the ladies, according to my pa. Pa always said, 'Hang a pair of women's bloomers off a cliff and Uncle Dan'll break his neck sniffing at 'em.'" He grinned.

"No kidding?" I grinned too.

The kid ducked his head slightly and looked around as if afraid he'd said something he shouldn't have. "But he ain't like that no more. That's why he gets mad—"

"When ya call him *Dandy Dan,*" I said, rolling my hand as I finished his words for him. *Interesting,* I thought.

"That's right." The kid's grin widened.

"But he told ya wrong about killing being easy, kid. It's *hard,* real hard."

His grin faded. "But he said . . ."

"I know." I raised a cuffed hand, stopping him. "That's the same thing I thought too. But boy oh boy, if I only knew . . . the nightmares, the times I've woke up shaking, seeing that dead man's face, hearing him scream, begging me not to kill him. I know his ghost is always close at hand, waiting for me. I reckon he'll soon get his chance at me in hell." I wiped my face with both hands and shook my head again. "But, hey, that's just part of the job, right? Can't let ghosts and eternal hell and damnation get the best of you, right?"

"Yeah. . . ." His voice faltered slightly. He gazed off out the window with his rifle lying loose across his lap. My first instinct was to grab it, butt-stroke his jaw, and skin out of there. But I thought of Jack and of the snowy land outside the window, and I put the thought out of my mind. Getting away might be the easy part, but in this country, getting

244

away was only the first step. This country was a killer of man, no less than the posse, no less than the bear.

I sighed, looking out the window with him. "There's times I'm sorry I ever chose an outdoor occupation, you know? Take my friend back there, for instance. See, he'd never be in such a shape if he'd become . . . say, a doctor or such. How is he anyway? He doing all right? Where've they got him? Next car back?"

His grin came back. "You crushed him flatter than a I-don't-know-what in that snow. He's in the last car back, still knocked out." Something flashed across his mind. His eyes turned caged, his hand tightened around the rifle. "Hey . . . Dan told me not to talk to you, so maybe we better hush here."

"Sure," I said. "That's probably a good idea. Who knows, any minute they might tell you to take me out on the platform, splatter my brains with a rifle slug, and throw me off like I was a sack of garbage or something, right?"

I smiled, letting him get a clear picture of it. "If you do, here's some advice. Look away as quick as you can. So you don't have to see me twitching and shaking, when the last of my life spills out of me. It's not a pretty sight. And I don't want it bothering you afterwards."

His face turned ashen, his mouth hung open an inch. "Gawd."

"See, what happens is—" I leaned forward a bit and tapped my finger against my forehead. "—that bullet smashes through the skull like it's glass, shatters the bone, and the splinters of bone tear through the brain and explode out the—"

I heard the rear door opening, and I stopped short and leaned back. "I'll tell ya later," I said.

The half-breed came walking up, tapped Ernie on the shoulder, and said, "Go on back, I'll watch him awhile."

The kid had to shake his head to free it of the picture I'd painted for him. "You all right, boy?" the half-breed asked as Ernie turned his drained face toward him.

"Uh . . . yeah." Ernie stood up, fumbling with the rifle, turned, and walked away quickly. The half-breed stood brushing snow from his coat sleeve, watching the boy leave.

Then he turned, stared down at me, and lowered himself into the seat. His rifle rested across his knee.

"Working on the boy, huh?" he said, eyeing me with a flat expression. His expression told me I'd be wasting my time trying it on him. I studied his eyes for a second before answering. They were blank and dark, offering nothing.

"All right, so I was, a little. Can you blame me? My life is on the line here. I'll do anything I can to stay alive. I admit it. Wouldn't you do the same?"

He didn't answer. His face was red from him being out in the cold, shoveling. Wet spots of melted snow dotted his flat hat brim. "They've sure kept you and the colored feller busy. Wasn't for you two I guess we'd be stuck here till spring, huh? Dan's lucky to have you boys."

Still no answer, no response. It was as if he were sleeping with his eyes wide open. I shrugged, and looked away out the window while the train struggled forward, going into the high rise of the mountain to Lodge Pole. Perhaps whatever division I'd seen among the men had ended once we got back to the train and out of the weather, I thought; and for a long time I stared out wondering what tactic to try next. But then, out of the blue, he said in a low tone, as if he'd seriously been thinking about it awhile, "I'm nobody's *boy."*

"Oh? Then don't tell me . . . tell Dan." I only glanced at him with a raised eyebrow, then turned back away and said nothing more.

When Spurlock came into the car and walked up to us, the half-breed stood up, and said before he turned to leave, "Silks was right about *one* thing, this one's a talker."

Spurlock grinned. "It's about time Silks was right about something." My ears perked at hearing that.

He swung down into the seat, laying his pistol across his lap. "I'll listen to anything ole Crowe here has to say. If I don't like it, I'll shoot a finger or two off." He grinned at me. "How does that sound ta ya?" Him and the half-breed both laughed. I just stared.

After the half-breed had left, I sat in silence for a while until the train throbbed forward. I glanced out the window, then all around, restlessly. "Damn, I shoulda relieved myself while we was stopped there. I don't suppose . . . ?"

"Forget it, Crowe. If you can't hold your water, you can catch it in your boot, far as I care. And don't waste your time figuring ways to get me off guard. It ain't gonna happen." He spread a sly grin. "I've handled more of your kind than you can count fleas on a Georgia dog."

I let go a breath and settled back in the seat. "Yeah, I reckon you're right. You boys are the best. Ole Dan musta taught ya everything he knows."

"Shiiiit . . ." He hissed low. "I knew more about manhunting coming in than he'll know going out. I was a scout for Selby back in the civil, when he was busy chasing ever skirt twixt Creed and Sonora. So don't tell me . . ."

I cocked an eye. "No kidding? You rode for Selby? I rode for the stars and bars myself."

"No you didn't. You rode guerrilla. You boys never impressed me much—just a bunch of dumb farmboys playing with your daddy's squirrel guns, is all."

"Is that a fact?" I stared at him.

"Well," he grinned, jiggling his pistol, "look who's holding the gun, and who's about to get their head clipped."

"You got a point there." I waited a second, then said, "Ain't it strange that a few years back, you and I fought for the same colors, and now—" I nodded at my chains. "—here we are on different sides of the fence."

"I learned my lesson in the war," he said. "From here on, the only colors I fight for is *green and gold.*" He chuckled; I chuckled with him, nodding my head.

"I agree." I said, then added quickly, "Of course, there ain't a doubt in my mind that you'll never see a dollar of the train money I hid." I smiled, shaking my head.

"Yeah? Why's that? You gonna get away? Go get it yourself? I don't *think so.*" He leaned forward, tweaked my nose with his pistol barrel, then leaned back.

"Come on Spurlock, anybody with one eye closed oughta see that Dan and that whore's planning on keeping that money for themselves. That's why he didn't want to go back for it till everybody sided against him."

His gaze wavered slightly. I knew he was considering it. Seeing an opening, I slipped into it quickly. "They ain't seen each other in years? But she finds out he's tracking me and just leads me to him? He knows her mind well enough to go around the mountain and be there waiting for me? Don't that scare you a little bit, seeing their minds clicking that close together? He's back there right now, bumping his roscoes, and ever time his ass rises and falls, she's breathing it in his ear, telling him: *Aw Dan! Aw Dan!* Let's keep that money ourselves. And he's saying, *Yeah baby! Yeah baby!* It's all ours!" I cocked an eye. "Tell me it ain't so. Tell me that ain't what you'd be saying." I leaned slightly. "Didn't I hear somewhere he used to be a real fool for the ladies?"

A silence passed; a nerve twitched in his cheek. "You're 'bout half crazy, ain't ya, Crowe?" He tried to smile, but it didn't take. I saw the picture I'd painted working on him. Now his mind would add stroke after stroke, till he colored it to suit himself.

"Half crazy? Hummpf." I leaned back, shook my head looking him up and down, and looked off out the window. "Yeah, you just go on thinking that. They're gonna burn your ass so bad, it'll pass for a side of bacon. . . ."

The train struggled and gained its pull, and we sat in silence for the longest time. *Ernie . . . the half-breed . . . and Spurlock,* I thought, gazing into the wall of ice-streaked rock. I had them where I wanted them. Now all I had to do was get the Deacon, Sparks, and big Dutch. *Three down . . . three to go.* I let out a breath and cleared my mind. I hoped Jack was coming around. *Damn,* I hoped he was.

CHAPTER

21

———•———

Darkness had set in by the time the train rounded into Lodge Pole. All the posse men stood gathered around me looking out the window, all except Deacon who I figured stood guard over Jack back in the last car, and Dan Silks who hadn't come out of the private car since we'd left the mountains. A wind had whipped in, full of snow and sleet, pelting the side of the car, building a thick scallop along the window edges.

"Man alive," said Sparks, running a hand across his forehead. "This is the *big* one coming . . . for sure this time."

"Yeah," Spurlock said. "Dan knows better than this. How the hell we gonna take him back and find the money in the morning?" I watched him run something through his mind. He bit his lip.

The rear door opened in a blast of wind. They all turned and watched Dan Silks bound along the aisle, cursing, shoving his shirt into his trousers. "Why in the *hell* didn't somebody tell me this storm was coming in?" His eyes were red, his hands shook. He looked exhausted, like a man who'd split rails all day, then wrestled an alligator.

"Why in *hell* didn't you see it coming yourself?" The half-breed jutted his chin. "You're the one s'posed to read the weather so well. Shoulda kept your face out from under the sheet."

"Don't tell me how to run this crew, *boy!*" A pulse thumped in Silks' red throat. "You and Ernie go get the horses off!"

"I ain't no *boy,*" said the half-breed. "I've done my share of broad-labor. Let Sparks help Ernie."

Sparks glared at him. "So, you're no *boy,* but I am?"

"It ain't exactly what I meant . . . but if the shoe fits, maybe you better—"

"Hold on," Silks said, stepping between Sparks and the half-breed. "The hell's going on here? I'm the one giving orders." He thumbed his chest.

"Yeah," Spurlock said in his Texas drawl, "and you're the one what's reaping all the rewards."

"What's that supposed to mean?" Silks glared at him. "What's eating you?"

Spurlock's jaw tightened. "Nothing." He looked at Ernie and nodded at the door. "Come on, I'll go check the damn horses with ya. Not that we'll be needing them come morning." He shot Silks a dark glance.

Ernie hesitated, leaning toward Silks as if something was pressing hard on his mind. Silks hissed at him: "Well? Go on, boy. You've been given an order. Now do it! What the hell's got into everybody?"

Silks watched them leave, then turned to the others with a bemused expression. "Can't I leave for a minute without this crew falling apart?"

"Minute, hell," big Dutch said. "You've been horning that squaw ever since you got on board. Now you've let the weather go sour on us."

"Let the weather . . . ?" Silks stared at him in disbelief, then at the other two. They stared back. "I ain't responsible for the weather now, boys. I mighta taken a little break for a while, to fill my natural needs—but by gawd! Don't go hanging the weather on me."

I sat quietly, glancing up at them from my seat. "Oh, I see," Silks said, shooting me a look. "This outlaw son of a bitch has been working his jaw, ain't he? I told you-all not to listen to nothing he says. The man'll say anything to keep his head on his shoulders."

"I ain't said nothing," I offered in a meek voice. "I made a deal with ya to keep me alive for a while. I've just kept my mouth shut, is all." I ducked my eyes down and stared at the floor, wondering if the woman had deliberately kept him distracted while the big storm rolled in.

"He ain't done nothing, Dan," Dutch said. "If he had, I'd have busted his head." He chuckled, laid a wide hand on my shoulder, and squeezed it until I almost winced. "Right, you little weasel?"

"He better not," Silks said, shooting me a burning stare. "I'll kill ya and say to hell with the money. I didn't want to go along with this in the first place." His hand went to the pistol under his arm.

"Easy, Dan," said Sparks. "We've gone this far with it. Let's play it out. The weather'll let up. We can wait it out a day or two if we have to."

"Yeah." Silks let out a breath, chafed the back of his neck, and spread a sheepish grin. "Boys, I rode that whore so hard, she'll be pissing steam for the next month." Quiet laughter rippled across them. *Crude bastard,* I thought. He leveled his shoulders.

"I suppose I better tighten up now though. I'll go see this *Colonel* Larr, and let him know we'll be accepting his hospitality for a couple days. We can all use a little rest here."

The rear door opened in a cold rush of wind. The Indian woman stepped inside and closed the door behind her. Gone was the doeskin dress, replaced by an expensive-looking robe thrown over a lacy nightgown that had to have come from Laura Larr's closet. She leaned against the door for a second, smiled, and walked to Silks, carrying his hat in her hand. Beneath the open robe, a fresh bandage circled her wounded shoulder.

The men stared like hungry dogs as she walked along the aisle, a different walk now, not the way I'd seen her trudge across the rocky land, but the seductive, loose walk of a woman for hire.

"Why, Dory Love," said Silks, "you'll catch your death of cold if ya ain't careful."

When she stopped before him, she flipped a speck of lint from his hat and held it out to him. Silks grinned, winked at the others, and took his hat from her. "See, boys, when you do right by 'em, they go out of their way to please."

She laughed softly, then looked at the whipped expression on my face and leaned over me. "Awww," she said in a teasing tone. "Why so gloomy? Your friend is doing much better, and has even drank some broth—"

"Sorry, lady," said Dutch, shoving an arm between her and me. "You can't talk to the prisoner."

She shot Silks a bemused glance. "Why Dan, who is in charge here, *you* or him?"

Silks looked at Dutch with a tight smile. "Settle down, Dutch, she's with *me. Dory* knows how to handle herself. Crowe ain't putting nothing over on *her.*"

Jack was doing better! She'd given me the message; and I lowered my eyes again, seeing Dutch step back grudgingly. I wondered if they realized just how important it was for me to hear that.

She stood back, and sighed, smoothing a hand down the flowing robe. "It has been a long time since I've known such finery as this. Wouldn't it be kind of the colonel to let us stay here until the weather breaks?" She touched Silks' arm, squeezed it slightly. "But I don't think even *you* could convince him to do that."

He glanced at his men, then back to her, widening his chest. "Oh? Well we'll just have to see about that. I can be very persuasive." He hooked a thumb in his belt and cocked his head slightly, glancing up and down the robe as the woman stepped slightly to one side and let her long dark leg reveal itself. "Yes siiirr," he purred in a long breath, *"very persuasive. . . ."*

When the woman had gone back to the private car, Silks and the others led me from the train to the lodge, surrounding me as I hobbled along through the wind and snow, with the brass knuckles pressing hard against the ball of my foot.

Inside the lodge we stood in the middle of the lobby. The riflemen pulled back a step but stayed around me while Dan Silks bounded up the stairs to Larr's suite. The desk clerk loosened his collar with a nervous finger and eyed the men closely. I caught a glimpse of big Eldon on his crutch. He peeped around at me through the beaded curtains, then disappeared. His crutch thumped off toward the rear of the lodge.

Ole Ponce stuck his head between Dutch and the Deacon and asked me, "Where are my dogs?" Dutch shoved him back, but Ponce leaned forward, staring around him at me.

"I sicced them on the bear," I said, standing there in my chains. "They never came back—"

"Quit talking," Dutch said, gigging me in the ribs. But I ignored him and said, "They're probably still on his trail, if they're alive."

"You must always call them off," said Ponce, a concerned look in his eyes. "I told you that—"

"I said, don't talk to the prisoner!" Dutch shoved Ponce hard. He crashed against the wall beside the window, and fell.

"You made . . . a terrible mistake," Ponce said, gasping. I didn't know if he was talking to me or Dutch. I heard Eldon's crutch thumping, coming back toward us from beyond the beaded curtain. Dutch turned back to me. "Keep your mouth shut or I'll get some fence wire and *wire it shut!"*

I nodded, hearing his words but looking over his shoulder into the mirror behind him. In the mirror I saw the curtains swing open behind me. "I ain't like the others . . ." Dutch raged in my face. Eldon stepped through the curtains, drawing back an ax handle with his free hand. *Jesus!* He was gonna crack my skull from behind.

"So one more word," Dutch was saying, "and I'll—"

His words came to a splattering halt as I ducked straight down and heard the ax handle whistle over my head. It sounded like someone smacked a tomato with a barn slat. The other riflemen jerked around with their guns pointed at Eldon.

The broken handle hung from Eldon's hand. He saw his mistake and his face turned green. "Oh God no," he whispered.

Dutch rocked back, turning, staggering into the Deacon with his arms spread. The two of them joined in a strange waltz, spinning arm in arm the few feet across the floor. Then they plunged headlong through the glass window, taking out the frame and a pair of fancy drapes on their way.

253

"Good Lord," said Sparks, cocking his rifle at Eldon's stomach.

"Please don't shoot," Eldon pleaded, his hands spread as he wobbled on his crutch. "I didn't mean to hit *him!*" The broken handle slipped from his fingers and dropped to the floor. "I swear to God!" He pointed a trembling finger at me. "It's this bastard! I hate 'im. You don't *know* how bad I *hate* 'im!" Spit flew from his lips. His eyes watered.

Sparks shot me a glance; I shrugged.

"On your knees, white boy—!" he bellowed at Eldon, gesturing him down with the rifle. "Or I'll blow your head off!"

Eldon struggled with the crutch, tried to go down but couldn't because of the tight bandage around his ribs and the other one around his leg. "I caaaan't," he sobbed. "Damn it! I didn't mean to hit him. Don't sho-ot me."

"It's true," I said quietly to Sparks. "We've had some trouble, him and I—personal stuff." I nodded slightly.

Sparks looked at Eldon's bandages, then at me. "You do this to him?"

"You had to be there to understand, but yeah, I did, in a manner of speaking—"

Silks pounded down the stairs. Deacon staggered through the open door and stood there covered with snow, blood, and broken glass. A small shard stuck from the tip of his nose in a bead of blood; his breath heaved. His eyes pinned on Eldon like poison darts.

"What's going on here?" Silks had his pistol out, fanning it back and forth. Cold wind whooshed through the broken window. Papers rose from the counter and spun away. Ben Larr stood behind Silks on the stairs, craning his neck. He looked around, down at the mess, then over at me in my chains.

Deacon stepped forward toward Eldon, his hands raised, fingers spread like claws. *"Vengeance is mine!"*

Big Eldon gasped. I raised my chained hands, feeling sorry for Eldon for some reason, and called out to Silks, "This is the man that tipped y'all off—don't let 'em kill him!"

Deacon stopped at the sound of Silks' voice: "Hold up, everybody!"

254

He looked at Eldon. "You're the one sent us the telegraph?"

Eldon gave me a strange glance, then nodded his head. "Uh-huh. That was me . . . I did it."

Deacon's eyes boiled. "He's hammered Dutch's nose into his face. Why'd he do that if he's on our side?"

"These men have trouble between them," said Sparks. He gestured his rifle toward Eldon. "Look what Crowe did to him. He was trying to hit Crowe, not Dutch."

"The Lord judges *actions,* not intentions," said Deacon. He started to take another step, but Silks' voice stopped him.

"Deacon, you and Ernie get Dutch and get him inside before he freezes."

"He ain't dead, is he?" Ernie's voice sounded hollow at the thought of handling a dead man.

"He's *alive,"* Deacon said, glaring at Eldon. "And if he wasn't he'd still have to be brung in, wouldn't he?" Silks cocked his head at Ernie. "What're you getting so squeamish about all of a sudden?"

"Nothing," said Ernie, ducking his face and heading out with Deacon.

Silks and Larr both looked at me. I looked away, and caught a glimpse of Brerton Beam stepping around from the dining room. When he saw us gathered there, he cowered back a step and said, "My goodness. What have we here?" He looked at my chains, then up at Silks on the stairs. He walked wide around us and over to the foot of the stairs.

"Who are you?" Silks asked in a gruff voice.

"Why, I'm Beam . . . Brerton Beam," he said with hesitancy. "I'm a whiskey drummer." He searched himself absently for a card but found none. "Why is Mr. Beatty chained? I demand to know what's going on here."

Silks studied Beam for a second. "Shit," he said, then turned from Beam back to Larr as if Beam was not worthy of an answer. "Colonel, we've been here less than an hour and one of *your* boys has perpetrated an act of aggression on one of *mine.* Am I gonna have trouble outa you?" He glared at Larr.

I watched Larr, wondering how he'd handle himself under his newfound circumstances.

"I told you," Larr said, his voice sounding weak. "I didn't know the men were fugitives, or I never would have hired them. They said they were big-game hunters." He shrugged. "How was I to know?"

Jesus, what a piece of putty. I slumped, and looked down at my feet.

Deacon and Ernie carried Dutch in, his arms looped over their shoulders, his big slack face hanging between them, his chin bobbing on his chest. Blood spread down from his face and covered his chest. His nose lay flat over on his cheek.

"Where do we take him?" Deacon asked. Bits of broken glass fell from Dutch's disheveled hair. He moaned. Blood dripped.

"Christ," said Silks. "Take him back to the train. Have Dory take a look at him." Then he turned back to Larr as they dragged Dutch out the door.

"Just so we understand each other, Colonel. Me and the boys are gonna take accommodation here till this blasted weather lets us leave—"

"Of course, anything," Larr cut in.

"The boys'll be taking rooms here. I'm staying in your private car, so I can keep an eye on Dutch, and take care of some personal business."

"I'm afraid that's out of the question," Larr said, trying to smile about it, but looking scared. "The lodge is open to you, of course, but I never lend my private car—"

"Oh? Well you shoulda said something before your boy ax-handled ole Dutch. Now I'm a man short, and I need to keep these prisoners separated. So you're either on the side of the law or you ain't. Which is it?" His pistol was still in his hand. He cocked it with the snap of a thumb.

Larr spread his hands. "But . . . but, you're not the *law*. You're a bounty posse—"

"We're the law for now, unless you've got other notions about it. If ya have let's get it settled right now."

"Well—" Larr ran a nervous hand across his cheek. "—I lost my sheriff. I have a jail here for your prisoner. You're welcome to our accommodations. But as far as my private car—"

"Good then." Silks cut him off before he could finish. "Sparks, when Ernie and Deacon get back, take Crowe to the jail. Keep a man on him at all times. I'll have the engineer keep the boiler stoked. Soon as this weather breaks, we'll head out." He turned back to Larr. "Go tell your cook to get busy and rustle up some hot grub . . . lots of it. And let's get some hot bathwater ready—and some whiskey, lots of it, too." He snapped his fingers at Larr. "Get busy with it."

Larr looked stunned. "But, I, that is—"

"Any problem?" Silks' eyes narrowed at him.

"Oh, well, no. I'll have the help get right on it."

"Good," Silks said in a gruff tone. He stepped down and over to the door. Then he turned back to Larr. "I have a big fancy rifle that belongs to you. I suppose you'll be wanting it back?"

"Yes, of course, please. It was custom made for me. I must have it back."

"We'll see how it goes." Silks glanced past his men with a slight smile of satisfaction, then left.

Larr took a deep breath, looked at the papers blowing about the room, and at the broken window. He glared over at Eldon. "Clean up this mess, then gather your gear and get out of here. You're finished!"

Eldon wobbled on his crutch. "I can't leave." He spread his free hand. "Where can I go? How will I get down the mountain?"

"That's your worry, not mine! You could have got us all killed, doing what you did." He shot a glance at Sparks, and said for Sparks' benefit, "Dan Silks and his men are *fine* people. I won't have you around causing trouble with them."

"At least let me stay until the weather breaks," Eldon pleaded. "I could die out there."

I, too, glared at Eldon, feeling better by the minute, seeing all kinds of possibilities opening up here. "Don't worry, *Eldon,*" I said, leaning toward him. "Nothing's gonna kill you but me."

He fumbled with his crutch, not facing me, and looked around at the mess on the floor. I chuckled and nudged the broken ax handle toward him with the toe of my boot. "Don't forget your weaponry. You might need it to fight off that bear."

257

Eldon shivered and swallowed hard.

Sparks put a hand on my shoulder, and pushed me forward a step. "Let's go find you a good cold jail cell."

Brerton Beam had watched quietly. Now he stepped in with us as Sparks shoved me toward the door. "But surely this man should have some food, some hot coffee? Perhaps I could bring both of you a bottle of warm spirits?"

Sparks glanced at him. "Why not? Bring it to us." He looked at Ponce over by the broken window. "Come on, Injun, show me the way."

Ponce stiffened. "My *name* is Ponce De Leon. Nobody calls me *Injun.*"

"Ponce, for godsakes!" Larr leaned over the banister, his voice hissing. "Do as these men tell you. We don't want any kind of trouble here."

"Boy oh boy, Larr." I shook my head. "I bet eating your leg made that bear sick for a month."

Sparks chuckled under his breath and shoved me on out the door. "You love seeing everything in an uproar, don't ya, Crowe?" He spoke above the roar of the wind, shoving me along, both of us hunched forward, leaning against the stinging sleet and snow.

CHAPTER

22

The jail was a one-room shack divided in half by bars. I looked it over good, stepping through the iron door. Even in the dark, I could see that the lock was of a kind easily opened by anything flat enough, stiff enough, and strong enough to turn the single tumbler. I stood still as Sparks plucked my hat from my head, closed the bars behind me, and walked over near a woodstove in the front corner.

"Colder than a witch's nipples," he grumbled. I gazed around in the dark, hearing him tinker with an oil lamp.

"I like the cold," I said, just to get him talking while we got settled in. "It keeps the mind clear and the blood working." From the cell I had a grainy view of the dark through a dirty front window streaked with ice. In the cell, there was a narrow barred window above a rickety bunk.

"*Shiiit,* I saw how you *love* the cold," Sparks said, brightening the wick on the lamp. A glow of circled light rose up in the darkness. "If the woman hadn't jackpotted you, you'd been dead in another day." I saw the light glisten on his black face. He smiled, took off his hat, and slapped it against his leg.

"We'll never know, will we?" I said.

"We don't even *need* to know," he said. He gestured toward my feet, and said, "Now get your boots off and pitch them out."

"What? Are you kidding me? As cold as it is? At least build a fire first." I didn't want him seeing the brass knuckles.

He grinned in the glow of the lamp. "It'll keep your *mind* clear and keep your blood working. Now skin out of 'em."

"Man oh man." I shook my head, stalling, stepping back to the bunk, getting out of the light as much as possible, hoping I could palm the knuckles without him seeing them. He watched me sit down and cross my foot over my knee. "Can't you get some kindling together and warm that stove—"

"Shut up, Crowe," he said, cutting me short. "I've never seen a condemned man act as ornery as you. Hope I don't have to wear you out with this rifle butt."

"So do I." I raised a hand toward him. "Boots coming off here, Boss," I said.

As soon as I took off the first boot, the door opened behind him and he turned. Beam stepped in; and while Sparks faced him, I quickly jerked off the other boot, snatched out the brass knuckles, and stuck them beneath the straw mattress. *Good timing, Mr. Beam.*

"I brought some whiskey," Beam said, holding a bottle out to Sparks. "As soon as some food's ready, I'll bring it too . . . and some coffee."

Sparks pulled the cork, raised the bottle beneath his nose, and sniffed it, glancing back and forth between Beam and me with a crafty expression. "What's the story here? Is Crowe a good friend of yours?" He watched Beam closely and stepped over near the bars. I stood, picking up my boots, and stepped over to him. "Have a snort, Crowe." Sparks stuck the bottle between the bars. I slipped the boots through the bars, dropped them, and took the bottle.

"Don't mind if I do." He watched me turn back a long shot; then he snapped his fingers toward me for the bottle.

"Is . . . is something wrong?" Beam spread his hands with a bewildered shrug.

Sparks still watched me closely as I wiped my hand across my mouth and let out a whiskey hiss. For another second he gazed into my eyes, then seemed relieved about something and smiled.

"No-sir, Mr. Beam," he said. "Not a thing." He turned up

the bottle and chugged down a deep swig. When he lowered it and caught his breath, he continued. "Just wondering why you're so concerned about our boy Crowe here."

Beam shrugged. "I don't know what this man has done, but he certainly treated me kindly on our way up here. He may have even saved my life on the train." He looked from Sparks to me. "I like to think there's some good in all men." He shrugged again. "Call me foolish . . . but it's just the way I believe."

"And a *fine* belief it is," I said, nodding, looking into his eyes. *Poor Beam. Naive, innocent . . .* I hoped he didn't get hurt here somehow. Whatever move I made, I'd be careful to keep him away from it.

Sparks grunted, stepping away and toward the pile of kindling and firewood beside the stove. "Save your sympathy on Crowe," he said, opening the stove door. "He won't be around long enough for it to matter. He's got a little task to do for us as soon as the storm passes; then he's going down the mountain in a gunnysack."

"My God! My goodness." Beam shook his head with a hand raised to his mouth. "You don't mean you're actually going to . . . ?" His voice trailed as he stared into my eyes. "That's barbaric beyond comprehension."

"Abso-damn-lutely," Sparks chuckled, breaking some kindling across his knee. He pitched it into the stove. "You can have the rest of him if you like . . . make some good fertilizer, if you'd grind him up. As much bullshit's as in him, he oughta spread a long ways."

"Have you no humanity, sir?" Beam hiked up his chest and spun toward Sparks. "This *is* a living breathing human being. Not some brute animal!"

"To each their own," Sparks said. "Still, I bet when his head rolls, the rest of him dances like a chicken."

"See here!"

I reached through the bars and tapped his shoulder. "Beam," I said quietly. "Let it go. These boys ain't to be fooled with. I appreciate your concern, but—"

"Get your hand back inside the bars," Sparks said, glancing around at us. I did, quickly. Then he said to Beam, "Better listen to him, mister. You're a whiskey drummer. You don't want to step over into our world. Right Crowe?"

261

I nodded at Beam and said quietly, "Just go, Mr. Beam. There's nothing more you can do here. I told them my friend's innocent. You might see to it that Silks checks it out. Other than that, just stay clear of all this, all right?"

"Well . . . I—" He rubbed his palms on his sides. I thought I saw his eyes water. "If you say so, Mr. Beatty. I'm just so very, *very* sorry. I feel like I should be doing something, *anything.*"

"Thank you, but go, please. It'd be better if you just left."

Before going to sleep that night, I managed to get the brass knuckles from beneath the mattress and slip them down inside my trousers. I was glad to see that it'd been Ponce instead of Beam who brought the hot food and coffee to us. I hoped Beam would stay away. For some reason I'd never been able to understand, it was always the innocent who got hurt the worst in such matters of man and their blood work.

When Ponce had slid a tray of food under the cell door, I'd asked about Beam, and Ponce said he'd been too upset to do anything but go to his room with a bottle of brandy under his arm. "Good," I said, hearing it. "This is no place for a feller like him."

"This is no place for *any* of us," Ponce replied.

I saw a strange foreboding look in his dark eyes and started to ask him what he'd meant. But Sparks had called from near the woodstove and told him, "No talking to the prisoner." So I took my tray and walked back to the bunk. Ponce had looked like he wanted to say more, but couldn't. He'd hesitated for a second, then left.

Come morning, I awoke to the sound of Laura Larr's voice and sat up on my bunk, seeing her and Dallas Renfrow talking to Spurlock over by the stove. Past them, through the dirty window, I caught a glimpse of Ponce and the Indian boy, Hasha. The boy sat atop a spindly roan. The roan pawed its hoof in the deep snow. Ponce stood in the white swirl, strapping supplies to a pack mule. I'd never seen him work so quick.

"Of course, we might have suspected something amiss," Laura said to Spurlock. "But I'm afraid my husband and I are both too trusting for our own good."

"Weeeelll, little lady," Spurlock said, stretching out his Texas drawl for all it was worth. "That's why there's good ole boys like us . . . so's we can keep things safe for folks like y'all."

I lowered my head, shook it, and looked up, over at Dallas Renfrow, who avoided my gaze. "If that's breakfast," I called over to them, "I'd like some before it freezes."

"Oh my!" Laura looked startled at the sound of my voice.

"Hush up, Crowe," Spurlock said. "You're scaring the little lady." Then, reaching for the tray in Laura's hands, he said, "I'll take that over for ya, ma'am."

Laura drew the tray back from him. "No. If you don't mind, I'll give it to him. Fear is best conquered by being faced, I always say."

Dallas and Spurlock nodded at each other as she stepped over to the bars in front of me. "So," I heard Renfrow say to Spurlock. "You barely made it here ahead of the storm."

Spurlock replied, "By the skin of our teeth . . ."

"Here, Mr. *Crowe*—" Laura leaned and shoved the tray beneath the bars as the two men talked to each other. "I hope you're ashamed of yourself . . . misleading my poor husband and myself. We both trusted you. *Believed* in you, you and your friend."

"I know, ma'am, and I'm truly sorry," I said, leaning down with her, hoping no one noticed my wry tone. I dropped my voice to whisper, fumbling with the tray. "How's my friend? Have you heard? Is he better?"

"A good breakfast is more than you deserve," she said. Then she whispered, "The offer still stands. If I get you out . . . will you kill my husband? Will you? Will you?" Her blue eyes shined in anticipation.

I pulled the tray to me. "Yes, deader than a mackerel," I whispered.

"There now," she said in a normal tone, standing, folding her hands across her stomach. She leaned slightly toward the bars, whispering again as Renfrow and Spurlock commented about the weather, "Beam saw your friend, last night. He was conscious, sitting up . . . he ate a little."

I took a deep breath, staring into her eyes. I nodded just to let her know I meant it. The deal was on. I hoped she couldn't see in my eyes that I was lying. I had no intention

263

of killing Larr for her. But right then I would have bargained with the devil if it got Jack and me off the spot. "Thank you for your kindness, ma'am. I'm sure your reward awaits in heaven."

A sharp glow lit her eyes; a trace of a smile passed across her lips and vanished. "Well, then . . . I'm all done here." She backed away, turned, and walked over to Renfrow and Spurlock. "Since you won't be leaving before the weather breaks, perhaps I'll have Mr. Renfrow bring over a noon meal for the two of you this afternoon?"

"That'd be fine, I'm sure, ma'am," Spurlock said. "Ernie will be guarding him, but I'm sure he'll be hungry by then."

Renfrow stopped before the two of them headed out the door. He glanced over and said, "I'm sorry you came to such an end here, Mr. Beatty, or Crowe, or . . . well, *whoever* you are."

"Not as sorry as *I* am." I offered a slight smile.

No sooner had the door closed behind them than Spurlock was standing before the cell. "Just for the fun of it, let's suppose what you said yesterday was true." He rocked back and forth on his boots, glanced over his shoulder at the door, then back to me.

I looked up from the bunk with my tray on my lap, deliberately took a large bite of biscuit, and said with a muffled voice as I chewed it, "Oh? About what?" I knew exactly what he was talking about but wanted to drag it out some. He expected me to start trying to convince him of something, but I wouldn't. This time he'd have to come to me with it. I stared at him, working my jaw slowly.

He cocked his head sideways. "Hell, you know . . . about Silks and the whore having something going on between them, about the money?"

"Aw, yeah." I nodded, looked away, seeming to consider it for a second. "I remember. There ain't much can be done about it though, whether it's true or not." I shrugged and took another bite. "Somebody just as well get some good out of it . . . since I'll be dead and gone. Might as well be them, I reckon."

"That's a hell of a thing to say. Why should it be them instead of me?" He lowered his brow and gazed at me, as if waiting for me to catch on to something.

"I don't know. Like I said, what difference will it make to me? I'm gonna die either way. I've resolved myself to it."

"What? You've given up that easy? After all the struggle you went through. Now you've *resolved* yourself to just dying, go to hell and be done with it?"

"I've thought about it all night," I said. "Then I woke up and saw the kindness showed me by that gracious woman, Mrs. Larr. I believe it was a sign from on high." I shook my head, took another bite. "It's just made me realize what a low-down, rotten dog I've been all my life." I shook my head slowly. "Yeah . . . I just as well end it here. Offer my miserable soul to the Lord on high and—"

"Now, wait a minute, hell. You ain't been all that bad. I've seen worse. The fact is, I've thought about it all night myself. I can see a way out of all this for you, if you're game to try it." His eyes gleamed toward me. "What do you say?"

I appeared to think about it, letting it come to me slowly, then raised a finger. "You mean . . . you helping me get away? The two of us getting the money?" I looked confused.

"Yeah, that's it." He nodded briskly. "Don't tell me you wasn't thinking about it yesterday." He leaned near the bars. "You and me, Crowe. Just two ole rebel boys making something happen for ourselves . . . like old times, you could say."

"Hmmmm. I don't know." I rubbed my throat, looking up at the ceiling. "I pretty much made my peace here. It's awful risky and rough out there, what with this new weather set in. I ain't even sure I can find the money, to be honest with you."

He grabbed the bars with both hands and hissed at me, "The hell are you saying? There's all that money out there, and you can't remember where? You're lying, Crowe. Silks and the whore are gonna get it, if I don't, and I can't stand the thought of that."

"Easy, Spurlock." I almost chuckled. "I mighta been wrong yesterday. Maybe it was all in my head. Hell, Silks ain't never mistreated ya before, has he? It could just be that—"

"Damn it to hell, Crowe! You brought it up, and it's the truth. They're making plans, and we both know it. I want that damned money! Now you put all that *dying* shit out of

265

your mind, or I'll blow your head off! I been coming up with a way to get you outa here. You're going, by God!"

"But there's a lot to be considered here," I said, sliding the tray off my lap. "There's two feet of snow out there and more coming. We need horses, guns, supplies. What about my friend? I can't *leave* him, and he's in no shape to ride—"

"Shut up, and listen. I can take care of horses and supplies. You just be ready, come nightfall. Your friend's doing all right. He'll be able to ride by then. We'll get ahead of them and let the snow cover our tracks."

"But how . . . how are you gonna get me out of here? I can't just walk out the front door."

"Damn it. Don't get softheaded on me." He nodded past me to the small window above the bunk. "I'll slip you a gun through the window while Deacon's guarding ya. You cover him, and I'll jerk that window out of the wall."

"Boy . . . I just don't know, Spurlock. It sounds awfully shaky to me. Silks is too damn smart to let us get away."

"Shiiit! He ain't nothing. You just get yourself primed for the getaway. I'll take care of everything."

Past him, I saw the door opening, and I cleared my throat warning him. He looked around at Ernie stepping in carrying a coffeepot.

Spurlock spun toward him. "Damn it, boy! What do you mean, sneaking around like that. You could get yourself shot!"

Ernie stopped wide-eyed, and stared at Spurlock, sticking the coffeepot out at him from across the room. "I—I wasn't sneaking. I just brung some coffee. I'm gonna relieve ya till Deacon gets here. Thought you'd be glad of it."

Spurlock's face reddened. "Aw. Well, I am glad. I just don't like being snuck on that way. Never did."

"Sorry," said Ernie. He walked cautiously to the stove and set the pot on it.

Spurlock turned back to me and spoke loud enough for the boy to hear. "Just remember what I've told ya, Crowe. Nobody better never say nothing against Dan Silks and let me hear it. Or I'll gut a sumbitch. Dan Silks is the finest, most decent—"

"What's going on?" Ernie asked, stepping over beside

Spurlock with two cups of hot coffee in his hands. "Somebody say something bad about Uncle Dan?"

"No. And they better never, around me," said Spurlock. "You keep a close eye on this bird, boy. I'm gonna go to the jake, then get some shut-eye."

When Spurlock had left, Ernie passed me a cup of coffee through the bars with his gloved hand. I took it and set it quickly on the floor, then stood up slinging my hand. "Damn! You coulda told me how hot it was," I said.

"Oh, my fault, sorry," he said with a sheepish grin. Then he nodded at the door. "What was he so worked up about?"

I grinned. "Aw, he just wants me to break out of here with him, but I turned him down. Told him it was too cold out . . . that I liked it here."

"Come on now, what was it really?" He grinned and sipped the coffee.

"Just like he said, kid. Evidently he doesn't want nobody talking ill of your Uncle Dan." I shrugged.

"Maybe *he* don't." Ernie's voice dropped low. "But I'll tell ya right now, this job ain't all Uncle Dan made it out to be. I'm sorry I took it . . . cold weather, all day in the saddle, maybe even have to kill somebody I don't even know, somebody like you that ain't done me no harm."

I just stared at him. "Oh? Is that a fact?"

"Dern right it is," he said, nodding, sipping his coffee.

I bent, and carefully picked up the hot cup, keeping my eyes on him. "Well, then. Maybe you just need to talk about it some, *Ernie,*" I said.

CHAPTER

23

---•---

For the next half hour, I stood sipping coffee, listening to Ernie tell me all the reasons why his taking this job was a mistake. He hadn't given much thought to killing a person until I'd spoken to him the day before. Sure, he told me, the others had mentioned it to him from time to time. He'd talked about it a little with his uncle Dan. But until he heard it from me—a man whose life he might actually have to take—the reality of the situation just hadn't struck home. He developed a nervous twitch in his jaw, just talking about it.

"Well, kid," I said when he finished, "look at it this way." I reached out between the bars and patted his shoulder, thinking how easy it would be to bang his head against the bars and get out of here. But I'd wait, and see how it went with Laura, and with Spurlock. "At least if I'm the first man you have to kill, I won't die holding it against you, no matter how gruesome and ugly it gets."

"Thanks," he said, and he lowered his eyes as I pulled my hand back inside the cell.

"If it comes down to you having to take that ax, or a knife, and lay my neck out on a chopping block, just do it and think nothing of it." I watched his face pale. "Even if I'm screaming, begging and quivering—as a man's prone to do at such times—just hack and cut . . . on through them

wiggling tendons and bloody arteries. Just get it over with."
I spread my hands.

He swallowed hard; I went on. *"Or . . .* if you have to
raise that pistol to my head at the last minute because I'm
convulsing so bad, and jerking and spraying you with
blood . . . just do it. And do it without letting it enter your
mind that only a minute before, I was a living breathing
human being, same as you, who only wanted to *live."* His
face turned a faint shade of green.

I sipped the coffee, let out a hiss, and gazed past him, off
through the window at the snow, still falling. Outside, I saw
no one on the boardwalk across the street, just the woman's
mannequin in the deserted store window. It stood there,
staring out blankly at the falling snow with its long black
cape flowing, and its fashionable wide-brimmed hat cocked
at a jaunty angle.

"Fact is, kid," I said, "killing gets a lot easier as you go
along. All you got to do is forget that the eyes looking at you
are eyes that will never again see the sunlight or the rain.
Don't even remind yourself that every *memory* that man
ever *had* is gone and lost forever . . . like times he remembered fishing with his pa, or scalding his sister's cat, or just
breathing, thinking, or feeling life run through him on a fine
summer morning—"

"Please! Please, stop it." He shook his head; his shoulders
shuddered. "I can't do it . . . I *can't."*

"Now, Ernie," I said quietly, leaning slightly, looking at
his lowered face. "I'm just trying to help you out a little
here."

"I know, I know, and I appreciate it. But I ain't cut out
for this kinda work. I never shoulda come along." His voice
cracked. "I was happy just tending my pa's farm in Ohio.
But there came Uncle Dan. 'Come on,' he told me. 'Get out
there and see what the world's all about.' I shoulda known
better. Pa always said Uncle Dan's a braggart and a nut-
head. I'm going right now and tell him I quit—"

"Whooa! Hold on." I reached through the bars and
grabbed the back of his coat as he turned. "I wished you
wouldn't do that, Ernie! Not right now."

"Why not *now?* Before I have to do something I don't
want to."

269

"Because, kid." I let out a patient breath. "He don't like keeping me alive anyway. What's he gonna think if you rush in telling him all this? He could go crazy and kill me on the spot." I shook my head slowly, turning loose of his coat, patting him on the chest. "No, I wish you'd let things settle here a little first. If something comes up where you need to do some shooting, just do like I saw lots of the boys do back in the war—take cover and fire in the air. Hell, who's gonna know the difference in a hundred years?"

He rubbed his face. "Yeah, maybe you're right. We're getting shorthanded as it is. Dutch is stove-up from that ax handle. Sparks and the half-breed are fighting back and forth, mad at everybody—"

"Really?" I cut him off. "What about?"

"Aw, it's stupid stuff. They both think the other is getting better treated . . . and that neither is getting treated as good as us white boys. You know how that goes."

"Yeah, I do. You just can't please some people." I looked him up and down. "Do me a favor, kid. If something *does* happen here, whatever it is, get out of the way till it's over. Will you do that, and keep your mouth shut about it?"

"Well, I don't see what it'd hurt." He smiled. I handed him my empty cup, and he said, "I won't say nothing . . . but don't you either."

"I won't, kid. Believe me, you've got my word on it."

I heard something in the distance, and cocked my head to the side. "Did you hear something, Ernie? Something far off?"

"Hunh-uh, what?"

"Wait, be still," I said, listening for it again. Somewhere, off a long ways, I thought I'd heard the ever so slightest sound of a baying dog. We stood silent until the wind settled; then I thought I heard it again.

"Well, what was it?" he asked.

I waited another second, heard nothing, and shook my head. "Never mind. Forget it. I thought I heard something but maybe I was wrong." I glanced at the pot over on the stove. "Would you mind pouring me another cup. Whoever made the coffee knew what they were doing."

"Sure," he said, grinning. "I made it. Pretty dern good, huh?"

"Yep. You could get a good job with the army, or a cattle drive or something."

I could've sworn I heard the sound again as he walked over to the stove, then once again while he poured the coffee. No sooner than he'd finished pouring us both a cup, Deacon swung open the door and looked around as if he might catch somebody doing something they shouldn't. A short-barreled ten-gauge hung from his hand.

"What are you doing, boy?" He glared at Eldon holding the two cups of coffee. "We ain't here to serve this black-guard heathen *coffee!*" He slammed the door behind him and stomped over to Ernie. "Give me that," he demanded, jerking one of the cups from the boy's hand. Coffee sloshed and splattered. "Now go on . . . get out of here." He nodded toward the door.

"I don't see why he can't have a cup of coffee. He's as human as the rest of us, even if he is an outlaw—"

"I said, *git!*" Deacon stomped a foot toward him; the boy backed away quickly, wide-eyed, and pawed frantically at the door. *So much for young Ernie,* I thought. *Now the Deacon.* What to do with the Deacon . . .

"There'll be no mollycoddling now that I'm here," Deacon said, as Ernie slung open the door and sprang through it. Outside somewhere, I once again thought I heard the sound of a dog in the distance. "Lucky I came early," Deacon added when the door slammed shut, "for there's no telling what dark evil you'd fill his head with. Myself . . . I'll just round a barrel of buckshot on ya and be done with it." He patted the ten-gauge. "Forget about the hidden money. I'd rather see your soul burning in hell. That's a sight money can't buy."

I listened, nodding as he spoke. "But, tell me, Deacon. Wouldn't you have to be there yourself, to see *me?*"

"Don't twist my words, *sinner, heathen!* I've seen the likes of your kind all over the West. Think you can outride the Lord, outshoot the Lord. Now look at ya. Ready to die like a dog."

He pointed his coffee cup at me, sitting down at the battered table. Swinging the ten-gauge across the table, he cocked both hammers and let the short barrel lie pointed at

271

me. "You best get on your knees and start letting me hear you beg his forgiveness, is what you better do."

"But if I do that, and get it, how would you see my soul in hell?" Even from across the small room, the barrels of the shotgun looked as large as a field cannon.

"Ha! You'll get no forgiveness. The Lord will have his vengeance on ya—"

"Then why would I ask for it? What would be the point? Just for your satisfaction? Just so you could see me beg?" I slumped on the bunk, staring across and through the bars at him. "How many souls have you won for Jesus with that kind of preaching?"

"Winning souls, *huh*. Good preaching ain't about winning souls. It's about sending sinners' souls to hell where they belong. That's what it's about." He raised a thick finger and said in a louder voice, *"Mercy* is what you better pray for, boy. Beg and cry for *mercy!* You'll get none, but you better pray and beg for it all the same."

Jesus. I shook my head, and started to say something more when the door opened and Laura Larr stepped in carrying another tray of food. "Here we are," she said, only glancing at Deacon, moving quickly over to the cell before he'd have time to think about it.

"Just a minute there, little lady," he said, getting up, following her. "Don't go near that man."

"What? Oh, don't be silly," she said over her shoulder. I could tell she was well stoked on cocaine. Maybe she had to be to get her nerve up. "I told Mr. Spurlock I'd be bringing Ernie and the prisoner some food." She glanced around. "Where is Ernie?"

"Never you mind. I've taken charge here. Let me see that tray."

I held my breath, hoping, as he raised a hand towel from the tray, that she hadn't put a pistol under it. She hadn't. "I'll have to take this," he said. "It's too early to eat anyway." He placed his thick hands on the tray and nudged it from her.

"Oh, well then—" She glanced at me and touched a hand idly against her midriff, just enough to show me the slight bulge of gun butt. Then she closed her coat across it and stepped back as I shot her a warning glance. "I should think the least you'd do is give the man some food . . . in this kind of weather."

"I will when I feel like it," he said, stepping back, squatting, and setting the food there in front of the cell where I could see it but not get to it. "Everything'll be good and hot where he's going. We'll just let him think about it first. Make him appreciate it more."

Behind him, Laura stepped around behind the wooden table while he poked a finger around on the tray. "Let's see here, Crowe," he said, taunting me. "We've got some stew . . ."

As he spoke, poking his finger in the food, I saw the small silver pillbox come out from under her coat. *Oh no!* I wanted to tell her to stop! But I couldn't say a word. All I could do was watch as she tapped a stream of the white powder into his coffee cup. She glanced up, saw the look on my face, grinned, as if misreading what my eyes were trying to tell her, then emptied the whole small box of it and tapped the bottom with her dainty finger. I rolled my eyes.

"And some good hot cobbler . . ." Deacon chuckled, poking his finger in it. He raised his finger to his lips.

Laura stirred the coffee quickly with her finger, then stepped back, wiping her finger on her coat. I just stared, shaking my head ever so slowly. "Aw," said Deacon, perhaps thinking I was shaking my head at him. "Don't worry, my hands are clean. I washed them yesterday before feeding the horses. You won't need this right now anyways. You had a good breakfast this morning." He spread a nasty grin. "We'll just leave it cool awhile—till the grease turns white. I heard outlaws don't eat but once every day or two."

"Tell me, Deacon," I said in a quiet tone, "when you was a boy did you pull the legs off little frogs, maybe drown a chicken or two? Did your daddy thump your head a lot?"

He raised himself up from a squat, and said in a low growl, "Don't you let my father cross your heathen lips again or I'll cut them off and jerk your loathsome tongue from your head."

"Um-hmm, I thought so," I said. Here it was, my way out. I could goad him over to the cell anytime, get him worked into a frenzy, crack his head with the knuckles, get the horse Spurlock was bringing, and be gone. But what about Jack?

273

Was he really able to ride? And if he was, how would I get to him? I couldn't leave without him; it was out of the question.

Laura cleared her throat to remind him she was still here. "Well, then, all done here," she said. "I'll just be on my way."

"Yes, ma'am, you just do that," Deacon said. He stepped back to the table as she left, raised the cup of laced coffee and took a sip. I watched to see if he noticed anything wrong with it, then smiled a little when I realized he didn't. "What are you grinning about, boy?"

"Nothing. Just trying to get a glimpse of the promised land before I gotta go there."

"Promised land? Huh! The devil's pacing hell right now, ready to throw hooks and horns in ya. There's *your* promised land." He threw back another sip, seemed to like it, then took a long drink of it and let out a coffee hiss. Somewhere out in the night, once again I heard a dog bark.

"Did you hear that?" I cocked my head.

"Yeah, I heard a dog. So what? Don't try to change the subject." He took a longer drink of coffee and seemed to fidget a bit in his chair. "When you get to hell, you're gonna wish—" His words stopped short; he wiped a hand across his forehead. "Whew! Sweet Jesus! It's *hot* in here." He batted his eyes and threw back the rest of the coffee. "Seem hot to you?"

I shrugged. "Figured it was just all that fire and brimstone you's conjuring up." Again I heard a dog bark, but didn't comment on it. Behind me, there was a scraping sound against the back wall beneath the barred window. *Not now, Spurlock! Not now—!* I clenched my jaws, hoping Deacon hadn't heard the sound. *Not with that splatter gun so close at hand!*

"So, Deacon," I said quickly. "Suppose I could have that plate of food now?" I nodded down at it through the bars, hoping he'd come over without the shotgun, hoping I could snatch him before Spurlock yanked the window out of the wall. But even as I said it, I noticed a glaze coming over his eyes, and he seemed to be too preoccupied with some deep inner thought to hear a word I'd said.

"Deacon? Deacon?" Still no answer. I watched him tug at

his collar and wipe a hand over his face. Outside, the scraping at the window stopped. My only hope was that Spurlock might've heard my voice and decided to wait for a moment. "Are you all right there, Deacon?"

He jerked straight up from the chair as if I wasn't there, and spoke to the air above his head as he tore off his shirt and slung it away. "Sometimes *theeee Looord!* carries a handful of spiders, and throws them on the back of them he loves the most!"

He pulled the top of his long johns loose, popping buttons, peeled it from his thick hairy back, and let it hang down from his waist. I just stared as he began pacing back and forth, rubbing his hands all over his naked chest and sides. The cocaine had him. It was starting to boil. "Amen," I said to myself in a hushed tone.

CHAPTER

24

---·---

For twenty minutes or more, I stood still as stone watching Deacon rant and rave, preaching to himself and scratching like a person lit with fleas. A thin trickle of blood showed above one ear where he'd actually dug through his scalp. He paced back and forth behind the wooden table, at times laughing, at times sobbing, but for the most part quivering and gritting his teeth. The sound was terrible. The shotgun still lay across the table, aimed and cocked.

I hadn't heard Spurlock at the back wall for a while and wondered for a moment if he had changed his mind and left. But then I heard once more the sound of a quiet scrape against the barred window, and I prepared myself to move fast as soon as he cleared a hole for me. Even with the cocaine boiling in Deacon's head, he could still manage to get the shotgun up and fill my whole cell with buckshot.

Just as I heard a tugging, creaking sound on the window bars and braced myself for escape, young Ernie threw open the front door and spilled through it with the big Catahoula circling his feet. "Oh Lord! Oh Lord!" His breath heaved; his face was flushed. He steadied himself back against the door and stared at Deacon as the Catahoula circled the room, sniffing and whining. "He's gone, Deacon! He's gone!"

"Who-ah-who-ah-whooose gone?" The Deacon stammered, his neck making sharp little jerks, tendons standing out, his ears redder than beets.

"His partner," the boy said, panting and pointing over at me. The Catahoula loped to my cell, leaped up, put his front paws on a cross iron, and sniffed toward me. His eyes were shiny, alert and searching. He whined under his breath. "He—he got away," Ernie continued. "The breed was sitting there beside his bed, deader than a rock, and the man's gone!" He shot a glance up and down Deacon's naked belly covered with fingernail scratches. "What's wrong with you, Deacon?"

Deacon's whole body jerked and trembled. "There ain't a wrong thing damn with me. Get he hell the how away?"

"What?" Ernie cocked his head and stared. I did the same. The Catahoula sniffed toward the wall behind me, and I prayed he wouldn't raise a fuss if he heard Spurlock out there. *That-a-boy, Jack! You made it. Now get the hell out of here.* I hoped now that he'd gotten away, he would forget about me and make a hard run for it. I'd catch up with him down the mountain once Spurlock made his move.

Deacon shook his head, steadied himself with a hand on the wooden table, and spoke one word at a time. "How, did, he, get, away? Where's, Spurlock, where's, Dan?" He raised his hand from the table and pressed his palms against his ears. "My head's cracking open!" The Catahoula whined, dropped from the bars, and scratched at the floor toward my cell. I reached my toe through the bars, tried to nudge him away. He growled and snapped at my foot.

"I ain't told Uncle Dan yet . . . Spurlock's gone too! I looked for him on the way here. His horse is gone!"

"Damn that Texan for what he is!" Deacon's voice jittered. He snatched up the shotgun so quick with his shaky hand, when he spun around with it one barrel exploded and blew the door off the woodstove. Sparks flew.

"My God, Deacon!" Ernie shouted.

But Deacon just slung the shotgun toward me, looking wild-eyed and insane. "This one won't get away!"

Behind me, I heard the wrenching of steel and wood ripping from the window frame. They heard it too. With the shotgun pointing at me, all I had time to do was hit the floor and roll toward the bunk as buckshot pinged off the steel bars and whistled above me in a fiery blast.

"Don't kill him, Deacon!" the boy yelled. The shotgun clicked open. *Hurry, Spurlock, hurry!* I scrambled under the bunk, catching a glimpse of the bars and frame being pulled from the wall as if sucked out by a terrible wind. *Come on come on Spurlock!* I snatched the bunk and turned it over, using the thin mattress as a shield between me and the splatter gun. The Catahoula barked in an endless wail at the cell door.

"He's bu-sting out . . . sho-ot him!" Deacon yelled. Chunks of wood fell from the window frame above me.

Ernie yelled, "I can't!"

"I can!" The shotgun snapped shut with a loud click. As soon as he pulled off both rounds, I'd have to make a lunge for the window before he reloaded, that is if there was anything left of me. The Catahoula tore at the cell door with his claws, bellowing.

"Get out of the wa-ay, you lou-sy cur!" The shotgun exploded. I felt the blast hit the mattress, heard the Catahoula let out a yip and scramble across the floor. Above me, the sound of Spurlock scraping away the remains of the open window frame.

"Look out, Spurlock," I yelled.

"Spur-lock?" Deacon screamed. "Why th-at dirty, rot-ten—" The shotgun exploded again, this time blasting the wall above me. I'd just started to make my leap as the shotgun clicked open; but I stopped cold in the terrible smell that filled my nostrils, and dropped back down as the long raging bawl of the grizzly roared through the window and shook the whole building.

"It's the bear!" Ernie screamed.

"Sho-ah, sho-ah, shoot it!" Deacon stammered.

"Get me *ouuut* of here!" My voice rose above the wail of the dog and the bawl of the bear; and I crawled frantically along the wall with the mattress covering me, to the front corner of the small cell. I grabbed a bar and tried shaking it. "Please!" I called out. There was a sound of boards being ripped and shattered from the back wall. *"Pleeeease!"* I screamed.

"Go! Go! We ne-ed rifles," Deacon bellowed. I heard him

scuffle toward the door, heard the bear's heavy breathing, the dog barking.

"What about Crowe?"

"Damn him . . . he's dead!" Deacon yelled.

Lord God! I peeped around the edge of the mattress and saw the bear stepping through the broken wall like a man stepping through a heavy curtain of beads. Splinters and board spilled about him. Under one arm he carried a bloody human leg with shredded trousers hanging from it— Spurlock's trousers. The Catahoula charged against the cell bars, his voice gone hoarse, foam spewing from his drawn flews, his teeth bared, his hackles quivering in fury. A blast of cold drafted from the open door as Ernie's and Deacon's boots pounded along the boardwalk . . . and I was alone! Alone with the bear.

He stood just inside the broken wall for a moment while the Catahoula raged. I smelled him, heard his deep powerful breath. My trembling hand found the brass knuckles and managed to slip them on my fingers somehow. I prayed, almost aloud, that he wouldn't see the quaking mattress, me huddled behind it, that he wouldn't smell the scent of me, or the odor of what I was apt to expel at any second.

Then I heard a deep growl mingled in his heavy breath, and felt him stalk closer, slowly. The Catahoula raged, flinging himself against the bars.

I dared not peep around, but I heard a thump and knew without looking that he'd just dropped Spurlock's leg to the floor. I heard a crackling of fire and smelled wood smoke, the cold draft of air fanning the embers from the broken stove. This was it. I knew it. I would die there, torn to shreds, what was left of my body cremated by a licking raging fire. A thin glow of heat swept past me on the cold draft.

The bear's breath was above me for a second, then warm on my exposed back when he leaned down and peeled away the mattress with his long claws as if uncovering a picnic basket. The Catahoula raged, slamming harder and harder against the rigid bars. The bear breathed slow and steady only inches from my trembling back. A drop of wet warm saliva spilled on me and spread on my shirt.

Deacon was right. I was dead, and I knew it; but knowing

it, I turned slowly, ever so slowly, cocking my fist in the brass knuckles and asking no more of *God* than to give me one last good punch at that big bastard's muzzle. Just one hard right, and maybe I could die knowing that at least he'd have to eat me with a pain in his jaw.

He dropped down slowly onto all fours as I turned, and his muzzle hovered back and forth only inches from my face. His putrid breath blew into mine while the Catahoula struck at the bars with no letup. Time, motion, and all matter stopped. The two of us had drifted to a high lofty place above world and worldly reason, where death and life were inseparable in their breadth and content. And I could only stare as he twisted his head back and forth with the curiosity of a lapdog. I may have even done the same in return.

Then, although he opened his jaws wide and reached his face close to mine, my face nearly covered and taken into his mouth, I could neither move back nor away. I stared, transfixed, and looked deep into the wet, pulsing throat as if studying the path to some dark new place where I was about to go—the beginning of a journey, destination unknown.

The brass knuckles were still on my hand, my fist cocked and ready, yet I made no move. The Catahoula still lunged, yet I heard not the sound of his hoarse voice. There was only the breathing, heavy and deep, from within that dark glistening world stretched wide before me. I saw the black and yellow stains on the bear's teeth, a scrape of something stuck back there, wet, soggy, and pale. It floated back and forth in a puddle of saliva against the edge of his thick tongue.

Then, he pulled his open muzzle back from my face, an inch, maybe two, but no more than two; and he let out a blasting bawl that blew my hair back from my forehead and stung my face with flecks of spittle. Yet, I did not move a muscle; perhaps I dared not, perhaps I couldn't. Or, if there be such a thing as teetering so close to death that death is no longer to be resisted, perhaps I'd found it . . . found it and felt it, and welcomed it somehow for a brief instant.

But something began to stir deep inside me—life maybe—as the bear took a step back, then another; and I felt a jolt of fear resurface—*run!* He turned his attention away from me and to the Catahoula still charging against the cell. *Jesus! Run, now!* I shook my head slightly, watching him draw in a deep breath as he rose up and blasted a bawl at the Catahoula through the bars.

Smoke thickened and blew through the bars. Slices of gray light swirled and spun from the orange glow of flames. Fire bellowed, licking and dancing up the far wall by the open woodstove.

The bear lunged, striking out a paw through the bars at the Catahoula. The dog veered back sideways, ducking the claws, then sprang forward again. The bear slammed against the bars, slashing out his claws as I slipped back a step—*For godsakes run!*—crouched, and slid backward along the wall in a draft of smoke until the open hole of jagged broken boards welcomed me like a mother's arms.

I ran like a man possessed, a man gone mad fleeing hell and the devil; slipping, falling, rolling in the snow, and coming back to my feet without missing a step. Behind me the Catahoula raged, crying out in some strange brutal harmony with the bawl of the giant grizzly. From the street someone yelled, "The damn jail's burning!"

Let her burn, I thought, feeling the cold air bite deep in my chest. Something dark and wet sloshed beneath my bare feet as I ran through it, and without looking back I had a feeling it was the remains of Spurlock the Texan.

At the corner of a building, I stopped and hung against a wooden barrel for just a second, long enough to get my bearings and slip the brass knuckles off my hand. My breath heaved; steam gushed like smoke from a bellows. "The hell's going on now?" I heard Dan Silks' voice call out from the darkness.

"The bear's in the jail, Uncle Dan! It's killed poor Crowe. He's dead and the other one's gone! Spurlock's gone too. The breed's dead! The jail's burning up! Nothing's what it oughta be."

"Shit-fire!" Silks yelled. "Can't I leave long enough to get me a little poon, without the whole damn place going—"

"Hurry, Uncle Dan!" Boots pounded through the snow, above the raging bear and dog and the crackling rolling fire. I ventured through an alley to the street; and with my back flat against the wall of a building, I peeped around toward the burning jail. In the flicker of firelight glowing out off the gray smoke, dark figures ran through the snow, forming a semicircle in the street around the sound of the animals inside. From the lodge, Ben Larr came limping through the snow.

Leaning there against the building, I realized that soon the bear would have to make a break for it, lest he and the Catahoula perish in the flames. He was too smart to charge out front into the rifle muzzles. No. He would do just what I would do if I were him. He'd come out the back and down the alley—straight in my direction. I crouched, pushed off from the building, and darted across the snow-rutted street. They could have spotted me in the darkness had they been looking, but I risked it, rather than tarry and have to face the big bear.

Across the street, I stopped long enough to hastily consider my situation. Spurlock was dead, but Jack was alive and gone. Gone where? What had he been thinking? Did he take a horse? Had he forgotten about me? No way, not Jack. He was somewhere, waiting, watching, seeing what was going on, same as I. But where? How would I reach him?

I couldn't last long here. I had to find shelter long enough to lay some kind of getaway plan. If not, Dan Silks would be right back on my trail. I thought of going to Laura Larr, but she was a pretty shaky bet. If the going got close, she'd point her finger straight at me, regardless that I'd agreed to kill her husband for her. *Beam. That's it.* Get to Beam. As bad as I hated bringing him into the game, he was the only solid card in the deck.

If I could get to his room, get a coat, some boots, a gun, then get to the barn, get a horse and flee . . . I would take all the other horses with me and scatter them into the wilds. Even Dan Silks and his men couldn't chase me down without horses. From the raging fire the Catahoula let out a long yelp. He hurled through the door of the jail in a spray of orange sparks and swirling gray smoke.

Now the bear would be coming, I thought, seeing the dog roll, smoking and yipping, in the snow. The men ran forward, circling him, firing rifles into the burning jail. The bear bawled.

I glanced once across my path behind me. My footsteps in the snow pointed my way like a road map. *Jesus!* I ducked into a crouch and slipped along the alley, hearing the men shouting. "The bear's kilt him, no doubt about it. Crowe's dead."

"Hunt for him . . . both of 'em, goddamn it! He might still be alive," Silks bellowed. "They're like two rats. They could be anywhere."

"But, the bear, Uncle Dan!"

"Fuck the bear! Shoot the bastard! Get them men caught and brought back here . . . damn this bullshit!"

I glanced all around, slipping back through the darkness of the alley. *Jack, where the hell are you?*

CHAPTER

25

With the sound of men, and the crackling fire roaring behind me, I ran, crept, and ducked along the alley, working toward the rear of the lodge. Wherever Jack was hiding, if he could hear, I hoped he didn't believe what the men had said about the bear killing me. Silks was right about one thing. Jack and I *were* like a couple of rats when it came to staying alive. Now that we were both free and moving, they'd have to take this town apart to sift us out.

At the end of the alley, I crept across the snow to the train and slipped along the side of it just like a . . . a *rat*. Somewhere in the darkness the bear would be moving about, unaware and detached from what was going on in the blood sport of man against man. I'd have to stay away from him. The best way to get to Beam was to slip along the train, then cut across to the lodge, keeping to the shadows along the line of storefronts.

The best place to start looking for Jack was at the point where he'd escaped. With everybody at the fire, the train sat dark and quiet, save for the light glowing in the private car where the Indian woman would be. I thought for a second about going to her, but I'd seen just enough of both her sides to keep me leery. She'd been playing *Dandy* Dan like a string instrument, but to what end?

I slipped up on the platform and into the next car back,

284

where I figured they'd been keeping Jack under guard. I was right. Inside the dark car, the half-breed's body sat still as stone in a wooden chair, his arms hanging at his sides and his head tilted back. His boots were gone. His gun was gone from his holster and his vacant eyes stared into the darkness above him. *Jack's armed himself . . . good!*

Four feet from the dead half-breed lay the bed where Jack's wrist must have been chained to the headboard. A baluster in the headboard was broken; half of it lay on the floor. On a small table sat a bottle of brandy with its cork beside it. I snatched a wool blanket from the bed, threw it around my shoulders, picked up the half-breed's hat from the floor where it had fallen behind him, and put it on.

I glanced around and moved on, searching for Jack's footprints leaving the train. But there were too many other prints now. They crisscrossed in the snow at the bottom of the platform—the sign of men running back and forth in confusion. I moved on. Somewhere between me and the distant glow of fire and smoke, I heard the bear let out a muffled roar and heard him puff out a deep breath. I moved quicker.

At the rear of the lodge, a steel drainpipe ran down the building to a frozen-over rain barrel. I tested the pipe with both hands, then stepped up on the barrel and began climbing. Crusted snow broke and fell around me. At the row of windows along the second level, I reached my foot over to a slippery ledge, scraped my heel until I made steady purchase, then reached a hand over to the frame and stretched over to it.

The window was stiff, nearly frozen shut, but I managed to raise it a foot and slide my leg in. Holding on by the frame, I bumped the window open farther and slipped in, down to the floor, and crouched there listening.

There was no sound save for that of the men in the distance at the burning jail. I heard Dan Silks curse in the distance; and I moved across the dark room, out into the hall, and along the dark hallway to the faint glow of light seeping beneath the door to Brerton Beam's room.

Listening, glancing around in the darkness, I heard the creaking of a floorboard inside as I rose up beside the door. I turned the knob softly and slipped in like a ghost. Beam stood across the room, staring out the window toward the burning jail. A flicker of the distant flames shone on the frosted window glass.

"Beam," I said in a whisper, "it's me."

I held a finger to my lips as he turned toward me. I'd expected him to be startled; yet when he turned and faced me, he did so quietly, almost as if he'd expected me to come crawling out of the darkness. "Mr. Beatty," he whispered, stepping toward me from the window with a finger pointing back toward it. "I—I heard the men . . . I thought the bear killed you. Thank heaven you're still—"

"I'm okay," I said in a whisper, cutting him off. "I need help. I need a gun . . . some warm clothes. Boots."

"But, your friend. Is he . . . ? I thought perhaps he was dead."

"He's all right, I think. I ain't sure. But they'll be coming, looking for me. If you don't help me, *I'm* dead, *that's* for sure."

"Well, I . . . that is, of course I'll help you. No man deserves to die that way." He raised a hand absently to his throat and swallowed hard. "What can I do?"

"Give me the pistol you carry," I said. He hesitated, fumbling, taking note of the brass knuckles on my hand. "Quick!" I snapped my fingers toward him. "And I need a warm coat."

"Certainly, here." He snatched the pistol out and handed it to me; I checked it and shoved it into my waist. "My coat will be a bit small, but—" He moved quickly to the large oak wardrobe, swung the door open, and pulled out his wool overcoat. "You're welcome to it, of course."

He watched as I dropped the blanket and pulled on the coat. "What are your plans . . . if you don't mind my asking," he said.

"I'm winging it, for now," I said, shaking the coat onto my shoulders. I stepped over, peeped out the window toward the jail fire, then back to him. Somewhere in the darkness came the bawl of the bear, followed by a rifle shot. I looked Beam up and down. Ordinarily I would tell no one my plans . . . but under the circumstances, why not, I thought.

Letting out a breath, I said, "I'm figuring to get all their horses someway, then skin out of here. There's some money hidden out there. I'm hoping to hook up with my partner and make a run for it."

"Let me go along," he said in a rushed voice. "I can be of assistance. I can help you find your friend."

"No way." I shook my head. "You've already been of help. I can't ask more of you."

"But, once you're gone, I'm afraid they'll know I've helped you, and Lord knows what they'll do to me for it."

"Uh-uh, Beam. I'm moving quick. It's life or death here. Just tell them I forced your gun and coat from you."

"What if I *insist* you take me along?"

"Forget it. I don't even have time to talk about it."

He sighed. "Very well then, I tried. All I can do is wish you Godspeed—" He stopped and raised a finger. "—and, oh. I do have something that you might take along, something that could help you *and* your friend, should you find him." He turned back to the wardrobe. "I'll just get it for you."

"What is it?" I fidgeted, impatient, wanting to get going. Outside, voices called back and forth. Once more the bawl of the bear roared in the darkness. "What could you possibly have that's gonna help me get—"

"Now, now, Mr. Beatty," he said, cutting me off. "You know how us ole bachelors are . . . always prepared." He rummaged for a second, then said, "Here we are," with his back turned to me.

Something flashed across my mind, something wrong here, something in his words. A realization stunned me for a second—but only for a *split* second, and I acted on it as he turned toward me, chuckling. "Here we are, Mr. Beatty. This will solve all your problems—"

"What about Vera and little Ellen?" I said in a resolved tone, cocking the pistol I'd jerked from my waist, holding it out at arm's length. His smile faded. The pistol he'd brought around toward me from the wardrobe was only half raised, and his hand froze there, his thumb across the hammer. "Don't raise it, you sneaking little son of a bitch."

Everything about him changed before my eyes. His voice actually dropped an octave, his expression turned from a clear brow to a dark level glare. His eyes narrowed. "That

287

was stupid of me, wasn't it, Crowe," he hissed. "One simple slip of the lip, just when everything was going so well."

"Offhand, I'd say it was the worst mistake you'll ever make, *Mister* Beam—if that's really your name."

I took a short step toward him. Outside, the men's voices sounded closer. "Damn the bear," I heard Silks say. "Find them bastards!"

"Oh, it's my name all right—" His free hand moved slowly inside his vest. I tensed my gun hand; but he stopped his hand to reassure me, then moved it on, pulled out a small leather wallet, and let it flip open. A small badge glinted in the dim light. "—and I'd bet twenty dollars you won't dare pull that trigger and give yourself away." He raised the pistol less than an inch.

"Easy," I said, and his hand stopped. "Midwest Detective Agency, huh? That's just another name for *bounty-killer.* Except Silks and his bunch is more honest about it. You had to pass yourself off as a whiskey drummer."

He chuckled, a dark, grim chuckle. "No, Crowe. *You* said I was a whiskey drummer. I just went along with you. That day on the train? I had you set up for a bullet in the back of the head, if Laura Larr hadn't showed up. I had your friend locked up good and tight in the stock car—he *shoulda* froze! I could've saved us all a lot of needless running around, taken the carpetbag *and* the bounty, and gone back to New Hampshire. But damn it all, the bear, the Larrs, then that posse horning in. It's been ridiculous."

"So, *that's* what the big deal was about your missing wallet. You figured it might've fell out along with your gun? We mighta seen the badge? You just wanted to make sure we hadn't?"

"Now you're catching on." His gun hand rose ever so slightly, then stopped. "I hate to break it to ya, but by now your friend really is dead."

"Oh?" My stomach tightened; my gun hand stayed tense. He saw it.

"Yep. *This time,* I put enough poison in his brandy to kill an elephant. The same poison the government traders used back when they killed off the Utes. It shoulda killed him before . . . but the man just *would not* lay down and die." He was talking to see if he'd catch me off guard, then he'd jerk the pistol up and burn me. But it wasn't going to happen. Jack was alive. Beam didn't realize it, but the poison he'd sent to kill him was the very thing that'd set Jack free. I almost shook my head to clear the irony from it.

"He's always been able to handle his liquor," I said. Beam's gun rose a fraction, then it stopped. He didn't think I'd noticed it move.

"You shouldn't have got so greedy," I said.

"Maybe." He shook his head slowly, smiling. "I admit, I've never had so much trouble getting a job done. Whatever Jesse and Frank paid you two . . . it really wasn't enough."

I heard boots shuffle along the boardwalk outside the lodge.

"We get by. Now pitch that gun over on the bed. You gave it a try, but it's over now."

"No, Crowe. It's *not* over now. I wanted the money from the carpetbag. Would've gotten it too, if you'd taken me along with you. Since you wouldn't, I figure I'll just stop the game right here and pick up the reward on you. Silks lost you, *I* found you, you're mine." The pistol in his hand rose higher, this time a full inch.

"Don't raise it," I warned, not wanting to have to pull the trigger on him and bring Silks' men down on me.

"Like I said, Crowe. I bet twenty dollars you won't pull that trigger. I'm betting you're tired of running, tired of fighting, betting you know when you're licked. Now pitch that little peashooter over on the bed and let's call it a night. That gun hasn't even been cleaned and fired since I hit your buddy Clarence Carter with that lucky shot back in Rawling Siding. It might not even fire now. Wanta chance it?"

I felt the skin tighten on the back of my neck. "You know all the wrong things to say, Beam." My fingers tightened around the gun in my hand. Downstairs, the door opened and slammed shut. I heard voices and the sound of boots.

"Like I said, Crowe . . . twenty dollars says you won't. I dare you to." His pistol rose slightly higher. I pictured poor Clarence Carter with the blood running down his head. The lucky shot he'd put in Clarence's head was the shot that had put the bag of money in my hand that day. That in itself was reason to kill him. *More irony here . . . enough to write a book—*

"Never bet on a dare," I said quietly.

"Twenty dollars, Crowe." The pistol came up, almost level with my stomach, his thumb ready to cock it. "Now bet or *fold."*

Boots pounded on the stairs.

"Fold, hell . . . *raise* you one." I snapped one shot, saw a tiny hole appear in his right eye, then watched him stagger backward, falling inside the open wardrobe with a stunned expression.

"I heard it," Dan Silks called out from downstairs. I snatched up the pistol that had fallen from Beam's hand, shoved it into my waist, and ran to the window, hearing the sound of more boots pounding up the stairs. "It came from Mr. Beam's room," said Ben Larr's voice from down the hall. I slung the window up and scurried through it. Even in my rush, I noticed there was no wind this night, but large flakes of snow had started to fall, heavy and straight down.

I hung by both hands and pushed out from the building with my bare foot; the snarl of the Catahoula clashed with the roar of the bear somewhere far up the street. *Good Lord!* Was there any letup between beasts and their battle?

I made the drop into a cushion of crusted snow and fell backward. "Don't mo-ve! Don't mo-ve a mus-cle, Crowe," cried Deacon's voice; and without seeing him, I felt the cold barrel of the shotgun jam into my neck. "I g-ot him, Dan! Got him co-ld! He's de-ad now!" Deacon vibrated like a plucked fiddle string.

"Don't shoot him, Deacon," Dan Silks called out, running off the porch and toward us. I caught a glimpse of him and Ernie in the corner of my eye.

"I-got-to! I-got-to!" Deacon's shotgun barrel trembled.

"No! Not yet." I felt the shotgun barrel shoved away from my neck, and heard them scuffle behind me. I almost bolted and ran; but as I jerked my head around, Silks stood with his pistol cocked and pointed. Ernie stood beside him, wide-eyed. Deacon fumed, struggled with the shotgun, but Silks had his free hand wrapped around the barrel, holding it away. Laura and Ben Larr stood watching from the porch. The sound of the dog and the bear still resounded in the night.

"Don't worry, Deacon," said Silks, "we're gonna kill him. You can bet your *Bible* on it. But we'll take him to the barn and cleave his damn head off."

"Sho-ot him first!" Deacon jerked at the shotgun; Silks held firm.

"The hell's wrong with you, Deacon? I've never seen you strung so tight. His friend's out here somewhere. I want *him* too." Silks turned and called out to the darkened streets. "Hear that? We've got your partner here . . . taking him to the barn. Gonna gunnysack this bastard." He waited for a second with a smug grin, but there was no reply, no sound in the night except the raging bear fight. "See, Deacon? See what I'm doing here? You just settle down and let me handle things."

Deacon eased down—or tried to. The cocaine had him boiling. "I see, I see." He rubbed his face with his free hand and let Silks take the shotgun from him. "I, just, ain't, thinking, straight. Don't, know, what's, the, matter. Thought, my beard, was on fire, but it, was snowflakes."

The sound of the dog and the bear stopped with a deep roar and a loud yelp. Then silence. Silks and Ernie pulled me to my feet, snatched the pistols from my waist, and pulled my hands behind me.

"Well, what have we here?" Dan Silks pulled the brass knuckles from my back pocket, slipped them on his fingers, and held them around in front of me. "Just what the doctor ordered. Every time I think of all the trouble you've caused me, I'm gonna bump you upside of your head." He tapped them against my forehead, and snickered.

I felt the cold steel cuffs snap around my wrists, and I heard Ben Larr call out from the porch, "If this town burns down, Crowe, it's all *your* fault. Hear me? You could've killed that bear, but you didn't. You thought only of yourself! Now look what it's caused!"

I just let out a long breath. Laura stood with a hand on her lips.

Silks tapped me soundly on my head with the brass knuckles and pushed me forward. "Come on, Crowe. Your friend will make a move now, if he ain't already left ya." He shoved me again and I bolted forward an extra step.

"Jack! Get out of here! Save yourself. Leave me—"

The brass knuckles hooked me sharply in the side, and I folded double and dropped in the snow. "Don't come out!" I yelled, my voice strained and lacking air. Then the shotgun swung around. The blow hit me full in the jaw, mashed the corner of my lip, and flipped me over in the snow. Blood dripped.

"Stop it, Uncle Dan!" I heard Ernie plead.

"He's ri-ght," said Deacon, his voice doing better as long as he steadied it. "If, you knock him out, we'll have, to drag him." He stepped over and leaned down near my face. "I want, this sinner wide awake, when the, blade falls."

"He's all right, ain't ya, Crowe," Silks said, pulling me up and shoving me on, the brass knuckles still on his hand.

"Never better," I said, across my numb, throbbing lip.

We walked along the middle of the snow-rutted street, them flanking me, me scanning the shadows, watching for Jack to make a move. "What about the bear, Uncle Dan?" Ernie's voice sounded shaky.

"I figure that bear's killed the dog and lit out of here," Silks said. "Just keep your eyes peeled."

At the burning jail, Freddie and Dallas Renfrow ran back and forth, throwing bucket after bucket of snow into the hissing flames. But the fire had spread to the building beside it. As we walked past, Sparks stepped out of the shadows with a rifle and fell in walking beside Silks. "I've looked everywhere, Dan, the stores, the barn—everywhere. Turned this town upside down. The man's hightailed it out of here."

"All right," Silks said; then he turned to me with his smug grin. "Maybe you and him wasn't as close as I thought. Looks like he's left ya hanging here."

I stared straight ahead. *Way to go, Jack.* At least one of us would make it out alive, I thought. We walked on, past the loading platform by the train, the heavy snow falling thicker, clinging to my shoulders and already piling along the tops of hitchrails and window ledges.

"Is this the big one coming, Uncle Dan?" Ernie asked as we trudged along.

"Yep. This is it. When the wind dies and the snow falls heavy and straight down . . . that usually means we've got a

292

deep one coming. All them storms don't mean a thing. It's this kinda snow keeps you pinned in the rest of the winter. We'll get laid up here and have to pack Crowe's head in ice till spring, right, Crowe?" He snickered, and tapped my head again with the brass knuckles. What could I say? What *could* I say?

PART VI

CAME THE
DARK ANGELS

CHAPTER

26

---·---

I'd heard it said that when it came time to die, a man should do so with dignity, showing a level of pride and courage that would speak well of him long after he was gone. Yet pride, dignity, and courage all seemed trivial now, of little comfort, as I walked barefoot through the rutted snow. Gone now was the resolve I'd felt those seconds when the bear's open jaws blew its hot breath on my face. I'd given myself over to death, cornered by steel bars on one side, a wall on the other, and faced by a predator from the wilds.

But in slipping past the bear, I'd found a thread of hope, enough to keep me holding on. To die now, after grasping that thin thread, seemed too ironic, too dark and ridiculous to fathom. If I *had* to die, why not *then?* Why must I have made this extra effort, suffered the extra cold and torment, if only to snatch these few meaningless moments of existence?

I don't deserve this, I thought, trudging through the snow, seeing the dim light from the barn in the distance and hearing, beyond it, the bawl of the bear. *I should have died an hour ago and been done with it.*

There was some small comfort in realizing that Jack had gotten away. In the end he'd done what is natural to man. He'd seen the hopelessness of our situation, and left—saved himself, as any man would do. And who could blame him? He would never have left had he seen one chance in hell of saving me. I knew that. My only regret at his leaving me here was the fact that I hadn't been able to tell him it was all right. But . . . I reckon he knew it.

Twenty yards ahead, I saw the barn door swing open and saw big Dutch come looping toward us through the snow carrying a rifle in one hand and an ax in the other. *Couldn't wait for us to get to there.* I shook my head and glanced around at the earth once more before leaving it. The bawling of the bear had stopped. Aside from the crackling of the raging fire behind us, silence fell as if falling with the snow.

"Keep moving, Crowe," Dan Silks said behind me, gigging me with the brass knuckles as I faltered on my cold feet and glanced around at the shadowed storefronts. I wanted to see one more living thing besides these men who would kill me. But I wouldn't. There was no other symbol of humankind except the lifeless mannequin with its long woman's cape, its fashionable flat hat, and its dull eyes staring straight past us into the night.

"Do you have to keep punching him, Uncle Dan?" Ernie's voice had a quaver in it. "He's dying, after all—"

"Then what harm is it?" Dan Silks chuckled. "Ernie, we're gonna have to have a long talk, you and me. I don't think you're cut out for this work. I'm thinking about sending you home."

"Suits me *fine,*" Ernie said.

"Fact is," said Dan Silks, "I never would have brought you if it hadn't been for—" His voice stopped short at the sound of a creaking door just behind us on our left. I even cut a sweeping glance around over my shoulder. In the instant that my eyes saw that the mannequin was missing from where I'd just seen it, realization struck me; and I dropped straight down instinctively.

The dark cape and fashionable hat darted toward us from the boardwalk, behind an orange blaze of pistol fire. *Jesus! Jack!* I tried rolling away in the thick snow, but could not, owing to the impact of Sparks' body slamming atop me when a bullet hit him high in his neck. I struggled to shove him off me, bucking him with my belly, my hands cuffed beneath me, digging for a grip in the snow.

Jack's gunplay was fast, faster than ever. But having me in his line of fire must've affected his aim. In a split second three shots had fired almost as one: the first killing Sparks, the second dropping Dutch at ten yards away, and the third spinning Dan Silks around and dropping him atop Sparks, on top of me. From there beneath them, I saw Ernie duck with his pistol out and cocked, but with his arms up, wrapped around his head.

"Don't shoot!" Ernie yelled. "I didn't want to kill him no dern way—"

"Then stand away," Jack bellowed.

But before Ernie could straighten up, turn, and run, Silks had scrambled off of Sparks, wrestled my head up under his arm, and raised me to my feet, using me as a shield. His pistol cocked against my head. Snow swirled.

"I'll kill 'im . . . *goddamn 'im,* I'll kill him!" Dan Silks' pistol wobbled unsteadily against my head; he was trying to adjust his fingers in the brass knuckles and hold the gun at the same time. "I mean it! Drop your gun . . . or I'll kill 'im!"

"I don't *drop* guns," Jack said in a quiet tone. "Why don't you just let him go? You're dead either way . . . dead as you'll ever be."

Ernie stood frozen, his pistol in his right hand, but his right arm still wrapped over his head as he crouched a foot from me.

"I've got some play left here," Silks said. "Ernie! Get around here! Get around here *now!"*

"Don't do it, kid," Jack said, his voice like the low purr of a mountain cat. "Or I'll have to burn you, too."

"Damn it, Ernie—!" Silks barked. I felt the pistol wobble some more, wondering if he could even pull the trigger with the brass knuckles in the way. Blood from his shoulder ran down warm on my chest. "Do like I'm telling ya, right now!"

I saw Ernie's pistol come down from around his head slowly, almost at face level, a foot from me. "I can't, Uncle Dan," he said. Even with my head pinned under Silks' arm, I saw Jack draw a bead on Ernie.

"Sorry, kid," said Jack; but before he pulled the trigger, I

299

heard something thump in the snow and saw that Silks' wobbling gun had fallen from his hand. Jack stopped and just stared.

"Shitfire," said Silks, and even as I twisted against his grip, he snatched for Ernie's pistol.

"No, Uncle Dan!" Ernie made a tug on the pistol as Silks grabbed it by the barrel. The cocked hammer fell, coming out of Ernie's hand, belching a blast of fire that streaked past my side, lifted Dan Silks and pitched him a backward flip. I spun and saw him land facedown in the snow with a terrible grunt, his arms spread and the brass knuckles lying an inch from his fingers. Smoke rose from the hole between his shoulder blades.

"My God Almighty," I said in a hushed tone, turning slowly in the snow, my feet gone numb and snowflakes pelting me.

"Oh no, oh no." Ernie stood with his arms spread, opening and closing his hands, lost in disbelief.

Silks rose up slightly on his palms, groaned as I stepped over to him and looked down. Jack walked up, stooped down with his dark woman's cape flaring around him, and pulled the keys from Silks' pocket. He unlocked the single cuff dangling from his left hand, then set me free. I worked my wrists one on the other, still looking down at Silks as he managed to wallow around and sit up in the snow.

Ernie stepped over beside me, leaning toward Silks; I stopped him with my arm across his chest. "Nothing you can do, Ernie," I said.

"I'm gonna get blamed," Ernie said, sobbing, looking down at Silks. "Dern it, Uncle Dan. You told me you'd make me a bounty-killer . . . but the only man I ever kilt is *you!*"

"It . . . weren't your fault . . . boy," Silks said in a halting voice. "I . . . never should've . . . hired kinfolk."

"Ain't that the damn truth," I said, watching his eyes glaze over, thinking that he must've been seeing memories flashing past him, maybe catching scenes and pictures from as far back as he could remember, seeing them now for the last time as they turned distant and dark and shut down around him. It struck me that these were *not* the kind of thoughts the bear would've had . . . had he stood watching me die amid his violent act. I shook my head to clear it, and turned around to Jack.

"My feet's frozen plumb up to my elbows," I said, feeling something well up in my chest, something that kept me from knowing what else to say. "What took you so long?"

"Ha! You thought I wasn't coming back *at all,* didn't ya."

"That ain't so. I knew you'd be here." Glancing up and down at him, I took note of the woman's cape and fashionable hat, shook my head, and grinned slightly.

He ran a hand down the flowing cape; his face reddened. His gaze narrowed and honed into my eyes, and he raised a finger for emphasis. "Don't you say *one damn* word."

"I wasn't going to, Jack. It's a very *fine* cape."

Dan Silks' boots were wet, and too small; but my feet were so cold, I feared I couldn't wait another second to get them out of the snow. Jack flipped the cape off his shoulders and wrapped it around me. He tried to put the fashionable hat on my head, but I ducked it, picked up Sparks' high-crowned Stetson, and put it on. Only then did I rub my stiff hands together, pick up Ernie's pistol, and wipe the snow off the barrel. Ernie sat in the snow beside his uncle, rocking back and forth, sobbing like a child.

Jack had walked on to where Dutch lay groaning in the street, his broken nose packed with gauze and a heavy bandage tied around his face. I barely made out his words when he looked at Jack and said, "You son of a bitch." Then Jack's arm rose effortlessly out from his side, and a jet of orange fire streaked down into Dutch's head.

Deacon had struggled and groaned and rolled over in the snow. He lay staring up at me, and didn't so much as flinch when I lowered the tip of the barrel a few inches from his face and cocked the pistol. The cocaine still had his eyes lit and shiny, his pupils large and excited-looking, like a kid watching fireworks going off, only Deacon's fireworks were all in his tight-strung mind. *There's worse ways to die,* I thought, looking down at him, watching his eyes flicker as heavy snowflakes plopped and turned to water on his face.

"Am I—am I de-ad yet?" His voice sounded dreamy and coated with candle wax, yet tense, excited about something.

"In a second," I said.

"Is this hea-ven?" He didn't seem to hear me. A strange—and I mean *really strange*—smile half formed on his lips. "It is! It's hea-ven. I see all the-se colors and sounds and waves of light all dancing together." His eyes swam in the rapture of it. "It is! It is hea-ven, isn't it?"

I let out a breath. "Well . . . if you say so. It's as close as you got, in *this* life." I steadied my arm, and tightened my finger on the trigger.

Before I pulled it, I heard a rustling behind me, looked over my shoulder, and saw Ben and Laura Larr come trekking through the falling snow. Behind them, Dallas Renfrow came loping over from the burning jail, looking all around.

I turned back with the pistol still in Deacon's face and started once more to burn a hole in him. But then I slumped the pistol and thought, aw hell, I couldn't shoot him, not with them running up seeing me do it. It wasn't that I didn't think he deserved it, being ready *as he was* to take delight in lifting my head from my body, nor was it that I was afraid to do so in front of witnesses. I reckon it was because of the Larrs being so convinced I was nothing but a stone-cold killer of man. Maybe I felt just contrary enough to show them I wasn't.

"Ain't you going to nail him one?" Jack asked, stepping up beside me in the falling snow. I looked at him, and just then realized that tears were running down my cheeks—thankful for being alive and having such life and death decisions still within my grasp, I reckon—and I was grateful for the falling snow that wet my face and hid those tears.

"Naw, I ain't gonna," I said, hoping Jack didn't notice my joy, my trembling, and my swell of gratitude toward all the unseen forces that had overcome me right then.

"Hell, look out," Jack said, swinging his pistol in slowly, "I'll pop him one."

I eased Jack's pistol away with the barrel of mine. "Let's not kill him," I said softly, hearing the Larrs come to a halt near us. Dallas Renfrow ran past them and kept running. I didn't see him anywhere.

"You ain't kilt me yet?" Deacon sounded confused, unbelieving. "You ain't even go-ing to?"

I looked down at him, wanting to laugh and cry out loud,

302

wanting to say something, many things really, but things no one, including myself, could possibly understand. "No," I said in my tight voice, "but I'm arresting you, you hophead bastard."

"Arresting me? Y-ou can't ar-rest me. Arrest me for *what?*" Snow streamed down his face in melting trickles. He blinked his shiny eyes.

I said, "For trying to kill a man—" I felt my voice sounding more and more shaky as I spoke, and I hoped Jack and the others didn't notice it. "For trying to kill a *man* . . . who didn't want to die."

"I've never even heard of such a charge," said Deacon.

"I *bet* you ain't, preacher," I said.

Deacon tried to spread a crafty cocaine grin. "You ain't the *law.* You ha-ve no authority."

"On this I *am,* preacher," I said, hearing my voice start to fail me. "On *this,* I do."

We stood there in the thick falling snow. Somewhere near the edge of town, the Catahoula started up again. It was good to know he was alive, but damned if I wanted him bringing that bear around again. "Please don't drive him back here," I said aloud, not realizing I'd said it until I heard Ben Larr's voice.

"If you'd killed the bear in the first place . . . none of this other would've happened." It was an odd thing for him to say, and both Jack and I cocked our heads toward him. "That is—what I mean is—" Larr stammered and looked scared.

"What he *means* is," Laura said, "if you had killed the bear, and then Dan Silks had *killed you,* my dear husband would've *killed* two birds with one stone. He'd have the bear dead . . . and not have to pay you the money he promised. Sweet deal, huh?" She stepped away from her husband and pointed a finger at him. *"He* sicced the posse on you, not Eldon."

"Now wait!" Larr wobbled in the snow, his crutch creaking from the weight of his struggle. I narrowed a cold stare at him. Snow fell straight down around us. "I was out of my mind on whiskey and 'edge.' You know how that stuff does. It makes me crazy. I wasn't responsible—"

303

"Now, kill him! Kill him, Mr. Crowe!" Laura's eyes shined, but not from cocaine. Hers was the wild shine of anticipation, of dark dreams come true. "I kept my part of the deal, now you keep yours. Kill this sickening, spineless *worm!"*

"Deal? What deal?" Larr looked confused, and shook his head in disbelief—the same look of disbelief Ernie'd had when he saw he'd burned the living hell out of Dan Silks.

I glanced at Jack as I leveled my gun and cocked it at Larr's chest. Jack shrugged. The look in my eyes told Jack it wasn't going to happen. It was just me wanting to see what Laura would do once she spilled her guts, then realized I wouldn't kill him for her. "I told her I'd kill ya, Colonel, if she'd get me out of jail. She blew Deacon away on cocaine—so I guess a *deal's a deal."*

Wobbling, holding both hands on his one crutch, he stared at her, still disbelieving. "You what? Made a deal? To—to kill me?"

Aw yeah, this would be better than killing him, and better than telling her I wouldn't do it.

"That's *right.* I did!" She jutted her chin. "You don't know how long I've waited to see this, *prayed* to see this . . . see your sorry guts blown out your spineless back, you rotten, despicable—" She stepped farther away to keep the blood off her. Snow fell heavier around us. "Kill him, Crowe! Kill him now!" Behind us the Catahoula bayed and growled, closer than before, coming back.

I leveled the pistol tighter, with the hammer back and my thumb across it. "Is there any more cocaine?"

"What?" Laura snapped her eyes to mine.

"Is, there, any, more cocaine? I want to know before I kill him." Even Jack's expression turned curious on that one.

"Yes." Laura snatched the silver case from inside her coat. "Here, take it, now kill him."

"Is there any more?"

"Huh? Why no, that's all. All there'll be until the weather breaks and the train—"

"Good." I opened the case with my free hand and let it pour out into the downfalling snow. Ben Larr groaned; Laura gasped.

"Come on, now," said Jack. "You could've just kept it from them. You didn't have to do all *that!*"

"Yeah, I did." I spoke to him, keeping my eyes on Ben and Laura Larr. Then I said, "Colonel. I've never seen a woman want a man dead as bad as she does you. She's told me some things about you that—" I shook my head slowly. "Well, I'm ashamed to even repeat them. And with you dead, she'll get everything you've got, the railroad, the mountain, right Laura?"

"That's right, all of it. It's all that's kept me with your sorry ass all this time. Now kill him, Crowe!"

"So long, Larr." I pulled the trigger, let the hammer fall, but then caught it with my thumb before it struck the bullet. *"Bang,"* I said; and Ben Larr seemed to melt halfway down his crutch before he caught himself. "Now you two go work it all out, clearheaded, with all the cards on the table."

CHAPTER

27

There came a long blasting bawl of the bear from over near the train platform, followed by a sharp yipe from the Catahoula. Then a rifle shot barked, sounding louder, more powerful, and of a finality that reigned above all else. The night fell into silence around us.

"He's—he's coming back," Larr said in a hushed voice.

"Not if I'm any judge," I said; and we all turned, our eyes searching through the falling snow as if within *it* and the darkness lay the missing piece to the puzzle of life. In a second, the Catahoula came loping out of the black-and-white swirl. Steam gushed in two streams from his muzzle, streaking up, mantling his head like misty horns and falling back in his wake.

He circled my feet and dropped against them, looking up at me, steaming, his breath beating in his throat and lungs like snare drums. "Good boy." I nudged him gently with my *deadman's* boot. This time he didn't snap at me. "The bear's dead," I said, turning from one to the other until my eyes stopped on Jack's and remained there.

"Yeah, I think so, too," Jack said softly.

"No! No, he's coming!" Larr trembled in place with both hands grasping his crutch. Laura stared off through the swirl, her hands clasped at her throat, perhaps wishing her husband was right, perhaps wishing the bear would sweep in and finish what it had started with Ben Larr years ago. But instead of the bear, the Indian woman walked slowly toward us from out of the falling snow, from the direction of the rifle shot.

I swallowed hard, wondering what to say as she stopped four feet from me. Larr's Swiss rifle hung from her hand. She looked at the others, then spoke to me as if they weren't there. "I killed him. I killed the bear—"

"Yeah, you did, ma'am. I don't know how I know . . . but I *know,* you did."

"—because the dog kept bringing him here for someone to kill, but no one would kill him . . . so I did." There was relief in her eyes, and if not for the snow falling full and wet on her face, I'd have sworn there was a tear there somewhere.

"How do we know it's dead?" Ben Larr asked quietly, but no one answered.

A silence passed; then Laura stepped toward the Indian woman and said, "Waaaait-a-damn-minute, here. That's my dress, my shawl you're wearing . . . my *shoes! Ben!* Look at this! No squaw whore's going to wear—"

Her words stopped short. The woman turned to her absently, but bringing, in her turn, the barrel of the big Swiss rifle. The rifle muzzle seemed to reach like a deadly kiss toward Laura Larr's bosom. "But it looks *really* good on you! I mean—it fits so well. You *do* have the figure for it. . . ."

"Thank you," said the Indian woman in a flat tone—no expression there, in either voice or eyes. Then she turned back to me. "Is everybody dead?"

"How do we know the bear's dead?" Ben Larr asked, raising his voice.

"Everybody that should be," I said, answering her, but ignoring Ben Larr. I reached out and took the rifle from her hand, saw the bolt was back, the chamber empty. I closed it to keep the weather out. "Ernie's alive. Deacon is too, if you call that living."

"You know who I mean," she said in a no-nonsense tone as if I might be teasing with her.

I nodded. "Yes, Dandy Dan is deader than hell . . . shot

307

by his nephew. Damnedest thing I ever saw. Last words were, he should've never hired kinfolk."

"Isn't that the truth." She smiled and seemed to ease down a bit.

"How do we *know* the bear is dead?" Ben Larr's voice kicked up a notch.

Seeing I now had the rifle, Laura Larr said, "I want those clothes back, you know—washed and pressed, just like you found them. . . ."

"How, do *we,* know the bear is *dead?"* He worked at controlling his voice. No one even glanced toward him. Jack only chuckled and shook his head.

The Indian woman looked into my eyes; and as if thinking I'd soon ask anyway, she said, "You knew nothing out there. Dan knew *everything.* I had to bring you here, to this world, to save your life—"

I raised a hand and cut her off. "I already figured as much, ma'am. You don't have to explain."

"How? Do we know? The bear *is* dead?" Larr was losing it.

"Still, I felt bad," she said. "Wondering what you must've thought . . . thinking I'd betrayed you after you two saving my life, and my son's. Thinking there was no one to help you, up here alone in the high country, trapped. I worried about it."

"Well, you shouldn't have. I'm just sorry about what you had to do with Silks—" I rolled a hand, felt my face redden. "I mean, you know, the things you did for him."

"How do we know the bear . . ."

"Oh?" She looked surprised, and shook her head. "No, you do not understand. Dan Silks could do nothing with a woman. He *tried.* He wore himself out, drove himself crazy *trying to.* But no." She shrugged. "That was his *weakness.* That is why I brought him here, to drive him to distraction. Dan Silks could *never* do anything with a woman. That is why they called him Dandy Dan, you see."

"Sure," I said, but then I ducked my face around and gave Jack a *can-you-believe-this?* look. The Catahoula still lay panting against my feet. Down the snowy street, Ernie helped Deacon to his feet, led him over, leaned him against a hitchrail, and stood dusting him off. Deacon moved a hand back and forth through the falling snow, seeming real interested in it.

"*How-do-we-know-the-bear-is-dead?*" Ben Larr yelled at the top of his lungs. He was really getting on my nerves.

I spun toward him, and yelled, "*Because she said she killed it!* Now shut up, Larr. I can still shoot you, you know."

His voice lowered. "But she might've only wounded him. How do we—"

I cut him off. "Because I feel it inside me!" I pounded a hand on my chest. "Right here! I *just* know it, all right?" No sooner than I'd said it, as if on cue, there came a long deep bawl through the swirling snow, and the hair on my cold neck stood up.

"Ohhhhh-shiiiit," Jack whispered, staring out toward the sound. "You better feel again . . . here he comes."

I spun, nudging the Catahoula. "Go boy!" But the dog just looked up, panting, then looked away. He didn't move. We backed away as the bear stood on his hind legs, lumbering out of the swirl toward us. I started to raise the Swiss rifle, but realized it was empty, and kept backing off. The bear faltered, nearly fell. His breath sounded broken. He was hit bad.

"Easy everybody," I whispered, "no sudden moves here."

As the bear stumbled closer, Ernie disappeared into the night. Deacon fell from the hitchrail and stared up at the bear. "Wh-at are you looking at?" Deacon seemed at peace with the universe. The bear just shook his head back and forth and lumbered on toward us.

"Jack?" I took a slow step back; the Catahoula just lay there watching, his breath still panting.

"I've got him," Jack said. Out the corner of my eye, I saw Jack had dropped down on one knee, his other knee up, left elbow resting on it, supporting his gun hand as if it were a rifle stock.

"Do not shoot him," the woman whispered beside me. "He is dead on his feet, just looking for a place to fall."

I glanced at her, then down at the Catahoula, and let out a breath. She was right. She knew it, so did the dog. The dog neither stirred nor growled. The bear stopped and teetered, twenty feet from us. "Kill him, Crowe," Laura Larr said in a hush.

"Yes, Crowe, kill it," Ben Larr said in the same tone. "You're the only one who can. Kill *it* before *it* kills *us.*"

I knew the bear was dying, and knowing it would soon fall, a strange thought—call it a flash of human greed—swept across my mind. I'd lost ten thousand dollars of the train holdup money. Jesse would want to know why. I wasn't sure he'd believe what really happened here if I told him. "Colonel, if I kill it the deal's still on, right? You'll match what's in the carpetbag as soon as I can go get it? Right?"

He didn't answer. I shot a glance over my shoulder as the bear took a halting step forward. "Right, Colonel?"

"No," he said, his voice sounding strange.

"No? What do you mean 'no'? You still want him dead, don't you?"

"Yes," he breathed, "kill him."

"The deal? The money? Colonel, tell me something here."

"No . . . I can't. I'm broke," he said. Laura Larr gasped, and whispered something under her breath akin to a dying woman's prayer.

"You're what?" My shoulders slumped. I turned toward him as the bear took another step. "What kind of shit is that, *you're broke?"* Jack even slid his eyes around away from the bear.

"It's true," he said, his voice going shaky. "I have no money left. It's a long story, all very complicated. But kill him, Crowe, for godsake, *kill him!"* A dark stain crept down Larr's leg and spread in the snow.

"Can you *believe* this?" I turned back, facing the bear, shaking my head. The Indian woman closed her eyes for a second, then opened them slowly, and let out a long breath.

The bear had moved closer, fifteen feet away now, rocking back and forth, almost making me dizzy watching him. Blood pumped from the hole in his chest, steady and hard, gushing with each heartbeat. There was nothing left of him, no need to run, no need to fear. The bear only saw us now through a wavering veil, I thought. We'd become the dark

310

still angels of his death, if a bear knew of death . . . if he knew dark angels.

He tried one last terrible bawl, just to threaten his dark angels away; but even his terrible bawl failed him. His breath clamped shut, his open jaws seemed to lock for a second in the pain of it. He twisted his head back and forth, letting out a low whine, too low, too meek for *this* bear's nature. The Catahoula watched, panting, perhaps remembering the bear had killed his friend . . . perhaps not; but whatever element had bound dog and bear in their single intent was now gone. Their waltz had ended.

"Don't shoot him, Jack," I whispered, hearing the click of metal on metal beside me.

"No, I'm just letting down the hammer," he whispered in reply; and in that small circle of swirling darkness, time stood suspended as a big, bad, ruthless creature from the plane of earth gave way slowly to the earth's pitch and sway, still standing, flaunting his existence in the face of his dark angels. His wild fading eyes passed across us—in them lay the shadow and substance of all things both holy and obscene.

"Jesus, God," I whispered, my voice feeling tight, back deep in my throat. But there was no Jesus he called upon, no God he answered to, nothing to console his blasphemous nature, only us, his dark angels, silent now. Both hunter and hunted, intertwined, wrapped as one—the waltz never ending . . . struck to one last note, that last note ending . . .

"By God, then," Ben Larr raged, shoving past me, snatching the Swiss rifle on his way. "I'll kill him myself! He owes me for a leg!"

"He's already gone, Larr," Jack hissed, as the bear rocked back then forward. "Leave him be."

"Like hell!" Larr hobbled forward, dropped his crutch, wobbled on one leg, raising the rifle, five feet from the dying bear.

"It's empty, Larr, you fool!" I yelled and started to step forward, wanting to snatch up his crutch from the snow and crack his head with it.

"Hunh?" He turned his red-rimmed eyes toward me, over his shoulder, working the bolt on the rifle back and forth, as if doing so would create a bullet out of thin air. The bear swayed forward, his big arms spread slightly. Larr still stared back at me, wild-eyed, tortured by all he'd ever been flashing back at him. Frantically his hand dug into his pocket and jerked out a silver bullet.

"Look out!" I yelled, my voice in tandem with Jack's and the Indian woman's. Larr snapped his face back to the bear . . . but too late. His silver bullet fell, disappeared in the snow. The big monster fell forward, down and down, his big arms spreading wider, his body crumbling Larr's beneath him like a paper kite. Snow swirled.

The ground beneath us trembled then settled, and we stood there staring down at the brown silver-tipped back of the dead grizzly. His fur stirred in the falling snow. "Yep, the bear's dead," I whispered.

"It'd take two mule teams to drag that bear off him," Jack said, standing, brushing snow from his trouser leg.

"I reckon it would," I said, "if a man was prone to do so." I looked all around in the swirling night, saw Laura Larr standing with her mouth gaped open. "I guess we're even, huh?"

She nodded her head slowly, still staring down at the bear. "He said, he's . . . broke?"

I rolled my eyes slightly—"I'm freezing"—turned, and started walking to the lodge. Jack fell in beside. I looked back as we walked. The Indian woman had taken Laura Larr by the arm, coaxing her along behind us. The Catahoula sprang up, shook himself off, and darted past us.

"Can you believe that, Jack! The man was broke!" I swung a hand up and let it fall. "Knows he's broke, sends us out there anyway, knows he won't pay us like he said—"

"I thought we only went because he'd turn us in if we didn't go."

"That's true, but still, he promised to match what's in the bag. Once it's over, I still gotta tell Jesse we've come up ten thousand short, you know, or make it up some way. Think Jesse'd believe all this if I tell him?"

"No, but you gotta tell him anyway."

"Well, I will. Only I gotta change it around a little, make it *believable* at least."

312

"Tell him what you want to. If he asks me, I'll just say I was drunk."

"Naw now, hell no! You've got to back me up on this."

"I'll be damn. You're on your own, especially the part about you smacking that bear in the jaw. That'll blow it for Jesse. It blew it for *me.*" Jack chuckled, shook his head.

I stopped in the snow and stared at him. "It's the truth, Jack. You don't believe me?"

"Sorry, mi amigo. I've seen you do some stup—I mean *strange* things . . . but smacking a grizzly, bare-handed?"

"Wasn't bare-handed. I had brass knuckles." I walked on, blowing warm breath on my numb fingertips. "See, maybe that's what you don't understand."

"No, I understand. Still. I rather tell him I was just drunk the whole trip."

I grinned. *It's actually over, thank God.* "Speaking of drunk, Jack. That brandy Beam brought over to you was poison. Think about that."

He tipped his collar up, shrugged. "Hell, I knew it."

"Come on now. *How'd* you know?"

"Well, when that half-breed took a shot and fell back dead in his chair, it was a pretty good indication—"

"Naw, Jack. What I mean is, Beam sent it over for you, to kill you with it. But it worked out all right. The half-breed drank the poison, you got away, I shot Brerton Beam."

"Whoa-whoa-whoa!" Jack stopped in his tracks, grabbed my arm, making me stop with him. "You killed *our* little Beam? Our little provider of fine liquor?"

"Yeah. But he was no whiskey drummer. He was a detective."

"My, my." Jack studied it, rubbing his chin. "You're gonna have to fill me in on all this."

"All right, then you're gonna back up my story when I tell Jesse and Frank. Deal?"

"Yeah, I suppose. All except the part about you hitting the bear. I didn't see it anyway."

"Man. You never will believe that, will ya?"

"Would *you?* Unless you saw it?"

"Well, you're my partner. I'd like to think I have enough faith in ya to—"

313

"Hold it. Do you believe I shot the bear, twice, that night on the train?"

"Aw hell. Are you gonna start that again?"

"Damn right. I'll get a knife and we'll go back and cut my two bullets out of him."

"I ain't doing that."

"Why not? It'll prove it."

"No. What if we go fooling with that bear and find out *he's* still alive?"

"He ain't alive. I guarantee that. He bled to death before our eyes."

I grinned. "Not him, Jack. I mean the son of a bitch underneath him."

We walked on to the lodge. On the way, Dallas Renfrow came running up carrying a block and tackle over his shoulder. His hat was gone from his head; soot from the fire streaked his face. His breath gushed steam. "Come on! Help me get to the colonel," he said. "He might be alive."

"You've got to be joking, Renfrow." I looked him up and down. "Your *'colonel'* died in a sea of bear, far as I care. Think you can change it? Be my guest." I sidestepped and gestured an arm back toward the rise of silver-tipped fur.

"I've got to *try,"* Renfrow cried out, running on through the falling snow.

I looked at Jack, hiked my shoulders up beneath the dark flowing cape, tugged the *deadman's* battered Stetson down on my head: "Don't we all," and walked on to the glowing light of the lodge in my *deadman's* boots, my breath—my warm breath—rising from my lips upward against the falling snow.

EPILOGUE

———•———

It snowed all that night, heavy and straight down, until by morning the bodies in the street were only smooth rises, like the drifts of snow, soon to melt and wed the earth beneath them. Above the lesser drifts rose that of the grizzly, a tuft of silver-tipped fur still visible and stirring in the breeze. The night before, after the first full and peaceful meal I'd had in a while, I'd crawled off to bed and slept like a dead man for four hours. But then I was awakened by Jack shaking my arm. "Wake up," he'd said, and my first thought was that there were still people wanting to kill us. When he assured me there weren't, I'd let out a long breath and wiped a hand over my face.

"It's my book," Jack said. "Some bastard has stolen my book! Can you believe that? It's getting where nothing's safe anymore. I left it under the bed when we went out to hunt the bear, and some asshole stole it."

"And you felt it's something I oughta be woke up over?" I just stared at him.

He shrugged. "How long was you gonna sleep anyway?"

"I'll never know *now,* will I," I'd said.

The next morning, Dallas Renfrow had stepped out beside me on the porch of the lodge. With a shovel under his arm, he'd stood there for a second, gazing longingly toward the tuft of fur. I saw what he had in mind, and I stopped

315

him, telling him that Ben Larr was as dead as he'd ever be, and that a few days of seeing undisturbed snow might pay better tribute to his colonel than any funeral service ever could. He took a deep breath and agreed; and we stood there in silence until Jack came out on the porch, followed by the young European with his skis over his shoulder.

The European bid us good morning, leaned his skis against the porch rail, and did a few brisk deep knee bends with his arms straight out before him. We just watched. Then, with no mention of the ruckus the night before, and taking no note of the burned hull of the jail sticking up from the snow, he spread a wide grin above his sharp goatee and traipsed off across the snow. I shot Jack a bemused glance as the young man walked away. "Light sleeper," Jack said, chuckling under his breath.

There was something mystical and unreal about being alive after such an ordeal, and for the first day I went around seeing things as if I'd never seen them before. Deacon acted the same way. Once Jack told me that Deacon and I were acting the same, I immediately took stock of myself and eased back into the everyday roll and flow of being alive.

Deacon, on the other hand, never quite got the hang of it, and spent the next seven weeks pondering whether or not all about him was death or a dream, or if he had *in fact* died, and here and now was some new place where he must make retribution for all he'd been, before going on to some greater place. I could make no sense of the man and even told Ernie if he didn't do something with him, I'd shoot him just to shut him up.

Ernie asked what had happened to Deacon. I'd shrugged and said, "Religion's a strange thing, kid." Then I went on to tell Ernie that a man of God might suffer many twists and turns in life but that God would always be at the core of his thought, for the better or the worse. Only man's perception of God changes, I'd told Ernie. In Deacon's case, he and God had done sort of a spiritual somersault together. It might take them both a little time to reconcile one another. "Meanwhile, kid, it's your job to make him keep his mouth shut, and see that he don't wander off and freeze to death. Can you do that?"

He said he'd try. And then he asked me quietly, "Is God mercy? Because to be honest, I never seen Deacon show mercy, never heard him preach any mercy. Do you reckon God'll show him any mercy in return?"

I only considered it a second, knowing I had no right to comment on such matters. Then I said, "Yeah, maybe God'll show him some mercy."

"How much ya figure God'll show him?"

I thought about that for another second, then smiled. "Oh, I'd say perhaps less than a man, but *surely* more than a grizzly. You can't beat that, can ya?"

Ernie seemed confused and scratched his head. "Don't worry about it, kid. Understanding mercy, whether it's God's or man's, ain't something ya learn overnight. I'm twice your age and still ain't got a handle on it. But I'm learning as I go." Ernie only nodded.

After a week, Ponce came trekking into town leading a horse with the Indian boy atop it. Behind them came the Airedale loping and limping through the deep snow. I felt great seeing that the Airedale had lived through the hunt after all. My eyes might have misted a bit watching him and the Catahoula romp around in the snow, "Painting the town yellow," I called it. But if my eyes *might* have misted seeing the two ole bear-hunting dogs back together, they most certainly *did* mist as I saw the Indian woman take her son in her arms and hold him against her.

The two of them stood there in the sunlight and snow for the longest time, while the dogs ran around them kicking up a swirl of white powder—small creatures, forever pursued by the finality of life, but for the moment, whole and complete. Something there about the circle of life, I thought. Something as real as a mother's touch, something as lasting as a son's embrace. Something as simple as two dogs running. *Precious life . . .*

I had to turn from the sight of them, lest I look foolish and melancholy in front of Jack and Ponce. "So," I said to Ponce, running a finger beneath my eye, "what brought you back here through all this weather?" I was certain he'd say it was to reunite the woman and her son, or perhaps even to bring the two dogs back together. But he only smiled and held out his hand.

"I came back for the brass knuckles."

"What? Oh, sure." I pulled them from my back pocket and laid them in his hand. "Here, you're welcome to them, free and clear."

"No," he said; but he slid them inside his coat as he spoke. "We will trade. I take the knuckle-dusters . . . you take the Catahoula."

"No, Ponce, I wouldn't think of it." I made it sound like I wouldn't think of taking advantage of him. Actually, I could just see that big dog back in Missouri, and picture Jesse or Frank reach out to pat him, and him snapping half their fingers off. "He's your dog. You'd miss him something awful . . . and think of how bad the Airedale would feel, losing his friend."

Ponce smiled a flat smile. "But it was the Airedale who told me to trade him to you. He said as long as they are together they will keep hunting bears . . . and the Airedale is *tired* of hunting bears. Better for you to take the Catahoula with you."

I'd started to say something else, but Dallas Renfrow walked up about then, and Ponce turned facing him with a dark gleam in his eyes. "You once said something bad about my hat, Renfrow. I dare you to say it again."

And so it went those few weeks until the weather broke, nothing to do but relax there high above the world, nestled in a warm lodge on the cold bosom of Mother Earth. Jack searched endlessly for his book, Ernie stayed busy keeping Deacon from wandering off to the wilderness, Ponce tried every subtle way in the world to goad Renfrow into a fistfight, and Laura Larr stayed up to her elbows in ledgers and overdue accounts, looking for a way to save what she could of the Larr financial holdings. Life goes on, I reckon.

We waited seven weeks for the weather to break, enough for us to ride up onto the high flatland and search for the stacks of money I'd hidden beneath an anonymous rock in the midst of a snowstorm; but strangely, once we got there, we rode straight to the spot. "There it is," Jack said, looking down at the damp stacks of dollars pressed into the soft ground, "the stuff that nearly got us killed . . . the same stuff that kept us alive."

"Maybe," I said. I waited a second, listening to the wind

across the mountain pass. "But I reckon you could say the same about a lot of things. The bear who nearly killed me is the one who broke me out of jail. The colonel sent us out here, and being out here kept Beam from sneaking and killing us. The woman *we* saved, saved *us* by leading us into a trap. The poison sent to kill you is what caused you to get away." I shook my head. "I don't know, Jack. I'd like to think we got away because I had Silks' men figured out and was ready to work them all against one another. But the way it worked out . . . well, it's almost enough to make ya believe in divine providence."

The day the train finally managed to make a run down to Elk Horn, Freddie helped us load our horses, and Jack and I stood looking around the retreat one last time. Laura came up just before we got on the train and told us that after some careful thought, she'd decided to go off with Dallas Renfrow and see the world on what money she could raise selling the railroad—even asked if I knew anyone who'd buy it. I told her I didn't offhand, but that I'd keep an eye out.

Renfrow stood off a few yards as if feeling guilty about taking up with his colonel's wife while the colonel's body still lay frozen to the underbelly of the giant bear. I just looked over and winked at him, and called out a congratulations. He blushed, but smiled and tipped his hat. "So," I said to Jack, turning, nearly stepping on the Catahoula standing against my leg. "I reckon that about wraps things up, huh?"

"Yep, it does," Jack answered, gazing away from me. Farther up the tracks, Ernie helped Deacon onto the train, and Deacon yelled out for all to hear that God forgave everybody of everything regardless what it was, and that all a poor sinner had to do was ask, and God would see to it a place awaited in heaven. "Even *outlaws,*" he called out; then, *"Especially* outlaws," he said as Ernie stuffed him through the door.

Jack looked back at me, grinned, and said, "What a long strange trip it's been."

"But not bad, as it turns out," I said, shaking the carpetbag of money hanging in my hand.

* * *

319

Halfway down the mountain that evening as we wound slowly around the sheer wall of rock, I heard the bawl of a bear, and shot a glance out the window beside me. Ahead of us, walking along a turn in the track, I saw the old man and his dancing bear lumbering through the remaining winter slosh, the bear walking a few feet standing up, then a few more feet down on all fours, as if unable to decide if he was man or beast.

On the other side of the old man walked a hulking figure in a heavy grizzly skin coat. Had it not been for a long walking stick thumping along beside him, I might have mistook him for a giant bear. Yet when we drew closer, I recognized his walk and said to Jack, "Look, Jack! It's ole *Eldon* . . . traveling with a dancing bear!"

"Sure is," Jack said, chuckling. "They look like brothers."

The train slowed down even more into the turn, and as it drew closer behind them, Jack leaned over me and looked out the window. "Wait a minute! What's that under his arm?" I thought Jack was going to climb out the window. "It's my *book!* That bastard's the one stole it. I shoulda guessed! I'll kill 'im!"

"Wait, Jack." I shoved him back and called out the window. "Hey there, *Eldon,* y'all wanta ride?"

The old man turned toward me, shaking his head, spreading a grateful toothless smile. The bear stood up and stared with an *I-don't-know-who-you-are-or-what-you-want* expression. Eldon saw it was me and jerked back a step, almost throwing an arm up as a shield.

"No hard feelings, *Eldon,*" I said, smiling. "Come on board. You don't still hate me do ya?"

"I don't hate nobody no more," he said, the three of them moving closer, keeping up beside the slow rolling train. "I spent the last month reading this." He waved Jack's book at us. The cover looked ragged and damp from the harsh winter. "This has changed my whole life."

"I'll change his whole life," Jack growled beside me.

"Be still," I whispered to Jack, then turned back to Eldon. "Good then, hop on and ride with us. We got lots of catching up to do."

The old man and the bear had already jumped onto the

slow-moving train, but hearing my words, Eldon hesitated. "What do you mean by that?" His eyes searched mine with suspicion.

"Nothing, *Eldon,* come on, get on board." I chuckled to Jack as Eldon grabbed a handrail and swung on. "Ever seen a man so distrusting in your life?"

But Jack didn't answer.

"Whew, boy, what a winter," Eldon said as he and the old man seated themselves across from us. "Hadn't been for Larr's coat, I'd froze to death." He waved Jack's ragged book in his hand. "Hadn't been for this book, I'd have gone crazy. I must have read it a dozen times. There's things here I wished I'd read years ago. Mighta saved me a lot of grief."

The bear stood in the aisle with its leash dangling down its side, its big eyes searching mine. I looked into those dark eyes, smiled, and for just a second started to reach out and pat the animal's head. But at my feet, the Catahoula growled low as if warning me. And it was a good thing he did, for I caught a glimpse of something in the bear's eyes that I have never been able to explain. The eyes said, *pat me at your own risk,* and seeing it, I pulled my hand back and tapped my fingers on my leg.

A man and a bear could live in the same world, respect one another, perhaps even ride the same train, I thought. But a wise man keeps his distance, and so I did, as the train gathered speed and chugged on down the hill. "Sorry I hit you, Eldon," I said. "We just got off on the wrong foot some way." I grinned, then asked him, "But why did you say it was you who telegraphed the bounty hunters, when it was really Ben Larr?"

He shrugged. "You *said* I was the one. I just went along with it because I thought they would kill me otherwise."

I chuckled and shook my head. "I understand. Staying alive makes us do some things without thinking, don't it?"

"It sure does," he said, smiling, looking back and forth between Jack and me for approval. "It *damn-sure* does."

I let out a breath. "But it's all over now, and we can all go on about our business, right?"

"Suits me fine," Eldon said; and he settled back, threw open the bearskin coat, and let out a long breath. We rode along in silence for almost a full minute before Jack

321

narrowed his brow, looked Eldon in the eyes, and said above the clack of rails and the pulse of the engine, "So, Eldon . . . what *are* you reading these days?"

"Oh, this is all about a man who grew tired of everything and everybody, and went off into the wilderness—sort of like I did, except under different circumstances . . ."

He rattled on until I finally said, "Eldon, he knows what it's about . . . it's his book."

Eldon's face turned sickly green. "Oh, I see." He cleared his throat and swallowed hard. "Well, then, here, I want you to have it back." He wiped a grimy hand across the ragged back cover and held it over to Jack. "I had no idea you two were interested in philosophy."

Jack jerked the book from Eldon's hand and wiped it across his trouser leg, grumbling.

"Philosophy?" I laughed under my breath, reached a hand down, and scratched the Catahoula behind his ears. I'd named him *Chance* for no particular reason. He growled under his breath but didn't snap at me. *"Philosophy?"* Across from me the old man grinned—a wise and knowing grin across empty gums. His eyes gleamed behind layers of wrinkles and time; and the bear stood breathing long and deep, swaying back and forth to the rhythm of the railcar. I smiled, leaned forward, and said softly, "Why, hell, *Eldon.* It's all we ever do."

Printed in the United States
By Bookmasters